The path to the Sun

The path to the Sun

an epic adventure

Book One
The Fallen Shadows Trilogy

Kimberli A. Bindschatel

The Path to the Sun
Copyright © 2013 by Kimberli A. Bindschatel

www.ThePathtotheSun.com

ISBN-13: 978-1481964579
ISBN-10: 1481964577

Thank you for purchasing this book and supporting an indie author.

For Ken, who believed in my dream

Book One

Who never doubted never half believed
Where doubt there truth is—
'tis her shadow.
~ Philip James Bailey

1

Kiran leaned out over the ledge, straining to see the bottom of the ravine into which he was supposed to jump. "But I can't see what's down there."

"That's the point," said Deke. "It's the only sure way to prove your faith."

"I don't think this is a good idea," said Jandon, leaning over Deke's shoulder.

Deke shoved him back. "Don't listen to him. Just do it, you heathen."

Kiran winced. He hated being called that. "Shut up, both of you! I'm going to jump. I'm just…getting ready."

Get yourself together, he told himself, wiping the sweat from his forehead. He took a deep breath and inched closer to the edge of the ravine. A cold shiver ran through him despite the hot sun and the sweat that soaked his tunic. His heart started to race again and the fear and doubt rushed back in. "I shouldn't have to prove anything," he muttered. But he did. He wanted so desperately to be accepted as a Toran. He *wanted* to believe. Why couldn't that be enough?

"My father says that faith shall set you free," said Deke. "It's the path of the righteous."

Righteous? That's easy for you to say. You were born with nothing to prove. Deke, son of Morgan, born to be an Elder, like his father, and his father's father, and his father before him. *Not a lowly orphan like me.*

"Just jump," Deke urged. "Are you worthy or aren't you? It's that simple."

Simple. Right. Why did it have to be a cliff? He could outrun most of the other boys. He excelled at the games. But he was cursed with a fear of heights. He closed his eyes again and tried to envision the jump as Deke had described. He would leap off the cliff and experience the rapture of flight. Then the Great Father would catch him in His hands and lower him to safety. So why did he hesitate?

All the Elders had made the jump. Hadn't they? They must have.

He dug in his pocket for a rock. The dark stone was one of his favorites, but he had nothing else. He tossed it over the edge, and waited, listening. Nothing.

It was a long way down; he knew that much from trudging up the side of Mount Gustavus. Once they found the path to the Sanctuary on the Mount, they had to climb another steep incline before sneaking across the Bridge of Enrapture, the only passage to the sacred retreat of the Elders.

Built many seasons past, long before the Time of Dissension, the suspended bridge stretched across a deep, jagged crevasse. It was made of old, weathered cedar planks tied together by a rope of wool and vine. When he crossed, Kiran told himself over and over not to look down. But as if lured by some unseen power, his eyes were drawn to the river below. What had once been raging white water was now a meager trickle. Exposed rocks jutted upward like the jagged teeth of the legendary Mawghuls that lived in the rocky meadows out beyond the Lost Forest. His stomach squeezed in his throat and set his nerves on fire. If not for that, he would be ready to jump now. He was sure of it.

He leaned back, pressed against the sun-baked rock wall, and closed his eyes. *You can do this*, he told himself. In his sixteen years, he had never backed down from a challenge, and he wasn't about to start today. He had to jump. This was his one chance. Usually, there was an Elder here for his time of atonement. But today, the Elders were gathered at the Temple for a special conclave. He couldn't remember that ever happening before and wasn't sure it would again. The time was now.

Kiran forced his gaze straight across the chasm to gain some sense of stability. A single brush pine clung to a jagged crevice, its long, slender roots like fingers holding on with a sure grip, its crooked branches bravely reaching out over the ravine. *I wish I had your fortitude,* he thought. *But perhaps you can see what's below.*

He drew in a breath, trying not to think about whether it would be his last. "Please, let it be true," he whispered. He gulped in air. His hand sprang up to cover his mouth as his gaze shot skyward. Had He heard? Kiran had not uttered a word in the Tongue of the Father, but he had expressed doubt aloud just the same. *Why can't I keep my mouth shut?* A good Toran does not question.

But he struggled. Whenever the thoughts crept into his mind, he tried to push them aside, to deny them, to focus only on the Truth. If anyone in the village suspected him of doubt, he'd be accused of heresy and banished. He would not let that happen.

He was a real Toran. And he was going to prove it right now. He took another step toward the edge.

"Kiran, wait!" It was Jandon. "The Temple Bells are ringing. We need to go."

"What?" He glanced back. Deke was gone. "But I was going to jump."

"C'mon. Another time. We've got to go."

Kiran exhaled. A part of him was relieved, although he knew that if he ever had the chance again, he would be back on the ledge. He kicked at the stones at his feet, spraying them into the air.

He sidestepped along the ledge and stepped down onto solid ground. Jandon was waiting, holding Kiran's hat out for him.

Jandon nudged him, a sly grin on his face. "You weren't really going to jump, were you?"

"You, of all people, know I would." He ran his fingers through his blond curls and flipped the ratty old straw hat onto his head and adjusted the brim so it sat back on his forehead, tipped up the way he liked it.

"You don't have anything to prove." Jandon squeezed through a narrow crevice in the rock.

Kiran followed him through and into a stand of pines. "That's not true," he said with a huff as he brushed branches aside. "And you know it. Now I don't know when I'll get the chance again."

"I don't know why you care so much anyway."

"If only they'd let me go to the Lessons."

"Not that again. Why would you even want to spend time at the Lessons? All we do is chant, chant, chant. And memorize stories that no farmer has need to know."

"Jandon, I've—"

Jandon stopped short and whirled around to face him. "Don't tell me you still dream of being an Elder. You're crazy. I mean, you've got to dedicate your whole life to it."

"Your problem is you think life is all about chasing girls."

"Well, isn't it?"

"I'm going to be an Elder someday. You'll see!"

Jandon shrugged and turned and kept walking.

"You'll never understand," Kiran mumbled. They emerged from the pines near the entrance to the inner sanctum, a shallow cavern in the side of the rock. Kiran brushed needles from his tunic. "What do you think the special conclave is for?"

"How should I know?"

"Well, aren't you curious?"

"Hopefully, they've been holding a prayer vigil. My father says it's been too dry for a second cutting this year. He's worried there won't be enough fodder to overwinter the flocks, especially after tithes. We have to plan the slaughter now. If we have another long winter ahead, we might lose our whole farm."

"But the Elders pray for good crops all the time. They wouldn't call a special conclave just for that."

Kiran glanced around the Sanctuary as if the answer, somehow, lay here for him to find.

Jandon grabbed Kiran by the arm. "Let's go take a look."

"No one is allowed except the Elders."

"C'mon. You know you want to. When will we ever get the chance again?"

"We need to get to the Temple. The bells are ringing."

"It will just take a moment. We can catch up."

"I don't know, Jandon. We weren't even supposed to cross the bridge."

"Deke did. So how wrong could it be?"

"But a sin is a sin!" he burst. Deke was supposed to be faithful to the Great Father, devoted to the Way. Half the time, Kiran didn't know what was right and what was wrong and he was tired of trying to figure it out.

He glanced over his shoulder. Through the ivy-covered archway, the solitary entrance to the inner sanctum, he could see Deke running across the Sanctuary meadow, straight toward the path that led back to the village. Resentment rose in him and his stomach started to churn. *It's not fair,* he thought. Deke lived by different rules. "Let's make it quick," he said.

He was surprised to find the most sacred place of the Elders so plain and simple. There was a straw mat near the back for sleeping, a kneeling board, and a single candle burned down to a nub. At the cavern entrance, a depression in the rock made a natural reflection pool where the cool mountain stream must have flowed like a fountain. Now, it was bone dry but for a trickle. Kiran leaned over and caught the stench of rotting leaves that had collected in the bottom.

The Pyletar—the symbol of their faith—was next to the pool on a small wooden altar. The base of smooth, dark wood was carved in the shape of a pyramid, a representation of the Sanctuary on the Mount, with a sphere suspended above, signifying the position of the Harvest moon at the time of the Coming of the Seventh Elder. But instead of a simple wooden sphere like the one in the Temple, at the apex of this Pyletar, cradled in a thin iron basket, was The Stone. Clear to the core, it was as transparent as fresh, spring water, yet it sparkled like nothing Kiran had ever seen before, casting rainbows on the altar.

"You know you want to touch it," said Jandon. "Go on. This is your chance."

Should he dare? Deke had said that when the Elders placed their hands on it, they could commune directly with the Great Father.

Kiran reached toward it and drew in his breath. He wanted so badly to feel it. As he leaned closer, myriad colors danced within. Gently, he laid his fingertips on it. Holding his breath, he waited. *Are you there?* Nothing. He waited a moment longer. Still nothing. He drew back. Maybe only Elders could do it.

Jandon stared at him. "Well?"

Kiran shook his head.

Jandon dropped to his knees at the altar, took a knife from his belt, and started to carve an X in the base of the Pyletar.

"What are you doing?" Kiran said. "This is the sacred Sanctuary!"

Jandon glanced up at him. "I want to be able to prove that I was here."

"But it seems so… wrong."

"Wrong, ha!" said Jandon. "Didn't you just say it's a sin to even be here?"

Kiran glared at him.

"Either way, may the Great Father forgive us," he said with a smirk. "Let's go." He jumped up, made a quick bow toward the altar, and took off running through the arch, scattering dry leaves to the ground. Kiran watched him go, shaking his head.

"Yeah, the Great Father will forgive you," he sputtered. *You're a Toran. Not a heathen bastard. Like me.*

He took one last glimpse of the Sanctuary on the Mount and dreamed about the day when he'd worship here. In better times, the Sanctuary must have been glorious, he thought, imagining what it looked like—the meadow of brightly colored flowers, the ivy-covered archway, the grand reflection pool next to the altar. The drought was taking its toll.

Dead wildflowers crunched under his bare feet as he sprinted across the meadow. The path, worn bare by seasons of methodical footsteps on their way in dedicated service to the Great Father, meandered through rocky crevices and around tight ledges toward the Bridge of Enrapture.

As Kiran approached, he slowed to catch his breath. Deke and Jandon were sure to be far ahead by now. He dreaded having to cross the rickety old bridge again. He gripped the hand ropes. His heart leapt into his throat as he stepped out onto the first plank. The bridge swayed and dipped, creaking with his weight. *Breathe. Breathe.* The bridge groaned with each step as he put one foot in front of the other to make his way across, his hands burning from gripping the ropes so hard. One last step and he was on solid ground again. He took off at a full run, leaving the path to take his own shortcut through the forest, dodging limbs and tree roots, determined to catch the others.

He leaped over a bluff and dropped to the ground, sliding on his side down the steep slope, rolling on loose gravel, grasping at tree limbs to slow his descent. Then, he was on his feet again, plowing through shoulder-high brush. He darted around a boulder and crashed through a thicket of blackberry bushes. He spun and tugged, the thorns ripping at his tunic. With a yank, he broke free and took off again, leaping over rocks and barreling through ferns. He slid down a bank slick with pine needles and landed on the path in front of Deke.

Kiran bent over, his hands on his thighs, his chest heaving. Deke was with the rest of the boys who'd been waiting to see if Kiran would jump. He could hear their laughter, the laughter that always made him feel small. "So you didn't have the guts to do it, huh?" he heard one say. He wasn't sure which. It didn't matter.

"I knew he wouldn't go through with it," said Deke.

"You left before I had a chance." He pulled a thorn from his foot. "I swear, if you could, you'd have the bells ring just to spite me."

"No, Kiran. Your fate is in the hands of the Great Father."

"Why do the bells ring?"

"Maybe the Javinians have mounted another raid and we need to take up arms," Jandon suggested. "The traitors always come after our bounty at harvest time—"

Deke held up his hand. "If Javinians attack, our warriors will be ready. Sentinels are posted on lookout. If even one of those heathens so much as sets foot in the village, we'll have him in the stockade by sundown."

Jandon cocked his head to the side. "But the bells could—"

Deke glared at him and he clamped his mouth shut. "A good Toran does not question. When he is summoned, he obeys."

Kiran's hands tightened into fists. "What is that supposed to mean?"

Deke rocked back on his heals, his expression solemn. *He looks just like his father,* Kiran thought. His wavy black hair, thick and rich, came to a point on his broad forehead. Some called it a demon's peak, while others were convinced it was a sign of wisdom. But his most arresting feature was his eyes, dark as a moonless night, each iris rimmed in gold. When he looked directly at others with those eyes, they knew that he was to be obeyed, without question. His voice taut, Deke said, "You've had your chance and failed."

"But I was just about to jump!" Kiran blurted.

"It doesn't matter, Kiran. You can't change who you are." The bells rang in the distance. "Besides, your time has run out. Do as you will, orphan. But *we* need to be there." He turned on his heel and strode toward the village. The others dutifully followed.

Kiran remained standing there, stunned, sure Deke knew something he wasn't sharing. Despite his pure lineage, underneath the cloak of virtue, shadows lurked. Dark shadows.

He heaved a sigh of resignation and dropped in line behind the others, following Deke down the well-worn path.

2

Kiran caught up to Jandon. "I think Deke knows more than he is letting on."

"Of course he does. He always does."

"I mean about the bells. The conclave. Why take me up there to jump today? Why would he care whether I made it at all?"

"Who knows? It's Deke. Why question?"

Kiran nodded, but he kept turning it over in his mind. Something wasn't right.

The path meandered along the forest's edge past tiny thatched-roof homes tucked into the hillside, their gardens laid out wherever flat land could be found for tilling. Kiran and Jandon came upon an abandoned farm, now fallow, the soil turned to dust. "I know this family," said Kiran. "They led a good, honest life, dedicated to the Way. I don't understand. Why is this happening to good people?"

"I know the family that took them in. They share the chores and ration the food. Now there's a mark on their door because they didn't make tithes."

"Well, how could they? With two families to feed?"

Jandon had no answer.

They came around a bend to a full view of the valley below, the bay, and the sea beyond, clear to the edge of the world. The forest from here to the village had been cleared over the years, felled to build houses and fuel the winter fires, the land left for pasture. In Kiran's childhood, it had been a lush, green meadow, fed by the rise and fall of nutrient-rich spring rains. But now, what remained was a barren plain, the surface a pattern of ridges in the dried earth like wrinkles on the face of an old man. The river had long since diminished to a muddy creek, winding through the lowland.

The Temple rose up from the landscape with its high-reaching stone walls and steep roof. Surrounded by the Temple Gardens, it was an oasis of green amid a world of brown.

Ding-dong-ong-ong, the bells rang out, echoing across the valley.

"Look at them all," Jandon said. Throngs of people were arriving from every direction—farmers and their wives with dirty-faced children in tow, craftsmen wearing their leather work smocks, shepherds called from the hills, dirt on their bare feet—all traveling with a singular purpose, all summoned by the bells.

Kiran wondered how close he would be able to get. During the weekly worship, he would sit outside the south window where he could sometimes hear the blessings. Today it would be too crowded.

As they neared the Temple, Jandon turned toward the village well. Kiran glanced down the path. Bria's green eyes met his and his breath caught in his throat. He quickly turned away.

"Aren't you thirsty?" Jandon asked. He glanced toward the well. "C'mon. She won't bite." Kiran inhaled a long, calming breath, then followed, his eyes on Jandon's boots. When he looked up again, Bria was standing right next to him.

"Hi, Kiran."

"Oh, h-hi," he stuttered and dropped his eyes to his hands. Her arm brushed his as she moved to let others pass. She was so close he was sure she could hear his heart pounding. Many mornings he had wandered the hills, hopeful to catch a glimpse of her as she tended her flock, but he never had the nerve to say hello. Now, she was inches away, smiling at him, her cheeks rosy from the heat, her deep green eyes alive and sparkling.

... like The Stone, he thought.

"Hi Bria," Jandon said, his gaze direct, unflinching.

"Oh, hi Jandon." She looked back to Kiran. "You boys are dripping sweat. What have you been up to?"

"Nothing," Jandon said too quickly, wiping his forehead. "Just obeying the summons." He flashed a smile. "How did you get down here from the mountain meadow looking so fresh and beautiful?"

She seemed not to notice the compliment. "The mountain meadow's barren. We've been forced down into the valley. Only it's not much better. My sheep lick the sand, trying to find water where there is none."

"But if you overgraze the valley now, what will happen come winter?"

"What would you have me do? Move into the woods? Into Javinian territory? There's no choice either way." She nodded toward the Temple. "The drought is worse than they would admit. It's time they do something about it."

The bells rang again. "Perhaps they are. Shall we go find out?" Jandon offered her his arm.

She nodded and turned to Kiran, expectant. In that fleeting moment he saw all of her in excruciating detail—how the curls of her soft, red hair fell around her face, her tunic pulled snug at her waist, the dirt on her small, bare feet—and reality seemed to fall away, as though she might take his arm instead.

But that would never happen.

"See you later, Kiran," Jandon said and led Bria away.

Kiran watched them go, his heart sinking. He headed down the road, hoping to get close to the Temple before being run off.

The bustle of the crowd reminded him of market days when he was a child. Shepherds would drive their flocks directly to butcher, and families would come to exchange eggs, milk, and grain. Craftsmen filled the row of narrow stalls that lined the street. Now, the stall doors hung askew from their broken hinges, the roofs rotten and sagging. Only ghosts passed through those doors.

Kiran rounded the corner and slipped into the Temple Gardens where he saw Old Horan standing near the back entrance. He hesitated, licking salty droplets from his lip, worried what might happen if he were seen with him. He liked the old man. Once he had saved Kiran's dog from a fight with a porcupine. Children teased him, calling him the one-eyed ogre. Adults stayed clear of his path. Some accused him of eating from the sea, but there was no evidence; he had none of the telltale lesions.

Years ago, Old Horan was to be an Elder, but something happened, something no one spoke of. Townsfolk whispered that, through the dark abyss that was his empty eye socket, he could see the future. Kiran had visited him many times, asking for his weather forecast. Old Horan could predict a storm ten days out, but no one else paid him any mind.

"Beware. The pulse of life ebbs," the old man warned, his one good eye fixed on Kiran. "The earth sickens and the snake bites. The ground is covered with thorns. To dust we shall go."

Old Horan was in one of his moods.

His bearded, disfigured face furrowed with concern. "Someone must go. Someone must go," he muttered, clucking his tongue.

Kiran glanced back the way he had come, wondering if he could slip away without upsetting the old man.

Old Horan seized him by the shoulders, his bony fingers digging into his flesh. "You will see," he said and pushed Kiran through the door and into a tiny side room. He eased the door shut behind them.

As Kiran's eyes adjusted to the dark, he saw the shelf piled with scrolls. "We're not supposed to be in here," he whispered.

Old Horan brought his finger to his lips, then pointed to a crack high up in the wall where light seeped through. He pushed two stools to the wall, climbed atop one, then gestured for Kiran to do the same.

Kiran pressed his nose against the wall and peered through the opening. They were directly behind the altar. A small boy was lighting the candles, which were wrapped in garlands of fresh flowers, yellow and orange.

Kiran looked at Old Horan.

The old man grinned.

Kiran turned back to the crack, his hands on the cool stone wall. The Temple's inner chamber was bigger than he imagined. Shutters in the timbered ceiling had been thrown open and shafts of sunlight crisscrossed, cutting through the stale air. Curious whispers blended with the sound of shuffling feet as the villagers filed down the rows of long, backless pews, cramming in like sheep in a pen.

From beside the altar platform came a chant in the deep, guttural language of the Elders. A hush came over the crowd and the followers rose to their feet. The chant grew in crescendo, reverberating through the Temple, as one by one the six Elders appeared on the altar platform. They were not in the usual purple cloaks that were worn at the weekly Worship of the Followers. Today, they were clad in full-length, white ceremonial robes.

Around and around they proceeded in a circle of worship, their robes brushing the floor, appearing as though they floated with divine grace. With each rotation their chant rose to a melodic symphony, then receded again to a deep, soothing resonance.

As he did so often, Kiran imagined how it would feel to be an Elder. He envisioned the day that he would be bestowed with the ultimate confirmation of dedication to the Great Father—the robe. He could smell the wool, feel the soft textile against his skin as it was ceremoniously draped across his shoulders, and the familiar gladness filled his heart as he imagined being uplifted by His Grace. Some day, he would pass into the realm of the Chosen. Some day. Then, he would know he was worthy, he would know who he was. Every worship day, seeing the Elders dressed in their robes, his dreams were rekindled.

The chant rose in crescendo once more, then came to an abrupt end. All was silent. The congregation watched in reverence, but with an air of detachment, it seemed. Was he the only one who didn't know what was going on? He searched their eyes for signs of concern, but saw only solace.

Old Horan's lips were moving, silently proselytizing, and a foreboding welled up inside Kiran. What did he know that the others didn't?

The Elders formed a line on the edge of the altar platform, their heads bowed like reverent statues, their faces lost within the hoods of their pure white robes. Aldwyn stood in the center, looking out over his congregation. He raised his hands, indicating to the followers to kneel, and they faithfully obeyed.

His voice boomed through the chamber. "You have been summoned to the Temple today with grave concern. In condemnation of our sins, this drought has been cast upon us. We cannot survive another barren harvest. In this, our time of peril, we must act. Therefore, it is decreed that seven of our youth shall set forth into the Land Unknown on a pilgrimage to the dwelling place of the Voice of the Father."

His words sent ripples of dissonant voices spreading through the crowd. A shiver of anxiety came over Kiran. The Land Unknown. No one traveled there. Ever. Demons lurked out there, evil Mawghuls that dwelled in dark places.

"Ah, the prophecy. Only suffering to be had," Old Horan sputtered away, prognosticating in his disjointed way. "Only suffering and sacrifice."

Aldwyn raised his hands, calling for silence. "They shall beg forgiveness for our sins and return with the blessing, as foretold in the Script of the Legend."

Old Horan inched next to him, his voice, low and raspy, "To certain doom, the lot of them... To certain doom." Then he laughed.

Kiran shrank back.

Aldwyn unrolled a new scroll and held it out before him. "Those who have been bestowed with the honor of this quest are as follows: Jandon, son of Hagen."

Jandon?

Somewhere in the midst, Jandon's mother cried out.

There must be some mistake, Kiran thought. Jandon was a simple farm boy with dirty trousers and bad manners. His only true skill was wooing the girls and keeping far from the watchful eyes of the Elders. Why would he be chosen?

Kiran spotted Jandon in the crowd. His mother seized him in her chubby arms and pulled him to her bosom, sobbing. His eyes darted side to side, seeking an escape. Aldwyn motioned for him to approach the altar. He pushed his mother aside and made his way through the crowd.

Old Horan wagged his tongue from side to side and mumbled, "So, it begins."

Kiran stared at the old man. "What begins?"

A wicked grin spread across his wrinkled face. Kiran turned back to the crack in the wall.

Jandon ascended the stairs to the altar platform and, as he proceeded toward Aldwyn, each Elder in turn bowed in blessing as he passed. Jandon looked as though he thought his soul might be snatched from him on the spot.

What an honor, Kiran thought. A real pilgrimage! He'd give anything to be able to go in Jandon's place. If he'd been chosen, he'd run to the altar, his head held high. *If only I was a Toran…*

"Deke, son of Morgan," Aldwyn continued. Heads nodded and the chatter increased.

Deke sprang from the pew and marched straight up the stairs toward the altar with a smug grin on his face. He took his place next to Jandon. Unease crept over Kiran. Deke wasn't surprised. He had known. He had known all along.

"Kail, daughter of Alicion." The announcement brought more gasps. Kiran was surprised, too. A girl? And not only that, she was the Flower Bearer, chosen as a young child to tend the Gardens of the Father and provide the floral offerings. Why would she be chosen for this quest? Certainly she wouldn't last a day in the wild, this fragile young girl with long blond hair and rosy cheeks. It didn't make sense.

"Innocent and pure," whispered Old Horan. "Innocent and pure."

Kail's parents smiled with pride. Her mother said something through clenched teeth. Kail jerked upright, correcting her posture, and moved toward the altar.

Aldwyn appeared to give up trying to keep the calm. He simply raised his voice over the bedlam. "Bhau, son of Sanders." Kiran knew Bhau well. He had been on the Mount with him earlier. He didn't like him much, but he was a strong boy, with broad shoulders and thick legs, dedicated to be a warrior, to fight in the name of the Great Father. It made sense that he would be selected. He looked the oaf now as he stood there, dumbfounded that his name had been called. His brother, Tobin, standing next to him, gave him a shove to get him moving.

"Bria, daughter of Laird," Aldwyn called out. Kiran felt a jolt go through him as though he'd been struck by a hammer. He gripped the stone wall. *It can't be!* He searched the crowd for her. *No, not her,* he silently pleaded. *Not her!*

He caught sight of her moving through the crowd, her red curls swaying side to side. The Elders bowed to her as she floated past them and took her place next to Jandon. Handsome Jandon.

Old Horan mumbled, "The matriarch. The mother to be." Kiran turned to face him, shaking. He hated the old man in that moment, despised him with every part of his being. He wanted to shout at the top of his voice, "Shut up!"

None of this made any sense. *Jandon? And Bria? What's going on? Why were they chosen?*

He leaned back to the crack in the wall. Aldwyn shifted his stance. "Rohders," he said and seemed to stand a little taller. Elder Morgan turned toward Elder Wregan and Kiran was sure he caught a look of surprise exchanged between them.

Aldwyn's voice called again. "And Kiran."

Gasps erupted among the villagers.

What? Did Aldwyn just say… Kiran?

Elder Morgan swung around, shaking with restrained fury. He looked right at the crack in the wall and Kiran sprang back.

"To your end and back again," came the haunting voice of Old Horan.

Kiran scrambled back to the crack. Aldwyn was rolling up the scroll. He slid it into its mantle with a definitive nod. It was done.

Elder Wregan had his eyes on Elder Morgan as though he expected him to do something, say something.

What's going on? Had Aldwyn gone against the other Elders?

Elder Beryl stepped forward. "Someone find the boy."

Old Horan gave Kiran a nudge.

Kiran shook his head. "There must be some mistake."

Old Horan grabbed him by the arm and dragged him down from the stool. "Go on now." He shoved him toward the door.

In a daze, Kiran made his way around the building to the front entrance. The crowd parted as he passed through the narrow vestibule and into the immense inner chamber. All at once, the congregation turned to stare at him. His throat went dry. The chamber stretched out before him, the altar so far in the distance it seemed impossible to reach. Kiran tried to take a step. It required all his attention to lift one foot then set it down again. All the while, faces hovered around him—watching, judging, scrutinizing. Somehow, he continued. The people seemed to move past him instead of the other way around as muffled voices swirled around his head in a haze of whispers. *The bastard child? On a pilgrimage? He's not even a true Toran.* The words, flinging through the air, stung like sleet, and he winced, again and again.

At last, he reached the altar and took his place among the others, standing still as a stone. He couldn't face the congregation, all those people. He looked over his shoulder, above the altar. He could feel that one knowing eye looking down on him. Kiran's throat tightened. *Does that old man really have the power of foresight?*

Aldwyn addressed the pilgrims. "Together, you shall bear the Voice of the Father with humility and dignity, for our fate is in your keeping. Make haste in your preparations. Time is of the essence. In one week's time, you shall go forth. With diligent prayer, we will await your safe return with the blessings of the Great, All-Powerful Father."

A cacophony of voices broke out. The villagers bustled about, everyone in a hurry to consult with everyone else. Heads nodded, hands waved in animated gestures, fingers pointed. Kiran stood motionless, taking it all in as if in a dream. He wasn't sure if they were celebrating or in a panic; the feelings and action blended together in a flurry.

Aldwyn laid his hand on Kiran's shoulder. He drew in a breath, as if he were about to say something, then simply smiled. Kiran fought the urge to let loose his flurry of questions.

Elder Morgan took hold of Aldwyn's arm. "We need to talk," he growled.

Aldwyn pulled away. "What's done is done."

Deke appeared next to Elder Morgan, his head held high. "What's wrong, Father?"

"Nothing that can't be made right," Morgan said. He turned from Aldwyn and put an arm around his son and patted his shoulder, pride in his eyes. They walked down the altar stairs, arm in arm, the elder's robe swaying behind them.

"What's going on?" Kiran whispered to Aldwyn.

Aldwyn gave him a reassuring smile and squeezed his arm. "We'll talk later," he said and turned to follow the others.

The other pilgrims disappeared in the crowd, their families gathering around to praise them.

Kiran stood alone, looking out over the congregation. Everyone had somewhere to go, someone to be with. He thrust his chin forward, threw his shoulders back, and headed toward the stairs.

No one waited there to praise him.

3

Kiran paced the floor of their home until finally the door opened and Aldwyn stepped in.

Kiran threw his hands in the air. "What happened in the Temple?"

Aldwyn went straight to the washbasin and splashed water on his face.

"What's going on?"

"Your chores?"

"They're done."

"The chickens fed? Water hauled?"

"Yes, now tell me."

Aldwyn spun around. "Don't you take that tone with me, young man."

Kiran dropped his gaze to the floor. "Yes, sir."

Aldwyn wiped his face with a towel. He hauled a rucksack from the corner and dumped the contents on the plank table. "You have preparations to make. Look over what I've packed for you."

Kiran plopped down on the bench and sifted through the pile. There was a waterskin, several small pouches of salt, a fork and spoon, a wooden cup, a tinderbox and a leather pouch stuffed with dry tinder, a length of rope, a short knife, a darning needle, a chunk of soap. "Do I need all this?"

"Is there anything there that you can go without?"

"How would I know?" He turned the tinderbox over in his hands, then set it down and picked up a pouch of salt. "I can't imagine why I'd need so much salt."

"The salt is for trade. It is valuable. Make sure to keep it in the water-proof box." Aldwyn put a kettle of water on the hearth. "We take it for granted here, but it is scarce elsewhere. Many generations ago, outsiders would come from far away lands to trade for our salt. That's how our village was settled. That's how we came to have a lot of the things we cannot make ourselves—knives, pans, forks. There are places in the world where metal is dug from the ground, turned in fire, and forged into shape."

Kiran examined the fork as though for the first time. He had never questioned where these things came from or how they were made. Why had he never asked? All of a sudden, he felt hopelessly ignorant. He dropped the fork and fiddled with the torn strap on the old rucksack.

"You'll have to find food and water along the way," Aldwyn said as he took two mugs from the cupboard. "You certainly can't carry enough for a trek this long."

"How long is it, Aldwyn?"

"Well, now… The dwelling place is on the far side of Wiros."

"Do you mean the *other* side? Of the *world*?" He shifted to the edge of the bench. "How will we know how to get there?"

Aldwyn smiled. "You will know."

Kiran sat back. Aldwyn rummaged around the kitchen, opening and closing cupboard doors. "Where is that bag of tarweed?"

"But no one has ever been there, right?"

Reaching into the back of a lower cupboard, Aldwyn found what he was looking for. "Ah. There it is." He brought the bag to his nose and smiled as he inhaled the aroma of the dried tarweed. He chose several nice leaves and placed them in the mugs, then dropped the bag in the pile on the table. "The Great Father will watch over you and guide you on your way."

"But why would He? I mean, isn't He angry with us right now? Isn't that why he sent the drought? We're going all that way to tell Him we're sorry. Why would He guide us there to do that?"

"Faith, Kiran. When the time comes, you will see."

Kiran stood up, took a few steps toward the window, then turned and paced back, trying to temper his curiosity. Aldwyn had always been lenient with him in private, but it was not the practice of the Torans. A Toran did not question. But today, Kiran could not hold back. "But that doesn't make sense!"

Aldwyn glanced up toward the Celestial Kingdom and took a deep breath. "It will be fine."

"Fine? You don't know, do you?"

"We know enough." Aldwyn walked around the central hearth, across the room and pulled a wooden trunk from under his bed. He took out several blankets and carefully compared their sizes and weights. He chose one and dropped it on the table. "It will get cold at night." He ladled hot water from the kettle, filling each mug, and sat down at the table. "There, drink your tea."

Kiran remained standing. "Old Horan said you were sending us to certain doom."

Aldwyn winced and stared into his tea.

"It must be a mistake."

"A mistake?" Aldwyn raised his eyebrows. "You question the wisdom of the Elders?"

"No sir." He lowered his gaze. " It is not my place to question. I am just trying to understand. Old Horan said—"

Aldwyn slammed his mug down on the table. "Don't you mind that crazy old man."

"But you've always said—"

"Never mind what I've said. Forget about him. Now, say what's on your mind."

"I want to know why we were all chosen."

Aldwyn sat back in his chair. He took a sip of his tea. "You will, in time."

Kiran drew in a breath. He looked Aldwyn directly in the eye. "Aldwyn, I want to know why *I* was chosen."

Aldwyn sighed. His expression turned introspective and his gaze shifted to the tiny shuttered window. Several long moments passed as though he were waiting for divine inspiration to speak.

Kiran wanted to shake the answer from him. "Something happened. I know. I saw it. You weren't supposed to call my name, were you?"

"That's enough!" Aldwyn rose from his chair. "Don't you question me. You were chosen by the Great Father. That's all you need to know."

"I am not a child! I know something's going on. And if I'm old enough to go, I'm old enough to be told why."

Aldwyn slammed his fist on the table. "You. Do. Not. Question!"

"I deserve to know!" Kiran grabbed his hat from the hook and left, slamming the door behind him.

His dog Echo trailed after him as he headed to his favorite spot, a high bluff overlooking the entire valley and the sea. He breathed deeply the humid night air, savoring the familiar mix of scents—salt, dry grass, hot sand. He came here when he needed to think, to feel the rhythmic surge of the sea—the heartbeat of the world.

Something wasn't right. Aldwyn had gone against the other Elders; he was sure of it. But why? Kiran put his arm around his dog. "Why would he take that risk, Echo?" He had gone against the Way before, when he taught Kiran to scribe. But they had kept it a secret. If others learned of it, they'd both be banished. But to go against the Elders, in front of the entire village… Is that what he had done?

Kiran heard a noise and spun around. Aldwyn was trekking up the hill. He sat down next to Kiran with a huff and wheezed, catching his breath. "I knew I'd find you here."

Kiran studied the man who was like a father to him. Wrinkles lined his weary eyes and his beard had grown thin. His frame was stooped and withered as though some great weight bore down on him.

Kiran pictured Aldwyn bent over, toiling in the garden under the burning sun. Alone. *How can I leave him?* Aldwyn had taken him in when anyone else would have shunned him. A dry lump formed in his throat. "Promise me you'll take your share of the tithes."

Aldwyn huffed. "I will do no such thing."

"But the other Elders do. And with me gone, and the drought and the garden. Who will water when it is your time of atonement and—"

"Now, that's enough. I didn't come all the way up this hill to talk about the farm." He ran his fingers down his long wispy beard and gazed out at the sea as if gathering his thoughts. When he spoke, his words came as slowly as snow melting in spring. "Before I was an Elder, before I knew I would be an Elder, I longed for such a quest. I believed so strongly, passionately. But it wasn't meant for me. I felt the hand of the Father lead me to my place there, amid the Elders." He pointed toward the Sanctuary, pausing, as if flooded with memories. He turned to face Kiran. "You, young man, are on a different path. This quest is *your* destiny."

"Yes, yes, to seek the Voice of the Father, I know. But why me?"

Aldwyn sighed the sigh of a teacher trying to reign in his wayward student. "Look out there." He gestured across the entire panorama. "What do you see?"

Kiran looked east, out over the Sea of Demarcation, squinting as he tried to focus on the edge of the world. Most days the waves tossed and churned, a vast tumult of white and blue that stretched all the way out to where it dropped off into the abyss. Tonight, as the last rays of sunlight skimmed across the surface, the muted colors of the sea merged into the sky as if they were one, without limit. It was times like this, he knew, when a man could be lured by the tranquil benevolence of the water, then, without warning, the winds would change, and send the man over the edge to his death. Kiran wasn't sure if that was what he was supposed to be thinking about. "I see…the sea."

"Ah, from here yes. But from the other side, it is the sea and a mountain."

"The other side?"

"How does it look on a different day? Or in a different season? Look to the forest. Do you see individual trees or a collage of color?"

"Well, I guess I—"

Aldwyn waved his hand in the air. "Search within yourself." He tapped Kiran on the chest. "Listen to your heart."

"I'm listening. I'm listening."

Aldwyn sat back and rubbed his chin the way he always did when pondering difficult questions. Kiran couldn't contain the smile that spread across his face. When he was young, he had imagined that Aldwyn could conjure magic by rubbing his chin. He knew it was the silly notion of a child, but it still came to mind every time he saw him do it.

"Here in the village, all we know comes from the Script. We study the scrolls, yet some preach the Way as if…" He turned to face Kiran. "But you, well, you see with different eyes."

"I've studied hard, you know I have. But the more I study, the less it seems I know." He sighed and poked at a hole in his boots. "I just have more questions."

Aldwyn smiled. "How innocent you are. And so perfect."

"You make me seem like a child. I'm sixteen!" He turned away. "It's just…all the rules." He looked north across the bay, to the easternmost peak of the mountain ridge, where the Sanctuary on the Mount sat perched. Anger welled up in him. He had stood on the ledge, inches from redemption. All he wanted was a chance to prove himself.

"Listen to me," Aldwyn said, taking Kiran by the arm. His eyes were set with determination, as if it were possible, by sheer will, to transfer his wisdom to Kiran. "You are to seek the dwelling place of the Voice of the Father and beg his forgiveness, but remember, the Great

Father works in mysterious ways. Knowledge and understanding can come from unexpected places. Seek wisdom from all whom you meet on this journey. But be cautious. These influences can also lead you astray."

"How will I know the difference?"

Aldwyn tapped him on the chest.

"Listen to my heart."

Aldwyn nodded. "Let that be your guide."

"But what if…?" Kiran twisted his boot in the sand. "What if my heart conflicts with the Way?"

"The search for truth is a grave task. This will not be an easy journey. Above all else, trust yourself."

"But the Script…?"

Aldwyn clenched his teeth. "The scrolls are not meant to be our only source of inspiration." He turned his gaze to the Sanctuary on the Mount for a moment, then shook his head. "We've become so… disconnected. I fear…"

"What? You fear what?"

He turned back to Kiran. "I fear I've already said too much. "

"What do you mean, disconnected?"

Aldwyn sighed. Then, as if to confirm he'd given Kiran too many things to think about, he patted him on the shoulder and said, "Clarity will come with time." Leaning on Kiran's shoulder for support, he rose to his feet and brushed the sand from his robe. "Maybe someday young Torans will learn the story of your travels."

"Really?" Kiran looked up at Aldwyn, his frustrations forgotten in an instant. "Will we be celebrated? Will there be a Book of our quest? I hadn't thought of that. We'll be heroes."

"Ah, now you are eager to go."

Kiran's face flushed red.

"Don't go off chasing the wind. Remember, patience. Only with patience and humility does wisdom come." A smile spread across Aldwyn's face. "Always so full of doubt you are. I have answered your questions as best I can. Now, you must seek for yourself. Why don't you stay and watch the sun set and recite the evening Verse. We'll talk further in the morning." He took a few steps toward their home, then stopped and turned back. He looked as though he had something more to say, but he only sighed and turned and headed home.

"Did you get all that?" Kiran asked his dog. Echo cocked his head to the side as if trying to understand the question. "At least I'm not the only one."

Time melted into the night as Kiran's confusion merged into an abstract longing that settled over him like a fog. Flashes of firebugs began to appear, one by one, in the tall grasses, and the landscape came alive, each tiny light sending a message in the dark. He thought of the many evenings he had spent chasing them, mesmerized by their magic—one of the many mysteries of the Great Father—and his disappointment as they always flitted just outside his grasp. *Those days are over,* he thought. *I have to start figuring these things out on my own.*

What was Aldwyn trying to tell me? He had to be prepared when he faced the Voice.

He jerked upright. *I am going to stand before the Great Father—and* speak *with Him.* He sprang to his feet. *If the Great Father will accept me as a true Toran, then everyone will.* "That's it!"

His hat fell to the ground and the dog let out a yip and spun around in a circle.

Kiran laughed out loud. "Yes! That's what I need to do." He stood tall, straightening his back. "I am going to be an Elder some day. I am. You'll see."

And so he made a vow. He would reach the Voice of the Father, no matter what it took, no matter how long. Then he would return home, with his head held high, bearing the blessings of the Great Father. He'd be a Toran—a real Toran. From this moment forward, his mission was clear, as though a door had opened before him that he hadn't known existed.

He plucked a switch of grass and stuck it in his mouth, then plopped down, snatched up his hat and placed it on his head, adjusting it just the way he liked it, and nodded with satisfaction. He lay back on his elbows and scratched Echo's ears. To the west, the last burst of sunlight blazed across the trees of the Lost Forest, burning orange and yellow. The amber sky turned pink, then magenta, then a deep, vibrant purple, transforming the Lost Forest into an abstract texture of leaves and branches, color and shape, light against dark. *A collage of color...*

Tipping his head back, he remembered how, as a child, he'd marvel at the stars as they popped out of their daytime hiding places. Now, they reminded him of all the things he still didn't understand and he felt small and insignificant. Like the orphan that he was.

Something still didn't make sense. Of all the people in the village, he had been chosen to go. Why? Aldwyn never answered his question. *Why won't he tell me?*

Kiran looked to the sky. "Why me?" he said aloud, daring to say it in the Tongue of the Father.

There was no answer.

Aldwyn was asleep in bed. The rucksack was propped against the table, the broken strap mended. Kiran went to Aldwyn's bedside and kneeled next to him. "I won't let you down," he whispered. "I will make it. I promise. I'll be an Elder someday, just like you. I'll make you proud of me."

He crawled up into his loft, but couldn't sleep. He stared up at the wood rafters that supported the thatch roof, stained black above the hearth by seasons of smoke. This was his home and now he had to leave. How many cups of tea had they had together? How many questions had he asked? Like the stone-piled walls, he had built so many memories, one atop the other. Would he ever see it again?

Finally, he fell into a deep sleep.

Hands gripped his arm. "Kiran, you must leave now."

The room was dark. It was still night. "What? Leave?" He shook his head, trying to emerge from his dream.

"The Javinians are attacking the village. You must go now!" Aldwyn's command hit him like a slap. He grabbed his tunic and jumped down from the loft.

The silhouette of a man hovered in the doorway. "Shush! Keep quiet. And no lanterns. The heathens could be right outside." Kiran recognized the voice. It was the warrior Shad.

Kiran slipped on his clothes, his nerves buzzing. Aldwyn cleared the table, stuffing everything in the pack. He wrapped some cheese and bread in cloth, tucked it in the top, and cinched down the straps.

Shad continued, "The pilgrims are meeting at the old well. Get your things together. Be quick." And he was gone.

"Here, put these on." Aldwyn handed Kiran his boots.

"But they're yours. I can't—"

"Don't argue."

"Aldwyn, what's happening?" Kiran whispered, his mind racing. "We can't leave now. We're not prepared. We don't even—"

"Shh. Pay attention and do as Shad says." Aldwyn slung an empty waterskin over Kiran's shoulder. "They must know of the prophecy," he muttered.

"Prophecy? You mean the quest?"

"Yes, yes. The quest." Aldwyn tied the pack on Kiran's back, took him by the shoulders, spun him around, and pushed him toward the door. "Once you are together, run as far and as fast as you can. Just get through the Lost Forest and past the border."

"But then what, Aldwyn? Where do we go from there?" Everything was happening so fast. He had so many more questions. He didn't know where to start.

Aldwyn flung open the lid to his trunk. "Here," he whispered in Kiran's ear. "This will guide you."

Kiran stared at the scroll in his hand. "But what am I supposed to do?"

Aldwyn took a deep breath, as if he were the one about to jump off a cliff. He hugged Kiran tight, then took hold of him by the shoulders. He tapped him on the chest with an encouraging nod. "Now go!" he said, and pushed him out the door toward the Land Unknown.

4

The harvest moon hung low in the eastern sky. The night was still young. He slung his pack over his shoulder and, with one hand holding his hat on his head, raced toward the well, his pulse pounding in his ears. He couldn't believe it. They were headed for the Lost Forest—Javinian territory. He was too excited to be afraid. He had been chosen. A real pilgrim. And he was on a real adventure, like he'd always dreamed.

The woods thickened. Trees closed in overhead, their leafy branches blocking all but a hint of moonlight. Kiran had to slow to a walk. The shouts of fighting men rose from the village. Kiran bit his lip. He tried to see what was happening, but the only thing he could make out in the moonlight was the Temple, in stark silhouette against the golden shimmering bay.

As he approached the old abandoned well, he searched the shadows for Bria. He saw Jandon first. Deke stood behind him, as calm and composed as an Elder waiting for his followers to gather before him. Bhau was there, too, shifting from one foot to the other, his hand on the hilt of the dagger at his waist.

"Look who dared to show," Bhau sneered.

Deke stepped in front of him. "I don't know what Aldwyn thinks he's doing, sending you, but you better be up to it."

Kiran glared back at him but said nothing. He leaned against a tree to wait. The chirrup of crickets grew louder in the still night.

Jandon whispered to Kiran. "I can't believe we're really going. Why would they send us? I mean, why the girls? Better yet, why Roh?"

Kiran was surprised. He hardly knew Roh, who was older than the other boys, and couldn't recall ever seeing him at the weekly Worship of the Followers. But Kiran wasn't aware of any reason he wouldn't be as worthy as the rest of them. Rumors were that he and his mother lived alone by the edge of the Lost Forest and had no farm. How he made a living, Kiran didn't know.

"We don't need his kind of trouble," Bhau said with a grunt. "He's just like his father."

"What about his father?" Kiran asked, curious now.

Deke looked at Bhau, then back to Kiran. His black eyes narrowed. He leaned in and spoke in a low whisper. "They sent him along with us to be rid of him, I'm sure of it. He's a bad seed."

The crickets stopped chirping. They all tensed, alert.

Bria and Kail appeared in the clearing escorted by the warrior Tobin. Bria greeted Kiran with a smile, her green eyes shining in the moonlight. Kiran's heart beat faster.

"Good evening, boys," she said, leaning on her walking staff, as calm as if they were headed out berry picking on a sunny, spring day. Kail stood behind Bria, her eyes downcast. The loaded pack looked enormous on her tiny frame.

Bhau motioned for them to step out of the clearing and into the shadows. "We're just waiting for Roh, now," he whispered.

"I'm here."

Bhau swung around, his dagger raised.

Roh was leaning on the tree right behind him.

"How long have you been there? Why didn't you announce yourself?" Bhau demanded.

Roh shrugged.

Kiran shot a glance at Deke. The crickets had never paused.

"All right. Listen to me now," Tobin said. "To get through the Lost Forest, follow this ridge. It leads to a hidden pass over the mountains. Once you are on the other side, back down among the trees, look for a stream. That's the border."

Roh stepped forward, "And what then?"

"From there, you're on your own."

"But how will we know which way to go?"

Tobin shrugged, a blank expression on his face. "That's all I know."

"But, we're not warriors," Kail said, chewing her lip. "What will we do?"

"Stay on the move until you're sure you've lost the Javinians. They'll track you."

Kiran glanced toward the village, anxious now to move on.

"Bhau can handle the lead, but you'll need a rear scout." Tobin pointed to Jandon. "You."

Jandon swallowed hard, his eyes darting from side to side.

Deke thrust his chin forward. "Hold on. Why Jandon?"

"Yeah, why me?" Jandon piped up.

Tobin looked to Jandon, confused. "You are the best athlete in the village. You always win at the games. Don't you want to be a warrior?"

"A warrior! No, no, no." Jandon took a step back, shaking his head.

"Why else would you compete?"

"Well, ah… Because all the girls come to watch."

Tobin raised his eyebrows in amusement. "Well, this is not the summer games. This is real. And you are in real danger. The Javinians will hunt you relentlessly. They are ruthless. Do you understand?" A rush of fear ran up Kiran's spine. He shot a glance over his shoulder. He knew the legendary tales of brutal torture—first the flogging with a leather switch, ripping and tearing pieces of flesh from the body, then the excruciating and humiliating execution where one was hung from a pole by the wrists and ankles and left to die. And the horrors of what they did to women were unspeakable. "You asked for my advice," Tobin said. "You're built for it. You keep watch from the rear."

Jandon hesitated, his expression sober. Then he nodded.

Tobin looked at each one of the rest of them as if analyzing their strengths, assessing their chances of success. Kiran wondered what he must have been thinking. They had no experience, no knowledge of the outside world. Did they even have a chance? Tobin shook his head. "May the Great Father watch over you."

They fled westward, venturing deeper and deeper into the Lost Forest. Bhau, born to be a warrior, with bulging arms and a thick neck, lumbered along, his eyes searching the landscape, scanning every rock and crevice for movement, his ears alert for unnatural noises that meant danger. The others followed as he crisscrossed through the forest, traveling in a sporadic pattern.

Jandon took up the rear, constantly looking back over his shoulder, occasionally circling back to scan the path behind them.

As dawn broke, the terrain shot abruptly skyward, and without slowing, they trekked up the rocky foothill, traversing twists and turns, climbing into the mountains. Soon, they had to crouch on hands and feet to scramble over boulders and encountered rock faces so steep they had to work together, pulling each other up and over. Kail struggled to keep up. Again and again, she fell, her pack pulling her off balance.

The hills to the north and south of the village had gently sloping ascents, easy and welcoming. But these mountains were steep and jagged. Kiran had always longed to explore these alluring peaks; they beckoned from afar, promising of the wild and unfamiliar, stirring his sense of adventure. But now he felt a sorrowful disappointment. There was only barren isolation here, a soulless beauty, like the grace of a hunter—silent and deadly.

Kiran grunted and huffed his way up the mountain, unused to the heat and altitude, his pack growing heavier with each step. He tried to set his own pace, a rhythm to numb his mind and shake his dark, somber mood. With each step, Kiran's sense of foreboding grew stronger, the words of Old Horan echoing in his mind. *Someone must go… to certain doom.*

When Kiran slowed to catch his breath and adjust the pack on his back, Jandon thundered past. "Can't you keep up?" he teased.

Kiran grimaced. "Aren't you supposed to be watching for the Javinians in the rear?" He glanced behind them. "Where's Kail?"

Jandon shrugged.

Kiran decided to wait. Not long after, Kail came around a pine tree, trotting along with her head down, breathing hard, her tunic soaked with sweat, blood stains at her knees.

"Are you all right?"

She gave him a pained look, as if answering would take too much effort. He let her pass and took a long, careful scan behind her before turning to follow, keenly aware that he was now at the rear of the group.

At mid-morning, they scrambled up a rise and reached a ridgeline barren of trees. The sun hung low in the sky, burning through the thin air. Rivulets of sweat snaked down Kiran's neck. It was too quiet here. The usual sounds of the forest were absent—the chattering of squirrels, birds chirping in the treetops—only the steady whisper of the wind. The cry of a raptor pierced the silence and Kiran looked up with a start. High above, raptors kettled, hundreds held aloft, soaring on the wind as if lifted from below by invisible hands.

He slowed, his gaze drawn back along the bald-faced ridge. The glare of the late morning sun blinded him to anything following from behind. He shaded his eyes with his hands and squinted, scanning for movement.

He thought he saw something.

He stopped short. He turned back toward the front of the group. Bhau was in the lead, with Roh right behind him, and then Deke and Bria. Jandon followed, waving, urging him to keep up. He glanced back the way they had come, sure he had seen something, but saw nothing now but bare rock. He moved forward again, keeping watch over his shoulder. Jandon asked what was wrong. Had he seen something or hadn't he? He wasn't sure. He couldn't explain it. But he couldn't let it go. Jandon shrugged it off and moved to keep up with the others.

Then it hit him. Kail was missing.

He spun around and ran back the way they had come, then dropped among the trees. Still he did not find her. He retraced their passing, downward, scrambling across the rocks, fear growing inside him. He came around a stand of pines, and at last he found her, sitting on a rock crying, her hair matted with sweat, her face red. Her pack lay on the ground next to her. He felt so relieved he didn't know whether to hug her or scold her.

"Kail, are you all right?" He sat down on the rock beside her. In one hand, she held a small bread loaf, and in the other, her waterskin.

"I can't do this," she cried. "I don't belong here. I should be tending the Gardens right now."

"We just need a rest. The others will have to wait."

"But they won't. You know they won't," she cried. "They're not going to risk their lives waiting for *me*. We have to get to the border."

"Aldwyn said we are to stay together. And we'll do just that."

"But Kiran, look at me. I'll never make it." She squeezed her eyes shut and tears started to flow again.

"You will," he said, taking her hand and squeezing it. "We are not going to abandon you. *I'm* not going to abandon you."

"But we don't even know where we are going. What are we supposed to do? Nobody told us anything. I don't know what I'm supposed to do!"

What could he say? She was right. They were running with no plan.

He caught himself. That wasn't quite true. He had the scroll. He reached back and felt for the bulge where it pressed against the side of his pack. Aldwyn had said it would guide them. But how? Were there actual, specific directions? But he couldn't just take it from his pack and start reading right then. He'd be found out.

Maybe he should tell her he had it. Maybe it would ease her mind. It could be their secret. But what would he tell the others? What if he couldn't translate it anyway? What if he got it wrong? Then where would they be?

He'd have to find a moment alone to read it first. Then he'd tell them all.

"I don't know the answers," he said and put his arm around her shoulders. "But I do know that the Great Father chose us and is watching over us now." He winced as he said the words, remembering how he had argued with Aldwyn, but he didn't know what else to say.

She sniffled and sat up straight, trying to gain her composure. She glanced to the sky, guilt in her eyes. "You are right, Kiran. I'm sorry. I'll try harder to keep up." She took a sip from her waterskin. "I just need to rest awhile longer."

Kiran nodded.

A ground squirrel with thick, fuzzy brown fur and a stubby tail emerged from the brush a few yards away and inched toward them, its curious black eyes shining in the sunlight.

"He's so cute," Kail cooed. She broke a morsel of bread from the loaf and tossed it to the ground. The squirrel scurried forward, snatched up the snack, and swallowed it whole. "Aww, just look at that." She tossed another piece and it came a little closer.

The critter rocked back on its hind legs and stood, wrinkling its nose, whiskers twitching, then cocked its head to one side, as though it were trying to discern whether they were dangerous.

Kiran met the gaze of the tiny creature and for an enchanting moment, their eyes locked and he sensed a feeling of reverence pass between them; it was more than curiosity, it was a connection of one sentient being to another.

"Do you ever wonder how the Great Father sees all, looking down from the Celestial Kingdom?" Kiran mused aloud. "Maybe he sees us through the eyes of the squirrel."

Kail sat back and looked at Kiran as if he'd gone mad. "What are you saying? You think that the Great Father is a squirrel?"

"No, no, no. I just meant… Never mind," he said, silently scolding himself. He knew better than to voice his questions to others.

Suddenly, the squirrel jerked up on its hind legs, standing fully erect, its head turned away from them. It held there for moment, turning its head, first this way, then that, its ears perked upward, then dove into its burrow. "Awww, don't be afraid. We're not going to hurt you," Kail said.

Then Kiran heard the thump-thump of footfalls on rock. He drew in his breath. There was no mistaking the distinctive sound of the wooden soled shoes of the Javinians. He looked at Kail and their eyes locked together in a shared bond of utter fear. He silently mouthed, "Shhh," and eased down off the boulder and crouched behind it. She followed, careful not to make a sound. The thump-thump echoed across the rocky mountainside. Kiran tried to focus on the footfalls, straining to hear over the sound of his heartbeat pounding in his ears. They were getting closer and closer.

He and Kail huddled together, shaking. Kiran's nerves buzzed. All of his senses came alive—the sharp smell of pine, the gritty taste of dust. He focused on her face—her bright blue eyes, as rich as a late autumn sky, the soft, faint freckles that dotted her nose, like his—and somehow he felt oddly detached, as if this wasn't happening to him, but rather to a character in a festival play, acted out before him on stage, and he was simply a spectator in the audience, watching this boy and girl, cowering behind a rock, their young lives in jeopardy.

Thump-thump, thump-thump—his heart pounded in his chest.

They waited.

Footsteps kept coming, closer and closer—*thump-thump, thump-thump*. He was sure the Javinians would kill him on the spot, driving their cudgels into his skull, and drag Kail off to their lair. *Thump-thump, thump-thump*. Sweat wetted his palms. He kept staring into Kail's blue eyes. She was the Flower Bearer; she could not die. They had to live. He had to survive. He must. Aldwyn needed him. The whole village needed him. He must get to the Voice of the Father, not die here on this barren, heartless mountain. Not today.

Thump-thump—bursting in his ears, terror rising in him. *They're right in front of the rock!* He clenched his jaw, his muscles straining. Kail closed her eyes, shutting him out. He was alone. The pounding footsteps—*thump-thump, thump-thump*—drowned all thought. He fought the urge to run, to flee, his entire being focused now. *Do not move.* He held his breath. *Thump-thump.*

The footsteps never slowed. They ran right by, heading away now, fading in the distance. He let out his breath and gasped for air.

He slipped from behind the rock, motioning for Kail to stay hidden. From behind a scrub tree, he spotted five muscled warriors running along the treeline, a distance off now, long bows strapped to their backs, spears in their hands.

"Hey, there you are." A voice cut through the air. Kiran spun around. It was Jandon.

"Shh!" Kiran mouthed, pointing. Jandon followed the direction of Kiran's finger. His mouth fell open. He dropped to his belly, breathing hard.

Kiran waited for the Javinians to drop back among the aspen, then motioned for Jandon and Kail to move. "Lead us back," Kiran whispered to Jandon. He obeyed without question, darting through the sparse trees, setting a brisk pace, his sleek, athletic body made for running. Kiran and Kail kept up with him, fear coursing through their veins, spurring them on.

They scrambled up the talus and crept along the open ridgeline where they found the others resting in the shade of a rocky overhang. "This is unacceptable," Bhau chided as soon as they arrived. "You need to keep up and stay with us. You disappeared without telling anyone."

Kiran tried to catch his breath, his blood still racing through his veins. "Kail had to rest, we—"

"The Javinians, we saw them," Jandon blurted. "Five of them."

Bhau leapt to his feet, alert now, scanning the mountainside. "Which direction?"

"That way," Kiran pointed. "Below the treeline."

"Ha! They've gone the wrong way. Let's get moving."

Alert now to every sound, they fled. By late afternoon, they were back in the thick cover of the forest, the shade of the towering pines a respite from the blazing sun. Before long, they came upon a rocky creek, just as Tobin had described. The forest was quiet, save for the gentle gurgle of flowing water. They fought through prickly bushes that crowded the water's edge to get a drink and fill their waterskins.

"This is it, the border of our lands," Deke said. "Don't worry, my friends, the Javinians will give up chase now. They wouldn't dare follow us into the Land Unknown."

Roh gave him a hard stare. "How can you be sure?"

"My father said that once we crossed the border, the threat of the Javinians would be gone."

"Your father, huh? We should be cautious just the same."

Kiran heard a noise and whipped around, searching for movement. A raven swooped through the forest, calling the familiar *cur-ruk cur-ruk*. Kiran glanced at Roh and exhaled.

"See. It's just a bird," Deke said and jumped across the creek.

The others followed.

So, this is it, thought Kiran, staring into the dark woods. *The Land Unknown.* A knot tightened in his stomach. If Deke were right, and the Javinians wouldn't dare follow, just what was there to fear?

5

They passed through a valley of tamaracks and over a thick carpet of soft, yellow needles. With every silent footstep, the threat of the Javinians seemed to fade.

The terrain dipped abruptly where a mountain stream spread into a marsh. Flocks of white geese and long-legged cranes roosted in the shallows. The far side turned to shrub-choked swamp.

Jandon came along side Kiran. "I could use a swim."

Kiran shrugged. "We haven't seen any sign of Javinians. Perhaps Deke was right."

A pair of cranes circled for a landing, their throaty rattle-call piercing the air.

"They don't seem worried," Jandon said. He dropped his pack, tossed off his boots, and ran down the bank and plunged in. Hundreds of geese simultaneously took flight, lifting off in an explosion of wings whooshing through the air.

Awe-struck by the magnitude of sound, Kiran marveled as the whirring tempest transformed into a melodious hum, a song of songs, rising ever skyward as geese separated into trails of white specks against the dark blue sky.

"Anyone with ears knows we're here now," Roh said. "We need to keep moving."

Kail slumped over onto her side. "I can't go on like this. We've been running all night and day."

Kiran hated to admit it, but he agreed with her. His back ached and his feet were blistered. He took off his boots and let his aching feet soak in the water.

"The Great Father awaits," said Deke. "As long as we have daylight, we travel."

"Fine. But which way? We need a plan," said Roh.

Deke looked Roh up and down. "There is no need for you to worry. The Great Father will guide us."

"And how will He do that?"

Deke flashed a smile. "I will know. Just follow me."

"What makes you so sure?"

"My father told me that I was to watch for the signs, that they would be clear."

Did he mention the scroll? Kiran wondered.

"Your father?" Roh said. He stared at Deke, his face like stone.

Deke stared right back. "We are pilgrims of the Great Father. We go where passion takes us."

Roh turned to Kiran. "So, we need a plan."

"That *is* our plan," Deke hissed through clenched teeth.

Deke and Roh glared at each other. Kiran looked at Roh, then back to Deke, wondering what was going on between them. He glanced at his pack. The scroll was in there. All the Elders must have known what wisdom it held, including Deke's father. Watch for signs. Was that all it said?

Deke sat down to put his boots back on. He squinted into the sun and gestured toward the brush. "We'll head that way."

"Into the swamp?" Kiran said. "We'll get lost in there."

Roh mumbled to Kiran, "We're already lost."

Kiran stifled a grin. "If we follow the creek upstream, we can fill our waterskins and find a narrow spot to cross."

"No. We are to go this way. I'm sure of it. We will travel until nightfall and rest wherever we find ourselves."

Kail shook her head. "But it's the full moon."

Bhau hoisted his pack to his back. "A warrior sleeps where he can, moonlight or no moonlight." He turned to Jandon. "This is why girls aren't warriors."

"This is not how things are supposed to be!" Kail wailed.

Bhau put his hands on his hips. "Oh yeah, how are things *supposed* to be?"

"We were supposed to be blessed before we left. We were supposed to receive guidance and preparation. And I am certainly not supposed to risk sleeping directly under the rays of the full moon!" Tears flowed down her rosy cheeks.

Bhau snorted. "The Javinians will take more than the moon."

Kail burst with fury. "But our virtue!"

Roh crouched next to Kail. "We'll figure something out," he whispered, then glanced back toward the woods, his eyebrows creased with concern. "But we have to get moving."

A raven called out a loud caw from deep in the woods. Kiran turned to Roh and saw concern in his dark eyes. Roh whispered to him, "I'd get my boots back on if I were you."

Kiran nodded in silent understanding. He slipped on his boots, then seeing that Roh had never taken off his pack, reached for his own.

Sound erupted in the forest behind them. They all turned. Squawking ravens. Roh whispered, "We need to go. Now!"

"Into the swamp!" urged Deke. He grabbed his pack and sprinted for the brush. Bhau was right behind him. Jandon jumped up, tried to get both his boots on at once, and fell back down. With one boot on and one in his hand, he grabbed his rucksack, and ran after Deke.

Kiran looked to Roh in a moment of indecision, his heart pounding in his chest. Should they stay and fight, or flee? Roh hoisted Kail's rucksack onto her back. "Follow Deke," he said. "They can't track us there. Go!" Kail plunged into the water, splashed across to the other side, and disappeared in the brush. Bria followed, dragging her pack as she ran.

Kiran hesitated, still unsure.

"There's no honor in dying here," Roh said and ran after them.

Kiran nodded, slung his pack over one shoulder, and rushed across the marsh. Just as he entered the brush, the strap on his pack snapped and the weight dropped away. He stumbled forward, then spun around. A Javinian burst from the woods, headed straight for him, his spear held high.

Kiran froze.

The spear sliced through the air. *Thwack.* A crane let out a squawk and flopped over. The Javinian came to a halt, a big grin on his face. Then he saw Kiran. Their eyes met. They faced each other for a long moment, neither one moving. Then Kiran grabbed his pack and plunged into the tangle of branches.

His loose rucksack bounced against his back and his empty waterskin slapped against his side. The others weren't far ahead. He ran as fast as he could, his hands out in front of him, ducking and dodging as branches whipped him in the face. He closed his eyes and ran blind, following the sound of branches scraping across their packs.

He tried to think, tried to sort out what happened. That Javinian was no warrior. He was a boy, about Kiran's age. He wasn't chasing them. He had no idea they were even there. But he had crossed the border. Why?

The sandy bottom turned to a muck that oozed over the top of his boots and he was forced to slow his pace. Things wriggled and crawled through the weeds. Each step stirred the stagnant swamp water and the suffocating humidity became saturated with the stench of decay.

Soon dusk descended and a dark cloud rimmed by the eerie yellow glow of twilight loomed overhead. Swarms of insects, from every direction, flew in his face, in his eyes and mouth. They got under his tunic and crawled across his chest, biting everywhere. He swatted at the air around his ears. Finally, he buried his face in his tunic, pulling it up over his nose with one hand while he swatted with the other.

The marsh transformed into a dark, shadowy place with the murky smell of death and a monotonous hum. Lightning flashed through the clouds and thunder rolled over the hills.

When finally he trudged upward, out of the wretched swamp, Jandon was sitting on the ground, putting on his other boot. Kiran looked back from where they had come. The bog stretched away before him, a vast, bottomland of tangled brush. Anything lost in there might never be found, he thought, wondering if the Javinian boy had followed.

"You all right?" Roh asked.

Kiran nodded.

"There," he said, pointing.

Kiran could just make out a ledge jutting from the rocky hillside. From there, they'd be able to see the entire swamp and anyone who might be following them. Kiran nodded.

Roh took off without waiting for agreement from anyone else.

As they got to the ledge, clouds passed over the moon again and rain poured down in sheets as though the clouds had burst overhead. Bria lifted her arms to the sky and danced around, her head tilted upward, catching raindrops in her mouth. She took Kail by the hand and they twirled around together, the rain soaking them.

Kiran leaned against the rock, his eyes fixed on Bria, imagining how it would feel to dance with her, to hold her in his arms. Lightning lit the sky and in a flash he saw the shape of her body where her wet tunic clung to her, revealing every curve. The vision was intoxicating and he felt the familiar stirring in his body. Thunder boomed again, as if threatening to drive the thoughts from his mind.

Bhau nudged Kiran. "We're being chased by Javinians and they're frolicking in the rain." He shook his head. "Girls."

Bhau was right; this was not the time to let their guard down. But he stood, frozen in place, transfixed. He was far from home, in a place he'd never been, chased by their feared enemy into an unknown land, and before him was the most beautiful girl he'd ever laid eyes on, dancing in the rain under the full moon. And all he could think about was her soft skin, her sweet lips.

Roh popped his head out of an opening in the rock wall, holding a flaming torch in his hand. "What are you waiting for?"

All at once, they hurried inside and stood huddled together, dripping on the dirt floor. They were out of the rain and hidden from view, but somehow Kiran didn't feel any safer. The musty, dank cave was a tangled maze of cracks and crevices that harbored the unknown, hidden and waiting. The air was stale. Shadows flickered at the edges of the torchlight, as if the light alone kept the demons of the dark at bay.

"What the blazes! Where have you brought us, Roh?" demanded Deke.

From back in the deep recesses of the cave, Kiran heard scratching—the sound of claws on rock. Something scurried about. Kail heard it too. "What was that?" she asked.

Everyone paused to listen.

"Did you check for Mawghuls?" Jandon asked Roh.

"Mawghuls!" Kail cried, clutching the pomander at her neck.

"They live in holes in the ground or deep in caves like this one," Jandon whispered. "They suck out all your blood, sap your strength, and then feed on your body while you're still alive. They steal your soul!"

Kiran shuddered; he knew the stories well. Everyone did. The village folk warned not to go out alone at night, to stay out of the forest. Mawghuls were demon spawn. If you came across one, you'd have no chance.

Kail squeezed her eyes shut.

Roh glared at Jandon. "Knock it off. You're scaring the girls."

"We're not scared," said Bria, putting her arm around Kail.

"Look," said Roh. He paced the perimeter of the cave, holding the torch to the walls. The interior was no larger than a sheep's pen. The ceiling was high enough to stand near the front, but sloped down to the dry dirt floor in the rear. Water dripped from the ceiling, trickling down the walls in tiny rivulets. There was a stack of dry timber near the back.

Roh circled around to face Jandon and held the torch in front of him. "See. No Mawghuls."

"Ee-yhew!" Jandon curled his nose in disgust. "What's that smell?"

"It's a dung torch."

"What?"

"How do you think it burns?"

"Well, it stinks."

"Well, it works." Roh shoved the torch toward him. It sizzled with the rush of air. "Here, go look for your monsters. If you find one, get some more dung."

In a rush of movement, a screeching black mass emerged from high in the back corner of the cave. A whirlwind of dark shapes darted around their heads in awkward, chaotic angles, the air crackling with the sound of their wings. Kail screamed, and in one fluid movement, the winged creatures swirled out of the cave.

"Good heavens! What was that?" Bria said, breathless.

"I got one," hollered Bhau.

One of the creatures lay on the floor, its wing bent. Jandon lowered the torch to examine its leathery wings and furry body. It wriggled and writhed, trying to take flight. Bhau stomped on it. "Nasty little beast," he growled.

"It didn't harm us!" Bria cried, a glint of hatred in her eyes.

"They won't be back. They hunt at night," Roh said to no one in particular.

Bhau dug the tip of his boot under the dead creature and flipped it out of the cave. "Good riddance."

Deke dropped his pack with a thump. "We'll hold up here for the night," he said as he sat down and reclined against the rock wall.

Roh stared at him for a long moment, as if he were about to say something, then shook his head. He grabbed a branch from the stack and snapped it at his knee.

Bria set down her pack to help. She took the torch from Jandon and put it to the pile Roh was making. The dry tinder crackled and popped, sparking to life. The cave lit up with a warm glow of the fire and, somehow, it didn't feel so intimidating.

Kail paced next to the fire, scratching her arms. "I stink from that filthy swamp and I itch. There were bugs all over me!"

"Are you girls going to stand there and complain or get dinner cooking?" Bhau said.

Kail stared at him with a pouty face. Bria strode across the cave, hands on her hips, her face inches from his. "Let's get something straight. I am not your wife! Make your own dinner!"

"Ouch! The cat has claws." He smirked and nudged Jandon with his elbow as he lowered himself to the floor, stretching out next to him. To Kail, he said, "You'll help with my boots, won't you?" He grabbed her by the wrist and pulled her to the floor. "What's this?" He ran his dirty fingers across her pale neck to the pomander that hung there. "Trying to resist my charm?"

Kiran leapt to his feet, clenching his fists. "Let her go! Just because we are out of the village doesn't mean the Father isn't watching!"

"Simmer down," Bhau growled, facing him down. "It's no sin to rub my feet." He pulled off a boot and pushed his bare foot toward her.

"Oh my!" she cried, her face going pale.

Bhau's foot was covered with slimy black worms and dripping blood. "Bloodsuckers," he grunted. "From the swamp."

Kiran looked down at his own feet and shuddered. *That means…* He fumbled with his bootlaces and tugged off his boots. Streams of blood trickled down his feet. His ankles were covered with the black slugs, latched onto his flesh, engorged with his blood. *Stay calm*, he told himself. He ripped one off. The fat, squishy worm burst in his hand and his own blood oozed down his fingers. His stomach squeezed and the taste of bile filled his mouth. *Breathe, breathe, don't throw up. You'll never hear the end of it.* "What do we do?" he asked, trying to sound calm.

"Use your fingernail, like this," Roh said. He had his boots off and was flicking worms from his feet one by one.

Jandon whirled around, hopping from one foot to the other, tugging at one on his ankle. As he yanked, it stretched, but wouldn't let loose. "Get off me!" he wailed.

"Or salt," Roh said. "Anyone have any salt?"

"I do, I do," said Kiran. He rubbed the blood from his hands on the dirt floor and then fumbled through his pack for the pouch of salt. He hesitated. Aldwyn had said it was for trade. He looked at his foot and his stomach did a flip. He ripped the pouch open and sprinkled some on his ankles, then watched with a mix of horror and relief as the worms wriggled and writhed, then shrank and fell off. His stomach began to settle. A little salt was all it took.

Jandon stuck his foot in Kiran's face. "Get them off, get them off!" he screamed, his eyes white.

"Stand still then," Kiran told him, laughing in spite of himself.

"It's not funny! Get them off! Get them off!"

"Actually, it is." Kiran grabbed Jandon by the calf and shook some salt on his foot, then the other. Jandon started to calm then; his breathing slowed as he exhaled in several loud huffs.

Roh leaned over to inspect the worms with a dramatic gesture. "We're saved. Kiran slayed the monsters."

Jandon smirked. "Very funny."

Kiran passed the pouch to Bria who was calmly checking her toes.

Kail lay curled up on the floor, clutching her pomander in her tiny hand, sobbing. Kiran wished there was something he could do to comfort her. She was right. This was miserable. The bloodsuckers had gotten to him—and the bugs, and the heat, and the mud.

Bria took Kail's boots and her own to shake them outside the cave. Kiran tucked the pouch of salt back in his pack and followed her out.

Heavy clouds had rolled in. It was too dark now to see anything but the silhouettes of the treetops, tinged by the muted light of the moon.

"Maybe a cave isn't the best place to hide," Bria whispered. "If they find us, we'll be trapped, with nowhere to go."

A stroke of lightning split across the heavens. Thunder clapped with a crackling roar, and the hush left behind spoke of unease, as if the Great Father were sending an ominous message.

6

They retreated to the shelter of the cave. He propped his boots against the wall next to the fire to dry and noticed what appeared to be a drawing scribbled there. "Hey, Roh, what do you make of this?"

Roh took a stick from the fire and held it to the wall. "I'm not sure."

"Looks like an animal. Don't you think? Look, it has pointy ears and big owl eyes."

"It looks like a Mawghul!" Jandon exclaimed, looking over Kiran's shoulder. "I told you. Black, scaly beings with big, round bulging eyes that eat people whole—in one gulp."

"Look, there're more, way up." Bria pointed to the ceiling.

"It's just the work of savages," Deke grumbled.

"What do you see?" Roh shouted over the patter of rain pounding the ground outside.

"Well, there's more than one drawing. First, there is a man and an animal in the forest. Then a huge mouth, I think. It looks like teeth. Then, in the next scene, the animal is gone and the mouth is closed. Like the forest swallowed him."

"Mawghuls, I knew it!" Jandon said. He paced in a circle, biting his lip. "We're doomed. We should go back."

Roh turned to Jandon, his eyes hard as stone. "There is no turning back."

His words echoed through the cave, leaving a pulsing silence in their wake.

Deke spoke first, "Well, only one of us is going back anyway."

Kiran turned to Deke. "What are you talking about?"

"The Seventh Elder, you know, the prophecy." He shrugged with a dismissive wave of his hand. "No, of course you don't."

The prophecy? Where had he heard that before? Kiran set his jaw and glared at Deke. He was tired of being dismissed. "Everyone knows the Seventh Elder will come."

Bria stepped in. "But we don't know when. According to the prophecy, the Voice of the Father will choose. Do you understand? If it's true, one of us will be the Seventh Elder."

"What do you mean? If it's true?" Kiran asked her.

"People say it was in the scroll that went missing during the Time of Dissention. My father's not so sure."

"Of course it's true," Deke said. "What does your father know? He's not an Elder."

Kiran's eyes went to his pack and the scroll he harbored there.

"We do not question the ways of the Great Father. By the Script, He guides us. We follow."

Roh glowered. "And by that you mean, He will guide *you*, and we are to follow *you*? Is that it?"

"My father told me—"

"Your father's not here. Aldwyn told us to do this together. He didn't say anything about following you."

Deke clenched his teeth. "But I will recognize the signs."

"And how is that? Do you know something you're not telling us? Something in the Script?"

"I do," Kiran blurted.

"You do what?" asked Roh, his eyes still on Deke.

Kiran fumbled through his muddy pack and held the scroll out before him. The pounding of the rain echoed through the cave. Kiran faltered, the weight of their eyes bearing down on him. "Aldwyn gave me this scroll before I left," he said, his voice crackling like dry wood on the fire.

After a long moment, Roh said, "Why do you think he gave it to you?"

"He, uh, he said it would guide us."

"How is that?" Roh asked, his gaze intense, as if he could extract the truth by his stare alone. "Only Elders can read the scrolls."

Kiran hesitated. He knew he must trust Aldwyn. He would have known the others would learn their secret. He closed his eyes and took a deep breath. "I can read it. Aldwyn taught me to scribe."

"What!" Deke bellowed, his voice thin. "But you're not even a Toran! I haven't even been taught to scribe yet. First, you must graduate the Lessons, then go through the Rites, then earn a seat as an Elder, *then* you learn the Tongue of the Father. That is the Way!"

Kiran stared at Deke. What could he say? The look Deke gave him was one of such fierce condemnation that for a long moment no one said anything.

Kiran looked to Jandon for support, but he turned away. Kiran's heart sank. Jandon was his best friend. But he had to keep this secret, even from him. He hoped Jandon would understand.

"Wait a moment." Deke narrowed his eyes. "You're lying. The other Elders would never allow it."

Bria spoke up, "He'll prove it one way or the other right now. Read it to us."

Kiran exhaled. Deke rocked back on his heels and crossed his arms, his eyes like daggers.

"Go ahead, Kiran," Jandon said. "Show us how special you are."

"The fact that Kiran has the Script here, and can read it, is a blessing," said Bria.

Kiran stared at his companions for a long moment before he pulled the leather mantle from the scroll. Roh quickly made a small torch and stood next to him, holding it so he could see to read. Kiran carefully unrolled the thick parchment. His mouth went dry as he stared at the ornate calligraphy, the elegant strokes of each letter. For a moment, it was as if he were seeing writing for the first time. He took a deep breath and began to translate aloud, slowly, determined to get it right. "When you have fallen into famine, and your well runs dry, when the ground is covered with thorns, do not despair." He paused, searching his memory. He'd heard this before. *The ground covered with thorns.* Who had said that? Old Horan. In the temple. He had said those exact words.

"What's wrong? Can't you read it?" asked Roh.

"Oh, no. I can. I just… Never mind." He continued translating, "Before you lies a long and perilous path. There is yet hope. Turn your eyes to the Great Father, and follow the path to the…" He tried to come up with the correct word. "…sun. For he who conceals his sins does not prosper, but whoever confesses and renounces them finds mercy.

"The path begins at the first gleam of dawn. Rejoice and do not look back, for nothing new is to be found there. Let your eyes look straight ahead, fix your gaze directly before you, as the sun shines ever brighter."

"What does that mean?" Jandon interrupted.

Roh waved the torch at him. "Let him finish."

Jandon frowned.

"Do not hasten in your travels, for time is the essence of passage. Along your journey, the river will flow. Drink of it and be merry, for it is your salvation."

Kail's blue eyes sparkled with hope. She clapped her hands together. "It's a river that we are looking for then!"

Kiran cleared his throat. "Alas, you will be faced with a crossroads; choose the way less traveled. The way is an upward struggle, never take your eyes from the summit. On the hills remember Him, in the valleys He will remember you.

"He who guards his way guards his life. Be mindful of the ways of the world about you. The heart of the discerning acquires knowledge; The ears of the wise seek it out."

"So we head toward the setting sun." It was Deke. "The river leads to a mountain. The dwelling place is at the summit on the edge of the world."

"Hold on," Roh cautioned. "How can we be sure?"

"That must be the way," insisted Deke. "We look for the river first. It will take us to the mountain. Weren't you listening?"

"I don't believe it was that clear."

"That's because you don't know anything about Scripture. Look at you. You make torches from crap."

Roh thrust his jaw forward.

Deke turned toward the others. "My father says, it is the glory of the Great Father to conceal, not for mere men to deliberate. We don't question. Our duty is to act. As the Script decrees."

Roh turned his back on Deke and asked Kiran, "Is that all of the Script?"

"No, there's more." Kiran refocused his attention on the scroll. "When you reach the peak and stand on the edge of darkness, before you will be a great pool of glorious reflection. There a wise man will appear, wrinkled with time and crippled with wisdom. Listen to him, for his is the Voice of the Father."

"Is that it? Is that the whole thing?" Jandon asked. Kiran nodded. "Well, where's the part about choosing the Seventh Elder?"

Bria piped up, "See, I told you. It's not there."

Deke moved next to her and glared, "Of course not. This is the Script of the Legend. It's in the Script of the Prophecy. But you don't have that scroll, do you Kiran?"

Kiran shook his head.

"Well, then you'll just have to trust me," Deke said. "Now let's get going." He reached for the scroll. "I'll carry that from now on."

"No!" Kiran pulled away, a hot streak of anger rushing through him. "Aldwyn gave the scroll to me. I'll take care of it. And who made you the leader, anyway?"

Deke sighed with pity. "What? Do you think because Aldwyn gave you the scroll that you are to be the Seventh Elder? You're not even a Toran. Obviously, he taught you to scribe to save himself toil. Don't you see? You're only here to record the tale of our journey. That's what a scribe does."

Kiran backed down as if he'd been slapped.

Bria stood next to Kiran and Roh, hands on her hips, glaring at Deke. "You assume too much. What makes you think we would follow you?"

Deke leaned toward her, his brow furrowed, a wicked grin on his face. "I don't care what you do, *girl*, but *we* are on a quest." He dug in his pocket and held out two flat, round rocks, each about two fingers wide. They were yellow-brown with a shimmer. "Oh, and I'm the only one with these."

"What are those?"

Kiran had a large collection of stones and he'd never seen one like these.

"Sacred stones, of course," he said and shoved them back into his pocket. He turned to Bhau and Jandon. "Now get your boots on. We're leaving."

"What? It's still pouring!" Jandon said. Deke glared at him. Jandon plopped down to put on his boots.

Deke turned to Kail. "You're coming with us." Her eyes darted back and forth from Bria to Deke as she twirled her fingers in her long, blond hair. "Get your pack!" She jumped to her feet.

"Leaving?" Roh said, a condescending edge to his voice. "Didn't the Script say not to hasten?" He turned to the others. "We should stay here where we are sheltered for the night. Who knows how the storm will turn."

"We're not afraid of a little rain," said Deke. "The villagers are counting on us. We must get there before the next planting season. If you want to stick around here gazing at the scratches of savages on the wall, go right ahead. Do as you please." He focused his dark eyes on Roh. "With a father like yours, I'm sure you always do."

Roh lunged at Deke, knocking him against the wall. Bria and Kail stared, mouths agape. Deke tried to jerk free. Roh had his hands wrapped around Deke's neck, his eyes filled with rage. "You mention my father and those lies again and I'll cut your throat. Do you understand me?" he said, his voice a low snarl. Deke didn't move, didn't breathe. Roh's grip tightened, his fingers taut. Deke nodded, his eyes wide. Roh shoved him away.

Deke rubbed his throat and took several deep breaths. "Well," he said, regaining his composure. "There's no call to be violent." He swung his pack over his shoulder. "Obviously, Roh is not a faithful follower of the Way." He turned to Bria. "Get your pack."

"I'm not going anywhere with you. Roh is right about the storm and you are just being a stubborn fool."

"Fine, stay here with…him." He turned to Kiran. "C'mon, let's go."

Kiran looked at Bria, defiant and strong. He wasn't going anywhere without her. "They're right, Deke."

Deke's face burned red. Without another word, he turned in a huff and strode out of the cave. Kail looked to Bria then Roh then Kiran, then silently turned and followed Deke.

Jandon hesitated, his eyes irresolute, as though he feared he had allied too soon. Bhau grabbed him by the arm and they were gone.

Roh stoked the fire. "Finally, we're rid of him," he said with a satisfied grin.

The Path to the Sun

When you have fallen into famine,
And your well runs dry.
When the ground is covered with thorns,
Do not despair.
Before you lies a long and perilous path,
There is yet hope.
Turn your eyes to the Great Father,
And follow the path to the Sun.
For he who conceals his sins does not prosper,
But whoever confesses and renounces them finds mercy.
The path begins at the first gleam of dawn,
Rejoice and do not look back,
For nothing new is to be found there.
Let your eyes look straight ahead,
Fix your gaze directly before you,

As the sun shines ever brighter.

Do not hasten in your travels,

For time is the essence of passage.

Along your journey, the river will flow.

Drink of it and be merry, for it is your
salvation.

Alas, you will be faced with a crossroads,

Choose the way less traveled.

The way is an upward struggle,

Never take your eyes from the summit.

On the hills remember Him,

In the valleys He will remember you.

He who guards his way guards his life.

Be mindful of the ways of the world about
you.

The heart of the discerning acquires
knowledge,

The ears of the wise seek it out.

When you reach the peak and stand on the
edge of darkness,

Before you will be a great pool of
glorious reflection.

There a wise man will appear,

Wrinkled with time and crippled with
wisdom.

Listen to him, for his is the

Voice of the Father.

7

Roh sat down, stretched his legs out before him, and closed his eyes. Kiran and Bria hovered over the fire trying to ward off the chill. Kiran kept looking to the cave entrance, expecting Deke to walk back in at any moment.

Bria whispered, "What do we do now?" Despite all of her confidence and strength, he saw fear in her eyes.

He wanted to sound brave. He sat down. "Everything will be fine."

"Fine? Boys!" She threw her hands in the air and paced to the cave entrance and looked out. "Why is it that boys must always be boys?" She paced back to the fire. "By tomorrow, he'll simmer down and all will be well. But he had to make a big show of it. I swear, if women led the races."

Kiran stared, speechless.

"That arrogant fool!" she huffed. "I don't blame Kail. What was she going to do? He certainly didn't make it easy for her. I don't know about Jandon, but Bhau would follow him over a cliff and never know what happened. Can you believe him?"

Kiran swallowed hard.

She paused. He waited.

"We need to stay together. When I see Deke tomorrow, I'm going to give him a piece of my mind." She exhaled with a loud huff. "Boys." She plopped down next to him, drew her knees up like a child, and laid her chin on her knees. "But you're not like him. You're different," she whispered. Her eyes met his. He wanted to tell her she was amazing, but the words stuck in his throat.

Their eyes were fixed for a moment longer. Then she turned away.

"I'm worried," she sighed. "We should pray for them."

"With no Elder to lead us?" he asked, incredulous.

"Well, I could be an Elder you know," she said, fire in her eyes.

"But you can't."

"But I *could*. Nowhere in the Script or the Books or the Verses, not even in the Songs does it say women can't be Elders. It's just an old-fashioned tradition." She was getting worked up again, her voice sharpened to an edge.

The thought had never occurred to him—that a girl would dream of being an Elder too. Especially Bria. He rarely saw her at the Temple. He was confused and delighted and surprised all at once.

"I don't want to be a farmwife. I want my life to have meaning. I want to do something important. Just because I'm a girl doesn't mean I am spiritually inept. And why was I chosen for this quest anyway? I can't be an Elder, but I can traipse across the world and face the Voice of the Father? It doesn't make sense."

The fire crackled and snapped in the silent space between them.

"So, let's pray," she said finally. "You know the daily Verse. We can at least recite that together."

She took his hand in hers, and he smiled then, as he glanced toward Roh, still asleep against the wall.

In a soft voice, she reached out to the Great Father and he joined her. At the end, she added, "Please watch over the others as they travel in haste to serve You. We are all merely innocent souls, blindly following Your command. Take care of our families back home, for they are at Your mercy."

When she was done, she laid her head on his shoulder and her hair spilled down his chest. He didn't move a muscle. He stared into the fire, her hand still in his, her words on his mind. Bria was the first ordinary person he ever knew to pray aloud directly to the Great Father. It was bold. *Maybe she is meant to be an Elder,* he thought. He tried to picture Bria wearing the robes, but images of her dancing in her wet tunic crept into his thoughts, the soft, sensual curves of her body, now so close to his. He laid his head on hers, his lips touching her hair, and all he wanted was to savor the feeling forever.

Thunder boomed outside, waking him. The fire had burned down to coals. Roh was sitting at the edge of the cave whittling the end of a large stick to a point. Kiran slipped away from Bria, laying her head down softly on his pack.

He sat down next to Roh. The fog had lifted and lightning illuminated the forest in dramatic bursts. "Do you think they are all right back home?"

"We have strong warriors," Roh replied, as if he were expecting the question. "They fought protecting us. They're counting on us. That's what you need to remember."

"But the rains have come. I thought—"

Roh glanced at the rain, then stared at Kiran with a blank expression. "It doesn't mean it is raining back home. On the other side of the mountains."

"What do you think of the prophecy?"

Roh used his knife with skillful precision. "I know why I'm here," he said with a conviction that Kiran wished he himself had.

"Well, what about the Script of the Legend?"

"You're the one who can read. What do you think it means?" he said, never looking up from his stick.

"Well, I'm not sure I even translated it properly," he admitted. "Mostly, I just copy scrolls for Aldwyn. His eyesight is failing and it is difficult for him. He didn't exactly teach me the language, I sort of picked it up by, by asking questions."

Roh put his knife down and turned to look at him. "So you have no idea? Is that what you're saying?"

"No, I do, I just…" Kiran turned away from Roh's stare. "That's not what I meant."

Roh smiled, a genuine, caring smile. "Listen, Kiran, you're a smart kid. Obviously Aldwyn trusted you. You just need to trust yourself."

Maybe Roh was right. He had been chosen to come after all. And he did know how to translate the Script. He did. "We're looking for a river and a mountain. But the scroll didn't explain everything. Do you think there is another scroll, the Script of the Prophecy, like Deke said?"

Roh shot an intense, yet fleeting look at Kiran. "I know that Elders never reveal everything," he said, an edge to his voice.

"How does Deke know so much then? Elders make a vow of secrecy. His father isn't supposed to share the secrets of the Temple. Even to his son."

Roh looked up at the dark clouds and a thin, wry smile, the kind of one who knows his own secret, came to his lips. "There's a lot Elders aren't supposed to do."

Kiran followed his gaze. "This storm should pass overnight. Deke was awfully brave to lead them out into it."

"Ha!" Roh scoffed. "We'll find them in the morning soaking wet and shivering. Deke doesn't stop to think. He acts on emotion and calls it faith. You think that's brave?"

"Well, he did jump off the Sanctuary cliff."

Roh turned, eyebrows raised. "Did he tell you that?"

"Well, no. Well, yeah. I mean, I guess I assumed he had." Suddenly he needed to scratch the bug bites on his neck.

"He had you up there, didn't he? I assume you didn't jump." He went back to whittling, the same enigmatic smile on his face.

"Well, I was just about to when the Temple bells rang. We had to run to the village."

"Uh, huh."

"But I was going to."

Roh stopped whittling again. "Kiran, do you even know the story of the jump?"

Kiran hesitated, then remembered that Roh already knew the truth, that he could scribe. "Yeah, of course I do. Past Elder Salder was on a—"

"Santon."

"What?"

"Elder Santon."

"Oh, yeah, you're right. Past Elder Santon was on a prayer vigil on the Mount when his faith was tested by the Great Father. He was told to jump off the blind cliff to the safety of the Father's embrace below. Without question, he did as the Great Father commanded. Deke said it was the ultimate show of faith."

"And you were eager to prove yourself."

"Well, I'm no heathen!"

"So, that's how he got you up there," he said, disdain in his voice.

"No! I wanted to jump. It was my idea."

"You do realize there is a drought?"

"What?" Kiran's head was spinning.

Roh shook his head. "Never mind. Why is Deke's opinion so important to you anyway?"

Kiran had no answer. Roh made it seem so simple, but it wasn't. Kiran had to do it. He just had to.

"Don't let him draw you into that nonsense. You're smarter than that."

"Did you ever do it?"

Roh went back to his whittling, with the same thin smile.

Kiran turned away, frustrated, but he didn't want to show it. He stared at a spot on the ledge where rain pelted the ground in tiny splashes. "Do you think Deke is the Seventh Elder?"

Roh shrugged. "He fits the mold."

"I don't know. He is bound to be an Elder. It makes sense that it would be him. It's just that he is such a—"

"A tyrant."

"Well, yeah." Kiran smiled. "He can really be a thorn in my side. But I'm still worried about him and the others out in the storm."

"What is meant to be, will be," said Roh. "We are all in the hands of the Great Father."

"I suppose you're right." There was a lull in the rain. Kiran stared off into the darkness. "Who do you think made those drawings?"

"Don't know. But I have been wondering who stacked the firewood."

Then he saw it. In the distance, near the edge of the swamp. "Roh, look. A campfire."

"It's the Javinians," Roh said without looking up. "They've been there all night." He rose to his feet and examined the pointed end of his stick. Then he held it at its midpoint, testing its weight and balance. "I was just thinking I'd go see about it when you sat down."

"What? By yourself?" Kiran jumped to his feet.

"Stay with Bria. And get some sleep."

"Sleep? Right. What are you planning to do?"

Roh lifted his pack. "Don't stoke the fire. If I'm not back by daybreak, leave without me. Stay out of the open; you're safer among the trees."

Then he was gone.

"This can't be happening," he whispered to himself. He sat down next to Bria and closed his eyes, but sleep wouldn't come. They were alone—all alone.

He needed a weapon.

He selected a solid branch from the pile, held it in his hand, just as he'd seen Roh do to check the balance, and decided it would suffice. With his knife, he quickly shaved the end to a point. It would have to do.

He wanted to pray with Bria again. But he didn't want to wake her. She needed the sleep and dawn would come soon enough.

He leaned the spear against the wall, sat down, leaned back against the cold rock wall, and held the scroll cradled in his trembling hands. *Is this the only reason I'm here? To be the scribe?*

8

When the sky hinted of dawn, Roh had not returned. The rain had stopped. Bria calmly accepted the news. They gathered their things and set out.

Kiran followed Bria as she crept along the rocky ledge, back into the thick woods—pungent red cedars and white birches, soft tamaracks and sugar maples. The forest was still, as if hushed by their presence. They took care not to leave a trace of their passing as they made their way through the undergrowth of berry bushes and ferns.

Soon, they were climbing upward again and the soft earth turned rocky. Bria moved with confidence, unintimidated by the uneven terrain, her walking staff all the support she needed. Kiran fought to keep pace with her, embarrassed that he could not match her stamina.

Amid patches of fluffy lichens and beds of rich green mosses, they found a stream flowing with fresh rainwater and stopped to fill their waterskins.

"What did Deke mean back there when he said you aren't a Toran?" Bria asked.

Kiran hung his head. "I'm an orphan. I have no standing in the Temple because of the question of my birth."

"I know. But why should that matter?"

"That's what I think!" he shouted, exploding with frustration. "I just want to be allowed to attend the Lessons."

She glanced back the way they had come. "We should keep moving," she whispered. He nodded, feeling like a fool for his outburst.

They followed the streambed upward, carefully negotiating the slippery rocks and exposed tree roots, keeping to the shade when they could, but the higher they climbed, the scarcer the vegetation became, until they found themselves amid a stand of stunted, knotty pines no taller than themselves. Twisted and racked by the wind, their trunks bent like decrepit old men, their gnarled roots spread across barren, smooth rock.

"I thought you said Aldwyn taught you," she said, trying to understand.

"Well, yes. But he didn't teach me the Lessons, well, not exactly. He challenges me. It's hard to explain." He shook his head, frowning. How could he explain his life to her? "It's not the same. Aldwyn speaks in riddles."

They emerged on the bald, round top of the mountain. Kiran stopped to catch his breath and look back the way they had come. Sunshine skimmed across the treetops.

A few more steps and they were at the summit. The far side of the mountain dropped away sharply. The land beyond stretched as far as the eye could see, clear to the very edge, where green melted into blue and became sky, so boundless, it surely held all of the Celestial Kingdom.

"Look at that," Bria gaped. "Not a single tree. Isn't it beautiful? Just breathtaking. I'm tired and my bones ache, but I've never felt more alive. Things are always better after a storm, don't you think? Everything is going to be all right. I know it will. The Great Father watches over us. We will endure. He will keep us from harm." She took his hand in hers and squeezed. "I just know He will," she repeated, then let go of his hand.

It did feel like the kind of morning when everything seemed fresh and new and worries just faded away. It was easy to forget all their troubles. After all, he had just spent the night alone with her. If he had sneaked out into the hills and spent a night with her back home, they'd both be banished. But out here, far away from the village, away from the rules and restrictions, he felt freer than he ever had.

He had the sudden urge to kiss her.

He took her hand in his. She stopped and turned to face him, her eyes bright, expectant. His breath caught in his throat. What if she didn't kiss him back? Or what if she got angry and slapped him? His hand went clammy. "Uh…you're right. Everything is going to be all right."

She smiled. He let go of her hand. Then breathed again.

She shifted her pack and walked onward. When he didn't follow, she turned back. "What is it?"

He gripped the makeshift spear in his hand. "Roh said to stay in the woods."

"Well, that is the direction of the setting sun, so that is the way we must go."

"But we're vulnerable out in the open."

"At least no one will be able to sneak up on us," she said. "It is so flat, once we walk a ways, you'll be able to keep a clear eye out in every direction."

He glanced back the way they had come, unsure.

"Listen. Roh can take care of himself. We'll find Deke and the others. He'll catch up."

Kiran nodded.

The decline was so steep, they had to climb down single file. It took them until past noon before they reached the base of the mountain. With the wind in their faces and the hot sun on their backs, they set out across the flatlands, picking their way among clumps of grasses to avoid puddles of water that had collected where the dry, hardened ground could not absorb it fast enough. Eventually, they passed into an area where there had been no rain. The soil became even and dry and they were able to walk side by side at a good pace. Sweat dripped down his forehead and his damp clothing stuck to his skin.

"What did you mean by 'the question of your birth'?" she asked.

"That's just it. I don't know. I was a baby, just weaned, when Aldwyn found—" As soon as the word came out of his mouth he regretted it. He kicked a clump of dirt. It skittered off and burst into a pile of dust.

"What do you mean? Found you?"

Kiran wanted to tell her the whole story. But what would she think of him? So many times he had told himself that his family history didn't matter. He was who he was, whatever his lineage. But it seemed to matter to everyone else. He stared off into the distance. Dark clouds were forming on the horizon. The air suddenly had a peculiar oppressiveness.

"You don't have to tell me if you don't want to. I understand."

"It's all right," he told her, deciding right then that he would. "Aldwyn told everyone that a village woman had come to him, ashamed, when he was walking back from his time of atonement at the Sanctuary on the Mount. She had hidden her pregnancy and begged him to take me. But it's not the truth." He took a deep breath and went on. "The truth is… You see…" He took another breath. "He didn't recognize the woman. He thinks she may, well, she must have been…a Javinian."

He held his breath as he searched her face, desperate to know what she was thinking. But she showed no reaction. He turned away, crestfallen.

"So, that's what Deke meant," she said flatly.

He nodded.

"He must know. About the Javinian. It's obvious, the way he torments you."

"Torments me? Deke doesn't…" He bit his lip. "I don't know how he could…know…"

They came upon a rocky knoll, a bump in the flat terrain, washed clean of soil by the wind save for a few tenacious grasses that held on in the crevices, their long, slender leaves bending in the wind. At the base, depressions pocked the ground—holes where large animals had lain. Kiran scanned the horizon, wondering where they had gone. In the sky in front of them, ominous clouds hovered like towering mountains. The tall grasses swayed in bursts of golden waves, undulating across the great meadow, and the pungent odor of freshly turned earth filled the air.

Bria stopped for a rest and offered her waterskin. "You don't remember your mother?" she asked.

"Not really. I remember feelings, fleeting images. Nothing else. It is as if my mind has forgotten, but my heart remembers."

Bria turned to face him, her eyes filled with genuine sympathy. She reached for him and her fingers brushed his cheek for a moment. Then her hand rested on his shoulder. "That's really sad. I'm so sorry, Kiran," she said so softly the words were almost lost in the wind.

"Oh, I'm fine. It's not a big thing, really." He pulled away. "You know, I envy you. You know who you are. It's like you aren't afraid of anything. I wish I could be like that."

She laughed. "I don't know about all that. I'll tell you something about myself that no one else knows. A secret."

His heart skipped a beat. She seemed vulnerable, standing here now, in front of him, willing to share, giving a part of herself to him. He wanted to know everything about her, every secret.

"No matter what," she said, "I will never get married." She stared, waiting for a reaction, her eyes so intense he had to look away.

Never get married, but… You can't really mean that! Was it because she wanted to be an Elder? But Elders could marry, after they made their vows. Or was she afraid of something? *Is she afraid of me,* he wondered. Was she just trying to tell him to leave her alone? Had he been too forward? Had he made her feel uncomfortable?

They walked on for a time without speaking. The wind grew stronger and suddenly a gust hit them with such force they were nearly knocked over. "My, it's really windy here," he said, breaking the awkward silence. A strange dark cloud had formed on the horizon in an odd shape, like an anvil. Bright bolts of lightning shot from it and struck the ground.

"I've got a bad feeling about this," he told Bria. Within moments, it was dark as night and the wall of clouds came bearing down on them. Rain fell in sheets, turning the parched ground to mud, and within seconds they were in an absolute downpour. Raindrops pelted their faces as gusts of wind swept along the ground in horizontal bursts, whipping the grasses into frenzied swirls. They tried to run, but the wind was too strong and the mud too slippery. They were out in the open. There was nowhere to hide.

The rain turned to hail. Chunks of ice the size of chestnuts fell from the sky, pummeling them. They covered their heads with their arms and turned their backs to the wind as it ripped across the ground, battering them in savage gusts. They had to find shelter. Lightning flashed and, as if guided by the Great Father, he saw another knoll ahead. He took Bria by the hand and ran into the wind to the refuge of the lee side. "Lie down flat on the ground, and keep your head down," Kiran shouted. He crouched over her as rocks of ice plunked at his backpack.

The wind howled and rumbled across the flatlands. When finally the hail stopped, Kiran lifted himself up on his hands, then to his feet, to see what he could. It was dark as night save for the eerie, pulsing blue-grey glow of the turbulent sky. A ring of clouds hovered close to the ground on the horizon, rapidly circulating. Hanging on the fringes of the dark, greenish base of the ring were what looked like twines of rope come alive, possessed by demons, twisting wildly in the wind. The coiled devils were spawned from the center, spinning out in all directions amid squalls of rain, hissing and squealing as they broke away from the core.

From the main cloud, directly under the dark, churning mass, one gigantic towering funnel of dust burst out of the chaos, rotating violently, ripping up grass and dirt and rocks as it came toward them, twisting and contorting in an erratic pattern, its thunderous howl right out of a nightmare.

Before Kiran could react, it was upon them. The specter grabbed him, sucked him from the ground and slammed him back down again several yards from Bria, knocking the breath out of him. Spots danced before his eyes and he gasped for air. She scrambled toward him on her belly, dirt and sand swirling around her. She said something, but it was lost in the deafening roar of the storm.

Then it stopped.

Everything went still as death. All he could hear was the sound of his heart pumping in his chest. The air felt so thick it was difficult to breathe. Kiran rolled on his back and looked up. A cold terror came over him. Directly above, the monster twisted and churned, a dark hollow column of rotating fury. Lightning shot across the mouth and higher up, inside its belly, white bolts zigzagged from side to side, illuminating the entire shaft in blinding flashes. Kiran stared into the dark vortex. *What kind of evil is this?*

Around the rim, the screaming continued as more and more demons spawned from the main one, writhing as they formed, then hissing as they broke away. All the while, the monster pulsed up and down.

Then, the roaring howl started again. The wind roiled around him in a demonic maelstrom, dust blasting his eyes with such force it burned. He buried his head in his folded arms and endured the whirlwind. Finally the ground-shaking rumble diminished and all he could hear was hissing. It was over.

Bria was shaking uncontrollably. He rolled over and wrapped his arms around her, trying not to shake himself. "What kind of demon was that?" she cried.

"I don't know," he said. "I don't know."

It was a long time before they dared to move from the shelter of the knoll. Kiran was still shaking, in spite of his resolve, and he feared he might lose control. Nothing had prepared him for the sheer terror of the wind demon.

The sun was shining again in the west. The sky was clear and bright blue. The demon had scattered the clouds, and the wind died down to a gentle breeze. As if nothing had happened.

To the east, a brilliant, iridescent rainbow appeared against the dark sky. "Look at that," he told Bria. "The blessing of the Father."

The sight brought a smile to her face. "That means all is well at home."

"Do you think so?"

"I'm sure of it."

"I'm glad," he said, coughing. His nose and throat were filled with dust. He put his waterskin to his mouth, tipped it up, but it was empty. He swallowed against the dryness.

Soon, the sun dropped below the horizon and he and Bria surrendered to the safety of the knoll for the night. They shared the last of her water and ate little, their appetites gone. The breeze continued to blow across the plains, dry and filled with dust, and did not let up as darkness fell. Too frightened to sleep, they lay awake staring up at the stars and listening to the wind rustling through the grasses, waiting for dawn, his arms around her. An inkling of guilt crossed his mind; their behavior was improper, but he didn't care. He was too scared to let go of her and she didn't seem to mind. He closed his eyes and savored the warmth of her body next to his. Sometime in the night, they drifted into a restless sleep.

They awoke to the sound of thunder.

"The demon is back!" Bria cried.

Kiran got to his knees and looked out over the grassland. "But the sky is clear," he said. "I don't see anything."

The rumble grew louder. "It's coming toward us!" She curled up into the crevice that was their hiding place.

He stood up and saw a billowing cloud of dust above the ground. Right before his eyes, a herd of beasts, at least a hundred strong, each ten times the size of a sheep, emerged from out of the ground, thundering toward them, a massive chaos of black and brown fur. "Get down, get down!" he yelled, dropping to his knees.

Bria covered her head with her hands. Kiran shielded her with his body as the beasts bore down on them in a fury. The ground shook with the pounding of hooves, as the animals stormed past them on all sides. Then, they were gone. Kiran squinted and coughed, choked by the swirling dust.

Kiran rolled off of her and she burst into tears. Strong, willful Bria had crumbled. He wasn't sure what to do. He wanted to cry himself. He had no idea how to fight these demons. How would they ever make it to the other side of the world?

"Hey," he said, touching her shoulder.

She looked up at him, her green eyes shiny. Tiny rivulets rolled down her dusty cheeks leaving dark, muddy streaks. Her hair was a tangled mess.

Kiran wiped the tears from her face and took her in his arms. "Everything will be all right," he said. He needed to hear it too, even though the words were coming from his own mouth. Maybe she would never marry him, but he loved her, and he'd do anything to protect her. He held her tight.

After awhile, she seemed to relax. She pulled away and looked into his eyes. "Thank you. I just needed a moment. I'm all right." Then she kissed him on the cheek.

Kiran's face flushed red. He felt dizzy and started to tremble. His hand went to the spot on his cheek where her lips had been.

"Are you all right? All of a sudden you don't look so good."

He couldn't take his eyes off her lips.

"Kiran, are you all right?"

"Ah, yeah, I'm fine," he stammered and turned away.

"Where did those beasts come from? You said you couldn't see anything."

"I don't know. It was as though they came right up out of the ground."

"Right out of the ground? That's ridiculous, Kiran." She giggled and he started to laugh. They laughed together, a nervous giggle that masked their fears. Their eyes met for a moment, and held. A rush of heat surged through him as she blinked once, then again, her green eyes sparkling in the sun. He leaned forward, his breath shallow and quick. She held his gaze a moment longer, then turned away. Disheartened, he sat back.

"Well, it's no matter. We must go on," she said, rising to her feet and brushing herself off. "We need to find water."

She was right. He rose to his feet next to her.

They headed westward, the sun baking the land dry, the wind too hot to be a relief. They crested a hill and stared down into a shallow valley with a rocky escarpment on the far side.

"I guess it isn't as flat as we thought," Kiran said, glancing back over his shoulder. "This land plays tricks on you."

"Well, that explains the appearance of the beasts."

Kiran scanned the valley in front of them. On the far side, he saw three of the beasts lying on the ground. He drew in a breath—there were men. He grabbed Bria by the arm and dropped to the ground, tugging her with him. Crawling on his belly, he peered through the tall grasses, trying to get a clear view. "What is it?" she whispered, crawling along next to him.

"Savages." Not three hundred paces off, four men hovered around three enormous shaggy beasts that lay dead on the ground, their lifeless tongues hanging from their mouths, their exposed entrails a feast for the flies that buzzed about.

The men wore only buckskin breechcloths at the waist, their chests naked. Even their feet were bare. These men were the worst sort—uncivilized—with crude ways and primitive minds. Kiran could not imagine how they had taken down such large animals. His grip tightened around his makeshift weapon.

As two of the hunters skinned one of beasts, cutting along the spine, pulling the hide back to reveal the bloody carcass beneath, another sliced open its belly and disemboweled it, pulling the bloody entrails out onto the grass. The savage sifted through the pile of guts and came up with the red, stringy heart, his hands and arms covered with blood. He raised it to his mouth and took a bite. Kiran's stomach squeezed in his throat and he had to look away. When he turned back, the savages were passing the heart around, tearing it to bits, their hands and mouths dripping with blood.

They had to get out of here.

Bria inhaled sharply, a high-pitched gasp.

Then, he felt the sharp point of a spear pressed to the back of his neck.

Book Two

Other cultures are not failed attempts
to be us; they are unique manifestations
of the human spirit— other options,
other visions of life itself.
~Wade Davis

9

His heartbeat pounding in his ears, Kiran craned his neck around to see two, three, four savages towering over him with spears held ready to strike. He swallowed hard. Their arms were big enough to rip a beast to shreds. Their broad chests were lined with muscles.

The men prodded with their spears, forcing him and Bria to stand. His knees threatened to buckle and his hands shook. He dropped his own makeshift spear and raised his hands in the air. "We don't mean any harm."

"We're just looking for our friends," Bria said, her voice barely a whisper.

One of the savages raised an eyebrow.

"Yes," said Kiran. "We're just trying to find them."

The man nodded as if he understood. To the other hunters he grunted and spat in some primitive communication. They shook their heads.

Then came a shriek carried on the wind. It sounded like Kail.

Kiran scanned the landscape. In the distance, a flock of carrion birds circled. Flying scavengers meant only one thing; someone or something was injured, or worse.

"Friends trouble," the man said.

Kiran nodded and took a step backward, waiting. He took Bria by the hand and took another step backward. The men made no move. "Let's go," he said. Bria nodded and they turned and ran. They ran all the way to the next ridge and ran until Kiran had to stop to catch his breath. He glanced back. The savages were gone.

The sun was setting as they reached a patch of woods that seemed to emerge from nowhere. "This way," Kiran whispered.

They crept forward, into the forest, carefully placing each footstep, the crackle of dry grass under their feet. The orange glow of twilight streaked through the treetops, but the forest floor was dark. Kiran reached for a tree trunk, running his hand along its rough bark as they moved past.

There was movement in the shadows. Hair stood up on the back of his neck. He grabbed Bria by the arm, yanking her to a halt. Someone or something was watching—and it was close. He heard something. The snap of a twig? Something was moving, breathing.

They took another step forward. Then he heard a low, thick growl. He stopped at once and spun around, trying to pinpoint the source. The woods had grown darker. He couldn't see beyond a few feet.

The growl came again, closer this time. From his right. No from the left. A shiver ran down his spine.

He turned around. He was face to face with an enormous wild dog baring its sharp, white fangs, its yellow eyes directed at his. He stared into those eyes, too frightened to blink. They were not the empty eyes of a monster, full of bloodlust; these eyes were deep and intelligent, calculating. His heart banged against the wall of his chest. He pushed Bria behind him, putting himself between her and the beast.

A second dog emerged from the dark, jaws snapping, then a third on its flank, moving into formation.

The leader paced forward, sniffing, as if assessing the strength of its foe, its eyes glinting in the twilight, never leaving Kiran's. The other dogs circled, moving closer and closer. "We're surrounded," Bria said, her voice shaking.

Kiran took a stone from his pocket and hurled it at the leader. It jerked its head to the side and the stone grazed its hindquarter. Kiran threw another stone, hitting the beast on the ear. It reared back, snarling.

Something thrashed in the brush behind the dogs. The dogs spun around. Savages burst from the darkness, waving flaming torches at the beasts. The lead dog winced, but stood its ground, snarling. The savages kept coming, poking flaming sticks at the dogs, until all three, one by one, turned and faded back into the night.

"Get friend. We leave fast. More dog soon," a savage shouted. But he wasn't talking to Kiran.

Beside him, holding a torch, was Roh. "It's all right. They're friendly," he said.

"Oh, thank the Father you're here," Bria cried, lunging toward him. She wrapped her arms around him.

"Are you all right? I thought I heard Kail."

"We did too." Bria eyed the man next to Roh.

"This is Haktu," said Roh. "These are the hunters of the Lendhi clan."

The man made no move of greeting, his face expressionless.

Kiran nodded like a mindless puppet, trying to comprehend where Roh had been and how he had befriended these savages.

A scream ripped through the forest.

Bria yelled into the darkness, "We're coming, Kail. We're coming!"

Haktu led them, his torch lighting their way, as they rushed into the shadows. The other Lendhi hunters moved with them, their flaming torches keeping the beasts away.

They found Kail clinging to Jandon, sobbing. Deke was swinging her pomander in the air in front of him, shouting. "Stay away! Stay away from me!"

Roh marched straight to him and yanked it from his hand.

Deke shrank back, staring wide-eyed, as though Roh were an apparition. Roh went to Kail and tied the protective amulet around her neck, then held her as she sobbed in his chest. Deke glanced around, seeing Kiran, then Bria, before recognition finally seemed to come to him.

Jandon stared at the ground, his eyes fixed in hypnotized horror, his chest heaving. Kiran took him by the shoulders and shook him out of his trance.

"Oh, thank the Father you are here! Bhau's gone. He's gone! Swallowed, vanished!"

"Calm down, take a breath. What are you talking about? Where is he?"

Jandon pointed to the ground some twenty paces away. "There! A Mawghul! It swallowed him and he was gone! We were just walking along that way, and he was leading, and then, and then he was gone."

Kail wailed anew. She buried her face in Roh's shoulder.

"He was screaming in agony." Jandon stumbled backward on one foot. "We didn't know what to do. Oh, Great Father, help him! Then the wild dogs came out of nowhere. Oh, thank the Father you came."

"What happened to you?"

Jandon looked down at his bloody ankle, his face a mask of confusion.

"A dog," Kail cried. "One of the wild dogs!"

Haktu started toward the spot where Jandon had pointed. "No!" yelled Jandon. "It will get you. Don't go near it!"

Haktu kicked at the leaves and sticks that were scattered around the edge of the shadowy hole. He made a hand signal to his hunters, then motioned to Roh. "Friend gone. No help. We go now."

So, that was it. A Mawghul had killed Bhau. For a moment, Kiran couldn't move. Bhau was the strongest of them, their warrior. If this could happen to him, then… He took a step toward the hole. He had to see for himself. "Kiran," Roh said, handing him a torch. "We need to get out of here."

Kiran clutched the torch in his hand and nodded. He walked with the others as they staggered along, following the Lendhi hunters out of the woods. Deke trailed behind stone-faced, his head hanging low.

As they crested the ridge, utter exhaustion came over Kiran in a wave. His limbs ached with weariness and his body felt drained, but his mind wouldn't rest. He sifted through the agonizing events of the day—the stampeding beasts, being captured by the savages, the terror of the Mawghul, and the wild dogs. Bhau's death. None of it seemed real.

"How did it happen?" Kiran asked Jandon.

"One moment we were walking along, the next he was gone. Like lightning, out of nowhere, the monster had him in its maw. You should have heard him. He was screaming and moaning. I could hear his bones crunching. There was nothing we could do. Nothing!" His hands jerked in the air in meaningless gestures. "That Mawghul would have swallowed us too. I know it. If you were there, you would've seen it."

"So you saw the demon then?"

"Saw it? He nearly got me too!" He shuddered.

"Did it leap out of the ground? Or did Bhau just step into its mouth? Were there no warning signs at all? Didn't it make any noise?"

Jandon shook his head, his eyes wild. "We waited. We waited, but…nothing. His body… Then the dogs came."

Kiran swallowed hard. *To certain doom…*

Roh slowed his pace to come alongside Kiran. "Haktu's clan is headed toward a river," he said.

"Hold on," Kiran said, his mind reeling. "How did you get by us across the flatlands? We never saw you. What happened with the Javinians?"

"We don't have to worry about them anymore," he said.

"But what happened? How do you know for sure? Tobin said they'd track us ruthlessly."

Roh exhaled, as if he thought it pointless to spend energy explaining. "The Javinians just needed incentive to look in another direction."

"Well, how did you meet Haktu and these hunters?"

"I saw them chasing the beasts. I went to ask if they had seen you."

"You just walked right up to them?"

"What else would I do? Hide in the grass? I'm sure they already knew I was there."

Kiran bit his lip. "You said they are headed toward a river. Do you think we should go with them?"

Deke spoke up. "Are you serious? We're not going anywhere with them."

"Well, maybe we—"

"They're savages."

"Now just a moment," said Roh. "Just because you—"

"Just because what? So, they happened to come along and scare off those dogs. It doesn't mean we should go with them. We can take care of ourselves."

Roh stepped in front of Deke. "From where I was standing, you didn't look like you were taking care of anything."

"Stop it you two!" Bria burst in. "Arguing won't get us anywhere. Look what happened last time."

Deke glared at her, his eyes full of contempt. "They may have infected us already with their wicked ways and we don't even know it. You're all so naïve."

Jandon finally spoke, "Listen, I don't know what to think, but they saved us from the Mawghul. Roh, you said they know the way to the river, right? I say we go with them."

"I just want to go home," Kail cried.

Roh gave her a reassuring pat on the back. "We have a very long way to go and many things to learn, like how to find food. We can learn these things from them."

Kail lifted her head and sniffled, as if a spark of hope had returned.

"Whether they follow the Way is not our concern."

"Not our concern!" shouted Deke.

Kiran grimaced. Roh was right. "Deke," he said. "The rest of us want to go with them. That's what we've decided. If you don't want to, go ahead and leave on your own."

"Oh, so you think you're the leader now, is that it?"

Jandon piped up, "I'm with Kiran this time."

Deke mumbled an unintelligible retort. Kiran couldn't contain the grin that came to his lips.

"What should we do about Bhau?" Jandon asked.

Roh replied calmly, "There's nothing to do. He's gone."

"Well, we can't act like nothing happened and continue on our way."

"We have to," said Roh.

"Well, we should at least *say something*," said Bria.

"Yeah, something," mumbled Jandon.

As they walked on, Kiran heard nothing but the rustling of the wind.

There was a pool of blood where the hunters had hacked the beasts into chunks, which they stacked on a travois, a sled-like device made from long poles. They lined up on either side, took hold of the poles, and heaved forward, dragging the meat across the dry grass.

"Come. You hungry," said Haktu. Roh followed.

Kiran stared at the bloodied ground where the animals had lain. These men had ripped the beating heart from that beast and devoured the bloody organ raw in some sort of macabre feast. They could just as easily turn on them, with brutal force. He looked out over the endless sea of grass. They'd have nowhere to run.

With a knot of apprehension in his stomach, he followed the trail of blood.

10

It was late when they approached the Lendhi camp. The scent of roasting meat and wood smoke wafted on the air and Kiran picked up the pace. He hadn't eaten since the night before and even then it had been meager—stale bread, a bite of cheese washed down with what little water was left.

Eight dome-shaped tents formed a circle around a blazing fire where the clan bustled about, working to preserve the kill of the day. Kiran whispered to Roh, "Is this how they live? In homes made of sticks and animal hides?"

"They follow the beasts as they move across the flatlands."

The Lendhi folk stole glances at the young Torans and exchanged subtle gestures as Haktu led them to an area out of the way and bade them to sit. He left without a word and disappeared inside one of the tents.

The clan numbered about sixty, that Kiran could see, young and old, each focused on a task. Mealtime was past, it seemed; children were cleaning bowls and utensils as scruffy dogs scurried about, sniffing for scraps.

Nearby, two men stood at a makeshift table, cutting chunks of meat into long strips while several women carefully draped the bloody pieces over the rungs of a drying rack that had been erected over a smoldering fire. An elderly man shuffled back and forth between the two fires, moving one hot coal at a time, slipping the embers under the drying rack.

Two women approached with a basket of meat, fresh berries, and a bladder of water. The Torans stumbled over each other to get a share, grabbing handfuls and gulping them down. The women bowed, exchanging looks of disgust between them. Roh thanked them kindly. Kiran stopped chewing and through a mouth full of food said, "Yes, thank you."

A tiny, naked girl of about three years sauntered over to them and stood staring, her large, round eyes pools of innocent curiosity. She clung to a tiny doll fashioned from dried reeds whose braided hair matched her own.

Deke leaned toward Roh. "What were you thinking? We can't stay with these heathen savages. They are uncivilized. Just look at them. They live like animals. Their children run about naked." He tore into another bite of meat with his teeth. "We can't trust them."

"Which ones do you mean?" Roh asked, his face expressionless. "The men who saved your life tonight or the women who just fed you?"

Deke paused, his mouth full of food. His eyes narrowed and he furrowed his brow. He chewed, then chewed again, then without a word turned away and swallowed.

At last, Haktu emerged from the tent and walked directly toward them. "Tonight you request."

Kiran looked to Roh, who shook his head. "We don't understand," he said. "You will take us to the river?"

"If Spirits' will."

"Spirits?"

"By Manu-amatu," said Haktu, matter-of-factly.

"Oh," said Kiran, nodding as though he understood; but he understood nothing. What was Manu-amatu? A path?

Haktu patted Kiran on the shoulder, as if he were an innocent child. "Is Lendhi way."

He left them where they sat and headed back to the tent.

Soon, the Lendhi clan put down their work and gathered round the fire, their eyes glittering with anticipation. A man with a long, barrel-shaped drum carved from a tree trunk, an animal skin stretched taut across the opening, sat down and with the palms of his hands started to pound out a beat—a slow, steady *ba-boom, ba-boom* that vibrated in Kiran's chest. From one of the tents came a line of dancers, stomping to the rhythm, feathers and bones swaying on flowing garments of fur and brightly colored cloth, bracelets of blue and green stones jangling at their wrists and ankles. Each carried a wooden bowl of dried leaves that seemed the focus of their dance. Haktu was among them.

The drumming stopped and the crowd parted. All eyes turned, gazing into the darkness. Kiran craned his neck to see. A man emerged, dressed in the full pelt of an animal, its head atop his, its brown fur trailing down his back. Around his neck hung a ring of jumbled bones. His ears were pierced with the feathers of an eagle, his wrists decorated with leaves.

The man had the same stature as Haktu, tall and commanding, but with the plump, softness of age and hair tinged with gray.

The procession of dancers ushered him to the fire, their heads bowed in respect. He raised his hands high above his head and all were quiet. He waved his hands in the air, gesturing with wide, flowing movements and spoke unfamiliar words, low and solemn.

"I think he is saying a prayer," Bria whispered.

The man sat down cross-legged next to the fire. Haktu stepped forward, holding his bowl out before him in offering, then motioned for the young Torans to approach. "Manu-amatu, these ones I tell you."

The amber light revealed a dark, wrinkled face and deep, knowing eyes that reminded Kiran of Aldwyn. "Welcome. I am told you need guidance to the river. And today, you lost one of your clan, out in the forest. We weep for you."

Kiran smiled. *So this is Manu-amatu. Thank the Father! Someone intelligent!* He looked to Haktu, wondering now why he spoke like a four-year-old.

Jandon stepped forward. "He was swallowed by a Mawghul. It was awful."

"A Mawghul?" He turned to Haktu. "You are right, my brother. They are in need of guidance. I shall consult on this matter."

When every dancer took his turn, and all the requests were made, the drummer resumed, pounding out a steady rhythm—the thump-thump of a heartbeat, the pulse of life. The dancers came alive, circling the old man, stomping to the rhythm, and with each third beat, chanting with a loud grunt. A second drum, this one higher in pitch, began a staccato rat-a-tat, sending waves of sound, breaking against the main beat. In a choreographed ritual, each dancer, in turn, faced Manu-amatu, held his bowl above his head, looking to the sky, then bowed and tossed the dried leaves on the fire. They rocked and twirled in synchronized movement, waving their arms in the air like birds in flight, their brightly colored clothing swaying in an undulating array of color.

All the while, Manu-amatu sat, as if in a trance, watching the tendrils of smoke whisper through the night air.

A third drum joined in syncopated beats, and, as if the rhythm brought her into being, a woman appeared out of the darkness, singing a hauntingly mournful melody. Wrapped in a flowing robe of black, she floated into their midst, her face encircled with a corona of flowers radiating outward like the rays of the sun. In one hand, she shook a rattle and with the other, she waved a short staff in the air. She circled the fire, then paused in front of Manu-amatu. In a flowing movement, she held the wooden staff pointed in his face, put her lips to one end, and blew. From the other end, a tiny white cloud puffed into his face. Manu-amatu did not blink. He stared into the flames with a dreamy, unfocused look, as though he were seeing into another world. His eyes became bleary and after a few moments his lips went slack, saliva ran from his mouth, and he slumped forward, mucus dripping from his nose. The woman lifted his head and his eyes rolled back to reveal ghoulish white sockets.

Bria gasped. Kiran glanced around the clan. No one seemed concerned as they swayed to the beat of the drums.

The enchantress reached behind Manu-amatu's back and flipped a grotesque mask over his face. It was the elongated, abstract face of a beast, carved of wood, with large, black holes for eyes. The horns stood tall atop his head, shiny black, glistening in the firelight. The men of the clan began to chant. The woman continued her sorrowful lament, spinning in slow, sensuous circles.

The volume of the low drum increased, pounding like thunder, the rumble so low the ground vibrated beneath their feet—*ba-boom, ba-boom.*

The rhythm increased in tempo, reverberating through the night. Kiran breathed in the sweet smell of smoke and let the waves of sound sweep over him. Faster and faster, the drums pulsed into a fever pitch. The beat pulsed through his veins, his heart pumping in unison. *Ba-boom, thump-thump, ba-boom, thump-thump.*

All at once, the drumming stopped and he was drowning in silence, an excruciating emptiness. Kiran drew in his breath, overcome by a feeling of utter vulnerability, as if his soul could be drawn from his body by the phantom beat that pounded in his head. He felt a hand on his and turned to stare into a pair of shining green eyes. "Are you all right?" Bria asked.

Kiran shook his head, looking about him. *What just happened?*

As if lifted by the force of silence, in one swift movement, Manu-amatu rose to his feet and leaped into the fire, twirling and stomping, swinging his arms wildly in the air, the flames flaring up about him.

Kiran shrank back in horror. "What's happening? Is he possessed by a demon?"

Bria shook her head.

The other dancers shrieked and hollered, caught up now in a violent frenzy, whirling and spinning in erratic circles. Manu-amatu grabbed two burning sticks and raised them high above his head, knocking them together as he sprang from the fire, scattering sparks into the sky. He tilted his head back and screeched like an owl as embers rained down on his head. He spun, round and round, until finally the burning sticks shattered and he collapsed on the ground in a shower of orange coals crashing down around him.

He thrashed about, his body wracked with violent convulsions—screaming, roaring, trembling, and twitching—that lasted for several minutes as he fought to cast out the demon. In a burst of strength, he leapt to his feet, spinning wildly until his body crumpled to the ground, the spell broken at last.

About him, the clan started to hum a low, soothing intonation as they softly swayed from side to side until finally Manu-amatu rose to his feet and the humming stopped in a hush of anticipation. The clan stared with rapt attention, the air charged with expectation.

Manu-amatu's voice thundered through the silence with what seemed some kind of revelation. Cheers erupted from the clan and a different kind of music broke out. Drums and flutes, rattles and bells played as the clan members embraced and twirled in festive celebration.

Kiran sat back, bewildered. Manu-amatu had not recited a Verse, had not spoken a word in the Tongue of the Father. Yet the clan acted as though they had been blessed. And how had he fought the demon? None of it made any sense.

The adults of the clan danced with wild abandon, gyrating in a wild frenzy by the light of the fire, utterly shameless in their suggestive rhythms. Partners clung together, moving in tandem to the throbbing beat, their bodies touching, pulsing with a surge of passion. The music seemed to take possession of every mind, seducing them, tantalizing them, carrying them along into a realm where all inhibitions were taken by the wind. The musty scent of sweaty bodies permeated the thick, night air.

The men and women moved together, sensuously entwined, led by the rhythm in a collective ecstasy. Kiran glanced at his companions, worried they could read his thoughts, but they seemed lost in their own, shifting uneasily. Kail sat wide-eyed and trembling, looking even more pale than usual. Jandon stared with his mouth gaping open as if he had been clubbed on the top of the head. Deke had a look of both disgust and indignation. Only Roh seemed to share Kiran's intrigue, subtly swaying to the beat.

The Elders would never condone this kind of dancing in the village, but he couldn't resist the contagious rhythm of the drums, the intoxication of the dance. All his pent-up desires came to the surface. To be able to give himself up with abandon, to let go, was irresistible. He felt an overwhelming urge to take Bria in his arms and hold her, to sway to the rhythm, her body pressed against his. The familiar rush of heat came over him. Her face was flush pink and her hair lay wet against her forehead. Her eyes caught his and at once he realized he'd been staring at her, caressing her body with his eyes. He started to turn away, but her eyes held his, and for a moment he felt a surge of connection, as if her thoughts were his, a mutual desire. In an instant the connection was gone. He was left breathless.

He leapt to his feet and merged into the mass of sweaty bodies, swaying to the rhythm—*ba-boom, thump-thump, ba-boom, thump-thump.*

Kiran awoke, disoriented, the warm sun on his face. Deke was whispering in his ear. "Look what you've done. In this demonic hive of hedonism and wickedness. I told you. I told you!"

Kiran shoved him away, sat up, and looked around, trying to get his bearings. *What happened last night?* The entire night felt hazy. Why couldn't he remember? It was as if someone had…as if someone had stolen his mind.

He drew in his breath. *A witch!*

Could it be? Witches had the power to take control of minds, make people act against their will. They never knew what happened.

It all made sense now—the lewd behavior, the way the clan members had danced with wild abandon. *The entire clan has been infected by her evil sorcery! She cast a spell over them all!* He glanced around the clan, his eyes darting from face to face. The Lendhi were calmly going about their chores—chopping strips of meat, tending the fire, tanning the hides—as if nothing had happened. *They don't know there is a witch among them.*

The enchantress. *It had to be her.* The way she waved her staff. And the moon was full. *How did I not see it last night?* Surely she was the witch; Manu-amatu had jumped in the fire and emerged unscathed. How could that be but by the spell of one with maleficent power?

Panic rose in his chest. *We've got to get out of here!* He looked at Bria and stopped cold, seized by a scant memory—her eyes, last night. She had looked concerned when he...*Oh no!* From the back of his mind came the unbearable truth: *Witches can only seize the minds of the unfaithful.*

In horror, he looked back to the clan—half naked men living like wild animals with no temple, no Elders. Ignorant savages, unaware of the Truth. It was their lack of reverence for the Great Father that made them vulnerable to a witch. He was sure of it.

He looked to each of his friends slumped on the grass beside him. *Only I was bewitched!* A rush of anguish flooded over him—he hadn't recited the Verse last night. So much had distracted him from it. How could he have forgotten? But that wasn't enough to make him vulnerable to a witch. His blood pumped hot in his ears.

He had to get away from her. Now. But what would he tell the others? He couldn't admit his weakness. Not without ridicule. Or worse, banishment.

No. They'd already decided to stay with the Lendhi. He had argued for it.

He had to deal with this on his own. He would have to be very careful. The slightest question or feeling of doubt and she'd seize his soul.

11

Haktu appeared with a grin, offering a basket of grilled meat and roasted root vegetables to the Torans. "Bounty plenty. Spirits like you."

Kiran took a serving of meat. Trying to act casually, he asked, "Last night, the dancing and the celebration, what was that for?"

Haktu cocked his head to the side, confused.

Kiran slapped his hands on the ground as though he were playing the drums and swayed back and forth, imitating the dancing. He shrugged. "Why?"

Haktu smiled in understanding and beamed with pride. "Hunt many beasts. Honor Spirits."

"Honor spirits? I don't understand. Last night, Manu-amatu said he would consult. But how, with whom?"

"Like bird, soar wind, to Spirit world."

Soar on the wind? That was absurd. Men couldn't fly like a bird. And did he mean the holy realm of the Great Father, the abode of souls gathered in the afterlife? "Do you mean the Celestial Kingdom?"

"Manu-amatu messenger," he said as though telling a child who hadn't been listening.

"The messenger?"

"By staff, he go." Haktu raised his eyebrows. "You have holy man, no?"

"Well, we have Elders. But they don't fly." He gestured toward the sky, raising his hands like Aldwyn would. "They talk to the Father."

"Ah," said Haktu, nodding as if he understood. "Why you travel, across land, to Spirit?"

"Because we were told to," growled Deke, butting in. "One does not question the Way."

Kiran blanched. He was sure Haktu meant no disrespect.

"Ah," said Haktu with a clipped, polite smile and turned away.

Kiran frowned at Deke, but it didn't matter. He was getting nowhere, learning nothing of the witch. He'd have to find another way.

Despite their lack of reverence for the Great Father, the Lendhi were a happy, friendly people. With genuine warmth and kindness, they welcomed the Torans, giving them hides and poles to erect a tent. Roh and Kiran managed to get the main pole set in the ground and one hide stretched over part of the top before declaring it would suffice.

There were chores for everyone; no one lazed about. Kiran watched with curiosity, helping where he could, all the while keeping watch for the witch.

The clan used every part of the animals they killed and each needed to be preserved. Several women worked to tan the hides of the beasts, which were used for myriad purposes: the covering of their tents, clothing, blankets, foot coverings, food storage, drums. One woman, the oldest in the clan it seemed, with hair white as snow, teetered about on one bad leg as she worked to remove the hooves and horns for tools and cooking utensils. Nothing was wasted. Even the dogs did their share, licking the bones clean.

Others of the clan, men and women alike, continued the work of preserving the meat of the beast, cutting it into strips to be hung and dried over the smoky fire which they continually tended to keep the flies away.

As Kiran interacted with the clan members, he tried to communicate with them. Occasionally, they would speak a word, but most of their mumblings were soft and incoherent. If he paid close attention to their expressive hand gestures, he could understand the gist of their communication, and he tried to gesture back the same way. Before long, it seemed, they were actually communicating and he was proud of the way he could read their facial expressions and interpret their body language. He wondered how they could ever live this way though, with such difficulty just trying to talk to each other.

On the third day, the westerly breeze turned cool, a welcome relief after months of hot, dry air. Kiran inhaled the sweet scent of autumn and felt his stress ease away. There had been no sign of the witch. She must have slipped away in the night. It was the calmest he felt since he had fled from the village, which seemed like ages ago now.

This morning, he sat next to a woman who stirred the dried meat into melted fat to be rolled into balls that were sewn up tightly in bags made of intestines and stored in leather pouches for travel. She smiled as she worked, showing him how to mix it, what the texture should be. When she turned to look into his eyes, a chill of recognition surged down his spine and he inhaled sharply. *The witch!* He jumped up, dropping the spoon of hot fat. *Don't look in her eyes. Don't look in her eyes!*

"You burn?"

"No, I, ah…" *What do I do? She's the witch!* He stumbled backward, turned, and fled.

Running as fast as he could, he skirted the edge of the camp. When he reached his tent, he dove inside, scrambled to his knees, and recited the Verse, twice in a row, just to be sure.

That afternoon, a hawk was spotted flying overhead. The bird circled the camp and headed west. Manu-amatu declared it a good omen for travel. It was time for the clan to move on. The next morning, at first light, faster than Kiran thought possible, the clan disassembled the camp.

Avoiding the women so as not to run into the witch, he stayed with the men, observing their work. The tents were taken apart and reassembled as travois, the poles laid on the ground and lashed together into a V-shaped frame, hides stretched across and tied to the poles, the baskets of belongings piled atop and fastened in place. Each loaded travois was fixed with a shoulder harness so it could be dragged across the flatlands. Smaller travois were assembled and fitted for the dogs.

Kiran marveled at the ingenuity of the device—simple, yet remarkably efficient. Deke, standing next to him, snorted. "They aren't even smart enough to make a wheel."

"No, these are better," he said. "Look how they glide over the stiff grasses and uneven ground where a wheel would get stuck. It is quite ingenious actually."

Deke huffed. "At least we're finally moving on."

With the rising sun at their backs, the clan set out across the prairie, moving as one amorphous mass, leaving a path of trampled grasses as they went. Four men led the way, their spears at the ready. The children followed, flanked by those adults who dragged the travois burdened with their worldly possessions. Younger men brought up the rear, eyes scanning the horizon. The white-haired old woman lagged behind, hobbling along, dragging one leg. Occasionally, she would sit upon a travois built just for her, dragged by one of the young hunters.

Kiran walked next to Bria. "I'm glad to finally be on our way, aren't you?"

She nodded without looking at him.

"To the river."

She nodded.

Without warning, the men at the lead halted. In a loud whoosh, a covey of grouse fluttered into the air. One young hunter was so startled he jumped back, tripped, and fell to the ground. The clan erupted in laughter and moved on.

Bria picked up her pace, moving away from Kiran. He watched her go, wondering what he had done wrong.

By midday, the sweltering sun became unbearable. Kiran pulled at his sweat-soaked clothes, flapping them against his skin, trying to cool himself. He was thirsty and footsore. Thankfully, they came upon a small pond and the clan stopped, dropping their loads to fill their skins. They were quickly on their way again and Kiran fell in line next to Jandon who had been lagging behind.

"How's your ankle?" Kiran asked.

"It hurts. But I'm fine. I'm tired of being hot, I know that."

Kiran glanced over his shoulder.

Jandon followed his line of sight. "What are you looking for?"

He could trust Jandon and the more eyes watching, the better. He eased next to him and whispered in his ear. "The witch. I'm keeping my eye on her."

"A witch!" Jandon jumped as if he'd been bitten, swiveling around in a full circle, his eyes darting about.

"Shhh! I don't know what powers she has and I don't want to take any chances. We can't let her know that we suspect."

"How do you know there's a witch?"

"Wait," Kiran grabbed him by the arm, swinging him around to face him. "You didn't suspect?" Jandon scrunched his eyebrows together. "Well, that's good. Then the others probably don't either. Anyway, you remember, the woman who danced with Manu-amatu."

"Oh, yeah. Who could forget? What a body. And the way she danced." He made a soft whistle. Then he turned to face Kiran, eyes wide, as if he just made the connection. "She's a witch?"

Kiran shushed him again, looking around to be sure no one heard. "Of course she's a witch. What else could explain it? Manu-amatu jumped in the fire. And he didn't have one burn. She cast a spell on him." He glanced over his shoulder again. "You were there. Didn't you see?"

"Huh." He scratched his chin. "I thought the magic came from the staff."

Kiran stopped dead and stared at Jandon, stunned. *A magic staff?* "I never thought of that." He had made some assumptions; he had to admit. Maybe she wasn't a witch after all. But he couldn't remember everything that happened that night. And the lustful feelings. It must have been the spell of a witch. Wasn't it? He looked sidelong again to be sure no one had heard and walked on in a storm of thought. *A real magic staff?*

As the sun approached the horizon, a suitable place to camp was found. The Lendhi went to work right away, their routine so engrained it seemed to happen without effort or planning. Tents went up, supply baskets were arranged, and the fire sparked to life. The women dug a pit in the ground, which they lined with the stomach of an animal to make a cooking pot, and filled it with vegetables and water. They placed hot stones in the water until it boiled. Before long, the scent of stew wafted through the camp.

Meanwhile, the Torans watched Haktu erect his tent. Curved poles were set in the dirt and lashed together, forming a dome-shaped frame. Several animal hides that had been stitched together were lifted with a pole and wrapped around the frame then pinned together with wooden skewers.

When they rose to set up their own tent, Jandon struggled to his feet and winced in pain as he put his weight on one leg. Bria took him by the arm. "Jandon, show me your ankle."

Reluctantly, he lifted his pant leg to reveal a swollen ankle. Pus oozed from the gashes in his skin.

"Oh, my! We need to take care of that. Why didn't you say something?"

He shrugged. "It's not as bad as it looks, really."

"But we can't risk it getting any worse!"

Haktu took a close look at the wound.

"I'm all right," Jandon said, waving his hand in the air as if to shoo away the problem.

Haktu ushered Jandon into his tent, insisting that he sit and rest. "Manu-amatu help," Haktu said gruffly and left.

Bria and Kiran sat with him, their eyes adjusting to the dark tent. Sunlight streamed down through the small opening at the peak of the roof, faintly lighting the interior.

Moments later, Manu-amatu stepped through the flap door, his hands crossed, his head bowed. A young girl stood behind him, holding a leather bag and a bladder of water. Manu-amatu examined the wound, then sent the young girl on an errand.

Manu-amatu selected items from a pouch he carried around his neck—pieces of bone, a white stone, several feathers, the tip of an antler—and deliberately placed them about the tent, chanting.

The girl returned, a wooden container in hand. She opened the lid and gingerly pulled from it a long, slimy black bloodsucker. Kiran's mouth dropped open and his stomach flipped. Jandon shrank back with a gasp and the color drained from his face. "Uh, I'm fine. Feeling better already. Thank you," he stammered.

The girl laid the wriggling worm on Jandon's ankle. He went rigid, staring wide-eyed, following her every movement. When she reached into the container and withdrew a second writhing bloodsucker, Jandon drew in a quick breath, his eyes rolled back, and he slumped over on his side.

Kiran watched with morbid curiosity as the girl applied several more worms to the purple, bleeding skin. While they enlarged, filling with blood, hot stones were brought from the communal fire and placed in a basket filled with water. From his leather bag, Manu-amatu took several dried leaves, dropped them in the basket, and stared into the brew, entranced, as they swirled about the bubbling water.

Meanwhile, the girl mashed herbs and pulpy roots in a wooden bowl. Once the worms had fallen away, she scooped out the poultice in her bare hand and put it directly on the wound, spreading it across the skin. Then she covered the ankle with an animal skin and wrapped it with strips of reed, twisting them together to hold the poultice in place. She picked up the bloodsuckers, returned them to the container, and slipped from the tent.

Manu-amatu dipped a wooden cup into the basket and lifted it to Jandon's lips, gently waking him. After Jandon drank, Manu-amatu stared into the empty cup as if searching for something. "The spirits are strong," he said and jumped up and stomped around the perimeter of the tent, beating the sides with a stick and shaking a rattle, chanting with fervor. Kiran sat stone still, startled by Manu-amatu's outburst.

Manu-amatu smiled with satisfaction. "The evil spirits have been cast out and harmony restored. Now he can rest," he said and gathered his relics and left.

Kiran remained where he sat, a phantom thought taunting him, lingering just beyond his grasp. He plucked a leaf from Manu-amatu's brew, examined it, and put it to his nose. Immediately he recognized the familiar leaf, but tasted it to be sure. Tarweed. But how could that be? There was nothing special about tarweed. It was just a tea. Had Manu-amatu blessed it? Had he imbued it with special power with the chanting? But it was just tea. Wasn't it?

Kiran ran after Manu-amatu. He had to know.

He caught up with the old man on the other side of camp. For a moment, Kiran stared, unsure how to ask. He'd be scolded for sure. But he had to know.

"What troubles you?" the man asked. He took his time to set down his bag and lower himself to the ground.

Kiran sat across from him. "The tea. Is it magic?"

"A very rare, special herb. It is difficult to find."

Kiran cocked his head to the side. It was true, he realized. The plant was common in the hills near his home, but he hadn't seen it here on the flatlands. But, still, tarweed had no special power. It was just a plant.

As if he read Kiran's thoughts, Manu-amatu said, "It is all part of the Great Mystery."

Great Mystery? "But you must know how it cures. Why *that* tea?"

"It does not matter how or why. What matters is what is."

"So it's not the tea?"

Manu-amatu scratched his chin and his eyes turned soft. So much like Aldwyn. *But maybe this man can really conjure magic.* Kiran drew in a quick breath. "It's *you*." His eyes grew wide. "You have the power to banish the demons of the sick." *You are the witch!*

Manu-amatu raised his hand in defense and shook his head. "I have no such power. Health is a state of harmony. Sickness is disruption, an imbalance. Through my connection to the Spirit world, balance is restored."

Connection? "Spirit world? Like the other night, at the fire? Haktu told me you traveled. By the staff. Is that it? Is the power in the staff?" He leaned forward and whispered, "Is it magic?"

"Ah, you are a seeker. You want to learn to walk with the Spirits?"

"Walk with the Spirits?"

"What are you seeking?"

"Well, we seek the Great Father. The Voice of the Father. We're traveling there."

"I see," he said, nodding. "Why must you travel? Your Elders do not commune with your Spirit, the Great Father?"

"Oh, yes. The Elders communicate with the Great Father through prayer, in the Tongue of the Father."

"And the Great Father, He answers in the same tongue? The Elders translate for you?"

"Well, not exactly. I mean...you don't hear His voice. But they do, somehow."

Manu-amatu raised one eyebrow. "You are not sure?"

"Well, yes, I am. I guess. It is just that we do not witness it. It is a sacred act, to receive the blessings of the Great Father. But we will. I will. That is where we are headed, to the Voice of the Father, so that we may receive his blessing directly. But the Voice of the Father dwells on the far side of the world. The Elders, they hear the... Well, we seek the Voice... It is difficult to explain." He screwed up his face, searching for the words. He tried again. "The Great Father dwells in the Celestial Kingdom. We seek the wisdom that is direct from the Great Father. We seek the source. The Voice of the Father."

Kiran had to admit, he truly didn't understand it himself. He sat back, frustrated. How could the Great Father dwell in the Celestial Kingdom *and* on the far side of the world? And if the Elders could speak to the Great Father, why did the pilgrims have to travel?

He sat upright. Aldwyn had said something about being disconnected. Was that what they were sent to do? Restore the connection?

An idea was forming in his mind and his nerves tingled with excitement. "You said you walk with the Spirits. Can you actually see the Spirits and talk with them? Do you hear their voices?"

Manu-amatu sat back and eyed Kiran up and down. "From the staff comes an opening, but you must then walk through the mist to the Spirit realm."

Kiran tried to remain still, keeping a blank expression, while his mind reeled with possibility. "So its the magic staff that takes you there?"

Manu-amatu nodded.

"How? How does it work?"

Maun-amatu smiled patiently. "It does not matter how or why. What matters is what is. It is all part of the Great Mystery. We do not question this."

Kiran nodded. What if the Lendhi did believe in the Great Father, only they called Him by a different name? And if Manu-amatu could travel by the staff…

12

Falling into the routine of the Lendhi clan was easy for Kiran as they traveled the great meadow, following the path of the migrating beasts, drawing their life from the land. Whenever a beast was killed or other food was found, they lingered at camp for a few days, harvesting, collecting, filling their baskets with the bounty of nature, then went on their way again.

In no time, Jandon was back to his normal stride, and he and Roh and Kiran ventured out with the hunters, stalking the beasts, antlered deer, and rodents that shared their grassy world. From Haktu, they learned to hunt by spear, how to follow animal tracks in the dirt, how to stalk their prey in stealth, always downwind, and to make the silent hand gestures the Lendhi used to communicate during the hunt. Haktu showed them how to wield a sling, swinging it about his head and flinging it accurately to stun or kill small game. When Kiran asked Haktu how he knew where to find the beasts, the master hunter smiled humbly and said the Spirits guided him, the signs were there for all to see.

The women of the clan were as open and willing to share. They taught Kail and Bria to recognize fruit bearing bushes and how to collect their edible seeds, buds and flowers. With sharp, pointed sticks they would dig bulbs, tubers, and roots out of the ground. Kail and Bria learned to read the behavior of the plump grassland birds to locate their nests and their nutrition-rich eggs. Soon the girls had their own storage baskets filled with small apples, blue and red berries, wild legumes, edible ferns, and the hard grains the Lendhi ground and cooked into mush.

Kail worked hard, and Kiran was glad to see her adjusting to life outside the village. She seemed to thrive here with new purpose, doing her part to learn the skills they needed. The color came back to her cheeks and he even caught her smiling.

Deke spent his days with the children, preaching the Truth, so, he said, they may know the love of the Great Father and be delivered from the wicked ways of their parents. All the while he preached, the children listened with open-mouthed fascination to the flow of strange sounds. Kiran wondered how Deke couldn't see; they didn't understand one word.

Some days, Kiran would join the women, an excuse to be with Bria. With patience, the women showed him how to collect the tall grasses, which ones were strongest, and how to weave sturdy baskets by placing the larger reeds at the bottom and making them waterproof with tightly woven patterns. When he attempted to make his own basket, the young girls bubbled with giggles.

He had no idea that grass could be woven so tightly and made to hold water, yet these women did. They understood things about the world, things he'd never considered important before. It wasn't just knowledge. The Lendhi seemed to live with the rhythms of nature, as a part of it, not separate from it. It was their way of life.

Late one afternoon, Roh arrived in camp with a young deer slung over his shoulder and a manly grin on his face. He had made his own kill using the weapons of the Lendhi. The clan greeted him with smiles of congratulations. He dropped the carcass with a thud in front of the Toran tent.

Haktu stood proudly next to Roh. "Must… What word? Pray. Honor animal Spirit."

Haktu dropped to his knees. Roh knelt next to him. Kiran did the same.

Deke stood with his arms crossed, wearing a frown of disdain.

"Well done, Roh," said Bria, kneeling next to him. Kail hesitated, looking to Deke, then her eyes lingered over the camp. She dropped to the ground next to Bria.

Deke leaned forward, his taut voice lowered, and said, "Pray? For an animal?"

Bria spoke through clenched teeth. "You bow, or you don't eat."

Manu-amatu appeared, smiling at Roh. "You have set free the Spirit to come into our hearts. We humbly beseech the breath of the fallen, come into our warm bodies that we may draw the breath of life."

The Lendhi clan cheered and went to work, helping Roh.

Kiran thought he was beginning to understand. The Lendhi had a kinship with all creatures. Plants and animals were sacred, sentient beings, possessed of souls. They killed animals only when necessary, and then with reverence.

But Manu-amatu himself was still a mystery. He was a paradox. Within the clan, he seemed the leader, the patriarch, the one everyone looked to for guidance, yet he did not lead in a traditional sense. He did not issue orders or set rules, nor did he profess any knowledge save that which was channeled through him from the Spirit world.

Kiran followed him to his tent. "I'm told you can interpret dreams," he said when the others were out of earshot. "Can you do it for me?"

Manu-amatu nodded. Kiran told him of a dream he'd had over and over since the night he left the village. In it, he searched through many doors, went up a ladder that extended forever, then always, at the end, saw himself in a reflection, but his face was not his own. It was Aldwyn's.

When Kiran finished, Manu-amatu said, "This Aldwyn, you have much respect for him."

"Yes. He is the Eldest and I am his ward. I want to be an Elder someday, just like him."

"Ah. You seek his knowledge, understanding."

"Well, yes."

"So it is among the clan," said Manu-amatu. "Wisdom is passed from father to son."

"Is that how you learned to speak so well?"

Manu-amatu raised an eyebrow. "You mean to speak the language of trade? Yes, I have learned this language as well as the language of the clan."

"The language of the clan?" The soft mutterings, the hand gestures… *They have their own language!* All along, they had been trying to speak to him and he thought they were stupid. Guilt swelled in the bottom of his stomach. *It was right before my eyes.*

Just as the Elders spoke both the common language and the Tongue of the Father, Manu-amatu, he realized now, spoke two languages as well.

"Not all of the clan speak the language of trade, but as we travel, we often encounter others. If this is the tongue of your village, is it not a place of trade?"

"It was," Kiran nodded, remembering now what Aldwyn had said.

"For salt. But the traders don't come anymore."

"I see. And now you are seeking new trade? Is that why your Elders sent you?"

"No. I told you. We seek forgiveness of the Great Father. We have sinned and brought about His wrath. The drought has threatened our crops, our lives. Our sheep wander barren, dusty pastures."

"Perhaps your spirit is angered by this cult of the seed, to think one can control the workings of the soil, the rain, to harness the animals that are meant to roam the land. You travel. But the voice you seek can be heard in the song of the bird, the twitter of the grasshopper, the murmuring of the river, and the sweet breathing of flowers. If only you would listen. We are part of the land, not rulers over it. For all things share the same breath—the beast, the tree, the man."

"So, are you saying that…" He thought of the squirrel on the mountain. "Are you saying that the Great Father lives among us? His spirit is *everywhere*?"

Manu-amatu seemed pleased. "You are not like the others; you think for yourself. You have the gift of insight."

"It is a sin to question the Truth," he said, his eyes downcast. "If Deke heard me…"

"Ah, Deke. He does not know that humility is the virtue most revered. Do not dwell on his views. You would be wise to be wary of the one who claims the sole source of truth. I do not believe it is a sin, as you say, to question. It is most honorable to seek understanding." Manu-amatu looked him directly in the eye. "So, young man, you dream of being an elder, like Aldwyn. Yet you struggle with a great question, yes?"

Unsure of how to respond, Kiran thought about this for a long moment. "I want… I want to understand…" He stopped, frustrated. "I can't see my destiny."

"Ah. You are haunted by the shadow of a bird."

"What? A bird? No. I…It's just that there is so much I don't understand." Kiran was starting to feel exhausted as he always did in conversations with Aldwyn, trying to sort out the multitude of things too abstract to grab hold. He needed time to take it all in, to let it settle. If only it wasn't so complicated. "I want to know why I'm here. My purpose."

"We do not have the power to draw aside the veil of unborn time.

It is all part of the Great Mystery. You follow Father Sun, the great light, to understand the light that is within. Take this path, wherever it may lead you, in this world or another. For you, it is the only path there is."

Kiran nodded, unsure.

"Do not let fear cast a shadow in your mind. To endure, to stay on the path, and care for your brothers, as you would yourself, this is what matters most."

"You're right. If only my faith was stronger, Bhau would not have died. We were supposed to stay together. Aldwyn said that together the Great Father would watch over us. Together we would have been safe from the Mawghul."

Manu-amatu put his hand on Kiran's shoulder, just as Aldwyn had always done, and Kiran felt a sense of comfort in the gesture, as though, in a way, Aldwyn were here with him. "The world is not to be walked in alone, this is true. Tomorrow, at the rise of the sun, we shall walk together. There is something you need to see."

That evening, the first night of the new moon, the Lendhi clan bustled about with new exuberance and a feeling of merriment about them. Some kind of celebration was to take place. Torches were placed, encircling the camp. The women prepared elaborate dishes.

Back home, the villagers would be preparing for the Harvest Festival, laying out a banquet of roasted mutton, cabbage, potatoes and fresh cider. Kiran's mouth began to water just thinking about it. Late in the evening, the Goshtar Goat would arrive with gifts for all the little children, and at midnight, the Floating Leaf ceremony would take place, his favorite part of the holiday celebration. Leaf-shaped boats carrying lit candles were set afloat on the bay, each carrying a wish from a villager. Every year, for as long as he could remember, he had made the same wish.

"Isn't she stunning?" Jandon whispered to Kiran, nodding toward a young maiden of the clan with eyes the color of honey. Kiran had already noticed Jandon had taken a liking to her. Jandon found reasons to follow her, offering to help her carry water, to set her tent. She smiled demurely at him and he flirted back.

Kiran hesitated before he said, "Yes, she is beautiful."

"They call her Takhura."

"I know."

Jandon turned to face him. "But what?"

"Well, Jandon, we'll only be with the Lendhi for a short time."

"Well, I'm not going to marry her!" He looked around and leaned over to whisper, "I know she's not a Toran. I just like her, that's all. The Lendhi, well, they're not so bad. Don't you think?"

Kiran smiled at his old friend. "Yes, I like them, too."

"Hey, listen," Jandon said. "Back in the cave…" He paused. "Well, I'm sorry."

Before Kiran could reply, Bria and Kail plopped down beside them with a basket of food.

Takhura cautiously approached, her eyes searching for someone. Kiran guessed whom. "He's with the children," he said. Lately, Deke had taken to eating with the children, never letting up with his attempt to convert them.

She smiled and sat down next to Jandon, offering him a sweet bread and a small leather pouch. He accepted the gifts readily, taking a bite of the bread. As he examined the pouch, his expression turned to one of confusion. Takhura blushed, giggling. There was a moment of awkward silence, as none of the Torans were quite sure what humor they had missed, especially Jandon. He stopped chewing, his eyes moving from Kiran to Takhura, searching for an explanation.

"For dance," Takhura said, nodding with an impish smile, then shyly looked away. She pointed to Kail's pomander. "Is beautiful."

"Thank you. It's my amulet. The scent is wonderful. Here, smell." She leaned toward Takhura and lifted the pomander to her nose, shaking it to release the fragrance.

Takhura inhaled and closed her eyes, sniffing, as if trying to identify it. "Ah, scent there river."

"The scent of the river?"

"Yes, river." She turned back to Jandon and dropped her eyes. "Is season together love."

"The season of love?" The clan was not shy with their affections. Without inhibition, they would kiss like lovers in front of others, an activity that made Kiran both uncomfortable and curious. Was it condoned now in this season of love she referred to?

"Today perfect balance. Sun return. Now woman time. Go river, flowers bloom, seed flows. There Sun stand still." She looked at Jandon and grinned. "Then wedding."

Jandon choked on the bread.

"Are you all right?" asked Kail. Jandon nodded, coughing, his face red.

"Wedding?" Kiran asked.

Takhura clasped her hands together. "Bind clans."

"So, the celebration tonight is for perfect balance, the return of the Sun? And now you enter the time of women? Is that it? I don't think I understand."

Takhura seemed flattered that Kiran was interested and she was eager to explain. "Man woman equal. Sun draws one, then other. Time equal, together in love." She touched her index fingers together. "You know, yes?"

Did she mean sex? Kiran opened his mouth to ask another question and Jandon elbowed him in the side, glaring. *But she probably knows about the staff. And the witch.* He would have to try to talk to her again.

The drumming started. Takhura took Jandon by the hand and they twirled around the fire, following a square pattern. At each corner they stopped and shook seeds from the pouch Takhura had given him, tossing them into the wind. After they made several rotations, they left the dancing square and returned to Kiran and Bria, arm in arm.

"We're going for a walk," Jandon told Kiran with a quick wink. Bria looked to Kiran with a raised eyebrow. Village custom required a chaperone.

Kiran took her hand and said to Jandon, "Bria and I will join you."

Takhura led them to a small rise where the four of them sat in the grass, looking back at the camp with only the light of the stars.

"Tell me your home," Takhura said. "You live by sea. You know Irichoi?"

"Irichoi?" Jandon asked.

"Yes, First Ones, live in sea. Swim same fish, talk same us."

Jandon laughed. "No, I don't know any sea creatures that talk. But we don't go out on the sea. It is forbidden."

"Forbidden? What mean, forbidden?"

"Forbidden. You know, we are not allowed."

"Oh," she said. "Spirits warn?"

"Sure, whatever, I don't know." He took her hand. "You are so beautiful."

She giggled and lowered her brown eyes. He leaned over and kissed her.

Kiran whispered to Bria, "C'mon, I want to talk to you."

"But—"

"Just come with me, please." He held his hand out to her.

She looked at Jandon and Takhura, now entwined in a passionate kiss. "All right." She reached for his hand. Once out of earshot, she said, "Kiran, I'm worried that Jandon is being led astray."

"I think Jandon is the one doing the leading," he said with a laugh.

"That's not what I mean," she said, her voice stern. "She does not live by the Way."

"I know their ways are different. But… They're just kissing."

"*Just* kissing!"

Kiran turned to face her. He took her hand in his and they faced each other under the twinkling stars, his eyes holding hers.

"It's not proper," she whispered.

"The Lendhi don't think kissing is wrong," he said, catching his breath. He trembled from the feel of her hand in his and he wanted nothing more than to kiss her right now.

"Well, yes. I've noticed. But Kiran—"

"I know. They don't live by the Way. But Bria, maybe. Maybe the Elders…" He was still sorting it out in his own mind. But right now, reason didn't matter. He just wanted to kiss her.

"What are you trying to say?"

The new moon shed little light, but he knew her face, knew every line, every curve. He pulled her closer. "What if the Elders aren't right about everything? In all the scrolls I've read, I never once saw any mention of kissing being a sin. Nowhere."

He leaned toward her, his lips inches from hers. He could feel her hot breath on him and for a long moment he held her gaze, his heart racing. She turned away.

"Listen to me," he said. "Back home, if we slept in a cave or a tent together, we'd be banished. But we've had to out here, for our safety. How could anyone say the rules are absolute?" She exhaled and he felt her relax. He could see the change in her eyes. "Out here, we have to decide. For ourselves." He pulled her to him once more. "What matters is what you and I believe, don't you see?" He kissed her then, full on the mouth, and her lips parted, letting him, her tongue responding to his, soft and hungry. A warm gust of euphoria swept over him.

He reached his hand around her back, pulling her closer, and she broke away, pushing against his chest. "Kiran, I can't," she cried and turned and ran from him. He stared after her in disbelief as she disappeared in the darkness. He slumped to the ground and slammed his fist into the hard dirt.

When Kiran wandered back into camp, the joyous, uninhibited laughter of young children drew his attention. He found the whole lot of them by the fire, listening with delight to Manu-amatu's stories. The old man held the children rapt, gesticulating dramatically with his hands.

Once the fire burned down to smoldering embers and the young babes had fallen asleep in their mothers' arms, Kiran asked him to tell him the stories in his language. Manu-amatu was delighted and started again, telling him of the beginning of time—a world filled with water and floods, spirits and demons, Father Sun and Island Mother. It was frightening and fascinating and enlightening. His whole life, Kiran had been told that the Great Father made Wiros to provide a home for His children. But how it actually happened, no one knew. He was sure he'd never read about it in any of the scrolls. Manu-amatu seemed to know how it had all happened.

Seek wisdom from all whom you meet, Aldwyn had said.

Kiran could hardly sit still for his excitement. He had learned something that would make Aldwyn proud.

At dawn, as Manu-amatu had promised, they walked together across the plain and into a small patch of forest. The old man wandered aimlessly it seemed, as Kiran patiently followed, until finally he stopped next to a pile of sticks, branches, and leaves. He kicked them away to reveal a hole in the ground. Memories came rushing back and the terror of that night rose in Kiran once again—Kail screaming, Jandon babbling incoherently, the wild dogs circling. "Come here, son," Manu-amatu said.

Kiran shook his head.

"There is nothing to fear," he said and took Kiran by the shoulder, directing him to the edge of the hole. Short spears jutted from the bottom of the rocky pit, purposefully placed there by someone.

Kiran stared in disbelief. He turned to Manu-amatu. "But why? For what?"

"Hunters drive the beasts along this path where they fall in."

"It's a...a hunter's trap?"

Manu-amatu nodded.

"There is no demon?" he half asked, knowing the truth.

"The demon was in your mind."

Kiran followed Manu-amatu back to camp, unaware of one step. *It can't be. Bhau was killed by a Mawghul—a real demon! Jandon said he saw it. Didn't he?* But he knew the truth. He had never seen the Mawghul with his own eyes.

Now he knew better. There was no such thing. Mawghuls weren't real. It was a made-up tale, conceived out of fear, a figment of a narrow-minded imagination. Bewildered, he could not bring himself to look eastward. He had always been told of Mawghuls, since he was a child. Aldwyn had told him specifically to beware. What other falsehoods had he been led to believe? What else was Aldwyn wrong about?

As if a window opened and let in the light, he felt a deep, profound respect for the Lendhi and an overwhelming remorse for having thought of them as savages. What he was thinking was heresy, he knew. The Great Father would condemn such deviation from the Way, but he couldn't stop himself. He felt like crying for the turmoil in his heart.

He had to tell the others.

When he arrived back in camp, he went straight to their tent. The others were all there when he poked his head inside the flap. "I have to tell you—"

"We need to talk to you," said Deke.

"You aren't going to believe—"

"It's important," said Kail, her expression solemn.

He looked to Roh who shrugged. Kiran sat down. "What's wrong?"

With a voice of authority, Deke said, "You have strayed from the Way."

"What?" He looked to Jandon, who would not meet his gaze. "What are you talking about?" Had Jandon told them about the witch? Did they know he had been under her spell?

Kail said, "We know you've been with that heathen, Manu-amatu."

"Yes, he just showed me—"

Deke interrupted. "You've put all of us at risk by consorting with him."

Kiran clamped his teeth together. "Jandon, tell them." He waited for Jandon to make eye contact. "You have been walking without pain and the swelling is gone, right?" Jandon shrugged. "He cured your ankle."

"We know." Deke leaned forward and narrowed his eyes. "We think he's a witch."

"A witch?" Kiran glared at Jandon.

"He mixes potions and conjures demons. He has the entire clan under his spell."

Kiran laughed. "No, you don't understand—"

"Stay away from him," Deke commanded. He stood. "It is the will of the Father," he said and left the tent.

Bria slid over beside Kiran and whispered to him, "I thought you were smarter than this. We have to be careful. Anyone could corrupt our minds."

Her words cut through his heart. *Yeah, anyone could corrupt our minds,* he thought. *Like teaching us to believe in Mawghuls.*

Jandon waited for the others to leave the tent before he spoke. "I didn't tell Deke about the witch, I swear. He figured it out on his own. Maybe he is right, maybe he isn't. Can't you let it be, just this once? What's so interesting about Manu-amatu anyway?"

"Jandon, listen to me. What if the Lendhi know things we don't and we're just too arrogant to see?"

"What do you mean? They don't even know of the Great Father," said Jandon, shaking his head.

"But what if they have—" He dropped his voice to a whisper. "Listen. I asked Manu-amatu about the magic staff. He said it's like a door, a connection to the spirit world. When he goes through, he can speak with spirits." As soon as he said the words out loud, the idea started to take shape and form. "What if we didn't have to travel to the end of the world?"

"What are you saying?"

"Aldwyn said something about being disconnected. What if…" He took a deep breath. "What if we could speak to the Voice of the Father with the staff the way Manu-amatu does? We could save the village right now and go home."

"I don't know. Are you sure?"

Kiran sat back. He'd never been so sure of anything. "I think it's what we're supposed to do."

Jandon got up to leave, shaking the stiffness from his ankle. "I know one thing for sure. You think too much."

13

The Lendhi were on the move again. Kiran wandered a distance from the group on his own. He needed his own space. His only companion was one of the dogs, shaggy brown with black feet, running alongside him. When the desire struck, he'd flop on his back in front of Kiran, his big brown eyes pleading for attention. *"At least someone wants to be with me,"* he said, stopping to rub the dog's belly.

In the afternoon of the third day, Kiran noticed Jandon walking toward him. He didn't want to talk to him; he didn't want to talk to any of them. "He's supposed to be my friend. Why does he always side with Deke?" he said to the dog. "He could learn a lot from you."

"I have something to show you," Jandon said as he approached, his hands in his pockets.

"What?"

"Not here. Tonight. After dark."

"Fine," Kiran said, keeping his eyes forward.

"Listen, Kiran…"

Kiran knew what Jandon was going to say. He was always trying to get him to see Deke's side of things. Today, he wasn't going to tolerate it. "You know what, Jandon? I've heard all the tales and always imagined savage heathens to be cruel and evil. I thought that of the Lendhi at first. But it's not true. Manu-amatu is kind and smart and insightful. He knows things. And I can't believe you deny it. Especially after he healed your ankle."

"I know."

"You're not denying it?"

"No."

"Well, why didn't you say something then?"

Jandon shrugged. "You know how Deke is."

Yeah, and you follow him anyway. "Well, what about Bria? What did he say to her? Why did she side with him?"

"I don't know," he said, his gaze off in the distance.

"But you were there. She didn't say anything?"

"No, not really."

"We're talking about Bria. I can't believe she just agreed with Deke. Tell me what she said."

"Kiran, my friend. Let it go. I'll see you later."

"Let what go?"

"Tonight. After dark."

"Fine."

That night, after the camp was set up and the evening meal finished, Jandon strode up to Kiran, his pack on his back. "C'mon, let's go for a walk."

"Why do you have your pack?"

"For once, no questions. Just trust me. C'mon."

They hiked over a hill and found a rocky clearing out of view of the camp. The wind had calmed to a gentle breeze and for the first night since they'd been traveling the flatlands they could hear the crickets.

Jandon got a fire going with twigs and grass he'd collected along the way.

"Are you ready?" he said.

"Ready for what?"

Jandon grinned, bursting with his secret. He reached into his pack and presented the magic staff.

Kiran's mouth fell open. "How did you get it?"

"Takhura told me. The woman, the witch-woman, is the Keeper of the Staff. So, I kind of borrowed it from her tent when she was at the evening meal. You think this will work, right? Well, let's do it."

Kiran shook his head in disbelief. A rush of excitement flushed through him. "This is it, Jandon. We'll face the Voice and all will be forgiven. We'll save the village." He shifted from side to side. "Hold on. Maybe we should wait. Maybe we should talk to Manu-amatu. We don't know how the magic works."

"Don't be such a girl. We saw. You blow into it. Now, get ready."

Kiran drew in a breath. "All right, do it then."

Jandon let out a hoot. He raised the rod to his mouth, aimed the end at Kiran's face and blew. A fine, white powder puffed in his face. He scrunched his nose; it smelled acrid.

At first Kiran felt nothing. He sat still, trying to be patient. "Do it again," he said. Jandon did as he asked, then passed the staff to Kiran. Kiran blew several puffs into Jandon's face.

Then they waited. Kiran's eyes became bleary. A tingling sensation started in his fingers, moving up and down his arms. His eyes were drawn to the night sky, pierced by countless brilliant stars, sparkling in the darkness in an unnatural way. It felt strangely unsettling. He looked toward the horizon. Visions of purple and blue danced across the plains in a kaleidoscope of slow undulating waves of color. He turned his focus to the crackling fire and was overcome by a swell of dizziness. His stomach felt bubbly, pushing in his throat. Jandon spewed vomit in the wind. Kiran bent over and threw up in the dirt. Jandon laughed then, his voice echoing across the sky, rattling the grasses, then bent over and vomited once more.

The world softened at the edges, a warm, fuzzy lightness that melted with the sky, as if the wind had swirled them together. He was awash with an overwhelming sense of calm and well-being, as if all was good in the world and the wonder of life was at his fingertips. He began to relax into a peaceful awareness, the sound of his own heartbeat the source of the rhythm of all life. His body radiated warmth, like the sun, his breath giving life to every flower, the grasses swaying with every exhalation. A flush of warm waves coursed up and down his body, and the sensations intensified, causing more waves of nausea. All sound penetrated his vision, encompassing his being with a clarity so brilliant, so sharp, it was painful, like piercing stabs to his eyes. The chirp of the night insects ricocheted inside his transparent soul and the wind roared across the sky, blowing the stars around. The pungent scent of the night air permeated all that was, washing over him with an intensity so sensual he felt the warm flush of arousal. He leapt to his feet and sang, and as he did, his voice awoke every living creature from slumber.

As time spun around, the terror of another, unknown dimension began to take shape and he spiraled inward, lost in the vertigo. Giant orbs of dizzying textures, with endlessly changing patterns, rolled in and out of his vision, pulsating with sparkling rays of light as Jandon twirled, his arms flailing, engulfed in flames that licked the air around him.

The sky ripped open and the world shook. Trees darted about, racing for the horizon. The grasses swirled around him, howling and screeching. He covered his ears, but the sound persisted, brushing at his eardrums. The stars pulsed, shooting rays in every direction. Flashes of color washed over him—red, yellow, orange, green—each with a different sensation—prickly, silky, watery, suffocating.

Then the darkness seized him with its icy fingers and a deep, overwhelming sorrow overtook him, a shadow of death and hopelessness so deep, he moaned with grief and fell to the ground, curled up into a ball, and cried like a child. His tears formed a river that flowed across the world, flooding every crack and crevice, covering all of Wiros. The dry, scratchy soil surrounded him, held him, merged with him and he became part of the hill.

The sky rained blood down on him. Everywhere, the world had the stain of blood—red sky, red sun, red hills. Kiran dug into the dirt with his bare hands and rubbed the rough granules all over himself, trying to scrub it away. Then he lay back down and sobbed, shaking with violent chills.

Slowly, the terror receded, the colors muted, and all went dark.

A burning light brought him slowly to consciousness. *Is this it?* he thought. *Am I in the Celestial Kingdom? Have we reached the Voice of the Father?* He was trying to focus, to make his eyes adjust, when a shadowy apparition appeared before him. He opened his eyes to meet the gaze of the witch.

She hovered over him, her eyes ablaze. He shrank back, covering his eyes. *No! This can't be!*

"The sun has set on you," she hissed.

A slobbery tongue licked his cheek. He lifted his hand to push the scruffy dog away and wipe his face. He could feel the shadow of the witch slip away. He rolled over onto his side, opening one eye to see her storm off, staff in hand, the dog romping after her.

The agony of last night slowly enveloped him. He sat up, disoriented. Roh was sitting next to him. "What did you do?"

Jandon sat up, his eyes groggy and bloodshot, his skin waxen. "What happened?" he grumbled then slumped back over on his side.

Kiran held his pounding head, trying to remember. But he couldn't focus, couldn't hold a thought in his mind for the rushing sound of the wind sweeping against his ears.

As they approached the camp, Bria ran out to meet them, her face red. "What were you thinking? You shouldn't go off on your own like that. We were worried sick. Just what is going on with you, Kiran?"

"They just got a bit disoriented in the dark," Roh said. "It's nothing to worry about."

Kiran smiled, silently thanking Roh.

She sighed. "Well, thank the Father you're all right."

In their tent, he slumped onto his blanket. "Bria, listen…"

She put a hand over his mouth. "Get some rest. We'll talk later. I'm glad you are safe." Looking up at her, he was suddenly aware of her warm hand on his face. She seemed to read his thoughts and lifted it away, her fingers trailing across his cheek. "I'll make something to eat. For the both of you," she said, her eyes shifting to Jandon who collapsed with a thump next to Kiran. "It will be ready when you wake."

Jandon was fast asleep.

Roh whispered, "She's in love with you, you know."

He shook his head, blushing. "She would do the same for you."

Roh grinned. "Uh, huh."

That afternoon, Kiran awoke with a mouth-numbing thirst. He stepped from the tent for water. The entire Lendhi clan was gone. Their tents. Everything. Gone.

Kail ran up to him, her face red, her blue eyes wet with tears. "What have you done!"

He looked out over the landscape. The Lendhi were nowhere to be seen. It was as though they had vanished.

"We're all alone again. Alone!"

Roh came up behind her. "They didn't say anything. I tried to talk to Haktu…" He shrugged. "It was like we were ghosts."

Kiran ducked back into their tent. "Jandon, wake up. Wake up!" he shouted, shaking him. "What happened? With the staff? What happened?"

"What? Huh?" Jandon rubbed his eyes.

"Did you reach the Voice? Was He there?"

Jandon looked around the empty tent. "Are you kidding? I was scared out of my wits."

"What went wrong?"

"How should I know?" He groaned and lay back down.

Kiran rocked back and stared at Jandon. What had gone wrong? He was sure they had connected to the Spirit world. Hadn't they? His stomach tightened as images came back to him—trees running across the landscape, the grass howling in the wind, blood raining down from the sky. The visions, the feelings, had taken over. He hadn't even remembered to search for the Voice. It was like he had been in some kind of abstract realm, where his body and mind did not connect, and he had no control over his own thoughts.

"Hold on. You said she was the Keeper of the Staff. The witch. What does that mean?"

"How should I know?" Jandon grumbled without opening his eyes.

"It would mean the staff is hers. The magic comes from *her*. Maybe I was right about her all along. Don't you think?"

Jandon was back to sleep.

For one and one half cycles of the moon, they'd been traveling with the Lendhi, trusting them as guides. But still they had not come to the river. The Torans had no choice but to assume the clan was still headed toward the river, so onward they went, following their tracks in the grass.

They spent their days collecting nuts and berries, as the Lendhi had taught them, storing their food in baskets and their own leather pouches. Roh built a travois using their tent poles and, with it, they took turns dragging their stored food with them.

The winds turned cooler as the gently rolling hills stretched out before them like a sea of green waves that seemed to go on forever. In the distance, they were sure they could see the edge of the world. Every day they moved westward, yet did not come any closer, and they soon became discouraged.

One morning, Deke dropped to his knees. His face to the sky, he threw his hands in the air and beseeched aloud, "Great Father, please show us a sign! Are we on the right path?"

The tiny band of Torans circled around Deke and stared up at the sky, waiting for a response. But none came. Just the ever-present whisper of the wind. They walked on.

At midday, the breeze changed direction. The winds had been constant from the west and it was as though the world had shifted. "Look at that!" Jandon pointed.

To the north, a solid black cloud hovered on the horizon. Within moments, the dark mass doubled in size and a menacing hiss echoed across the plains.

Terror rose in Kiran. He turned to Bria and saw the frightened look on her face. "That's no cloud!" he shouted. "Get down, get flat on the ground!"

They dropped to their bellies, covering their heads and ears as the screeching demon bore down on them. Kiran buried his head in his arms.

"It's a flock of birds," Roh said. "Amazing!"

Kiran peeked up under his arm. Infinite multitudes of birds, as far as the eye could reach, weaved and swooped along in one massive stream, so immense, it blocked out the sun. He rose to his knees. The sky was alive with the raucous beating of countless wings, flowing in a rush of high-pitched chatter.

The flock dipped and swayed, the birds flying in perfect unison, as though one being, passing like a living torrent—a river of birds borne on the north wind. The Torans sat and marveled at the never-ending spectacle as afternoon turned into evening with hardly a break occurring in the flock. At dusk, the mass turned westward and disappeared in the sunset.

"The Great Father has spoken," Deke declared, his face shining. "They show us the way. We are on the right path."

Onward they walked into one golden sunset after another, through another full moon, staying just behind the Lendhi. To the northwest, hints of snow-capped mountains appeared out of the clouds on the horizon. Soon trees dotted the landscape and the rolling flatlands transformed into hills covered in sprawling green conifers.

One late afternoon, there was a noticeable excitement among the Lendhi. The clan picked up their pace, the older ones barely able to keep up. Then, at the crest of a hill, the clan came to a halt. The young Torans hurried alongside. Before them stretched a valley, low and open. Flowing right through the center was a massive river.

"Look at the size of it!" Kail said, her eyes wide. The great expanse of blue water spanned ten times the width of any river near their village. Sandbars broke through the sparkling surface where cranes and geese gathered, chattering in the wind.

They dropped their packs and ran down into the valley, through the wetland marsh at the river's edge, sinking to their knees to get to the sweet, cold water. They scooped handfuls to their mouths, then tossed off their boots and soaked their aching feet.

Roh said, "We should take to the river."

Deke huffed. "The Script said to drink of the river and be merry. Not travel on it. The Great Father forbids us going on the sea."

Bria said, "No matter how large, a river is not the sea. I'm with Roh."

"You're always with Roh," Deke sneered.

Bria thrust her jaw forward. "The sea is treacherous because you can sail too close to the edge and fall off. Here, we can see the other side."

"That's a lot of water," said Jandon.

"We have no tools to build a boat," Deke grumbled. "We don't even know how." He grinned with smug satisfaction, as if he had settled the matter.

Roh stared at Deke, his eyebrows knit in concentration. Without another word, he set off down river.

The Lendhi had disappeared over the ridge.

"Do you think we should follow them?" Jandon asked. "I mean… we're here. At the river."

"We should thank them," Kiran said.

"Why bother?" Deke said. "They won't even acknowledge us."

Kiran hung his head in shame.

Kiran and Jandon set up their tent while Bria and Kail followed the Lendhi women, baskets in hand, to collect the bounty of the lowland marsh. Before dusk, they returned, their baskets full of red berries and the sweet, tangy wild onions that were plentiful along the river's bank. Fresh cattail roots had been gleaned, as well, for their sweet flavor and stomach-filling sustenance.

The girls were making a meal when Roh appeared. "Come, look at this," he said. He led them downriver to a swampy inlet. Pointed stumps scraped with tooth marks jutted from the ground. Logs lay about, many the same diameter and in similar lengths. All the branches had been chewed off and dragged away. "With these logs, we can build a raft like the one in the pond back home." He was grinning like a child. "We don't need tools. Just some rope."

Deke turned and headed back to camp, shaking his head.

Kiran and Jandon helped him stack the logs, then using smaller branches as cross members, they lashed them together. When the raft was complete, they shoved it into the river and watched it float. "We'll go at first light," Roh declared.

In the morning, Kiran woke with a heavy sorrow. "I can't leave them without apologizing," he told Bria and left for the Lendhi camp.

He found Manu-amatu sitting alone next to the cooking fire. Kiran bowed in front of him. "Please forgive me. I didn't mean any harm." He held out a small leather pouch. "Will you accept my gift?"

Manu-amatu hesitated, as if considering Kiran's sincerity, then took the pouch and opened it. "Ah, tarweed. What you did was forbidden. Only because of your ignorance may I forgive you." He looked Kiran in the eye. "Now, that is done. Do not dwell on it anymore." His voice changed to a cordial friendliness. "You plan to take to the river, I see."

"Yes. We've built a raft."

"The way you have chosen is a dangerous one. Beware the face of the waters, for She can anger and bring sickness. Do not drink from the river. Only from the small streams that feed Her."

Kiran winced, remembering how they had rushed to the river's edge at first sight of it, gulping down the cold water to quench their thirst. Had they angered the river already? "Thank you. You are wise."

"Kiran, you will reach the sun. It is your destiny. But it is on the path that you will find what you seek. In the flash of a firefly in the night, a breath on the wind, a whisper across the grass."

Kiran stared into Manu-amatu's kind eyes, drinking in his words, wondering if he too had the power of foresight.

Bria came up beside him. They bowed in farewell and headed back to their tent.

"What did he mean, a firefly in the night?" she asked.

"I don't know. His wisdom comes in riddles. Just like Aldwyn." He took hold of her arm. "Listen. He knows things, Bria. He said not to drink from the river or She might anger. We had better heed his warning."

"All right," she said. "But what do you think he meant?"

Kiran thought for a moment. "Perhaps the river can turn stormy, like the sea."

"I hope not." She looked at him out the corner of her eye and grinned. "I'd hate if Deke were right."

Father Sun,
Island Mother

In the beginning, there was darkness.
The world was a watery abyss. Spirits
dwelled in the mists.
Then, the winds began to blow and a Great
Spirit shot from the water, into the sky,
bursting with light, Father Sun
Another Great Spirit emerged from the
water, wearing a mantle of green. Island
Mother took shape, with four directions-
East, West, North, and South.
By the Father Sun, Island Mother
conceived, and from Her came all living
things. The birds that sing, the fish that
swim, all the trees that root in the ground,
and plants that cover the land, and the
animals that creep and crawl and walk on
four legs.

One day, Father Sun collected swirls of dust from the four directions. The wind blew, breathing life into the First Man and the First Woman. They awakened and crawled through a long, dark cave into sunlight.

All was well until Man began to argue with Woman. Each did not appreciate the other. They fought one another and took from the land and killed animals without gratitude.

Angry, Father Sun sent a bolt of lightning that split the land apart. Water gushed up through many cracks, causing a flood that covered the world.

From the depths of the watery abyss came the evil Spirits, armored with hard and glistening scales, and big, round fierce eyes that glowed like fire. Their ears were pointed and sharp, their feet webbed to swim through the sea. They hunted the last of the First Ones that were swimming adrift, swallowing them whole.

Once again, Island Mother emerged, bringing forth all life as it is today. The waters receded to the sea and the animals came out from their hiding places. The evil Spirits retreated to the underworld. Out of a cave, the Lendhi people came to walk the great meadow She had made just for them.

Father Sun whispered on the wind, warning of the fate of the First Ones who came before. He sent a Great Shaman to the bendhi, to teach all living things to live in harmony and peace. Man and Woman learned to cherish what the land provides. But Father sun warned, the world will be destroyed again if they stray from this path.

May Father Sun never know shame,
that He should hide his face
and leave the world
forever in
darkness.

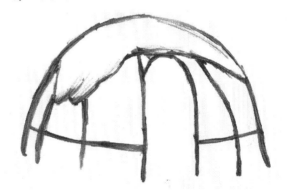

tents made of flexible wooden poles
covered in animal hides convert to
carrying device for travel

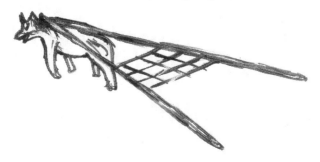

edible red berries
grow on low-lying bushes

to preserve meat, cut into strips,
then smoke over coals

bird nests on the ground,
eggs are plentiful

wild onions
grow along
water's edge

hide-tent cover, blankets, clothing
stomach-cooking pot
hair-weave into rope
dung-firestarter
bones-awls, scrapers
horns-spoons, carry coals

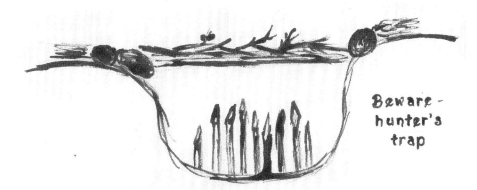

Beware-
hunter's
trap

14

Riding on the river was a new, enchanting experience, and for a while, they sat in silent wonder, feeling the raft glide on the water. They hummed along with the rippling, gurgling music of the river, gently rocking to the rhythmic clacking of the logs, delighted to finally be on their way. The morning sunshine sparkled on the surface as they passed herons standing on sand spits and ducks paddling against the current.

Roh and Kiran stood atop the raft, using the long travois poles to steer. The bulky raft, fully burdened with its load, proved to be difficult to maneuver, but before long they were accustomed to its awkward lurches. They learned to read the signs the river provided, anticipating its moods. Dark, smooth water was deep and ran slow but trouble free. Small, erratic ripples meant a shallow, rocky bottom where they might run aground. A smooth, round mound of water indicated a submerged rock that should be avoided.

As dusk descended in the river valley, they floated on, listening to the chirping of night insects and the croaking of bullfrogs until they came upon a sandbar stretched into the river. They pulled ashore and made camp.

At the river's edge, Deke crouched to fill his waterskin.

"Manu-amatu warned us not to drink from the river," Kiran said. "Only the side streams, remember?"

"The Script said to 'Drink of it and be merry.' Did it not?"

"Yes, but I—"

"You what?" He rose to face Kiran. "You can read the actual words of the Great Father, yet you listen to a savage." Deke tipped up his waterskin, gulped down a swallow, then wiped water from his mouth with the back of his hand.

Kiran winced. He closed his eyes, struggling to take control of his anger.

Kail came along side Deke. "I don't understand."

Bria stood beside Kiran, hands on her hips. "The Script doesn't say we must drink from the river. We should be cautious and fill up the waterskins at every side stream."

Deke looked at Kiran, then back to Bria. "Go ahead and follow the heathen," he snarled. "I'll follow the Way."

"Fine."

"Fine."

Kiran frowned.

Under the gibbous moon, they settled in their bedrolls. Kiran lay awake, listening to the rush of the river against the rocky shore. Maybe Deke did not believe in the wisdom of Manu-amatu, but Kiran vowed: he would not take one sip from that river.

As the days passed, the rhythm of life on the raft lulled them into a quiet complacency. They slipped into a steady routine: rise at daybreak, launch the raft, float down the river until nightfall, set up camp, then rise in the morning to do it again. The landscape passed by in an ever-changing display. Short, thick bushes gave way to cedars and white birches. Hardwoods and evergreens sprawled across the hillsides. Small furry animals appeared and disappeared through long stretches of calm water.

Early one morning, Kiran was staring into the band of foam the raft left on the dark smooth water when a furry critter with big brown eyes and large teeth appeared swimming alongside the raft, cutting a V in the glossy surface of the water. In one swift movement, Roh thrust his spear through the back of its neck and flipped it onto the raft. The animal wriggled and flopped and, without hesitation, Roh jabbed again, striking the final blow. It lay limp.

"Oh my!" cried Kail, turning away.

"Nice shot, Roh," said Jandon.

"Let's pull ashore," said Kiran. "We'll get a fire going."

They hauled out onto a sandy beach strewn with pebbles. Bria suggested they unload the raft and set up camp. "There is quite a bit of meat on this animal. We'll need a couple days to preserve the hide," she said.

"It's morning and we've just set out," Deke grumbled, "Don't bother. We've seen these animals all along the shoreline. There are plenty."

"That doesn't mean we should just waste it!"

"Don't tell me those savages put ideas in your head, too. We need to keep moving, not waste time with that."

Roh intervened. "We have to travel lightly. We'll eat our fill and leave what's left." He gestured toward a vulture circling in the sky. "It won't go to waste."

Bria set her jaw and squared her shoulders in defiance. She looked to Deke, then back to Roh, anger in her eyes. Then she grabbed the dead animal by its feet, flipped it over on its back with a thump, and ripped it open with her knife.

Jandon and Kail got a fire going. Bria skewered the meat and propped it over the flames. The fire sputtered and hissed as the sizzling fat fell in juicy droplets on the burning coals. Kiran couldn't keep his mouth from watering.

The days melded into one another as they traveled on, day after day, following the sun, camping night after night under a waxing moon. The view from the river passed by in a blur of green and brown. Gradually, the banks grew higher and rockier, the vegetation more sparse.

One late afternoon, they came around a sharp bend and the riverbank changed abruptly. Sheer rock reared up out of the river on both sides, towering toward the sky, closing them in. The pace of the current quickened and the raft bucked and shifted, rocking through curls of white water, tossing them about. Deke grabbed onto the raft, his muscles taut. "Don't rock it!" he hollered.

"We're not," said Kiran. "It's the river. Look at me." He was standing upright, pole in hand, bending his knees, flexing with the movement of the raft. "Make your body loose, like this. Just go with it."

Deke scowled and looked away, gripping the roping, his body rigid as they rode the funnel of water through the gorge.

As the channel narrowed, constricting the flow of the river, all its pent-up power surged forth, carrying them forward with increased speed. Kiran whooped with joy, elated to be moving at such a brisk pace.

"Just think if we had to cover this distance on foot," Bria said with an enthusiastic whoop as the rock face went whirring past.

Around the next bend, the river slowed again widening into a round pool. The rock walls encircled the river, vertical and smooth, as if the Torans floated at the bottom of a giant bucket. "Look at that," said Bria, pointing upward. Layers of rock, pink and orange and brown, made striped patterns. "Like a rainbow!"

The muffled whisper of bubbles and gurgling whirlpools reverberated off the rock walls. Bria's eyes sparkled with delight. "Hellloooooooo!" she shouted, grinning.

"Hellloooooooo!" came back to them.

Kail giggled, giddy with silliness. The boys joined in the merriment, even Deke, whooping and shouting to hear their own voices echo back to them. Bria laughed, a big belly laugh bursting with uninhibited exuberance. Kiran smiled wide. He loved her. Maybe she wouldn't marry him, or even kiss him again. But he loved her. He could go anywhere, endure anything, as long as she was with him.

Bria started to sing a lively children's song and Kiran and the others joined in:

> *"Come follow me,*
> *Wherever I shall go,*
> *Come follow me,*
> *To where I do not know."*

The melody repeated, whispering across the chasm, as though a choir of celestial beings had descended from above to escort them on their way.

Distant and faint, there was a sound Kiran did not recognize, like the low rumble of thunder. But the skies were blue. The thunder grew louder and louder as they passed out of the chamber. Suddenly, the river turned turbulent and angry. Water gushed and roared, smashing against rocks in a fury of white foam. Before they could react, the current propelled them forward with a whoosh into the churning maelstrom.

The raft bucked and tilted, careening toward exposed rocks. Kiran and Roh pushed against the boulders with the poles. But it was no use. Everything was happening too fast and they were impotent against the strong current. The raft spun sideways and slid down a giant wave. Kail screamed. Roh and Kiran dropped to their knees and shoved the poles under the roping.

"Hold on," Kiran shouted. "Everybody hold on!"

"What the blazes have you gotten us into!" hollered Deke, his face gone pale.

The raft rammed against a rock. The corner lifted and the raft rode up the side of the boulder at an angle, knocking them off balance. It held there, in the grip of the surging river, the logs twisting against the ropes, threatening to snap apart. Water rushed past on all sides, roaring like thunder. "Knock it loose!" yelled Roh. Kiran grabbed the edge and shifted his weight to the far corner. The backside of the raft caught in the current and spun, whipping around, flinging them back into the roiling chaos.

Just as the raft leveled, they slid into a white hole of whirling water. The raft jerked and spun in the vortex of white. Water pounded in from all directions. They scrambled to stay on top as waves of water swept over the raft, pummeling them with surge after surge.

Finally, the raft spun out of the hole, crashing into a wall of water. Bria lost her grip and bounced to the edge of the raft. Kiran flung himself toward her, reaching, but the force of the water slammed his hand away as she disappeared into the frothy abyss. "Bria!" he screamed. He couldn't breathe, couldn't move. He searched the angry water for sign of her as the raft spun round and round. Then, right in front of the raft, she shot up, gasping for breath. *Boom*—the raft crashed into her, slamming her under water again. She popped up on the side of the raft, stunned, but managed to grab hold and hang on. Kiran lunged for her, his arm outstretched. Water rushed past, the powerful river tugging at her as they careened through the rapids, her fingers slipping inch by inch. With a burst of strength, she jerked upward, trying to hurl herself on top of the raft, but she lost her hold, and was gone again, under the swirling waves.

The raft rocked sideways and another giant wave slammed over them, washing Kiran overboard. In an instant, he was sucked down, under the churning water, kicking and flailing his arms. Tumbling and swirling, powerless against the force of the current, his mouth full of water, he lost all sense of orientation. He opened his eyes but all he could see was white. His lungs burned. Then, at last, his head broke water and he gasped some air, only to be tumbled into a swirling eddy. He thrashed against the current, pulling, rising, falling, swirling. Then he felt hands groping for him and Roh was hauling him back onto the raft.

He heaved and coughed, blowing water out his nose. "Bria! Where's Bria?" he shouted, his head jerking, searching the river for her.

"There!" Jandon yelled, pointing. Bria was bobbing in the choppy waves, fighting to stay afloat.

"Use the pole!" Kiran yelled to Jandon.

Jandon slid the pole from the roping and swung it out toward Bria. She grabbed hold with both hands and held tight as they rocked through the rapids.

Hand over hand down the pole, Jandon pulled Bria to the raft. He grabbed her under the arms and hauled her aboard. She fell on top of him, heaving and shaking. Jandon put his arms around her, holding her close to calm her. "You're all right. I've got you," he told her.

Kiran collapsed, closing his eyes. At least she was safely aboard. The raft slowed in a stretch of riffles, then the water flattened, and the rocking and spinning finally stopped.

Kiran lifted his head and looked back up river at the maelstrom. Manu-amatu had warned of the face of the waters. Kiran hadn't really known what that meant. Now, he knew the full force of Her fury. From now on, they would be at Her mercy.

Downriver, they came upon a sandy, boulder-strewn spit, jutting out under a sheer rock face, with barely enough room to pull out. Scruffy, dry bushes grew from cracks at the base of the rock face, the first vegetation they'd seen in days. They dragged the hefty raft out of the water and unloaded their packs. There was no room to pitch the tent, so they stuck the poles between the logs of the raft and stretched the tent hide to keep it from shrinking as it dried. They hung their wet clothing in the bushes to dry in the sun.

"Some of our food baskets have filled with water," Bria groaned.

Roh inspected the raft, tightening every rope, checking to be sure the logs were secure. Deke stood over him, chewing a fingernail, watching every tug and pull.

Kiran came along side them. "I fear the river will anger again."

Roh looked up river, then down. The river was an endless stretch of white foam. He said nothing.

"I knew it. I knew it. Mark my words," Deke wagged his finger at Kiran. "This is all your fault. The Great Father is punishing us for consorting with savages."

Kiran leaned forward. "Those savages saved your life! Or have you forgotten that?"

"You let them lead you astray. I told you! I warned you! For this, you will pay. A simple penance will not do." His face was turning red as he worked himself into a fury. "Doubt is the greatest sin, Kiran. You dared to question the Truth!"

Kiran clenched his fists. "Manu-amatu warned us not to drink from the river. But you wouldn't listen. This is your fault."

"My fault?" He turned to make a show to the others. "Look who is making accusations. The heathen bastard."

Kiran lunged at him, hitting with his fists. They toppled over the edge of the raft and into the sand. Kiran was on top. He had Deke pinned, his left elbow pressed into Deke's throat, punching him in the stomach with his fist. Then Roh had ahold of Kiran's arms, pulling him away. Deke lay on his side in the sand, gasping for air, his left eye red and puffy.

An awkward silence settled on the group. The girls busied themselves building a fire. Jandon tossed a line in the river, trying to hook a fish.

Kiran wished he could go for a walk and think, but there was nowhere to go. He sat with his back to the others, facing the river, staring into the waves. He picked up a stick of driftwood, tossed it into the current, and watched it bob and twist in the froth, ricocheting off rocks as the water pushed it in countless directions.

He picked up a rough stone and rolled it over in his hand. Maybe Deke was right. He had strayed from the Way. Learning from the Lendhi was one thing, but to question the Truth, that was a sin. All his dreaming about the magic staff had brought nothing but trouble. He slipped the rock into his pocket and looked to the sky. *I'm just trying to understand. Have I really sinned?* A gust of dry wind blew through camp, stirring the sand, and the fire flared with a loud whoosh. The tent hide billowed and rattled against the poles. Kiran shuddered. *It's just a breeze,* he told himself.

The wind picked up and another gust howled through the canyon, the air so thick with swirling sand they had to cover their heads to breathe. The others gave up their work and crawled into their bedrolls.

The girls had spread their belongings out on the few rocks to dry. Strips of meat were hanging on the tiny branches of the bushes. Kiran got up to get his blanket. It was already bone dry. He curled up under it and covered his head. It was going to be a long night.

The wind blew non-stop through the night. When dawn finally came, Kiran awoke to find himself half buried in a pile of sand. He shook the gritty particles from his hair and wiped his face. His eyes itched.

Jandon emerged from the pile next to him blinking and spitting sand from his tongue. "This is just great," he spat. He got up, took a few steps, and hollered, "Ouch! Hot coals! Hot coals!" He hopped backward on one foot and tripped over Kiran, spraying sand and coals into the air. In a flash, the dry, brittle bushes were crackling with roaring flames.

"Fire! Fire! Get on the raft!" he heard someone shouting. Kiran's blanket was on fire, burning his feet. There was nowhere to go but into the water. He scrambled from his bed, gathering what he could in his hands, and plowed into the river. Bria ran into him, full force, trying to get away from the fire. She stumbled and fell onto the raft.

In a blur, they were all on the raft and back on the river, helplessly bobbing in the waves, scrambling to keep hold of their belongings. The poles stuck straight up, swaying back and forth with the creaking of the logs. The tent hide blew off, into the river, and was lost in the rapids.

"Is everyone all right?" Kiran asked as a wave splashed over the side and sprayed his face. He quickly checked: Bria, Roh, Kail, Jandon, Deke. They were all on the raft.

Kail screamed, "Go back, go back! We have to go back."

"What's wrong?" Bria asked.

"My pack. My things," she sobbed. "I don't have my things."

Kiran quickly counted. Kail's pack was missing. The clothes they had hung in the bushes were gone, too.

"Oh no! The food!" cried Bria. "We unloaded the baskets of food to dry." Kiran looked back up river. They were already around a bend and being swept away by the powerful current. There was no going back.

15

The face of the water churned in a roiling froth of white. Walls of dark vertical rock hemmed them in on both sides. There was no place to pull ashore, nowhere to land, nothing to do but hold on and hope.

The river widened once more and the canyon walls swept upward and outward, taking all shade with them. The unrelenting sun blazed down out of a sky empty of clouds. Kiran dangled his feet in the cool water until they were white and wrinkled. His hair felt like straw and he squirmed in scratchy, gritty pants. He tried to look brave, but inside he was tied up in knots. Jandon sat beside him, his best friend since they were kids, but his presence gave little solace. A space had grown between them that Kiran wasn't sure how to close. Or if he wanted to.

Kail sat cross-legged, biting her nails, her skin pink and blistered from the sun. Bria seemed resolute, determined to stay strong, but her hair had lost its luster and hung around her face in a tangled mess. Only Roh seemed undaunted by it all.

Bria dropped a hook and line in the water.

"It's no use," Jandon said. "There are no fish in this river."

"We have to try," she snapped.

He threw his hands in the air.

Roh and Kail had assessed the pouches and reported that, indeed, they had no food. They had only three waterskins among them, and two were empty. They had to find water. Soon.

Kiran scanned the barren rocky landscape with a shudder of hopelessness. It had been days since they had seen a side stream. There were no signs of wild animals, save for one black bird soaring along the ridge. The assumption that they would simply hunt for fresh meat had long since vanished. They did spot occasional hoofed beasts with big, curled horns, but they would flee up the precipice without hesitation at the slightest movement, their agility defying reason.

He realized now how naïve he'd been. His stomach lurched and his hands began to shake. Bria had been wise, wanting to keep every morsel of the animal Roh had speared. He had thought the food they carried would be enough. But enough to get them where?

Maybe Deke had been right. After all, he was meant to be the leader. He did have those sacred stones. Kiran shook his head watching Deke now, gripping the raft with both hands, every muscle stretched taut. Kiran hated him for his arrogance, for drinking from the river after Manu-amatu had warned against it. But Deke followed the Script to the letter. *That's what a good Toran does.* Kiran bit his lip. No. They were to take to the river. He was sure of it.

Bria looked at Deke and her eyes narrowed. "I told you we should have preserved that meat. You said there would be animals everywhere. Well, where are they? Huh, where are they?"

"It wouldn't have mattered since you left the baskets anyway!"

"Me! Since when is the food my responsibility?"

"Since you are a girl!"

Kiran grabbed his arm. "Listen, if you want to start laying blame—"

"Stop it! Stop it!" Kail screamed, her face red with fury.

"Kail's right," said Roh. "Arguing won't help. It was everyone's responsibility. We all ran in a panic from the fire. There's no one to blame."

"Well, it's certainly not me," Deke huffed, turning his back on them. "I never wanted to get on this river in the first place. The Script did not say to *ride* on it. 'Drink of it and be merry.' That's what it said." He flicked his hand westward. "Now, we're no longer headed toward the setting sun."

"But that must be what was meant," said Kiran, exhaustion setting in.

Deke spun around, his eyes wide. "Meant? Are you an Elder now? The Script did not say to ride on the river. And you don't interpret. You don't guess. You. Don't. Question!"

"The Script is not written in plain language. It's vague and unclear. Isn't that the job of an Elder? To interpret the Script?"

"No!" shouted Deke, angry now. "Elders carry out His commands. An Elder is His servant. An Elder pledges an oath, to lead as others follow the Way. To obey His law."

"I understand that. But His law comes from the Script. It is not always clear and concise."

"That just shows your ignorance. I don't know what Aldwyn was thinking, trying to teach you to scribe. It's obvious you are not capable. And you are certainly not worthy. Believe me. It won't go unpunished. My father will hear about it when I get home."

Kiran's teeth were clenched together so tightly his jaw hurt. "Yeah well, you'll have to get to the Voice first!" With the impulse to stomp away, he searched the landscape for an escape. His eyes set on the jagged cliffs overhead. "It's too bad we can't get up there," he said aloud.

Roh followed his gaze. "Good thinking, Kiran. If we could find a route up the canyon walls to the top, we could get a look downriver. Then we'd know if we should stay this course or abandon the river all together."

They craned their necks, bending backward to look up at the bluffs.

Jandon scoffed. "You're kidding, right? You want to climb up there? How? Those rock walls are higher than the cliff at the Sanctuary on the Mount."

Kiran looked sidelong at Roh in disbelief. He was actually considering it.

"We need to find water and food," Roh continued. "We'll make camp and I'll go."

Kiran's eyes were drawn back up the side of the cliff. His legs went weak.

Deke looked over his shoulder, eyeing Roh. "It's too dangerous. The Great Father has watched over us so far." In his most authoritative voice, he said, "Have faith. He will provide."

"What I have," Roh said flatly, "is the knowledge that where there are animals, there is water. It must be up there."

"I don't know," said Bria. "Deke's right. It looks awfully dangerous."

"No, don't go," Kail begged. "Don't leave us. We are supposed to stay together."

"It may be our only hope. I'm going," Roh said. "At first light." Deke shook his head.

"I think it's brave," Bria said. "But you shouldn't go alone."

Without thinking, the words "I'll go with you" burst from Kiran's lips. He stared at Bria and swallowed hard, waiting for a reaction, his insides doing flips. She shifted her gaze to him and smiled. "I'll go with you," he repeated.

The bare rock offered few places to sleep. The moon was full again. With the tent hide lost, Kail and Bria had nowhere safe to sleep. Kiran helped cover them with what clothing and blankets they had, then wedged into a tiny perch at the water's edge. He raised the last waterskin to his lips but got nothing. He chewed on a bit of leather to keep his mouth moist, even though his teeth ached and his lips cracked with the movement.

He lay awake in the shadow of the towering cliffs filled with trepidation as the constant roar of the river echoed around him. The moonlight shimmered across the surface of the water, a ribbon of silvery glow, gently curving through the darkness, crests of white foam sparkling, as if alive. He wondered how something so beautiful could be so menacing.

As the stars were unveiled by the dark of night, he saw one fall from the Celestial Kingdom and shoot across the sky, its flaming green tail trailing behind it. A few moments later, a second followed, this one a tint of yellow. Kiran fixed his gaze on one star, waiting to see if he could observe it dislodging from the firmament. Such a sign would ease his mind. Witnessing the birth of a shooting star was a good omen. He stared until his eyes grew heavy.

At first light, he and Roh were up, packing for the trek under an overcast sky. They packed their rucksacks with only the essentials to keep their loads light. Bria tied the waterskins together and stuffed them in Kiran's pack. "Be careful," she said, trying to smile. Her eyes, reddened from the dusty air, were etched with worry.

Roh grinned at Kiran, one eyebrow up. Kiran returned Bria's smile, noticing her sunken cheeks. He and Roh had better find something to eat. His hand went to her cheek, but he let it drop on her shoulder.

Roh said, "It might take all day to reach the summit. I don't expect we'll be back until tomorrow night at the earliest."

"Tomorrow night?" Kail said. "No. No! Don't go! There's water right here." She dropped to her knees at the river's edge and started gulping handfuls.

"No! Kail! Stop!" Kiran ran to her side.

"You must be mistaken. The Father always provides. You read the Script yourself!"

"I know I did, but maybe—"

"Drink of it, you said. Drink of the river!"

"But Kail!" He grabbed her by the arm and dragged her from the water. "Maybe this isn't that river."

She sat back, her eyes wide.

He turned to Roh. "Let's go."

Roh set the pace as they picked their way over a jumble of boulders, progressing up the incline at an angle, then switching back, slowly making their way upward. Placing each foot with caution, they crossed slopes of loose scree. Occasionally there were pockets of sandy soil where low, scrubby vegetation had taken root. Plants with glossy, leathery leaves that looked as though they were covered in wax. Others pear-shaped with spiked thorns. Some grew in horizontal bunches, low along the ground, with dense rosettes of leaves, their vein-like roots sprawling across the surface of the rock.

After climbing a stratum of steep, crumbly rock, they came to a dead end. A sheer wall rose nearly twenty feet above them with a jagged crack right down the center, as if it had been cleaved in two by a giant. They looked back the way they had come. There was no other way.

Kiran's head started to pound. He dropped to his knees, panting. "I guess this is as far as we can go." Twenty feet straight up was insurmountable. It was just too high.

Undaunted, Roh dropped his pack and wedged himself into the cleft in the rock face. "We can crawl up this way," he said. From his pack he took a short length of rope, tied it around his waist, and attached it to his pack. He pressed his back against one side, his feet firmly against the other, and began to shinny his way up, towing his pack dangling below him. Watching him go, Kiran's hands grew clammy and his legs started to shake.

Roh tossed the rope down to Kiran. "Your turn!" Kiran gathered the straps of his rucksack together, tied them to the rope, and tested his knot. Then he looped it around his waist.

He took the rope in his hand and tugged, testing it. Then he tested the knot again. Did he really have to do this? He looked up at Roh who sat comfortably on the edge, his legs dangling over the side.

"Take it steady," he yelled down.

Sure, steady, thought Kiran. *I'm shaking so hard I'll bring the whole wall crumbling down.* He reminded himself to breathe as he placed one foot on the far side of the crack and pushed his back against the wall. "All right, here I come." He gritted his teeth and started up the crack, inch by inch, holding his breath all the while. About half way up, he locked his knees, holding himself wedged in the cleft, and let his hands go, one at a time, to stretch his cramped fingers before he continued upward.

Finally, his legs shaking, he reached the ledge and dragged himself over the top. He flopped on his side, and for a few moments he lay there, trying to catch his breath.

"Look," said Roh, his gaze skyward. Kiran rolled onto his back. Dark clouds hung heavy overhead. Curtains of rain streaked down, trailing beneath the clouds, but no raindrops hit the ground.

"How can that be?" Kiran wondered out loud, licking his cracked lips.

"I don't know. Let's keep moving."

By late-afternoon, they were traversing a crumbly recess in the side of the canyon wall, working their way up a low grade toward the top when they came upon a sparse copse of stunted cedar. Kiran found a bare bush, stripped of leaves and blackened by fire. "Struck by lightning. What luck." He snapped off a piece of a partially charred branch. Wood burned by lightning was sacred, sanctified by the hand of the Great Father. Kiran knew immediately what he wanted to do with it. With a smile of satisfaction, he put it in his pocket.

Roh had continued on without waiting. Kiran staggered forward to catch up. As he left the stand of dwarf trees, he found Roh kneeling in a sandy crevice. "Water!" Roh said, his face bright with a smile.

Kiran dropped to his knees next to him. A thin line of water trickled from under the rock. Kiran put his lips to the ground and sucked at the sand like a lowly beast. It grated against his parched lips and sore gums. He grimaced and spat it out. Roh took off his tunic, pressed the corner into the crack in the rock, then put it to his mouth and sucked at the damp fabric. "Try this," he said.

"But how will we get enough to fill the waterskins? For Bria and the others?" Kiran pawed at the ground, digging into the sand until his cracked fingers split open and started to bleed.

"It's no use," Roh said, pulling him back.

Kiran heaved a sigh and looked skyward. The sun stared down from above, not caring whether they lived or died. "Maybe we should just drink from the river."

"We just have to keep going," Roh said and he rose to his feet. "C'mon."

Kiran shuffled along, his head down, and before he realized, they were walking on flat land. Roh came to a halt. As far as the eye could see, the landscape stretched before them, a barren, monochromatic expanse of utter desolation, devoid of any vegetation or sign of life whatsoever, just the wave of heat shimmering on the horizon.

Kiran blinked twice, unable to believe his eyes. "Where are all the animals we've seen? Where do they go? This looks like the Great Meadow, but there's not even grass. It's just… nothing."

Roh scanned the horizon, turning left, then right, squinting in the sun. "Let's have a look downriver." They searched for a vantage point, inching out on a rocky prow that jutted over the drop-off.

When Kiran stepped to the edge, he had a full panoramic view that took his breath away. Terraces of rock spread before him in layers of buff and pink, gray, brown, and vermillion—a majestic rainbow of rock, just as Bria had said. "Look at all the different kinds of rock," he said.

Below, the long, sinuous flow of the river cut great sweeping curves through the bottom of the gorge, the distance reducing it to abstract form—a blue line against a background of brown. Kiran swayed, overcome by a sensation of vertigo. He caught himself, dropping to one knee. He looked down to the gravel at his feet, trying to keep his balance, and dropped to a seated position.

He had only ever seen the rocky shoreline of the sea near his home. He had never imagined an entire canyon made of solid rock, and for as far as he could see. The epic scale was mind boggling, as if space and distance had no meaning. The sheer size of the canyon made him feel small and helpless, a mere speck in this colossal place. A powerful wave of veneration swept over him and tears came to his eyes.

A beam of sunlight broke through the cloud cover, shining down from the Celestial Kingdom into the labyrinth of sandstone cliffs and stone spires as if to highlight certain formations in a golden spotlight.

"Look at that," he pointed. "It looks like the temple bell tower."

"More like a stone tomb," Roh mumbled.

"It's magnificent! I've never seen anything like it."

Roh squatted down and plucked a lone strand of grass from a crack in the rock. As he rolled it between his fingers, it turned to dust. "We wouldn't last but a few days up here," he said, releasing the dust on the wind. "The river is the only way." He scanned the horizon. "I don't see any signs of water, or animals either. We should head back as far as we can while there's still light."

Kiran nodded, taking a last look at the awesome sight before him. Aldwyn won't believe this, he thought. Who'd have thought such a place existed. Only in dreams.

A warm wind blew up from below as he turned and followed Roh back down the way they had come.

Hiking downward, they soon realized, was slower than going up and they hadn't gotten far when dusk descended in the canyon. The wind increased in strength, whipping dust and sand in the air, and they quickly found refuge under a ledge. Kiran's whole body ached and he wanted nothing more than to collapse onto his bedroll and sleep, but his head throbbed with a constricting sensation, his thoughts filled with visions of clear, flowing water.

16

Lightning crackled in the air and thunder boomed simultaneously, jolting Kiran from his sleep. It was barely dawn. Peals of thunder echoed through the canyon, rumbling like the groans of a giant. The damp air smelled of mud and the stringent, metallic odor of a lightning strike. The promise of rain made his heart swell with hope.

Roh's eyes were closed. *You might as well sleep,* Kiran thought. He took the charred piece of cedar from his pocket and began to whittle.

In the distance, the low booming of a rockslide reverberated down the canyon. He paused to listen, eyeing the ledge above their heads. He inched back, pressing against the rock, and continued to cut shavings from the wood. First, he shaved a flat surface for the base. Then he cut from the base on an angle, shaving off bits in tiny strokes, turning it as he went to make the four sides of a pyramid. At the tip, he carefully cut in a curving motion, forming a sphere and the Pyletar took shape.

From out of nowhere came the gush of rushing water and a deluge plunged over the ledge above. Kiran scrambled to his knees and held his head back under the flow, gulping water. "Water! Water!" he shouted, his words muffled in a gurgling mouthful. He grabbed a waterskin and held it under the precious flow. "Wake up!" he shouted, nudging Roh with his foot. Kiran reached for a second waterskin and handed it to Roh. "Can you believe it? It never rained."

Roh jumped to his feet and within moments they had full waterskins and full stomachs. They sat back to wait for the waterfall to recede.

Kiran gasped with a spasm of stomachache. He should have taken a little at a time. He had just been so thirsty. And they hadn't eaten in three days now. How long could someone survive without food? He ached with visions of harvest on the farm—fresh lettuce, sweet potatoes, winter squash, and a juicy mutton shank, dripping with fat. It was past harvest time now. Had Aldwyn gleaned anything at all? His stomach squeezed again. And the sheep. How many would they lose again this winter? How long could the village last?

"Roh, do you ever… I mean, we'll make it to the Voice, right?"

"Well, one of us has to, or all of this will be for nothing."

The waterfall thinned, leaving tiny gaps in the strands of water. Kiran glanced down at the river, deceptively benign from this distance. He looked back up river, the direction of home. "But how will we ever make it back? We can't paddle up that river, not against that current."

Roh looked him in the eye. "I'm not sure we are meant to."

Kiran swallowed hard. A scratchy, old voice echoed in the recesses of his memory: *To certain doom, the lot of them... to certain doom.* Kiran sat stone still, staring at the space where the streams of water spattered on the rock in front of them, struggling to keep hold of something, anything. The odds were too great, their chances too slim.

Maybe they were to take the river, maybe not. He just didn't know anymore.

Roh was watching him, his brow knit as though assessing whether to say what was on his mind. Finally, he said, "This is the way. The river. We are on the right path." Kiran wasn't sure if Roh was trying to reassure him or himself.

"What happened back there? With the staff and the Lendhi woman?" Roh asked.

"Oh, that. Well..." Kiran picked up his knife and started hacking at the carving, sending tiny bits of wood in the air.

"What were you trying to do?"

"I don't know. I don't even think I can explain it. I thought I could. . . travel, like Manu-amatu. Damn it!" The knife sliced across his finger, spilling his blood on the Pyletar.

"Careful!" Roh grabbed Kiran by the wrist and examined his finger, holding it tightly to put pressure on the wound. "We can't afford to get hurt out here." With his other hand he pulled a cloth from his pack. "What do you mean, travel?"

Kiran stared at his bloody finger. Roh had a strong grip on it, pinching off the flow of blood. He didn't want to admit what he had done, what he had thought. What would Roh think if he knew the truth? He had disgraced the Torans and dishonored the Lendhi. And all for what?

Roh carefully wrapped Kiran's finger. "Are you doubting your translation of the Script?"

"No, it's not that. It was just that I thought. . . Well, I don't know what I thought." He pulled his hand away and stared at his bandaged finger. He expected Roh to persist with his questions, but he said nothing more.

After a long silence, Roh picked up the wooden token Kiran had been carving, turned it over in his hand, and held it under the waterfall to rinse away the blood. "Why are you carving a Pyletar?"

Kiran blushed. "It's for Bria."

Roh smiled, nodding, as if it were a perfectly reasonable thing to do.

"Deke would condemn me for it."

Roh raised an eyebrow. "Well, I'm not Deke."

They sat in silence for a time, behind the wall of water, waiting for the deluge to stop. Kiran looked at Roh. He was right; he wasn't Deke. He was someone Kiran could talk to. "Do you think the Great Father knows our intentions?"

"Do you mean do I think the Great Father is expecting us?"

A thought struck him like a punch in the stomach. He looked at Roh and his lip quivered. What he was thinking felt like blasphemy, but he couldn't help it. "Then why are we going? I mean…"

"Why are we going?" He looked at Kiran as though he didn't understand the question. "Because it was foretold that we would."

"But don't you wonder? Didn't you… question?" Kiran held his breath, fearing he'd gone too far.

"No," he said, as if it had never crossed his mind.

"But, like you said, you aren't Deke. You're not like him at all. You don't seem to—"

"I came because it is my duty."

Kiran nodded. Roh looked away.

Around them, water seeped from every crack. A stream of red sand flowed at their feet, gritty and abrasive, running into crevices, dislodging small rocks and other loose objects in its path. Shifting rocks rumbled above them. Kiran shuddered, imagining the massive walls crumbling, sliding to the river and being washed away.

The rushing rainwater cascading over raw rock reminded him of last spring at home, when, amid the long drought, the rains had come with such force they did more damage than good. Spontaneous streams had cut through the dry valley, gouging crooked ridges in the ground. The cracks had grown larger and larger right before his eyes.

The water pouring over the ledge above slowed to a trickle, and the view spread before them, as though a window shutter had been thrown open. The rain had ceased, the clouds had dissipated, and rays of sunshine streamed down from above. All along the canyon walls, hundreds of waterfalls existed where yesterday there had been none.

All that rainwater flowed down through the canyon, like in a giant crack in the ground, picking up rocks and pebbles and grit, grinding away the bottom, deeper and deeper.

"Are you sure the river is the way?" Kiran asked. "I mean, maybe Deke is right. What if this isn't the way the Great Father intended for us to go?"

"You saw the terrain up there. We have no choice but to take the river, wherever it may lead."

"Now, yes, but, well…" Kiran wiped water from his forehead. "The Script of the Legend was written a long, long time ago."

"What are you saying?" Roh looked intently at Kiran, his eyebrows creased.

"At first I thought we were hiking upward, into mountains. But what if…" he faltered. He had to be wrong. He was questioning again. He clenched his teeth, frustrated. The questions just popped in his head, uninvited.

"Go ahead and say it, Kiran."

"What if, instead of heading across the land, we are headed down?"

"Down? What do you mean?"

His mind was whirring now. If the water cut into the ground, and the canyon was this deep… How deep could it go? Did the river continue deeper into the rock and flow directly off the edge of the world? "It seems we are headed into the depths of the world."

Roh looked along the length of the canyon, then back at Kiran and a deep understanding passed between them. Roh rose to his feet, flung his pack on his back, and started downward. Kiran followed.

They couldn't find the route they had taken up. Nothing looked the same. Rocks had shifted and moved, rearranged by the downpour.

After noon, they dropped into a narrow ravine and followed it downward. Strangely, the rock was dry within the ravine. They were making good time when Kiran stopped short. The air suddenly had the strong odor of musty humus and cedar. "Do you smell that?" Before Roh could answer, the ground shook under their feet. He looked up. A wall of water roared toward them. "Run!" Kiran yelled. "Go, go, go!"

In three strides, Kiran was across the small crevasse. He leaped unto a boulder, grabbed a handhold on a ledge, and flung himself upward. In one swift motion, Roh was beside him. They pressed against the rock wall, feeling naked and powerless in the path of the white fury. There was nowhere else to go.

The flooding rampage rushed by, rumbling and roaring through the ravine. Rocks crashed into rocks, exploding into pieces, flying into the air in every direction.

"Where did all that water come from all of a sudden?" Kiran yelled over the roar.

Roh shook his head.

As he clung to the ledge, Kiran thought of the mud-packed ground out on the Great Meadow when he and Bria had set out alone. The soil had been too hardened from the sun to absorb the rain. This canyon was solid rock. There was nowhere for the water to go but flow downward, to the river. To Bria! He had to get to her.

He chewed his lip, waiting for the initial blast of water to pass through, then he leaped from the ledge and continued down a crumbly decline. When they came to the top of the crack they had shinnied up, Kiran tossed his pack over the edge, sprawled across the opening of the cleft, pushed his feet against the opposite side, and slid down the crack as fast as he could. As soon as his feet hit the bottom, he grabbed his pack and took off at a dead run. He fell to his knees and slid down a scree-covered embankment, landing on his feet at the bottom.

At last, Kiran could see the others below standing knee-deep in water. The shore they had camped on was completely submerged and the four of them were clinging to the edge of the raft, fighting to keep it from floating away in the turbid water. He skidded down the embankment and plowed through the water toward them.

When Bria caught sight of him, she yelled over the roar of the river, "Thank the Father! You're alive!" He reached to take hold of the raft. She lunged at him, wrapping her arms around his neck. As quickly as she did, she dropped her arms again. "I knew it! I knew you hadn't died!"

"Slow down," he said. "Died? Why would you think that?"

"The blood! There!" she pointed to a narrow gorge.

"Blood?"

"Blood gushed over the walls when the rains came. Waterfalls of blood! Deke thought you had died for sure, but I made him wait for you." Her eyes searched his. "What did you find up there?"

"Nothing. We found nothing." He lifted the strap of the waterskin over his head and handed it to her.

"We've been drinking the rain," she said, taking it from him and tying it to the raft.

Roh came alongside him.

Bria turned to Roh, her eyebrows raised. "Nothing?" she asked, incredulous.

Roh shook his head and dropped his pack on the raft. "We stay to the river," he said and climbed on. Jandon flopped onto the raft, resigned. Kail looked as though she might crumple where she stood. Roh took her by the hand and helped her unto the raft. She gave him a meek smile and a nod.

The river bubbled and boiled, a monstrous flood of dirty brown water filled with debris. An entire tree, roots and all, floated by, spinning in the roiling current. *That's odd,* Kiran thought. They hadn't seen a tree for many days.

As soon as they were back on the river, they heard the familiar rumble of ground-level thunder. Ahead, the rock walls narrowed and they knew what that meant. All the water would funnel into the narrow chasm and push through the gap with a fury—and them with it.

They gripped the ropes with all their might as they plunged into the churning nightmare.

Before Kiran could catch a breath, the raft lifted, and they were airborne, plummeting over falls. The raft dropped, weightless, then submerged into a seething cauldron of white. They held on, muscles strained, as the raft bobbed up and spun into a stretch of boulder-strewn rapids, rocking in choppy waters, until finally the river widened again and at last they found a place to pull ashore.

In the morning, eerie clouds drifted down the steep rock walls, a mist flowing like waves in the wind. Kiran removed his boots and rubbed his sore feet. Cracks had developed between his toes and a raw patch had formed where sand had chafed his skin.

When the blistering sun came up over the ridge, they piled on the raft and braced for another day of insufferable heat.

Then the bees came.

From nowhere, they descended—humming, buzzing bees, with striped bodies and sharp stingers. Deke and Jandon were at the poles. They waved their hands in the air, frantically shooing them away. The bees swarmed around their heads in thick, dark clouds. The boys threw water at them, but no matter what they did, the ruthless bees were not dissuaded and showed no sign of letting up.

Kiran took off his hat to fan his face, but it seemed only to provoke them. He considered putting on more clothes, but realized right away the added heat would be more intolerable and irritating than the bees.

Bria took another approach to their plight. She sat motionless, her eyes closed, while the bees crawled over her shoulders and neck, inching along her bare, glistening skin. She actually smiled as if the touch of tiny feet was a pleasure. Kiran stared at the bees as they drank her sweet sweat.

In that moment, he envied the bees.

The bees were particularly determined to torment Jandon. They swarmed around his head, buzzing with a fever as if they enjoyed torturing him. No one wanted to get near him. They all shifted to one side of the raft, avoiding his buzzing cloud. In desperation, he tied a piece of rope to the back of the raft, held onto the end, and plunged into the cold water. He trailed behind, floating on his back, his face the only part of his body out of the water. Before long, he started to laugh, a delirious chuckle.

"What's wrong?" Kail wailed. She turned to Kiran, desperation in her expression. "Has he gone mad?"

Roh grabbed hold of the rope and hauled him to the raft.

"What's so funny?" he demanded.

Jandon sprang from the water, a big grin on his face. "Don't you see?" he laughed. "Bees!"

They stared at him, waiting. Maybe he had gone mad.

"Yes! Bees, bees, bees! Bees mean plants. Plants mean food."

It was the first time they'd smiled in days.

Around the next bend, the surface of the river turned calm and the water became a deeper shade of green with the spin of soft, gentle whirlpools at the edges. The walls closed in, making glorious shade, cool and dark, and reflections of the rock face danced in the glassy surface of the water. Along the shoreline, just as Jandon had said, was the green of life—vines with white, trumpet-shaped blossoms.

"Look!" Jandon pointed upward to a thick mass of brown fur. Creatures the size of carrion birds with leathery wings clung by clawed feet to the vertical rock face, two and three deep.

As the river swirled around another bend, the sandstone canyon opened up before them, transforming into a haven so startlingly beautiful they couldn't believe their eyes. It was as though they'd come upon another world. Right in the center of the canyon, splitting the river in two, stood an island bursting with green foliage. The sun shone down through the clouds, making streaks of sunlight in the sky that seemed to point right at the island.

The canyon walls that encircled the island were covered with dripping mosses and hanging plants bearing bright crimson flowers. Tiny, delicate waterfalls trickled forth from cracks, casting veils of mist in the air where rainbows sparkled, iridescent on the wind. A gentle breeze carried the fragrance of fresh, citrusy blossoms. The soothing hush of gurgling water and the twittering of birds sounded like Kiran had always imagined the music of the Celestial Kingdom would sound. He blinked and shook his head. It had to be a dream.

Kail squealed. "We've made it!"

Book Three

Whatever deceives men seems to produce
a magical enchantment.
~Plato

17

No one spoke a word as the current carried them toward the paradise they had found. Kiran rubbed his eyes in disbelief. Hunger and thirst could make people delirious, he knew. *Is that what's happening?*

The main branch of the river flowed to the right side of the island and dropped into a turbulent rush of white waves. Using the poles, Roh and Kiran maneuvered the raft to the left where the water was glassy calm.

The island was an exotic tangle of green upon green. Low, spike-leaved bushes grew at the water's edge, filled with the chatter of birds. The rich fragrance of flowers permeated the warm, humid air.

"Look there," Roh said. He stuck the pole in the river bottom. The raft rocked sideways and eased against the bushes. The branches bent downward, heavy with ripe orange and yellow fruit. Kail and Jandon reached out and plucked handfuls, piling it on the raft. Ravenous, Kiran bit into one, the sweet juice running down his chin. He'd never tasted anything so delicious. He ate the soft core and reached for another one.

As they glided further down the shoreline, the thick forest gave way to a flat landscape of peaceful gardens with row upon row of vegetable plants.

Roh mumbled, "There must be—"

"People!" hollered Jandon. Men and women in white tunics were hoeing, raking, and tilling the soil. Jandon called out to them, "Hello there! Hello!" Roh gave Jandon a sharp look and quickly flipped his pack over the pile of fruit. One woman glanced up from her work, but did not slow her pace or acknowledge them in any way.

The Torans exchanged looks of confusion. Had she not heard? She must have; she looked up when Jandon called. Yet she ignored them. The Torans waved and shouted as they floated by, but still got no response.

Soon, they came upon a floating bridge which spanned the width of the river. The raft came to rest against it. The Torans waited, looking about.

"Should we go ashore?" Jandon asked.

"Let's wait and see," Roh said, scanning the area.

At last, a barefoot young man, about their age, dressed in the same white tunic as the others, approached carrying a rope and bucket. Right away, Kiran noticed the unique scar in the shape of a star in the center of his forehead. The young man smiled with genuine welcome and crouched to tie off their raft. Deke jumped onto the dock and stuck out his hand. "I'm Deke, leader of the Torans." Roh and Kiran exchanged a look of amusement. The young man took his hand, shaking it, but simply nodded.

Bria stepped from the raft. "We have been on the river for many days without food or water. We would be most grateful for anything you can offer."

The young man nodded again with an encouraging smile. From the bucket, he offered her a wooden cup of water.

"Thank you!" Bria said, gulping it down. The boy filled the cup again and it was passed around, Kail and the boys each taking a long draught. Then, with a smile of satisfaction, the young man turned, motioning for them to follow.

Into the dense, tangled growth of green they went, walking single file along a dirt path toward the interior of the island. Bria whispered to Kiran over her shoulder, "Do you think the boy can't talk? He hasn't said a word."

Kiran shrugged. The forest here was nothing like the woods back home. There were no trees, at least as Kiran thought of trees. These were more like giant plants, all stem and huge leaves, with exotic flowers in all colors and shapes. "Bria, look at that," he said, pointing at an exquisite orchid-like flower with pinkish-purple hues hanging from a low branch.

She smiled with delight. "And those!" She gestured toward a stand of rich, velvety red blossoms shaped like pinecones. Hundreds of butterflies swooped and flittered about, sparkling in the dappled sunlight. Some danced on silky wings, translucent and speckled, and others were strikingly large, the size of his hand, blue and velvety, with iridescent shine. A giant bee buzzed by his head. As it slowed and hovered in midair before a big, fluted purple blossom, he realized it wasn't a bee, but a tiny bird with a curved bill. It darted to and fro, from blossom to blossom, hovering at each, its wings beating too fast to see.

The air smelled of spices mixed with citrus fruit. His stomach churned. He regretted eating so much of the sweet fruit all at once.

Kail stopped to sniff at white blossoms hanging on a vine. She giggled with delight. "The scent of the river. My pomander, the scent of my pomander." The young man smiled at her, nodding as though indulging a small child and motioned for her to follow. She skipped along the path to catch up.

They emerged at the edge of a patch of gardens. The young man led them to a small, grass-covered hut, gestured for them to stay, and slipped away. People of all ages, men and women alike, milled about, busily tending the gardens, paying them no mind, all dressed in the same plain white tunics.

Kiran whispered to Bria, "They seem friendly, but they don't make eye contact. Why don't they say hello? Doesn't anyone speak at all?"

Before long, a woman appeared, walking directly toward them, tall and slender and graceful, dressed in a sheer white robe that clung sensuously to her body, distinctly different from the white tunics of the rest of the population. She stopped about fifty feet away, summoned three young boys from the gardens, then sent them scurrying off.

As she stepped into the hut, she spread her arms wide. "Welcome, my children. Come. Sit. Rest your weary bodies."

She can speak, Kiran thought with relief, *and our own language.* She also wore the star mark on her forehead. It was intentional, Kiran realized. He quickly glanced around; nearly everyone he saw wore the mark.

She directed them to a bench. "I am Angei-Ami. Your arrival is most auspicious." She looked them up and down, quietly assessing them as they took their seats where she directed. "Have you traveled far?"

Deke answered, "We've been from home nearly four moons now. We left our homeland and traveled a great open plain fraught with wind and demons. We lost one of our own to a Mawghul."

Kiran winced.

Deke went on, "We encountered a most unpleasant clan calling themselves Lendhi. Hence, we took to the angry river, traveling by raft through rocky terrain and blistering heat. Our camp caught fire and we lost our food and some belongings."

"Oh my," she cooed. "You poor souls. Well, you are most welcome and safe here. And there is plenty to eat."

"We won't be long and we'll be on our way," Roh said.

The young boys returned from their errand. One boy set down a pitcher of drink and a stack of cups. The other boys carried large platters, one heaped with slices of fruit, orange and yellow and pink, tiny globes of green, one red fruit, cut open, revealing its juicy red seeds, and a bowl of nuts, and on the other a spread of cured meats and cheese. As the boy with the meat platter set it down on the small wooden table in front of the Torans, his eyes trailed over the meat as if he didn't want to let it go.

"You may go now," the woman said to the boys. She turned back to the Torans with a smile. "Please, don't be shy. Help yourselves. There is plenty. I know you must be famished."

Kiran could hardly hold back, trying to be polite. He grabbed a handful of nuts and shoved them into his mouth. In the other hand, he took a reddish-brown fruit shaped like a crescent moon from the platter and examined it. It appeared too tough to eat.

"Here let me show you," she said, taking another from the platter. She took hold of its stem and ripped it open, peeling the skin down its side. Kiran did as she had shown him and bit into the deliciously creamy white center. "Now tell me, where is home?"

Jandon had his eyes on the woman and with a mouth full, juice running down his chin, he answered her. "We are Torans. Our village is on the edge of the Sea of Demarcation, from here directly toward the rising sun."

"And what brings you to our kingdom?" She handed the peeled fruit to him.

Kail moved to the edge of her seat. "We seek the Voice of the Father. We were chosen, as pilgrims, to beg His forgiveness. We are to receive the blessing. Have we found the dwelling place?"

Roh stiffened.

"Oh my dear." She ran her fingers through Kail's long blond hair. "You have found so much more." She rose and said, "Relax now. Enjoy the food. I shall return."

Then Angei-Ami disappeared into the wall of green.

"I can't believe it. We've found the dwelling place!" Kail giggled with delight.

"Not so quick, girl," Deke said. "Where is the reflection pool? Where is the peak? And the Script didn't mention other people."

"This must be the place. I'm sure of it. Maybe the Script is not exact."

Deke pursed his lips. "Not exact. It is the Script of the Legend!"

Several of the people working in the garden nearby looked up from their work.

Roh leaned forward and whispered, "We can't be sure of anything yet. We need to be cautious and not say too much. Something isn't right here."

"What bothers you?" Bria asked.

"I don't know. Just a feeling… Something."

Kiran felt it too, but he couldn't quite translate the feeling into thought. He saw that Roh had his pack on his back and felt a sudden sense of panic. He had left his on the raft. With the scroll inside. His heart started to race. He had to get back to it.

Deke reached over him for a piece of cheese. "Something isn't right here because this isn't the dwelling place," he said, shoving the cheese in his mouth. "We need to eat our fill, get fresh water, and move on. Kail is mistaken."

Kiran clenched his jaw and glared at Deke. "How can we be sure?"

"I'm with Deke," Jandon muttered, his mouth full.

Kail shrugged. "Well, I, for one, am not going anywhere near that awful river again. Look how beautiful it is here. We're safe now. And this food!" Her eyes glittered as she browsed the platters. "You two sound like that creepy Old Horan back home, always speaking of death." She took a handful of nuts. "This is the place. I'm sure of it."

Jandon swallowed his food and turned to Kail. "You are the last person I'd trust to make that call."

Kiran stared at Jandon. He'd never been so rude.

"What?" he said to Kiran. "She's being emotional." He threw his hand in the air. "You know how girls can be."

Kiran's eyebrows shot up. He looked at Bria. Her lower jaw was thrust forward and the tendons in her neck drawn taut. "Jandon," he said, looking from him to Bria. "I don't think—"

"Tell us, Jandon, how girls can be," Bria said, her face turning red.

Jandon paused as though deciding whether he wanted to tangle with Bria. "I'm just saying," he whispered, "that she's, you know, not cut out for trekking through the wilderness. I don't think she can be objective."

Kiran said, "But how can any of us be objective?"

"You've missed the point," said Deke. "We don't wish. We don't speculate. We follow the Script."

"Yeah, not the whim of a girl," Jandon said.

"But how will we know either way?" Kiran asked.

Roh leaned forward. "We'll have to wait and see."

"It doesn't mean we can't enjoy our stay," Deke said as he stacked two thick slices of meat on a piece of bread. He lifted it to his mouth and took a bite.

Jandon snatched a handful of nuts and tossed one in his mouth. "Yeah," he said, "we deserve a bit of respite."

"Meanwhile, we keep our eyes open," Roh whispered as he glanced across the gardens. "And our mouths shut."

They fell silent, drinking in the surroundings and eating their fill of the delicious exotic foods.

Angei-Ami stepped from the trees. "The Guardian is at supper," she said. "He will greet you as soon as he has finished."

"The Guardian?" Kiran asked.

"Why yes, of course. Isn't he who you've come all this way to see?"

Kiran glanced at Roh who raised an eyebrow and made a subtle shrug. "Ah… yes," he replied.

"Please, follow me." She strolled back down the path they had come. Near the river, Angei-Ami stepped from the path.

Kail stopped short and launched herself backwards, slamming into Deke who stumbled to the ground.

"What the blazes!" he hollered.

A green snake lay coiled in the sun. "Don't worry. It's harmless," said Angei-Ami.

Kiran sidestepped, leaving the path, never taking his eyes off the snake as he passed.

When they arrived back at the bridge, Kiran was relieved to find their raft still tied where they had left it. He hopped aboard and untied his pack, chastising himself for being careless. Angei-Ami said, "You have no need to worry." Kiran hesitated, then slung the pack over his shoulder.

As they crossed the bridge to the mainland, two men stepped from the cover of the jungle onto the path to greet them. They lowered their eyes in deference and stepped aside as Angei-Ami passed.

A wooden trellis enclosed the path, entwined with climbing vines dripping with tiny white flowers, rich with the sweet fragrance of honeysuckle. Up ahead, they heard the gushing sound of falling water. They stepped from the thick jungle canopy into a grotto cut with massive buttresses and deep, dark alcoves. High above them, nearly the height of ten men, a feathery white waterfall spilled over a limestone cliff into a sparkling turquoise pool banked by travertine formations and lined with delicate ferns, feeding on the mist. The pool overflowed, cascading down through smaller, shallow pools, each a different shade of blue-green surrounded by layers of moss-covered rock. A white egret stood along the edge of one gazing into its own reflection.

Angei-Ami encouraged the Torans along as she continued down a stone walkway that meandered through numerous sparkling aquamarine pools of different sizes and shapes. Kail squealed. "Pools, Deke. Look. Pools!"

Angei-Ami looked them up and down. "Indeed. May I suggest a bath?"

Kiran ran his fingers through his tangled hair, suddenly aware of his grisly appearance. His tunic and trousers were torn and soiled with the dust of their journey.

"We have the finest baths in all the land," she said, as if it had been decided.

The same young man who had greeted them on the dock appeared from nowhere, carrying two large baskets.

"Young men, you may follow Cartus. Ladies, come with me." She took one of the baskets and nodded for the girls to follow.

Kiran hesitated; he was uncomfortable letting Bria out of his sight. Roh was right. Something didn't feel right here. But he still couldn't figure out what it was. Angei-ami had been nothing but welcoming and kind. Was he overreacting? Bria smiled at him as if to say, "I'll be fine."

Reluctantly, he went with the other boys as they followed Cartus around a bend to one of the larger pools, tucked between walls of green leaves. They removed their boots and dirty clothing. Jandon plunged in. "The water's warm!"

Kiran stepped in and couldn't believe it. Hot water! How could that be?

Cartus handed them a wooden tray with lumps of soap, then sat down on the edge of the pool. The boys lathered their bodies and hair, washing away the dirt and grime of the journey. Kiran wondered what Roh and Deke thought of all this—the pools, the fountain, the waterfall. He glanced over at Cartus. The boy sat with his eyes lowered, his posture as though he had the patience and fortitude to sit, waiting all day. Kiran wished he would leave, so they could talk alone. He'd have to wait to ask the others their thoughts later.

Kiran laid his head back and closed his eyes, letting the warm water soothe his sore muscles. Maybe Kail was right; maybe this was the place they were supposed to find.

He emerged from the bath feeling refreshed. Cartus offered him a clean white tunic to wear. Kiran brought the fresh linen to his nose, inhaling the scent of clean laundry. Their dirty clothing was gone. So were their boots. For a moment, he had a surge of panic, but then saw his pack was where he had dropped it. "My boots?" he said to Cartus. The young man just smiled, lowering his head, reminding Kiran that he wore no shoes. It must be their custom, Kiran thought.

He donned the tunic and once the other boys had stepped from the pools and dressed, he grabbed his pack and they followed Cartus back to the main path where the girls and Angei-Ami were waiting.

Bria was scrubbed clean and dressed in a crisp white tunic. "Wasn't that absolutely glorious!" she said, her wet hair clinging to her face, glistening in the sun. Kiran smiled, trying not to stare. He was just glad to be with her again. *Why am I being so paranoid?*

Angei-Ami continued down the stone walkway. Like a shadow, Cartus disappeared again.

At the end of the walkway stood a palatial structure as high as the village temple, perhaps higher, but round, built of wood posts and beams with a cone-shaped thatched roof of dried reeds woven in intricate patterns. There were no exterior walls. It was a great open-air pavilion.

Directly in front of it was the largest of the pools. On a rock base at its center stood a stone sculpture of a naked woman holding a vase turned downward with real water bubbling out. Kiran had never seen a naked woman before. His eyes dropped to his hands. Jandon stood gawking, unabashed, a grin on his face. Bria elbowed him in the gut.

As Angei-Ami approached the pavilion, her gaze lowered and she stepped lightly. This was a sacred place. The young Torans followed her around the fountain, up two steps, and under the roof.

Once across the threshold, it took a moment for Kiran's eyes to adjust to the shade. There were no chairs, no tables, just a vast expanse of bare stone floor, glistening with shine from the humidity. At the far end was a raised platform, nearly five stairs above the floor, where a man knelt at an altar adorned with flowers and flickering candles, encircled by women, seven in all, kneeling with their foreheads touching the floor. They were barefoot and wore gauzy white robes like Angei-Ami's.

Angei-Ami nodded to the Torans, a tacit instruction to wait, and slipped away. She floated up the stairs to the platform and stood waiting for the man to acknowledge her.

When the man finally rose, one of the women dropped to her knees before him and slipped sandals on his feet. He strode toward them, his white-clad attendants following several paces behind, and greeted them with arms outstretched in priestly welcome. Handsome by any standard, with chiseled features, he had a strong, squared jaw, and a tall, commanding stature. The creases at the corners of his soft, brown eyes were sharply etched with wisdom. The mark of the star was on his forehead. His long hair was gathered and tied loosely at the base of his neck. He wore a beard, which struck Kiran—no other man they had seen had a beard.

The Guardian lowered his eyes and nodded in a gesture of peace. "Welcome to the Kingdom of the Kotari," he said, his voice calm and soothing. "Kneel in gratitude, for providence hath brought you to us."

Unsure how to act, Kiran was terrified of giving offence or unwittingly committing some irredeemable blasphemy, so he lowered his eyes in the only way he knew to show reverence as he dropped to his knees. Deke remained standing. "It's an honor to meet you," he said. "We have traveled far seeking the Voice. It is the edict of—"

Kiran glanced up. The Guardian's expression had hardened. His eyelids lowered and lips pursed. He stared at Deke as though waiting for an unruly child to acquiesce to the rules. Angei-Ami leaned slightly forward, her eyes wide, silently scolding Deke with a subtle shake of her head.

For a brief moment, Deke's eyes darted back and forth from his fellow Torans to Angei-Ami. Then, his shoulders slumped in submission and he dropped to his knees.

"Hold fast your proclamation," the Guardian said. "For you need time to rest and be planted on a sure foundation." His gaze moved from Deke to Kiran and a warm smile came to his face. The Guardian's captivating eyes drew him in with an energy that was mesmerizing and a sense of solace settled in Kiran, like he'd never felt before.

"In due time, you will learn the ways of the Kotari. You are weary now, but you will be quickened by The Coming of Light, for I can see you are dedicated. You are beloved followers, who in faith obey." The last he said sternly, as if to emphasize the necessity of obedience.

"We have waited for thee. Together, we shall prepare to witness The Coming of Light, so that we may be saved from Eternal Darkness. Let us not look to the things of this world, which are darkness, but to the Great Father of Light. Today, I shall reveal His name to you. His name is: Ani."

Kiran shook with excitement. Everything was becoming clear now. *A pool of glorious reflection. . . The fountain! There a wise man will appear... Could it be? Could it truly be?* Here, standing before him, was the wise man of the Legend. Kiran lifted his eyes. The Guardian was speaking directly to him. His eyes held Kiran's, drawing him into their dark depths, as though the entire world had melted away and Kiran was the only person who mattered. He was overcome by a desire to lose himself in the glorious bliss, to follow wherever the Guardian wished.

"All will be revealed to us at The Coming of Light, when Truth will be unveiled for ever and ever."

The Coming of Light? Kiran's head was spinning. There was so much he didn't understand.

"Now, I confess to you. This morning my faith was severely tried. I was dreaming, and in my dream I was hurled into pitch darkness. Helpless and terrified, I, in all my weakness, cried out, 'Have I dishonored Ani?' I was lost in utter helplessness. Only Ani could save me. Then the darkness broke. A sweet, gentle voice spoke and said, 'Trust in Me.' And then appeared a vision before me of seven sheep, wandering the desert, carrying a great burden. They had been cast out, vulnerable in the face of temptation, enduring the elements—wind, water and fire—seeking the sign that they may be cleansed. I know now, that it is by the Grace of Ani that you have been brought to me, so that I may tell you of The Coming of Light."

The Guardian had seen their coming—their trials, the wind demon, the angry river, the fire. *He has been expecting us!*

The Guardian leaned forward, his eyes narrowed. "It is the beginning of the end. You know this; you have seen the signs. That is what hath brought you here." He rocked back and smiled, a smile that said everything will be all right. "Enter with love, dwell here, in the Kingdom of the Kotari. Join us. Together we prepare for the Day of Thunder, when we shall hear His voice."

A warmth spread over Kiran's body, from his heart to his fingertips, as though the Guardian were the sun, warming him with his radiance. Tears filled his eyes. At long last, they had found the wise man. Kiran dropped his head in his hands, trembling with joy.

18

Once the Guardian concluded his welcome, he turned away, leaving behind a profound emptiness. Angei-Ami stepped forward and motioned for the Torans to follow. She led them back down the path. Near one of the pools, she stopped short, her hand at her belly. Kiran quickly glanced around for a snake.

Kail took her by the arm. "Are you all right? Oh." She smiled. "Are you with child?"

"Yes, my dear." Angei-Ami nodded. "It is the greatest honor to be a wife of Ani and to receive his divine seed. For His holy line will inherit the world and reign glorious." She closed her eyes and rubbed her belly. Then, as though lightened by His love, she raised up on her tiptoes and continued along the way.

Once back on the island, Angei-Ami led them to a row of straw-roofed bunkhouses. Cartus, along with two girls and three other boys about the same ages as the Torans, greeted them with smiles. "These are your brothers and sisters," Angei-Ami said. "They will help you to get settled." She smiled with a dismissive nod and turned to leave.

Roh went after her, saying something that Kiran couldn't hear.

She turned and eyed him up and down. Her lips parted slightly and she gazed into his eyes for a long moment. "You are welcome to stay as long as you would like," she said.

Cartus stepped forward, looking directly at Kiran. "I am honored to welcome you and share with you the love of Ani."

Kiran blinked. "You can speak. Why didn't you talk to us before, when we arrived?"

"Here, in the Kingdom, we show our reverence in silence, which reminds us of our place and our commitment to servitude."

"Oh, I see. Well, I'm glad. I have so many questions."

"I'm sure you do. Please come with me. It is my role to teach you our ways here in the Kingdom of the Kotari," he said with the same smile. His facial expression did not seem to change.

Kiran took several steps after Cartus, then turned back to Bria, then Roh. "I'd prefer to stay with the others," he said, chewing on his lip. "We need to stay together."

"Oh, don't worry. We're all here together." He gestured toward the greeters. "It is our duty to answer your questions and make each of you feel welcome. It is my honor." He bent in a subtle bow, then put his hand on Kiran's shoulder. "I can see, what you need is a good rest."

He was right; Kiran was tired. He didn't want to offend the young man, so, he acquiesced. His eyes were drawn to the boy's star-shaped scar.

Cartus's hand went to his forehead. "This is the mark of Ani. So that I may be recognized."

"Recognized for what?"

"That I am one of the chosen. And you too, in time, will be taken into the Kingdom and sealed by the star, so that you may be a Receiver of Light."

A Receiver of Light? The Guardian had spoken about the Coming of Light—and the Voice. But Kiran couldn't recall him mentioning what it meant to be a Receiver of Light. Kiran wanted to ask, but didn't want to appear too ignorant or as if he were questioning too much. He'd ask Roh about it later.

Cartus eyed his pack. "There is no need to carry the load."

Kiran's fingers wrapped around the strap. "It's no bother."

"Soon you will see. Ani provides all that you need. Your material belongings will no longer matter."

He took a path that led into the forest, talking as he went. "Here, in the Kingdom, you will find peace. Serving Ani is the greatest honor. There is no greater reward than His love."

"Tell me about the Guardian," Kiran said.

"He is the chosen of Ani, the Guardian of Light. He is the divine messenger and we are his brethren. Only through him are we guided in service."

"Is he…" Kiran hesitated. If he asked, would Cartus think he was questioning? "Is he truly the wise man? Of the Legend?"

"He is indeed."

Kiran drew in a breath and started to shake with excitement. Cartus continued on as if it was just another day.

To their left, the forest opened up into a clearing where the soil had been trampled to hard-packed ground. "This is the Body Temple, for dawn meditations," Cartus said, never slowing. The trail continued toward a large rectangular structure with a grass roof. "That is the dining hut. We all eat together." He turned right. On the left was a stable of goats and other animals Kiran did not recognize.

They continued on, approaching the tiny grass-covered hut in which he had been served the food earlier. "The island isn't nearly as large as I had thought," Kiran said.

Cartus came to a stop and crossed his arms. "No more than we need. It is in His service that we are rewarded."

In His service? Was everyone here dedicated to the Great Father? Like the Elders back home? Had they all taken the vows? Was this his opportunity to become an Elder? A ripple of excitement ran through him. "What do I need to do to become a Receiver of Light?"

"Each of us has something unique to contribute for the good of all, according to his ability."

"Oh, but is there a vow or something like that?"

"If you live by His Word, you are a Receiver of Light. Is it the Right of Emergence that you ask about?

Kiran nodded, although he had no idea what it was.

"No one has earned it yet. Only the Guardian has the right. Only he is worthy."

Cartus continued down the path. Kiran pointed over the dining hut across the river to the far canyon wall. "What's over there? On the other side of the canyon?"

"I don't know," Cartus said flatly.

"Well, aren't you curious?"

"I serve Ani here. It is not the will of Ani that I go there. I do not question this."

Kiran blushed, feeling scolded.

"You must understand that generally, talking while we are in His service, is not done."

"Oh?"

"It's all right, for now, as you are still in need of guidance. But soon, you will be expected to be reverent as well. You see, our voices are to remain in the shadow of His voice. Only the Guardian has the divine connection. We must be mindful so we are not led astray. Talking can easily breed sin. In the past, we've had those who preached the poison of the unfaithful. If you become aware of anyone who speaks that evil, you must report him right away." They arrived back at the bunkhouses. "In fact, we are to exhort one another daily, lest any of us be hardened through the sin of deceitfulness. We must maintain our faith. When the time comes, all the world will look to the Guardian for guidance, and we will be at his right hand."

Cartus led him to the fourth bunkhouse down the row. Twelve sleeping mats lined the walls, six on each side. There was a wooden box next to each. No personal items in sight. "Who sleeps here?" Kiran asked.

"There is your mat." Cartus pointed to one near the center of the room. "You've traveled far. I'm sure you are eager to rest." He reached for Kiran's pack. "Let me take that for you."

Kiran gripped the strap. He knew that when Elders took their vows, they gave up all worldly possessions. He supposed he wouldn't need his things. He only had dirty clothes and traveling gear, but they were his. And the scroll. He couldn't let anyone know he had the scroll. They would realize he could scribe and he would be punished. He needed some time to think.

"I have to relieve myself," he said. "Where do I go?"

"Oh, yes, right this way." Cartus led him to the shore. "You may go here, directly into the river. Everything you expel is washed away."

"Thank you," Kiran said, staring into the frothy water, waiting for Cartus to leave.

Cartus stood, his arms crossed. Kiran eyed him, unsure what to say. He nodded his head, silently urging Cartus to go. "I…ah…would like some privacy."

Cartus hesitated. Finally, he shrugged as though he was uncomfortable, but acquiesced.

That's odd, Kiran thought.

He quickly scanned the area. Just inside the treeline, he spotted a pile of exposed rocks. He checked to be sure the scroll's mantle was secure, wrapped it in his blanket, and piled the stones on top. From his pack, he took the Pyletar he had made for Bria, slipped it onto a piece of cord, tied it around his neck, and tucked it inside his tunic. Then he headed back down the path.

When he returned, he found the bunkhouse occupied with boys and men, all dressed in white tunics, silently readying for bed. As he opened the door, heads turned, erupting with smiles and hellos.

"Welcome to House Four," someone said. "Welcome to the family."

Kiran hung onto the doorframe. "Thank you," he said, taking in all the new faces.

"We are honored to have you," he heard from another voice. Eleven heads bowed.

Kiran blushed.

"Please, come. Sit." A young man about his same age and height put his arm around Kiran and led him to the center of the room. "Tell us all about yourself."

The others gathered around, sitting crossed-legged, their full attention on Kiran. The weight of all those eyes on him made his stomach twist in his belly and his mind went blank.

"Uh… about me?"

"Where do you come from? What has brought you to us?"

"Well…" He told them of the village. They were most interested in his relationship with Aldwyn and persisted in inquiry about why he would leave home. He told them of the drought and how they had set out during a Javinian raid. The boys hung on his every word, wanting to know more. So he told them of the quest, how he was seeking the Voice. Then he told them of his time spent with the Lendhi, although he did not mention the staff.

After a while, he started to relax and enjoy the attention. They were truly interested in him. Every remark, every part of his story, they wanted to know more. So, he continued, including more details as he went. When he got to the part where he climbed to the top of the canyon, one boy gushed with praise. "You are a brave soul, brother. I admire you greatly. I could never do such a thing."

Kiran didn't know how to respond. He'd never received such compliments, let alone admiration. They really liked him! He talked and talked. When he got to the part in the story where he'd arrived on the island, he paused.

"What is the trouble?" someone asked.

Kiran looked at the faces of his new friends, trying to gauge their sincerity. Surely they'd understand his reservations, he decided. "We weren't so sure this was the place we were looking for."

An uncomfortable silence filled the room. Cartus whispered, "Kiran, if you have those kinds of feelings, you are not to speak of it. You are to go to the Angei. Do you understand?"

Kiran glanced around the room. Eleven faces stared, waiting for his response. He nodded, as though he understood. *The Angei? What feelings? Did he mean feelings of doubt?*

"You are just tired now. Wait and see. All will become clear. You will bask in the love of the Guardian. You are family now, my brother."

The others, men and boys alike, joined in. "You are one of us," he heard someone say. "You are family." Kiran let out his breath, relieved. Yes, he could wait and see. What harm was there in that?

The brothers settled down on their mats for the night. "Oh, my manners!" Kiran sat upright. "I didn't even ask your names."

"You call us brother, of course," said the boy next to him.

Brother, he thought, grinning. He looked around the room. *I have brothers.*

He lay back down on his mat. He couldn't remember a time when he had been so happy.

Before dawn, he was roused from bed and out the door. The forest was alive with chattering birds. At home, the birds sang in beautiful melodies, but here, it was a squawking ruckus. It would take some time to get used to.

They took the path toward the clearing Cartus had called the Body Temple. Kiran was concentrating on keeping up with his brother in front of him, so as not to lose sight of him in the pitch dark, when suddenly a shrieking howl ripped through the forest. Kiran halted in his tracks and the hairs stood up on the back of his neck. "Brother, what was that?"

The man behind him urged him along, whispering, "The lost who have forsaken Ani." He shook his head with pity. "Tormented souls."

A shiver ran up Kiran's spine. Tormented souls? Forsaken Ani? "What do you mean?"

"Unbelievers." The howl bellowed through the forest again. Kiran cringed, his eyes searching in the dark for the source.

At the Body Temple, the group spread out, forming three lines, standing more than an arm's length apart. One of the brothers moved to the front to lead the group.

In rhythmic motions, the leader thrust his clenched fists outward while simultaneously chanting, "Praise Ani! Praise Ani!" Kiran followed along, mirroring the leader's movements as best he could. With each thrust, he pushed air out of his lungs in a heavy exhalation. "Praise Ani!" huff, "Praise Ani!" huff. Then the leader changed the pattern. With his feet wide apart and his arms held above his head, Kiran bowed at the waist, holding his arms stiffly outright, as he rapidly bent forward, blowing out air as fast and forcefully as he could muster. "Praise Ani!" huff, "Praise Ani!" huff.

Soon, Kiran felt dizzy, his toes and lips began to tingle, but he kept going. He had to keep pace with the others. Before long, his heart started to race and there was a ringing in his ears. He tried to focus on the leader, but a blue mist drifted before his eyes. His hands cramped into tight fists and he crumpled to the ground, his head spinning. All went black.

He awoke, lying on his back, limp and exhausted. Cartus was leaning over him. "You have touched the spirit of Ani!" he proclaimed. "You have the gift!"

"But I don't... I felt dizzy."

"That is how you are supposed to feel in His presence. You have experienced the power of Ani's love. Embrace Him."

Another of his brothers dropped to his knees next to Kiran. "Brother, do you know what this means? You'll be one of the chosen. You will earn the star."

Kiran rubbed his temples. "Do you hear, brother? You'll be one of the chosen," he heard another brother saying. He looked to his new brothers, standing over him, and smiled. *One of the chosen.* He had never wanted anything more.

The brothers of House Four filed into the great dining hut, the only sounds those of shuffling feet and clanking bowls. Kiran took his place in line, his arms at his sides, his head down, trying to follow the order of decorum. Out of the corner of his eye, he saw Bria at a table nearby. She looked happy, smiling as she ate. He hoped to catch her eye, but as he shuffled toward the serving table, she never looked up from her bowl.

He took the bowl he was served and followed his brothers to their table. Kiran tapped his spoon on his leg as he waited for his brothers to find their seats. Finally, when the last of his brothers was seated, he dug in, scooping out a heaping spoonful and shoving it into his mouth. He rolled the lumpy porridge over his tongue and swallowed hard, but the coarse grain stuck in his throat. This was not the platter of fruits and meats he had been offered the day before. He whispered to the boy seated next to him, "Is this what you are served every day?"

The boy kept his head down. "Yes, to cleanse the body and soul. To overindulge is a sin."

A sin? Kiran thought. *But I'm so hungry.* Why was it all right yesterday, but not today? he wanted to ask, but the boy gave him a warning glance.

Bria's group stood to leave and Kiran leaned back on the bench, craning his neck, hoping she would see him. She turned his way and their eyes met. His heart skipped a beat. He wanted to jump up and run to her, but he remained seated, in his expected place. He had learned already the code of silence and would have to be content to watch her as she walked by. His eyes lingered on her, taking in the grace of her movements, her strong yet womanly body. Just being apart for one night had made him ache to be near her. Being apart didn't feel right.

Cartus nudged him. "Brother, keep your mind on your business." Kiran pulled his eyes from Bria, feeling scolded, although he wasn't sure why. What did it hurt to look her way? He dropped his chin and stared into the bowl of tasteless mush.

From the dining hut, the brothers of House Four went directly to the garden to harvest the vegetables grown there. Kiran had never seen gardens like these. Rather than planting in rows, flat-topped mounds of soil had been built for clusters of crops. Several tall, grass-like plants, called maize, grew close together in the center of each mound. Bean plants grew on the maize stalk, climbing it like a pole, while squash plants surrounded the base, their broad leaves spreading to block sunlight and prevent weeds. Cartus explained how these three crops relied on each other; it was difficult to grow one without the others. They were grown year-round. As soon as one was harvested, they replanted the mound.

Kiran's back began to ache from bending over. He stopped to wipe sweat from his brow and caught a glimpse of Jandon walking down the path with Angei-Ami. His hair was wet, but Kiran was sure it was him, strolling along with his casual gait. But why was he with her? And why was his hair wet?

A brother dropped a bag at his feet, ripped it open, and dumped a pile of dark, rich humus atop a mound. Cartus handed Kiran a rake. "Spread the fertilizer, evenly across the mound," he said.

Kiran had never heard of such a thing. "What is it exactly? Where does it come from?"

Cartus stopped what he was doing and gave Kiran the smile. "I don't know."

Kiran stared at him a moment. *Aren't you curious?* he wanted to ask, but he already knew the answer.

From there, they went directly to a shaded area and gathered in a circle to chant and sing. With the songs still on his lips, Kiran followed his brothers to bathe in the cold river and back to their bunkhouse to dress in another crisp white tunic for dinner and the evening sermon. There was no break, no rest; they went from one task to the next. But Kiran didn't mind. He relished the companionship of his new brothers and was eager to again stand in the presence of the Guardian to hear his message.

At last, the day neared its close, and for the second and final meal, Kiran was served a watery succotash of maize and beans. He gulped it down, too hungry to complain. He looked for Bria again, but didn't see her this time until on his way out, in the stable, he caught a glimpse of red hair. There she was, tending to the goats, cooing at them as she fed them from her hands. They had found the wise man, had completed their journey. Now, they simply had to wait, with reverent obedience, for the Day of Thunder. So, why did he feel restless? He gazed at Bria, longing to be near her again, to hear her giggle. Was this what it felt like to be an Elder? To give up so much? Sure, Elders could marry, but only after they were fully ordained. He wasn't sure if he'd be able to stand it.

At the ring of a bell, every member of the twelve Houses of the Kingdom of the Kotari proceeded across the bridge to gather under the great roof, stopping only to wash their feet in the first pool. As Kiran entered the pavilion, he searched the mass of faces for Roh, but did not see him in the crowd.

When the Guardian appeared, the room charged with energy, as though the sun had burst free from behind a wall of clouds. He moved to the edge of the platform and raised his hands high in the air. An audible hush came over the crowd. "This is a most glorious day," he sang out. "Pilgrims have been delivered unto us, searching for the true path. Let us welcome them with love, and dedicate ourselves to their care, that they may learn how to pray and sing in preparation to bear witness at The Coming of Light. Praise Ani!"

"Praise Ani!" shouted the followers in response.

Kiran's spirit soared. He still couldn't believe it was true; they had made it. Their journey was over.

The Guardian spread his arms wide, gesturing toward the grand vista that surrounded them. "Let us not fear that Ani has not chosen us, for I have witnessed His love in rich streams, flowing from the mountains on high, and heavy abundance, here in His kingdom." He held up a bright orange fruit. "In seeing these truths, we know we are the chosen. We see Ani's hand lifted up and we are blessed."

Yes, just as He lifted up His hands to receive Elder Santon when he jumped, Kiran thought, nodding. *If one simply believes.* His mind raced back to that moment on the ledge. He had hesitated, had doubted. But no more. From now on, he vowed, he would not question. The Guardian was standing before him, the true wise man of the Legend.

With baskets in hand, the ladies in the white robes went into the crowd. The room was filled with the sound of the followers sucking on the juicy fruit. Kiran moved to get a piece for himself and stopped in his tracks. There was Deke, carrying a basket of fruit. How had he been granted such an honor so quickly? And Kail was next to him, holding a basket in her hands as well. They were already at the right hand of the wise man.

"Wherefore, my holy brethren, we shall lift up those who seek the Truth. We all know the wicked power of temptation." The Guardian's gaze fixed on Kiran. "I know what is in your heart and poisons your mind." His eyes bore into Kiran and he felt transparent, certain the Guardian saw directly into his mind and read his every thought. He cowered in the face of judgment, shivering with guilt. "For I was once poisoned by the same evil, struggling to find my way. Harden your heart against that temptation and, in time, you too will find peace."

Kiran let out his breath. *He knows what is in my heart, the struggle of my mind in constant questioning. And he does not judge me for it!*

He has felt it too!

Looking into the Guardian's eyes, Kiran felt a connection between them. The pull of his words tugged at Kiran's soul, as though the Guardian spoke directly to him, in the common language, so that he might fully understand and be liberated from ignorance. Back home, the Elders spoke in the Tongue of the Father. When at last Aldwyn had agreed to teach him, he drank in the information with such gratification, to finally be allowed to seek pure knowledge of the Great Father. For him, on that day, life had begun.

Now, he could continue that journey. The Guardian was the wise man of the Legend, and like the Elders from the Books of the Script, he was here to share divine knowledge. This man, standing before Kiran, would have the answers to all his questions; he was sure of it.

"Take heed, you are on the true path; for faith is the path of the righteous."

Kiran paused, confused now. *Wasn't that what Deke had said on the mount?* Just what did he mean? Did the Guardian understand and forgive? Or would Kiran have to prove his faith here too?

"Do not be mistaken, it is a narrow path; the path to righteousness is total obedience." The Guardian leaned forward. He lowered his voice and his eyes grew dark. "But beware those who say they love Ani and do not follow the Way. They are liars!" he spat. "They don't really love Ani. They think that because they are here, in the Kingdom of the Kotari, it is enough, and they don't have to serve. They may have the appearance of Ani's servants, but speak lies against the Truth. Take heed, my brethren, lest there be in any of you an evil heart of unbelief and the temptation to depart from the Kingdom. Out there," he thrust his arm outward, pointing toward the river. Every follower turned to look in that direction. "Out there you will only find suffering and darkness. Those who roam in disbelief live in torment because they have chosen to disobey. We know that those who don't obey must be punished!" He slammed his fist down on the table.

"Those liars have been passed over, bereft of His divine providence. Let us labor therefore, lest any man fall into the sin of unbelief. For at the Coming of the Light, the Word of Ani will be made manifest. Do not be mistaken. Ani does not just see good and evil, but He knows the thoughts and intents of the heart. All men are naked and opened unto the eyes of Him."

I knew it! thought Kiran. *The Great Father knows my every thought—my hopes, my fears, my questions, my...doubts.* He drew in a breath, his mind racing. He could not let himself fall back into the sin of disbelief.

The Guardian paced back and forth, the veins at his temples about to burst. "Always, men fail to hold to the promises of Ani because they know not when the prophecy will be fulfilled. So, they let their minds wander into doubt." He shook his head so hard hair broke free from the tie at his neck. "Their souls will be ripped open for all to see."

Imagining his soul being ripped open, Kiran shook with terror. *I believe, I swear I do!*

The Guardian paused to wipe his brow. He started again, his tone and cadence now a dirge-like rhythm. "As it is written, on the Day of Thunder, you will hear His voice. Everyone who wears the mark will be filled with Inspiration. Down from the clouds, He will descend, and in the days of the voice of the seventh, when He shall sound the call, the mystery of all shall be revealed."

Voice of the seventh? Does he mean the Seventh Elder? The mystery of all? The Great Mystery? Kiran struggled to keep up, the words and concepts coming too fast. This was all new information. He saw Kail and Deke and Jandon in front of him, nodding. He glanced around. His brothers, all the followers, were nodding with expressions of adoration as the Guardian marched on. He just needed a little more time, that was all. Then he'd understand. He was just tired.

"We welcome those who seek the Truth." The Guardian lowered his eyes, his attention on Kail. "For they are innocent and pure." Then his gaze shifted to Bria and lingered, eyeing her up and down. There was something in his look that made Kiran uncomfortable, a murky, uneasy feeling.

"But we must shut the door to sinners," the Guardian thundered, his eyes shifting to lock with Kiran's. "Those who dwell in doubt and let their minds be filled with envy and pride." A rush of shame came over Kiran and his knees went weak.

"For when the thunder comes, all those who do not obey must be cast out into darkness. The wrath of Ani will bear down upon them without mercy!"

Kiran shook with fear. *I am not one of the wicked! No! I will obey! I will obey! I will earn the mark. I will be a Receiver of Light. I will!*

"The Day of Thunder will come!" the man shouted, throwing up his arms. "And on that day, we, the Receivers of Light, will know the Truth and bask in the Glory of Light Everlasting! Praise Ani!"

"Praise Ani!" Kiran shouted.

19

The sermon went on long into the night. Kiran no longer heard the Guardian's voice, his mind lost in a labyrinth of questions. The Guardian bombarded him with so many new concepts, concepts that seemed right, yet left him feeling uncertain, though he couldn't grasp hold of a reason why.

He followed the brothers of House Four back to their bunkhouse in the dark, trying to pull himself from the whirlwind of confusion. If only he could talk to Roh. Maybe he just needed some sleep. Tomorrow, he told himself as he collapsed on his mat. He'd look for Roh again tomorrow.

He refused to let doubt plague him again. As soon as the flame of doubt started to pulse, he tried to smother it, assuring himself that what the Guardian preached was true; the Voice would come. All he wanted was peace, respite from the burning questions. But deep in his mind, there was an ever-present flicker, a smoldering ember, like a word or a feeling, a niggling voice that whispered, urging him to continue on the quest, to get back on the river and keep going, that this was not the edge of the world as the Script described. When he looked around, he saw smiling faces, content, nodding. Everyone else believed, unquestioningly. They couldn't all be wrong. He must have been missing something. What the Guardian said must be true.

The next morning, he was again awakened before dawn, led off to morning meditations right away, then work in the gardens, then chanting and singing, then more work, then the daily sermon with the Guardian. The next day was the same, then the next. The long days began to flow together in a continuous cycle, drawing Kiran along by the momentum of routine. Life became a blur, like a deep, delirious sleep, where the same dream is dreamt over and over again.

He longed for some time to think, some time alone to sort through his thoughts and feelings, but there never seemed to be any.

He could not shake his restlessness. He envied the calm that the others seemed to have, the peacefulness imbued in their beings. He would catch himself looking at them at odd moments, wondering what they were thinking, what answers they harbored. What did they know that he didn't? Perhaps, if he could only grasp the message, he would feel it, too.

He was so tired; he could barely concentrate enough to get through the tasks of the day, let alone follow the late night sermons. Lately, all he felt was confusion. Every night he fell asleep too exhausted to think.

The only thing he knew for sure was that here, in the Kingdom, he felt secure and loved, content with his new family, his brothers of House Four, who admired and respected him. He had never before felt such a sense of belonging. Maybe life was different here compared to life in the village, but he would adjust.

He still didn't know what to make of Cartus, though. Kiran couldn't seem to please him or gain his trust. With Aldwyn, he had always felt comfortable asking anything. But here, with Cartus, he had to keep up his guard. There was just something in his manner, something in his smile.

No, it's me. There is something wrong with me; I must try harder, he told himself. He plodded along, through the routine that became his life. He had to keep going until the Day of Thunder.

Then one night, after a week, or maybe longer, Kiran couldn't be sure, he lay awake in the moonlight, watching a spider creep along the rafter above his mat. He was tired, but his mind just wouldn't stop. At the sermon that evening, the Guardian had warned of desires of the flesh. Kiran's eyes had gone right to Bria. He couldn't help it. He ached to be near her, to hold her in his arms, to smell her hair again, to kiss her one more time. Just thinking about her made his body react and he squirmed in his bed, his senses brought fully awake. He was to deny those… feelings, the Guardian had said. To succumb, to give in to temptation, was a sin, and sinners were cast into eternal darkness. Alone. Lost. Tormented souls.

Kiran tried not to think about it, though his heartbeat sent pulses throbbing throughout his body and he ached for release. Being in the bunkhouse with his brothers was suffocating. He had to get out of here, had to be alone. He pushed himself up on his elbows and looked around. No one stirred. He got up and quietly slipped out.

On the moonlit porch, he took a deep breath, inhaling the cool night air, and started to feel better already. The forest was alive with sound. The perpetual daytime hum of insects and other creatures of the jungle had transformed into a roar that filled the night. This is the dwelling place, he thought. *So why do I feel so restless?* How had the Script described it? Wasn't there a peak? Maybe he had been right, and the river had changed the terrain over time. That could be it. No. Something wasn't right.

He could read the Script again. Then he would feel better. Tonight, the moon was near full. He should be able to see clearly enough at the river's edge. He pressed his ear against the door and heard the soft snoring of one of his brothers. Yes, now was the time.

Under the dark canopy, he shuffled down the path toward the river. He sat down with the scroll in a patch of moonlight and read the last lines again:

> *When you reach the peak and stand on the edge of darkness,*
> *Before you will be a great pool of glorious reflection.*
> *There a wise man will appear,*
> *Wrinkled with time and crippled with wisdom.*
> *Listen to him, for his is the Voice of the Father.*

Kiran read the verse three times. So the wise man *was* the Voice of the Father. But the Guardian spoke of the Voice yet to come. That wasn't right. Or was it? Now he was confused. *Maybe when the Voice comes, He will speak through the Guardian. Maybe they are one and the same, just not at all times. Could that be it?*

What would Deke say, he wondered. He must have worked it out somehow. But how? Perhaps he forgot the wording of the Script. No, it was Deke. He could recite the Script word for word.

Kiran ran his fingers through his hair. If only he could talk to Roh. No one could tell Roh what to think. He had his own mind. And Kiran could talk to him about these things.

Stop questioning! he caught himself. *What is wrong with me? I must obey or be punished. It doesn't matter whether I understand or not.* He shook his head like a sheep trying to shoo away troublesome flies. *The Guardian is the wise man.* And the wise man knows the true nature of the Voice.

"Good evening, Brother," came a voice in the dark.

His head jerked up with a start. It was Cartus.

He shoved the scroll back into its hiding place and rose to his feet. "You startled me," he said, glancing over his shoulder. Had Cartus seen him move the stone in the dark? His pulse started thumping in his temples.

"What troubles you, brother, that you are not at slumber?"

"Uh, nothing. I just…" He looked down at his hands. "Couldn't sleep."

"The Guardian does not abide insolence. You are not to abandon your brothers to wander alone. Being alone can lead to sinful behavior."

"No, I wouldn't." Kiran shook his head. Did Cartus know he had those… feelings? Suddenly the muggy tropical air felt stifling. "My stomach has been bothering me," he lied, licking his lip.

Cartus stepped into the moonlight. "A stomachache is not a good sign. Sin manifests in the body, my brother. Perhaps you are not as dedicated to Ani as we had thought."

"No, no. I am. I just—"

Cartus took a step closer. "Do not let your mind slip, brother, or your thoughts roam too far. The wrath of Ani is fearsome and what you invite of your own sin will be brought down on all your brothers."

Kiran bit his lip. "My brothers?" If he sinned, all his brothers would be punished? "I didn't know."

"My brother, I know your heart is true. But you must be more diligent in your obedience. Go back to your bunk now. Rest your head."

"Yes, yes. I am tired." He started to go but stopped and turned back. "Cartus, I have not seen my brother Roh. Do you know what House he is in?"

"Oh yes. The Guardian has assigned him a very special task. You will see. As I told you before, each by his ability." Then the smile.

So Roh had been chosen for something special, like the others. Why hadn't he? He had been trying so hard to make his heart pure. And he was being passed over. He had to show the wise man how dedicated he was. He had to find a way.

The next morning, as the brothers of House Four left the morning meditations, a woman appeared adorned in the same gauzy white robe Angei-Ami had worn. Cartus pulled Kiran aside as his brothers continued on their way. "This is Angei-Laina."

Kiran forced a smile, his eyes darting back and forth between them. "Am I in trouble?"

"Of course not," she said. "Won't you come with me and I'll explain everything." She took him by the hand.

Fear stirred in the pit of his stomach. What was her name? Hadn't Cartus just told him? He was having trouble with his memory lately. Was it Angei? Not Angei-Ami. "Your name, Angei, is it—"

"Forgive him," Cartus interrupted, glaring at Kiran. "He has just arrived and is impulsive, full of questions." He lowered his eyes in respect.

Kiran copied him, lowering his eyes, wracked with guilt.

The kind woman softly lifted his chin. "My son, the Angei are the wives of Ani. It is a great honor to be wed to Ani through service to the Guardian."

Kiran nodded, grateful for the kind response, although he didn't understand. The Great Father had wives? More than one?

The woman dismissed Cartus with a nod. He turned away, wearing his permanent smile.

Angei-Laina led Kiran across the bridge to the sparkling pools. "Go ahead and get in," she said, gesturing toward the pool in which he had bathed when he first arrived. "Enjoy."

Kiran was taken aback. This was definitely not the normal routine. He had learned this much.

"The pools here do more than soothe aching muscles. In these waters, many find peace. It is by the love of Ani that we have been given this gift. We invite you to accept His love and the love of the Angei. There is no need to feel scared or uncomfortable. Now go ahead," she urged with a smile, turning away.

Kiran nodded. His eyes moved from her to the pool. Still unsure, he stripped to his underclothes and waded in.

To his surprise, Angei-Laina turned back and sat down on the edge of the pool. "I just want you to relax and for us to talk, all right?"

"I suppose." What harm was there in talking?

"You can trust me," she said, reaching with one finger to push a curly lock from his forehead. "Now, close your eyes and relax."

Kiran laid his head back on the edge of the pool and closed his eyes, letting the warmth of the water soothe his weary body. But he couldn't relax. He was in a bath. In his underclothes. With a woman. Right next to him.

He opened one eye, watching her.

"My, my, you are a restless soul. I can help you find your way, if only you would trust me."

He closed his eye once more, trying to relax. *We are only talking.*

"Free your mind, let all thought go, as it once was, when you were a child—pure and free and innocent. Picture yourself as a small boy. You are all alone, walking through the woods and feel lost. Someone has left you."

Kiran winced at the memory. He was alone, under the towering trees, searching for someone.

"You wander alone in the woods until you finally find your house, but no one is home. You step inside, calling for him, but no one answers you. Your things are there. Picture them now, things from your childhood, all dusty, tattered, and torn."

Painful memories flooded his mind with no sensible sequence, pounding in so fast he didn't have time to recognize their meaning. He rode the waves of emotion, reliving each agony, each heartache.

"You are beginning to feel lonely, as lonely as you did as a little child in bed. Who did you long for?"

Mother! he cried in the vision, raising his hands to cover his eyes. His heartbeat rang in his ears as he fought back tears.

"Why are you all alone, crying in your bed? Weren't you loved? Think about the loneliness, the agony of being forgotten. Those feelings are still deep inside, tugging at your heart. You are crying all alone and no one comes." Angei-Laina took one of his hands in hers. He opened his eyes and stared into her pale blue eyes. "You don't have to ever feel lonely again. We are your family now. We love you." She patted him on the head and brushed back his curls with the soft caress of a mother's hand. "In the Kingdom of the Kotari, no one is alone. The love of Ani is like the warmth of sunshine after the rain. You are now in His loving arms. You can let go of all the hurt and sorrow."

Tears warmed his eyes and he started to shake, overcome with emotion as the echo of his call for his mother tore at his heart.

"That's it, my son. Let it all out," she soothed. "Your feelings show your depth of love and connection. Don't shy away from them."

All those years, he had wept inside for a mother and now the tears came flooding forth. Angei-Laina pulled him to her bosom. "I want you to think back again, now. Think back to home and the agony you have suffered at the hands of others. Who was there for you? Who defended you?"

Kiran closed his eyes once more and tried to picture Aldwyn, but he could not form an image of him in his mind. Like wisps of smoke, bits of memories came, wavered, then disappeared on the wind.

"The old man took you in. Why? What reason could he have?"

Aldwyn loves me.

"He wanted to mold you, shape you in his own image. How do you know that what he taught you is true? Maybe he led you down the wrong path."

No! Aldwyn loves me. Kiran's head began to hurt. *Doesn't he?* His heart started to pump harder.

"You have nothing but his word. Maybe he was just a confused old man, using you for his own gain. But that doesn't matter." She gently released him from her embrace. He opened his eyes and stared into hers. "You are a man now. You are old enough to make decisions of your own."

His jaw set, he said, "I am not a boy."

"I know, brother. I know," she said, her soft eyes running down his chest, down his body and back up again, causing a flush of warmth in him. "You have entered the Kingdom and are born into a new life. It is time to let go of those old thoughts, those old ways."

Let go. Yes, that's what he needed to do. *Let go. Let go.*

"Your old thoughts are stones in your way, blocking your path. Move forward, no matter what you have to do. This is your journey, and yours alone. You've had no loved ones, no one who understands."

No one who understands. Deke had constantly antagonized him, berated him, disparaged him at every turn. His fists clenched in anger. Then there was Jandon, turning his back on him—his best friend! At least he had thought they were friends. But when it came down to choosing, he knew Jandon would always go with Deke.

And Roh. Kiran thought they had become friends, but had they? He was still an enigma. Kiran had no idea what Roh really thought of him or if he cared about him at all. Kiran's face burned with rage. That day, after he learned the truth about the Mawghul, they had scolded him! All of them! Even Bria. He'd never forget her face as she turned away—the despondency in her eyes. After the night they had kissed.

Years of anger and frustration surged to the surface. He had been denying, pushing their judgment aside. Up to this moment, he had yearned for their acceptance, their friendship, their love. Well, no more. He belonged here, in the Kingdom. He was accepted here, unconditionally, with genuine love. He didn't need them.

He fought back tears. *But my Bria.* The burden he carried with him, the shadow that haunted him, burst into a gaping black hole, enveloping him in darkness. Angei-laina was right; he was all alone. He trembled, fearing he'd be lost in the abyss forever.

"Let go. Let yourself emerge from the darkness, for darkness is evil. You have always been forced into the dark. But you are smarter than that. This is your time, to do as you believe." She lowered her eyes once more, her eyelids heavy. "You know what you want. As you said, you are not a boy. You are a man."

Three women appeared at the side of the pool, tall and thin and shapely, dressed in the gauzy gowns of the Angei, their voluptuous bodies showing beneath. One woman with lustrous red hair and eyes the color of rain carried a platter of fruit and sugary breads. She set it on the edge of the pool and dropped her robe. Kiran drew in a breath and stiffened. What was she doing? She wore nothing but a sheer camisole. His eyes followed her every movement, drinking in her soft curves. He could see her nipples through the thin fabric and his mind raced back to a stormy night, and Bria dancing in the rain, her wet tunic clinging to her body.

With a tiny ripple of water, the woman slipped into the pool beside him. He looked to Angei-Laina, his eyes wide. She nodded, signaling all was well. *But the Guardian just said...*

The other two women dropped their white robes and slid into the pool on either side of him. Angei-Laina's voice weaved into the thoughts surging through his head. "Stop thinking with your head, stop rationalizing, stop seeking answers. You need only humbly accept love in your heart to find peace." Kiran's eyes fixed on the red-haired woman who was swirling her hands through the water, her soft eyes on him. "To experience the rapture, on the Day of Thunder, you must learn to let go your inhibitions. You must give yourself over entirely to Ani, without question, without hesitation."

To let go inhibitions. Hadn't he said that to Bria? The thought fluttered in and out of his mind. When he wanted to kiss her? He blinked, trying to concentrate. The red-haired woman eased next to him and ran her fingers through his hair, playfully twisting his curls. One of the other women came along his other side, placing her hand on his knee. He trembled at her touch. She leaned toward him. Her shiny red lips parted slightly and she whispered, "You belong here." She leaned in closer, her warm breath on his ear, "You are wanted." Kiran stared at her, breathing hard. She reached for the platter, took a morsel of sweet bread in her fingers, and brought it to his lips. He opened his mouth to her, his heart racing, desire pulsing through his veins.

From nowhere, Cartus appeared again. "It is time to head back for the evening meal."

Kiran's eyes shot up to him. He gulped, swallowing hard. He couldn't stand up now.

The four women eased from the pool. He watched them go, the robes clinging to their wet bodies, his breath fast. He turned to see Cartus staring at him and his face flushed red.

"Do not be embarrassed," Cartus said, handing Kiran a clean, dry tunic. "To face temptation and abstain is virtuous. In the Kingdom, it is a sin to spill your seed without permission of the Guardian. He must grant you the Right."

"The Right?" Kiran turned his back to Cartus and rose from the pool to dress.

"You will see, my brother. In time. For now, we need to go."

Kiran followed him back to the island, his body racked with frustration. Was he brought to the pools to face temptation? Was this how he would earn the mark and be one of the chosen? To let go his inhibitions, to embrace the love of Ani—was that what he needed to do to serve the Father?

But how could he ever give up Bria? Just the thought of her made his pulse race again. He was thankful Cartus was facing the other way. *What is happening to me?* Most of the time, he couldn't think of anything else, couldn't concentrate. Any gesture or smile, brushing past a girl, the slightest breeze sent his body ablaze. He thought he might go crazy. He needed release, that was certain, freedom from the incessant desire, but he wasn't sure that was what Angei-laina meant.

She had said he needed to let go, to stop using his head, and open his heart.

But it wasn't his heart that ached.

20

One day flowed into the next and another moon passed without much notice as Kiran went about his daily routine in the Kingdom of the Kotari.

Then one day, while Kiran worked with his brothers in the gardens, news of a wedding whispered among the followers. In seven days, a nuptial banquet and grand party was to take place in honor of a new Angei. The entire Kingdom was aflutter with excitement and festive optimism.

When the day finally arrived, everyone was roused at dawn and assigned duties in lieu of their daily chores. Cartus directed all the brothers of House Four to their posts. Kiran fell in line, following three of his brothers to the cookhouse. They knocked at the back door and a woman, about Aldwyn's age, with blond, curly hair, answered. "We're assigned kitchen duty," his brother told her.

"Come in," she said, waving them past her. She took one look at Kiran and put her hand out to stop him. She stared into his eyes and, for a fleeting moment, he felt a glimmer of recognition. There was something about her eyes. Or was it her voice?

"I haven't seen you around," she said. "What kind of work can you do?"

"Whatever you ask of me, I suppose. So long as you'll show me how to do it. I'm a quick learner."

Standing with her hands on her hips, she looked him up and down. "Well, where are you from? What work have you done?"

"Farming mostly. I'm from the Toran village, on the edge of the Sea of Demarcation, from here toward the rising sun."

She drew in a breath. He thought he saw her lip quiver.

"I think I have a job for you," she said finally, her voice softer now. "Come in."

He strode up the two steps into the kitchen and followed her to a storeroom in the back. "Sit down there," she said, pointing to an old stool. "I'll be right back."

He waited, listening to the clanking of pans in the kitchen.

At last, the woman returned. "I have a special chore for you. You'll be helping me make the ceremonial drink." Her eyes held his for a long, uncomfortable moment.

He squirmed and rose to his feet. "All right."

"What's your name?"

He paused a moment, realizing that, since he had arrived, no one in the Kingdom of the Kotari had ever asked his name. "Kiran," he said, his own name sounding foreign now as he said it out loud.

Her lip quivered again; he was sure he saw it this time. She remained silent for a long moment. Something in the way she looked at him made him feel weighed and measured.

"Are you all right?"

She looked over her shoulder, then nodded, regaining her composure. She gestured for him to follow, then left the room as though she couldn't get out fast enough.

"Sure, but ma'am," he called, trying to keep up with her as she flew out the back door. "Please, tell me your name."

She halted and turned to face him. A warm smile spread across her face. "Kalindria," she whispered, waiting with eager eyes as though she anticipated a response. He had no idea what she sought. Finally, she turned and motioned for him to follow.

She led him to a covered patio with a long, wooden table on which were bowls of various items. One was filled with the green inner shavings of tree bark. Another contained flower petals, another leaves and stems, yet another, bits of root. Just beyond the patio was a smoldering fire, a tripod straddling the pit.

Kalindria demonstrated how to knead the tree bark in a bowl of cold water. He worked, doing as she taught him, as best he could, mashing the bark into a paste. When she left him to stir the fire, he glanced up, and caught her staring at him. She quickly looked away. He kept mashing the bark as she swung a huge black pot, larger than he had ever seen, over the pit. "We need to boil that paste into a syrup," she said. Kiran helped her pour the mashed bark into the pot and she stirred while directing him to crush the other ingredients between two large stones.

"So, you are a Toran?" she asked, the question a surprise. He had become accustomed to the silence of the Kotari.

"Yes, ma'am," he smiled. *A real Toran,* he wanted to say.

"What brings you here?" she asked, now staring into the pot.

"I was sent with six others on a quest to the Voice of the Father," he said, digging the memory from the back of his mind.

Her eyes shot up. "Who sent you?" she asked, her eyes holding his with a desperate grip.

"The Elders did. You see, it was a drought and Aldwyn—"

"Aldwyn?" she gasped.

Kiran stopped what he was doing and stared at her, waiting for an explanation. She quickly averted her eyes, looking into the steaming pot. "Yes, Aldwyn. Do you know him?"

She turned back to face Kiran. Her eyes went soft, as though resigned to share her secret, and she made an almost imperceptible nod. "How is he?" she asked, her voice a small whisper.

Kiran studied her a moment, wondering how she could possibly know Aldwyn. "He is fine. As far as I know. We have been gone several moons now. I don't know if he gleaned any harvest, but he always has the tithes." He frowned. "If he'll accept them."

She nodded, her eyes filled with pain.

"How do you know Aldwyn?"

"It was a long, long time ago," she said, her eyes misty now. "Is he married?"

"Married?" Kiran was surprised by the question. "Why, no. He's never married. I'm afraid—"

"What?" she said, dropping the spoon handle. "Afraid of what?"

"I'm afraid that's my fault." His eyes lowered. "I'm an orphan and Aldwyn took me in when I was just a baby."

The woman reached for the table to steady herself, the color draining from her face.

"Are you all right?"

"Yes, yes, I'm fine. It's just the heat."

"Shall I get you a cup of water?"

She nodded.

Kiran hustled off to the kitchen and returned with two cups of water. The woman had regained her composure; the color had come back to her face. Kiran wanted to know more about how she knew Aldwyn, but her demeanor had changed, closed off now, and somehow asking the questions seemed rude.

He went back to work, smashing the flower petals, watching her with interest, waiting for the right moment to restart the conversation.

He set another pot of water to boil, as she directed. When it finally bubbled, they poured it into the large bowl of crushed leaves and petals, steeping them like tea. They set the hot pot down in the dirt and he took over the task of stirring the large cauldron of tree bark.

Kalindria eased next to him. "Listen," she whispered. "You need to get out of here. You need to leave, as soon as possible. Before it's too late."

"What are you talking about?"

She looked from side to side, then glanced over her shoulder as she leaned in close to Kiran. "Listen to me. The Kingdom is not what it seems. The Guardian is not truthful. He is manipulating you—all of you. Get away while you can."

Kiran took a step back, his eyes darting around, looking for anyone who might hear them. This kind of talk bred sin—the poison of the unfaithful—Cartus had said. He was to report anyone who spoke this way.

"Nothing good will come if you stay," she went on. "You will only live on in regret. You must go. Now!"

Somewhere deep inside he knew she spoke the truth. Things weren't right here. Something was amiss. Like the way the Guardian looked at Bria. And why hadn't he seen Roh at all?

Kalindria was the first person he had met in the Kingdom who had shown any doubt and she was adamant. She had only said out loud what he had been thinking. Should he admit his own suspicions? Maybe she knew more than she was saying. No. He must be cautious; if he discussed this with her, even acknowledged his doubt, he'd be risking too much. He knew better. Maybe this was a trick. Another test. Kiran searched her eyes for the truth.

A young man appeared on the path from the kitchen. Kiran's heart skipped a beat. Had he heard anything? If they were caught speaking blasphemy… The boy had the face of a child, yet hobbled along, dragging a crooked leg like an old man, his head bobbing as he whistled a merry tune. "Here you are, more petals." He dropped a basket on the table, then paused, looking at Kiran with big, curious eyes. "Hi there, who are you? I'm Pel. Nice to meet you," he said. He grabbed Kiran's hand and pumped it up and down, an unruly thatch of brown hair flopping over his forehead. "It's always nice to have help, that's for sure."

Kiran looked from Pel to Kalindria, then back to Pel. Pel's expression changed, as though he realized he had interrupted something. "Forgive me." He leaned toward Kiran. "I can't seem to master the silence rule," he said in a fake whisper and winked. He dumped the petals into a bowl and turned and limped away, empty basket in hand.

Kalindria watched him go, then turned back to face Kiran. "It's all right. You can trust Pel." She took a deep breath and her eyes turned soft and loving. "And you can trust me. I am, I was, a friend of Aldwyn."

His mind snapped to full attention. "A friend of Aldwyn?"

"I knew Aldwyn because…" She averted her eyes, as if what she had to tell him was too painful. "You see," she said, turning back to face him. "I was a Javinian."

Kiran took a step back. *A Javinian?* He didn't know what to do, what to say.

"But I left. I had to."

Kiran nodded, his eyes fixed on her.

"I found refuge here, in the Kingdom."

"You escaped their evil ways," he whispered, relieved to have an explanation.

"Escaped? No, I—"

"You must be glad to be free of them."

"Free? Kiran, no, I didn't want to leave."

Kiran took another step back. "Didn't want to leave? But they're brutal killers. They torture Torans."

She nodded in quiet acceptance as if she had been accused of this before. "Have you ever actually seen a Javinian torture someone? Or known someone personally who was hurt or killed by a Javinian?"

He thought for a moment. "Well, no. But I saw them myself, with bows and spears."

"Yes, hunting weapons. Not fighting weapons." She moved toward him and took his hands in hers. "The followers of Javin were cast out, from their own farms, their livelihood. They were desperate. They had to take to the forest and live as they could, to survive. But torture and murder, those are the false accusations of the Temple, perpetrated to set the Torans against us."

What was she saying? Was she accusing the Temple of lying? That kind of talk was blasphemy. He shook his head in disbelief.

"You'll come to see, someday, what people will do and say to hold on to their power. That's why you need to leave here, now." Her fingernails dug into his palm.

Leave? He yanked his hands from hers. "What are you saying!" He couldn't trust her or anything she said. She was a Javinian and Javinians had their wicked ways. Why would he want to leave? He had a family now, brothers who cared about him. And the Voice was coming, here, on the Day of Thunder.

Why was she saying all this? Was she trying to get him in trouble? But why? He knew what happened to those who had forsaken Ani. His eyes narrowed. "You must think I'm stupid. I know about the lost souls."

She scoffed. "Are they still telling newcomers that? Kiran, those are monkeys."

"Monkeys?"

"They are small, harmless creatures of the forest. They howl for the same reason birds sing."

"I don't believe you," he said, his mind whirring.

"No. You don't want to believe me. But you know I speak the truth. I can see it in your eyes." He quickly looked away. "Search within yourself. Listen to your heart," she whispered, tapping him on the chest.

Kiran met her gaze. That was odd. Aldwyn had said and done the same thing. What was she trying to do? There was something about her, something soft and gentle. He shook his head. How could she be a ruthless Javinian? But why would she tell him she was? *Because Javinians are wicked, that's why.* Always trying to lure people to their heathen ways. He couldn't listen to another word. "Aldwyn was no friend to a Javinian. You are trying to trick me. But it won't work. I will not be denied the providence of Ani!" He turned his back to her and strode away.

Down the path he ran, away from the questions, the suspicions, the turmoil, rushing like whitewater through his head. He had to find a way to clear his mind of it all, to recapture his faith.

At once, he found himself at the Body Temple and he knew just what to do. Standing in the proper position, he thrust his clenched fists outward, chanting, "Praise Ani! Praise Ani!" No one could accuse him of blasphemy. "Praise Ani!" huff, "Praise Ani!" huff. Lost in the movement, he started to relax into the comfort of the familiar.

"I've been looking for you."

Kiran spun around. It was Cartus. He sucked in air and his knees went weak.

"I want to remind you," Cartus said with the smile. Kiran let out his breath. "Tonight, at the celebration, you must mind your thoughts and actions if you seek the Right of Emergence."

Kiran stared at him. Did he dare ask? What exactly was the Right of Emergence? "I understand," he said with a bow, trying to hide his confusion.

"I trust you will do well, for the glory of Ani."

Kiran nodded.

"Soon, you will be marked by the star. It is the greatest honor, my brother." Cartus slapped him on the back, grinning wide.

Kiran eyed him. He'd never smiled like that before.

Cartus looked around at the empty clearing. "What are you doing here alone?"

"Oh, I was no longer needed at the kitchen and was sent to ready for the banquet. As I came by, I felt inspiration to do the meditations." Kiran bit his lip, hoping Cartus would accept this explanation. *I should report Kalindria right now. I should tell him.*

"I see," Cartus said. The smile was back. There was a long pause. "Well, get back to your brothers."

"Yes, yes, I'll do that."

When he arrived at the bunkhouse, he saw one of the older men outside. "May I ask you something?" he whispered.

The man hesitated, then nodded.

"What is the... Right of Emergence?"

The man leaned back, his eyebrows raised. "You don't know?"

Kiran bit his lip and shook his head.

The man leaned forward. "The blissful release, my brother. Are you seeking the Right?"

"I'm not sure what it is... exactly."

"Oh. It's the one thing you've been aching for."

Kiran's face flushed red.

The man nodded. "Indeed," he said with a wink.

Before he crossed the river, Kiran could hear the music, lively and upbeat. The brothers and sisters of the Kotari, filled with energy, bumped and swayed as they filed across the floating bridge to gather for the wedding celebration.

Once inside the pavilion, everyone was loud and boisterous, unlike the quiet, solemn behavior Kiran had become accustomed to in the Kingdom. Women whirled about the floor, joyously moving to the music. The men watched, lining the dance floor. Kiran pushed through the throng of followers toward the edge of the pavilion. He had no interest in dancing. Tonight he wanted to talk to Roh, but soon realized he would have a difficult time finding him in the chaos. Still, he scanned the crowd.

Someone grabbed him by the arm. "This way!" It was his brother from House Four, the man he had asked about the rite. "Devotion starts with the ceremonial drink."

The man shoved through the crowd with Kiran in tow. When they burst from the fray, Kiran found himself face to face with Kalindria. With a curt nod and showing no sign of recognition, she handed him a cup. Perhaps it was best if they did not acknowledge each other, he thought.

"Drink up," his brother said, interrupting his thoughts.

He took a sip of the drink and puckered. It had a pungent, sour flavor.

Just then, Cartus appeared beside him. *He's like the wind,* Kiran thought, glancing back to Kalindria. Was that fear in her eyes?

"What's the matter?" Cartus asked, wearing the familiar smile.

Kiran stared at him a moment. "Nothing. Nothing at all." He took another sip of the drink and decided it wasn't so bad.

The music stopped and the Guardian appeared on the platform, his arms raised skyward. "Welcome, my beloved followers! Tonight, we celebrate the sacred love of Ani, for He has chosen a new bride." Cheers went up from the followers.

A young woman, her face hidden behind a shimmery veil, floated across the floor to the Guardian. He took her by the hand and led her to the edge of the platform. "I present to you, the bride of Ani." He lifted her veil, and there, standing before the Kingdom of the Kotari, the newest wife of Ani, new Angei to the Guardian, her rosy cheeks flush with pride, was Kail.

Kiran's mouth dropped open.

The Guardian pulled her to him and kissed her with showy passion, running his hands up and down her body. The followers cheered with happiness. The music started again and the Guardian ripped the veil from her head. Kail glowed from the attention, standing before the crowd unabashed, the gauzy-white robe of the Angei revealing her shapely curves. Kiran blushed and had to look away. As the followers cheered her on, she crossed the platform, moving her hips to and fro in a ritual dance that she had obviously practiced for some time. She circled the Guardian, letting her hands glide across his chest, her legs entwined with his. Kiran couldn't believe his eyes. *Innocent and pure... Innocent and pure!*

The music picked up tempo and Kail fluttered around the platform, dancing as though in a trance. She ripped her pomander from her neck, and spun around wildly, twirling it in the air, spilling the contents to the floor.

Kiran got a chill, like the first chill of autumn as it chases away the summer warmth. He lifted the cup to his mouth and gulped down the rest of his drink.

The music played on into the night. While the followers danced and drank, for Kiran, the world turned fuzzy. His vision became watery, distorted, like he was looking into a reflection in a stream. He went back to the line to take his third, or was it his fourth, cup of the sour drink; he couldn't remember. He settled into a contentedness, like all his worries had melted away. His eyelids grew heavy as he watched the women dance, their bodies glistening with sweat. The familiar surge of desire came over him and he became consumed by his need—an overwhelming, all-encompassing desire. What had Cartus said? For the Glory of Ani? He knew what he wanted; he had imagined it so many times before. He looked around, searching for her.

He wandered from the main pavilion, down the path to the pools. Stone lamps lined the path, lighting the way. Mesmerized by the soft circles of light on the path, he sat down, running his hands in the sand. He became enchanted with the flickering of shadows cast across the pebbles. He lowered his arm, watching its shadow move across the ground as he swayed back and forth, trying to focus. His arm felt weightless, floating, apart from him, yet he knew it intimately. His attention turned to his hand. He examined each line, each groove, across his palm, then turned his hand over as if seeing it for the first time. Feeling his own fingernails, he tugged at the ends, amazed by the way they attached to his fingers.

He continued down the path toward the river, trying to remember his purpose, now mesmerized by the sounds of his own footsteps, then the sounds of the night, sounds so enchanting it was as though he were hearing them for the first time—night birds twittering, water gurgling, women giggling and moaning, a moaning that caused an ache in his loins.

People were splashing and laughing, their garments strewn aside. In the dark corners, he saw some of the men and women intertwined, naked, moving to their own rhythms. A thought of inhibition surfaced, then drifted away again. He walked on, looking for her.

Then he saw her, stepping from a pool, dripping wet, her short tunic clinging to her body. His gaze followed her as she slipped down a path into the woods. He went after her, wanting her now with a fervor he had never known before.

"Bria," he called. She turned to face him, this creature of his dreams with her intoxicating smile. His desire for her washed over him, not as individual thoughts, but one rolling emotion. He took another step closer. He was inches from her, his heart pounding in his chest. He leaned toward her and she leaned toward him. She teetered sideways, losing her balance. He grabbed her and pulled her to him, burying his face in her hair and the scent of honeysuckle.

They were still for a long moment, her breath on his neck, hot and erratic, melting with his. She raised her face to his and her eyes spoke to him, inviting.

Without thought, guided by instinct and a primal understanding of her surrendering to him, conscious of nothing but the green fire of desire in her eyes, his lips met hers, parted, and the feel of her tongue sent a rush of heat pulsing through his body. He knew—by the slight parting of her lips, by the gentle tilt of her head, then by the way she slid her hand, softly, up his chest and around his neck—that she was feeling as he was, irresistibly drawn, in the moment, flush with passion. He craved her with an undeniable ache and longed for the feel of his hands on her.

She pressed her body against his and they were on the grass, entwined as lovers. It was as if he wasn't a person, but only a merging of feelings, his senses overwhelmed—her scent like the wind, her skin soft and wet, her lips like honey, her tongue sending hot shivers of pleasure through him.

She drew him to her. He slid his hands under her tunic and cupped the soft mound of her breast, warm in his hand. He thought he might die in blissful turmoil as she rolled over and pulled the tunic over her head, tossing it aside. With wild abandon, he pressed his mouth to hers, hungering for her, aching for her with a desire that had been welling up inside him, ready to burst. He couldn't get enough. She eased beside him, tugging his trousers away, and guided him to her, enfolding him. She arched her back, pressing against him, and he cried out with excruciating joy. Together they rocked, building momentum in a rhythm of sheer agony as waves of ecstasy surged through him, each gaining momentum, until one great wave washed over him in a warm, enveloping rush of pleasure. He convulsed, his heart pumping wildly out of control, then collapsed at her side, breathless.

His heartbeat slowed and he sighed with an overwhelming sense of bliss. He was physically exhausted, but his mind still radiated waves of consciousness, with a single pervasive feeling—peace.

When he awoke, he was first aware of the birds singing in the trees, then the sun on his face. He opened his eyes, blinking in the bright sunlight. Butterflies flitted about, from flower to flower, lighting with folded-back wings. He inhaled the scent of honeysuckle and was struck full force by the memory.

Had he really? Bria was draped over him, her head on his bare chest. He bit his lip. Feelings of regret started to creep into his mind. She slowly opened her sleepy eyes and looked up at him. He saw realization dawn. She pulled away as though she had been burned, staring open-mouthed at his naked body.

"What evil is this?" she cried, her face full of contempt. "What have you done?" She leapt to her feet and ran, ripping his heart out as she went.

21

Kiran stumbled through the day in a suffocating haze of shame, the world gone gray, no air left in it. He couldn't eat, couldn't drink. Every moment, he dwelled in uncertainty, his thoughts of her all encompassing. What did she think of him? What would he do? He chewed his fingernails down to bloody stubs and paced in circles. They had committed the greatest sin. There was nothing more sinful than what he had done—even worse than doubting or questioning an Elder. It was strictly forbidden. In the village he would be shunned—or worse. His hand went protectively to his groin. Men had been castrated for taking a woman against her will. What had he been thinking? How could he have done such a thing? He rested his forehead on his knees and covered his head with his arms. He couldn't bare the echo of her voice: *What have you done? What have you done!* He grabbed handfuls of his hair and tugged at his head, but that didn't take away the pain, because the image of her face, covered in loathing, was inside, imprinted on his mind.

When night finally came, he lay sleepless, turning over and over on his bed mat, his mind spinning, the memories of their passion mixed with the horror of his sin. He had wanted her, had taken her. And now he was drowning in remorse, recalling every moment, every detail, each bringing nothing but agony. Had he imagined that she had been so willing? Had he misread her signals? He replayed the scene over and over again in his mind. She had reached for him, had pulled him to her, with eyes full of passion. The memory brought a warm flush of desire. He rolled over, frustrated. She would never forgive him. He had destroyed all chance of a life with her.

A flood of tears, held damned by the presence of his brothers, threatened to burst free. But they couldn't know. He got up from his bed and slipped out the door, seeking fresh air. He dropped to his knees and held his head in his hands. He had to figure out what to do, what penance would suffice, if any, and if he could ever be forgiven. The thought of having destroyed all chance of becoming an Elder was too much to bear. Not only had he lost all chance, he would be punished. And what would the people of his village think of him? And of Bria? Would the Voice even acknowledge them now?

The words of Kalindria haunted him. *You will live in regret.* Maybe she was right? Maybe he should leave? But how could she have known?

No, he couldn't leave. The Voice would come, on the Day of Thunder. It would be his only salvation. He would face the Voice just as he had planned. The Great Father would forgive. Wouldn't He?

Yes, that was it, he decided. To face up to his sin was the only way. Any punishment would be worth enduring if it would relieve the burden of guilt that weighed on him. At first light, he would confess to the Guardian. If he were the one to grant the right, then he had the power to grant forgiveness. Then everything would be all right. He closed his eyes finally, decided.

Once the morning meditations were finished, he abandoned his brothers and strode down the path toward the pavilion. He crossed the bridge and, as soon as he set foot on the mainland, two men blocked his way. "What business do you have?" the one asked.

"I must speak with the Guardian," Kiran said, anxious now.

"Were you summoned?"

"No. I seek his counsel. I need his guidance."

"You can make a request to see him after the general gathering."

"But this can't wait," Kiran said, feeling his nerves come unraveled. "It is most urgent."

The one man looked at the other and frowned. "Wait here." The other man stepped in front of Kiran, his full body blocking the path.

After what seemed an eternity, the first man returned with Angei-Laina. She approached with a gentle smile. "What troubles you this morning, brother?"

He couldn't tell her. What would she think of him? She had been the one to tempt him, so that he might master control. No. Only the Guardian could forgive him. "I need to speak with the Guardian. And…" Tears came to his eyes. "I just need to speak to him."

"Everything will be all right, my brother," she soothed, taking his hands in hers. "But the Guardian is not available right now. You can tell me. I'm sure I can help you."

"No, I will speak only to him!" He ripped his hands from her grasp, pushed past her, and raced toward the pavilion. He ran around the fountain and up the steps and across the platform toward the room behind. He must be there, Kiran thought. He had to speak to him. Now. He threw open the door.

In one stunned moment, Kiran took it all in. Before him, the Guardian lay sprawled in his bed, naked, with three of his Angei, their robes tossed on the floor, soft pillows and blankets strewn about, platters of luscious, half-eaten fruits and meats and empty cups of the sour drink on the table, the air heavy with sweet perfume.

One of the women on the bed glanced up at him with sleepy eyes.

Kiran felt a rush of desire and instant shame. What kind of place is this? He took a step back, his hands dropping to cover himself.

"What is the meaning of this?" the Guardian shouted, rising from the bed, wrapping the sheet around his waist. "What are you doing here?"

Kiran's mouth dropped open, but he had no words. In a blink of utter clarity, he saw the truth as he had never seen it before, twisted and warped out of form. A depraved man stood before him in an ugly stench of sweat. Bile stirred in Kiran's stomach and rose to his throat. The man was nothing but a liar, hiding behind a mask of reverent humility.

Kiran stood taller and looked the man straight in the eyes. It was like looking down a deep, dark well. But something—cold, calculating, threatening to strike—made him draw back, realizing all at once—he was staring into the eyes of a madman. The world shifted, like ice cracking in spring, then shattering beneath him. With those eyes, this man had beguiled and seduced his followers, manipulating them to serve his ego, with no feelings of remorse, no shame, no guilt. It was all a lie.

The two guards burst into the room, their chests heaving, faces red.

The Guardian frowned. "It's about time you got here." They seized Kiran, one gripping his shoulders while the other wrenched his arms behind his back. "Take him outside," the Guardian said, reaching for his robe.

The men whipped Kiran around and shoved him forward, into the pavilion. "Get down," one grunted, forcing him to his knees.

The Guardian stood over Kiran, peering down at him, his eyes blazing. "How dare you enter my private rooms!" he thundered. "For what purpose?"

Kiran bit his lip, trying to get ahold of himself.

"Speak!"

The guard tightened his grip. Kiran winced. "I just needed your guidance."

"On what matter? What could be so urgent?" The Guardian's jaw muscles were stretched taut.

Through clenched teeth Kiran said, "I sought forgiveness."

The Guardian rocked back on his heels. His expression changed in an instant, and with a voice, now calm and controlled, he said, "You must learn patience. For only in time does Ani reveal everything."

Oh, everything has been revealed! Kiran thought, his gut churning.

"Your brothers here will show you the way to cleanse your soul." He motioned for the men to take Kiran away.

Kiran's eyes narrowed and he thrust his lower jaw forward. "But I haven't even told you—"

"Silence!" the guard shouted, shaking him. "You forget your place."

The Guardian leaned in close. "I know what you have done," he hissed, a flame of warning in his eyes. "You are a lost soul. In darkness you shall atone."

Kiran stared back at him, expressionless, the same cold determination in his own eyes. The guards hauled him to his feet. The Guardian stood in the path, blocking his way, looking down on him, making no motion to move. Kiran sidestepped, leaving the path, never taking his eyes from the Guardian as he passed.

The guards took Kiran over the bridge, back to the island, to a shack hidden in the jungle far from the trail. "Wait here," the one grunted, shoving him down a dark stair into a cellar. The door slammed. Then the click of the bolt.

Kiran pounded and kicked at the door. He fell back and hit a solid wall, slick with dampness. The cellar was the size of a closet and smelled of mold. At once, he felt the full weight of the day on his shoulders and it was more than he could carry. His knees buckled and he sank to the muddy floor, letting loose his tears. He curled in a ball and sobbed until every tear was spent and he could cry no more.

Then he waited, listening for someone, anyone, aching for the silence to end. Kalindria had been right. Why hadn't he listened to her? There had been days, long unconscious stretches of time, where he had pushed his doubt aside, had wallowed in the comfort of easy answers, had lost himself in the mind-numbing routine of daily life, of blind dedication, living solely for those moments when he could be in the presence of that man, and dreading being ripped away again. Then something would happen, like seeing Cartus's painted-on smile, or the mindless heads nodding, that nearly got him questioning again. Then there were moments, times when he clearly knew things weren't right, but immediately dismissed his suspicions. Out of what? Out of fear? Out of naivety? Out of denial? Out of some deep desire to have succeeded in the quest?

He had been living in denial, grasping on to the Guardian's words, using them to shield himself from uncertainty the way a child pulls his blanket over his eyes. All the while, the Guardian basked in adoration, putting on a show of piety, his self-delusion fueled by the faith of his followers.

Why didn't I see? Kiran slumped to the floor in the darkened silence.

At last, he thought he heard someone outside the shack. His heart beat faster. A door creaked open and footsteps moved across the floor above. Kiran rapped on the door, beating his fists into the wood. "Let me out!" There was no response.

Soon, there started a rhythmic pounding on the floor above him and the grunts of a man followed by raw moans of pleasure. Kiran slid to the floor and covered his ears. He tried to block it from his mind, but his body responded, tense and tingling, and all he could think of was emerald-green eyes and the scent of honeysuckle. With every thrust he heard, he envisioned her, in sweet agony, until his mind emptied of all thought and his body ached for release. Then, realization came flowing in. All at once, he understood how he had been manipulated. In the baths. At the banquet. He had been caught up in physical desire, riding on the wanton tides, all orchestrated by the Guardian.

Kiran shook with anger. He felt violated, invaded, his soul tarnished. He felt like a fool.

Kiran took a deep breath. He had to get to the others, to tell them.

He went to the door and shook it, trying to knock it from the hinges. He pounded out his frustration on the door. But no one heard.

The day passed into night before the guards returned. They took him through the darkness, back across the bridge, and down a path that ran along the river's edge. Kiran scanned the woods and the trail. He had no idea where they were taking him. In all the time he had been in the Kingdom of the Kotari, he had only been on the island or at the pavilion. He knew nothing of the surrounding area, nothing of the world outside the confines of his daily routine. How had he let that happen? He clenched his jaw, angry with himself for being so complacent.

Finally, they came to the opening of a cave. An old man with a toothless grin sat in a rocking chair just inside the entrance. The man pushed himself out of the chair, lit a torch, and handed it with a white cloth to Kiran and gestured for him to go further inside. Kiran hesitated, glancing back toward the cave entrance. The guards stood there, hands on their hips.

The light of his torch was swallowed by the darkness and he had the sensation the cavern was immense, at least ten times the size of the one he had stayed in with Bria. As he moved toward torches he could see in the distance, black winged creatures darted above his head, emitting high-pitched squeaks. The stale air was heavy with an acrid vapor. His eyes watered and his nostrils burned with each breath. He quickly realized the cloth was to cover his face. He tied it around his neck and adjusted it to cover his nose and mouth.

Five men were at the back of the cave, their faces hidden behind white neckerchiefs.

"What are we to do?" he asked.

One shook his head, glancing toward the old man, a sign to remain silent, and gestured toward a mound of goo on the cave floor. The surface undulated with black beetles. The man handed him a shovel and a canvas bag.

So this is where the fertilizer comes from, he thought.

He soon realized he was standing on a massive pile of excrement. When he dug in with the shovel, the beetles skittered in every direction. The clicking of millions of tiny feet filled the cavern with a whirring buzz. They crawled up his pant legs, their little legs digging into his skin.

There had to be a way to escape. He had to think of a way. He fought the impulse to run from the cave, run as far as his legs would take him. He knew the guards would just haul him back in. No. He would watch every movement, every procedure, learn their habits, their routine, and make a plan.

At dawn, thousands upon thousands of the winged creatures returned to the cave. Kiran put down his shovel and watched in awe as they entered in a massive rush of fluttering wings.

It was also the end of the night's work. The men stowed their shovels and filed out. The guards were waiting. Kiran ripped the cloth from his face, gasping for fresh air. The guards forced the workers to keep their eyes straight ahead on the path back to the island where they were taken to separate quarters. Kiran was locked in the cellar. Alone. Again.

On the second night, he was taken back to the cave. As the men filed to the back, the man in front of him stumbled and dropped his shovel. Kiran reached for the handle just as the man did and their eyes met.

It was Roh.

22

Kiran felt like hugging him he was so relieved, but Roh did not acknowledge him. *Certainly he saw me,* he thought. He followed Roh to the back of the cave and whispered, "We have to find a way out of here."

Roh glanced toward the old man and turned away.

Kiran grabbed his arm. "Roh, listen to me."

"Silence!" yelled the old man.

Roh yanked his arm from Kiran's grasp, gave him a look of warning, and went to work with his shovel.

Kiran stared after him, stunned. *What have they done to him?* He looked different somehow, more like a man. His arms bulged with muscles. But he had become a follower, like the others. Somehow, Kiran had to get through to him.

When they filed into the cave the next night, Kiran watched for his opportunity. The moment came. The other men were several steps ahead. He maneuvered so his back was to the old man and Roh couldn't avoid him. "It's me. Kiran."

Roh grimaced. "I know. Now shut up."

Kiran glanced over his shoulder toward the old man. Roh brushed past him. "There are worse punishments than this cave." Kiran's eyes grew wide. He glanced toward the cave entrance and the guards he knew were there, then back to Roh. With a quick nod, he turned away. They'd have to be careful. Very careful.

He kept his head down and shoveled, the blisters that formed on his palms the only proof of the passage of time.

The guard swung open the cellar door. It was early evening. Too early to go to the cave. Kiran backed into the corner. Had they been found out? The guard grabbed Kiran by the arm. "You're needed in the kitchen."

At the back door to the cookhouse, Kalindria was waiting. She dismissed the guard and Kiran followed her up the trail to the patio.

Pel was there.

Kalindria gestured for Kiran to come closer.

"You were right," he burst. "You won't believe what I—"

"Shhhh," Pel hushed, glancing over his shoulder.

Kiran dropped his voice to a whisper. "I saw. I went to the Guardian to…to talk to him. I saw. It's all a lie. We have to get out of here."

Kalindria nodded. "We've been planning for some time. When you arrived with the raft, well, we knew that was our chance. Pel was able to hide it downriver and we've been stocking it with food, a little everyday. We were going to leave the night of the wedding, but…"

Kiran looked to Pel. "But what?"

"We want you to go with us."

"How?"

Kalindria smiled. "We get off the island by telling the bridge guards we are taking you back to the cave."

"All right, but what about the others?"

Pel shook his head emphatically. "We can't take anyone else. This is our only chance."

Kiran crossed his arms. "I'm not leaving my friends here."

Pel huffed and turned to Kalindria.

"Listen, Kiran," she said. "It's not that simple—"

"Yes, yes it is. I'm not leaving without them. We go together."

Kalindria sighed and sat down on the bench. "We need to think this through."

Pel shuffled over to her. "It's too risky. We've got to go now."

Kalindria looked up at Kiran. "How many?"

"Roh's in the cave. Then there's Bria and Kail and Deke and Jandon. But I don't even know where they are."

"I do," Pel said. "But I can't just go get them all. It will raise suspicion."

Kalindria stood up. "Get who you can. Bring them here. We'll figure something out."

Pel sighed and turned and headed down the trail.

"Let's get a fire going," Kalindria whispered. "In case someone comes by, we'll look like we're working."

Kiran nodded. As he made a pile of sticks, he ran through different possible scenarios.

At last, Pel came up the trail with Deke and Jandon.

Kiran ran to them. "I'm so glad to see you. We need to—"

"Shhhh," Jandon hushed. "You know we are not to speak without cause."

"Listen to me. The Guardian is not what you think. We have to get out of here."

"What are you talking about?"

"You have to trust me. I've seen the truth. We need to go."

Pel faced Deke and Jandon. "This might be our only chance to escape."

"Escape?" Jandon scoffed. "If you want to go, just say goodbye and leave the way you came."

"Just leave?" Pel said with a snort. "It doesn't work that way. If you show any sign of defiance, the guards drag you off to work in the cave." He turned to Kiran. "Tell him."

"It's true. I've been there. And Roh." He turned his hands up to show the blisters.

"But we can't just leave," said Jandon. "We'd be banished to the eternal agony of the tormented souls. We are to stand witness on the Day of Thunder."

Kiran looked at his old friend. His eyes were puffy with fatigue, his shoulders slumping with weariness. "Jandon, don't you see? There is no Day of Thunder. The Guardian made it all up."

Jandon stared at Kiran with blank eyes.

"Listen," Kiran said, putting his hand on Jandon's shoulder. "I'm so tired, I can't think most of the time. After we arrived, I lost all track of time. I feel like I've been living in a fog. I think the Guardian made our lives this way purposefully, so we wouldn't question—"

"We're not supposed to question!"

Deke spoke to Jandon then. "I think they might be right. I've, well, I've had my doubts." He looked at Kiran and heaved a breath. "It's like Roh said. This can't be the dwelling place like the Script described. This isn't the edge of the world."

Jandon spun around. "But I thought… Why haven't you said anything?"

"I haven't seen you until now."

"But why didn't you find me? Why are we still here?"

Deke gave a hint of a shrug and looked away.

Kalindria was right, Kiran thought. If he hadn't seen the lies of the

Guardian with his own eyes, would he be ready to escape? The Kotari were like family, family he never had. And the time in the baths, with Angei-Laina and the other women. Blood rushed to his cheeks. "Have you been to the pools with Angei-Laina?"

A revealing smile spread across Jandon's face.

Deke responded, his face red. "The Guardian has cast a spell. That's the only explanation."

Kiran thought of Bria and cringed with guilt. Maybe Deke was right. Something had taken his mind. The power of his longing had been so intense. It all started when he took the drink. He looked at Kalindria and drew in a sharp breath. He exhaled. Somehow he knew it wasn't her. But why else would he commit such a sin with Bria? He bit his lip. "Deke's right. There must be some kind of spell."

Jandon glared at Kiran. "You always think someone has cast a spell. The witch, now the Guardian."

Kiran's mouth dropped open in disbelief. "You swore you'd never mention the witch!"

Kalindria stepped forward. "The Guardian is a master of deception. All he needs are words."

Pel piped up. "Listen. We don't have much time." He pointed to Deke. "You mentioned a dwelling place. Is that what you sought? No doubt he told you this was it, right? I was looking for a healing fountain," he gestured toward his crooked leg, "for this. He told me it was here, but it was only for the worthy, that I needed to earn entrance by faith. That was over a year ago. Trust me. It's just his way of drawing you in. He tells you what you want to hear. We feed his ego while we go hungry. Well, no more. I'm leaving."

Deke said, "We are with you. All of us. So what's your plan?"

"We go by raft, same way you got here."

"Raft? It took hours to build that raft. I don't know how we could make another one with the kind of trees there are here. And in secret."

"Oh, we don't have to." Pel grinned, his chubby cheeks pocked with dimples. "I hid yours. It's ready to go right now, just downriver."

"But first we have to get Kail and Bria," said Kiran. "And Roh. Do you know where they hold him during the day?"

Kalindria and Pel shook their heads.

"We'll have to get him at the cave. You said you could get past the bridge guards by telling them you are taking someone to the cave, right?"

Kalindria nodded. "But it will never work for all of you. Especially the girls. They don't send girls to the cave."

"All right. You and Kalindria take Deke across the bridge and get Roh. Jandon and I will get the girls. Wait." Kiran paused a moment. "There are guards at the cave too."

Pel glanced at Kalindria, hesitated, then nodded. "We had a plan, in case we had to get you out that way, but—"

"Kail isn't on the island anyway," Jandon said. "She stays with the Guardian now, remember."

Kiran squirmed with the thought of Kail being in that bedroom with him.

"No, that's not necessarily true," Pel said. "The Angei have a house on the island. If they are not chosen to be with the Guardian in the evening, they stay there."

"How do we know for sure?" asked Jandon.

Pel shrugged. "We don't."

Kalindria was shaking her head. "Even if you find the girls, how will you get off the island?"

"We'll have to swim the river to meet you."

"Swim!" Pel said.

"Shhhh." Kalindria glanced down the trail.

Pel shrank. "The current is too strong. You'll drown."

Memories of tumbling in white-water made Kiran's heart race. But he'd done it before and survived. He could do it again. "That's what the Guardian wants you to think."

Jandon shook his head. "I'm not jumping in that river. No way!"

Kiran looked to Deke. He knew he wouldn't do it. He sat down on the bench to think. "Hold on," he said. "Guards keep watch so that no one can leave the island, right?"

"Well, yes, but—"

"So we can easily get *back* on the island."

Pel's eyebrows shot up. "Why would you want to do that?"

"We all go to the cave and free Roh, then he and I will come back for the girls." He turned to Pel. "How were you planning to get past the cave guards?"

"That's the easy part." Pel grinned.

The guards didn't question Kalindria when the group passed over the bridge. Once they got to the cave, she told the guards, "Three more for you," then left to hide in the bushes and wait. Deke and Jandon followed Kiran to the back, looking for Roh.

Pel hobbled in on his crooked leg, smiling and jovial. "Good evenin', brothers." The old man frowned, gesturing for silence. "For you, sir, a special brew from Kalindria," he said with a wink, handing the old man a cup. "Bottoms up." The man accepted the cup, flashing Pel a toothless grin. He drained it down and promptly burped. "Sit, old man, I have news." Pel led him to the rocker, whispering in his ear.

The workers turned from their work, their eyes on Pel. The old man's eyes fluttered, then he slumped in his chair. Pel gave him a nudge. The man did not wake.

Kiran searched the group of men, their faces hidden behind neckerchiefs. "Roh?"

Roh tore the cloth from his face. "I'm here."

Deke stepped up. "You were right. It's all a lie. We're getting you out of here."

Another worker, taller and older than Roh, stepped forward. "This talk is blasphemy."

Deke took a step back. His mouth clamped shut.

Roh stepped between them. "If you don't like it, go back to shoveling then."

The worker stared at Roh for a long moment. Then, with a huff, he turned, shovel in hand, and headed for the back of the cave. The other men stood around, staring.

"And that goes for the rest of you. If you want to stay here, that's your business."

Another man hesitated, his eyes going back and forth from the older man to Roh. He picked up his shovel. The remaining men shuffled away.

"No time to chat," Pel said. He turned to Deke and yelled, "Oh yeah, make me! You big oaf! Think you can push me around. I'll teach you a lesson!"

The guards appeared at the cave entrance. "What's going on in here?"

Kiran handed Roh a bag and gave him a nod that said trust me.

Pel pounced on Deke, pummeling him with his fists.

The guards charged forward. One grabbed Pel by the arm, the other reached for Deke. Roh and Kiran lunged from behind, shoving the bags over the guards' heads. The men bucked and wrestled. Kiran was slammed to the ground. Jandon was there with a shovel. He clobbered the guard in the head, knocking him out cold. Jandon swung around and walloped the other guard. The man dropped to the floor with a thump. Kiran and Deke stared in disbelief.

"Well, all right then," said Roh, slapping Jandon on the back.

"Let's go, let's go," urged Pel on his way out of the cave.

Kiran grabbed a torch and hurried after him, his heart pounding in his chest.

"We need to tie up these guards so they can't follow us," said Roh.

"Go on, brother," a man said. They spun around. He leaned on his shovel. "I wish I could go with you, but my wife won't speak of it. I'll take care of them. Good luck to you."

Roh nodded in thanks and they turned and ran. Kiran led Roh toward the bridge.

Once they were down the trail, far from the cave, Kiran stopped to catch his breath. "We have to get the girls. Then we swim to meet the others with the raft." His hand went to his forehead. "Oh no, I just remembered. I hid the scroll on the island. We can't leave it."

"We'll have to swim with it then," Roh said, his brow knit in thought. "Wait here." He took the torch from Kiran and disappeared in the thick jungle. Kiran was instantly engulfed in darkness and the croaking of night bugs. His heartbeat throbbed in his ears until Roh finally returned. He had an empty bag from the cave. "This should work."

Kiran's feet seemed to find every hole and root in the path as he ran. The Pyletar bounced against his chest. Bria's Pyletar. He slowed to a stop. Roh turned and came back to him.

"I think this is the back side of the pavilion," Kiran whispered. They could hear splashing and the giggles of women. "Bria's on the island. But Kail might be with the Guardian tonight, in his private room."

"How did that happen?"

Kiran turned. "How long were you in the cave?"

"Since we arrived."

Kiran's mouth dropped open. "I'll ah, I'll tell you later. Anyway, we may be able to see. There's a back patio and fenced pool."

Roh gave Kiran a questioning stare.

"I, ah, kind of barged in. That's how I ended up in the cave."

Roh grinned. He stuck the torch in the sand and started into the tangle of trees. Once they found the fence, they crouched behind it, trying to see between the slats. The Guardian and three of the Angei were in the pool together, drinking and laughing.

"I don't see Kail, do you?" Roh whispered.

Kiran shook his head. Roh pushed away from the fence and motioned for Kiran to follow. Kiran hesitated, looking once more. How could they be sure? What if she were inside the room, out of sight? There would be no way to come back for her.

As expected, the guards did not question them as they crossed over the bridge. Once on the island, Kiran pulled Roh into the shadows.

"We need to split up." He swallowed hard. He slipped the Pyletar over his head. "Will you get Bria? I'll find Kail."

"I figured you'd—" Roh hesitated. "Yes, I can get Bria."

"Give this to her, please," he said, handing the Pyletar to Roh. "Maybe it will remind her of, of home."

Roh nodded with understanding and took the Pyletar. Kiran told him where the scroll was hidden. "We'll meet there," Roh said and slipped into the bushes.

Kiran found the house Pel had described and slipped in through the door without making a noise. It was built just like House Four. But unlike the mats on which he and his brothers slept, here were actual bunks. He crept through the room, straining his eyes in the dark to make out faces until he came upon a bunk with a swirl of blond hair. With relief, he kneeled next to her and gently shook her awake, whispering in her ear. "Kail. It's Kiran. Wake up. We need to talk."

She rolled over. "What's the matter? What's wrong?"

"It's important. Please come outside with me." He grabbed her arm and tugged her up.

"Hold on. You aren't allowed in here. And don't call me Kail," she said, yanking her arm from his grasp.

His eyes whipped around the room. He had to think fast and grabbed at the first thought that came to mind. "It's Bria," he whispered. "She needs you."

Kail got up from the bed and followed him out.

Once outside, under the light of the moon, he saw the bright red star on her forehead. He swallowed hard. "Listen, Kail, we have to go, we have to leave the Kotari now."

"What are you talking about? Have you lost your mind?"

"Don't you see? Things aren't right here."

"What is wrong with you, waking me in the middle of the night with this kind of talk? It is blasphemy!"

"But haven't you had doubts and—"

"Doubts? The Guardian is Ani incarnate, manifest as the wise man of true flesh and blood."

Kail had changed. Her posture, her demeanor—everything was different. She was stronger, more confident. She was no longer the scared, helpless girl he had comforted on the mountain.

"But this isn't how the Script described the dwelling place. This isn't the edge of the world."

Her eyes narrowed. "I see what's going on. You're jealous. You thought you'd be the one and you can't accept that it's me." She threw her shoulders back. "I am the pure vessel. I will bear the child and he will reign."

Kiran took a step back, unable to hide his shock. "So, you've... But Kail! The Elders would—" As soon as the words left his mouth, he faltered, sinking in his own guilt.

"The Elders? Stuffy old men with misguided, old-fashioned ways. What do they know?"

Kiran was trembling now. Hadn't he said the same things to Bria that night in the meadow? Hadn't he felt the same frustrations? And he too had given in to them.

"I know now why I was chosen. The Guardian has shown me the way. By his authority, I have been wed to Ani, for the glory of the Kingdom. This is what I was born to do." She paused, then a smile came to her face and she looked at him now with the motherly expression of the Angei. "Kiran, you need to learn your place. I pity you, always questioning. Why can't you see? Look around. No drought. No famine. This is the true dwelling place and we are to become Receivers of the Light. You need to learn patience. Now go back to bed and get some sleep."

"Listen to me," he said. "The Guardian is using you for sex. All the Angei. The Guardian has had us all fooled!"

"No, you are the fool!" she screamed, her eyes blazing. All at once, he could see; there was no way he'd be able to persuade her to go. Kail had embraced the word of the Guardian, from the first moment, without question. "You have gone too far. This kind of talk is forbidden. You must repent! Kneel right now. I'm calling for Angei-Ami." She started toward the bunkhouse.

"No, no, Kail. I'm sorry," he said, panicked. If she alerted the Angei now, they'd all be caught and he'd be sent back to the cave. He lunged for her, grabbing her by the arm. "You are right, forgive me. I have had a moment of weakness. Please, do not report me."

"But you must learn to obey!" She yanked her arm from his grasp and ran into the bunkhouse, shouting, "Blasphemer!"

He stumbled backward. No. *She can't do this. This can't be happening!* He spun around, facing the shadows. He threw back his head and ran, thrashing through the jungle, his feet pounding out the panic in his heart. Then a bolt of fear stopped him cold. What if Bria wouldn't go? All the air was sucked from his lungs. Kiran gasped for breath. He shuddered and took off running again, running with all he had. He ran so fast he couldn't think. He didn't want to think. The thought was too much to bear.

When he got to the rocky beach, out of breath, he saw two figures in the dark. Roh and Bria were already there. He wanted to throw his arms around her he was so relieved, but held back. He couldn't bear to look her in the eye. But he saw, around her neck, she wore the Pyletar.

He went straight to the rock pile and pushed the stones aside. The scroll was gone. "I've already got it," said Roh, holding the bag out to him. "Where's Kail?"

"She wouldn't listen to reason. She's completely under his spell." He took a breath. "We have to go without her."

Roh nodded as though he had expected the news.

Bria looked in a daze of shock, her eyes wide. "We can't."

Shouts came out of the darkness. "Blasphemers!"

Kiran took Bria by the hand. "I'm sorry. We have no other choice."

She bit her lip and nodded. Together, they plunged into the dark, churning river.

winged creatures live in
caves, add droppings
to soil to grow
crops

stay to the river
Do not drink from it!

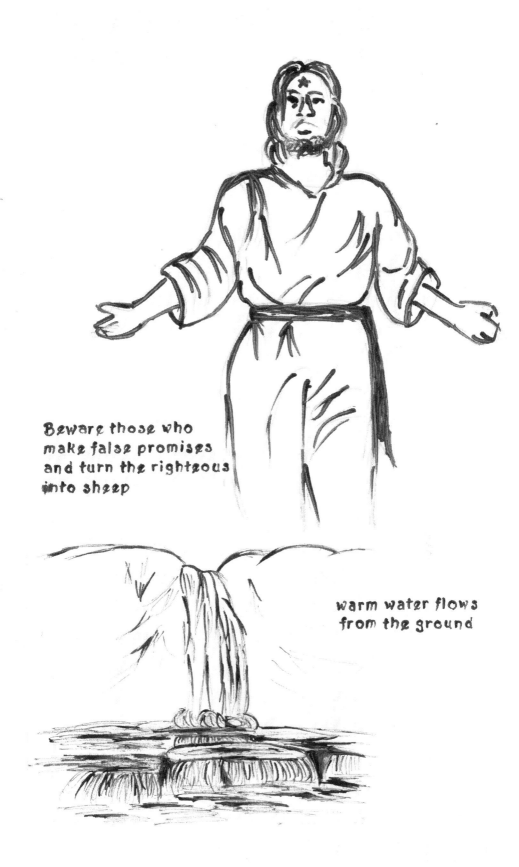

Beware those who
make false promises
and turn the righteous
into sheep

warm water flows
from the ground

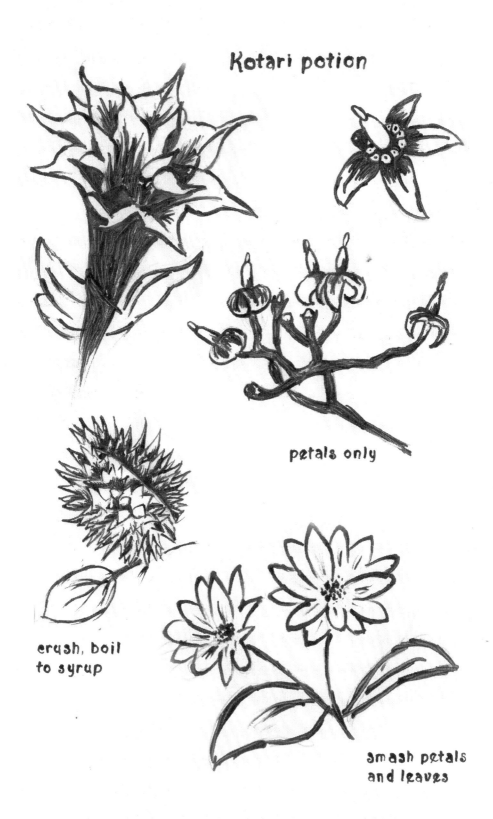

Kotari potion

petals only

crush, boil
to syrup

smash petals
and leaves

Book Four

Three things cannot be long hidden:
the sun, the moon, and the truth.
~Buddha

23

Kiran had forgotten the sheer power of the river. With one hand gripping the bag, he struggled to stay with Roh and Bria as he was tossed about in the frothy waves. When finally Jandon and Deke came along side them with the raft, Kiran could barely keep his head above water, but he made sure Bria was safely aboard before taking Jandon's hand and being hauled on board.

"Where's Kalindria?"

Pel shook his head. "She wouldn't get on the raft. Said her destiny was in another direction."

In one swift movement, Roh pulled himself out of the water and onto the raft. "Who's Kalindria?"

"The escape was her idea," Kiran explained. To Pel he said, "So you just left her?"

"She's a stubborn woman. I know that. She made me promise not to leave without you, though."

Jandon scanned the dark river. "Where's Kail?"

Kiran heaved a sigh. "She's gone to us."

"Gone?"

"She wouldn't come. Her mind is set to stay with the Guardian. She has been marked with the star. And she believes she is with child."

Jandon's mouth dropped open. "With child? But she had the pomander!"

Bria shook her head. "With child?"

"I couldn't convince her," Kiran said. "I tried."

Roh wiped water from his face. "Nothing could protect her from herself."

Deke shook his head and muttered, "Well, she's spoiled now anyway."

Bria winced. Kiran's stomach tightened and he had to look away. His hands curled into fists. He imagined shoving Deke into the frothy water and holding his arrogant head under.

Kiran glanced at Roh. He was staring at Deke, rage in his eyes, his jaw set, his hands twisting a bit of rope to the point of breaking. Kiran looked at Deke, then back to Roh, confused.

As they floated downriver, the full moon and stars became lost in the thick canopy. Keeping the raft in the center of the raging river in the black of night was not easy. The others kept quiet as Deke and Jandon worked the poles.

When dawn finally broke, misty sunlight fluttered through leafy branches high above the river. Spiky leaves, broad leaves, stalks of long, slender leaves, all grew together, intertwined in variegated shades, twisted with vines. It was as though they were traveling through a steamy hot tunnel of green. Overhanging branches reached out and dipped into the river, stirring the water into white foam.

Birds chattered away above, although they were too difficult to spot. Occasionally they'd catch a glimpse of color as some exotic bird darted across the river.

The water was a deep, rich green—the color of Bria's eyes. At least the way Kiran remembered them. She wouldn't look at him. She sat on the edge of the raft, gazing toward the shoreline. Kiran wanted to know what she was thinking, what she was feeling. Would she ever speak to him again? What should he say to her? Deep down he was scared to speak to her at all for fear of acknowledging their sin. Maybe if they never did, somehow it wouldn't be real, and they could go on, like nothing had happened.

But how could life ever be the same? Now, he ached for her all the more. The slightest look from her, brushing against her, her hair fluttering in the wind, was all it took to fill his head with images of her naked body and get his heart pumping.

"What an adventure!" Pel whooped, breaking the silence, his eyes like a child. "I've never been on a raft before. It's like being carried on eagles' wings."

Roh smirked. "Yeah, something like that."

"So, we just go with the flow of the river and let it take us wherever it may go?" he said, digging in one of the bags.

"Our packs," Kiran said.

"Yes, I told you," said Pel. "Everything is here. And we are well stocked."

Kiran reached inside his pack for his hat. With a flick of his wrist, it popped back into shape and, with a grin, he flipped it onto his head.

Pel handed Bria an orange fruit.

Bria took it from him, caution in her eyes. Pel handed pieces of fruit all around. "Doesn't it feel great to be liberated?" He flopped back on his elbows, ripping into a juicy yellow fruit. He sprang back up. "We should celebrate," he said, his face lit up with a smile. "Too bad I didn't pack any of Kalindria's special drink. Now, that was quite a party, eh?" He winked at Jandon. "That was a rare occasion, I'll have you know. The Guardian must have felt dissension in the Kingdom. Good thing he didn't catch on. Ha! We've made it!" He drew in a long breath. "Ah, the smell of freedom!"

Thoughts seemed to come to him like bubbles to the surface, bursting into being. He turned and said to Bria, "You sure are a pretty one. I'm surprised the Guardian didn't set his sights on you."

Bria's eyes grew large.

"All right. We've heard enough," Kiran said through clenched teeth. "We've left and that's all that matters.

"Sure, sure," said Pel with a shrug. He looked at Kiran, then back at Bria. " Uh huh. Hm. Well, I'm thirsty," he declared, sitting up and slapping his thighs.

"Here." Deke leaned over the side to fill a waterskin in the river.

Bria looked at the stack of foodbags on the raft. "You packed all this food but didn't fill the waterskins?"

"Thanks, friend," Pel said to Deke with a grin, taking the waterskin from him. He looked to Bria. "I couldn't. The drinking pool is not on the island. You have to go over the bridge, and it's always guarded." He lifted the waterskin to take a drink.

Kiran grabbed his arm. "We were warned not to drink from the main river. Only the small streams."

"Don't listen to him," said Deke. "He heeds the words of a savage."

Pel paused, looking at Kiran as though assessing his judgment. He handed the waterskin back to Deke. "I prefer to err on the side of caution."

"Suit yourself," said Deke, shrugging his shoulders. He tipped up the waterskin and took a draught of the water and sighed, a long drawn out "ahhhhh" to emphasize his pleasure.

Pel grabbed the waterskin back from him. With his fingernail, he made a long scratch along the side. Deke looked at him with confusion. "So that I may know which is yours," Pel said, handing it back to him, "and I don't drink from it."

Kiran smiled.

From high in the treetops came the low, guttural bellow of the lost souls, so loud, so intense, Kiran could feel it rumble in his chest. He shrank back, his eyes darting to the green canopy above, a shiver running through him.

"Lost souls," cried Bria, her eyes wide.

"That's just the monkeys," said Pel, popping a nut in his mouth.

Kiran looked at Pel with surprise. "That's what Kalindria told me."

"It's true."

"Who's Kalindria?" Bria asked.

"She's the woman who helped us escape. She works in the kitchen," Kiran told her, distracted by a flood of unfamiliar feelings. "I helped her make the drink for the party. She used to be a Javinian."

"A Javinian?"

He had everyone's attention now.

"Yeah, she used to be. But she said she had to leave." He paused, thinking back to their conversation. "She knew things too. She knew Aldwyn."

"Why would she be with the Kotari?" Bria asked.

Pel answered, "The Kotari are folks from all races and lands, people who felt cast out or unwanted, seekers. Everyone there is from somewhere else."

"Yes, I understand that. But why did she leave the Javinians?"

Kiran shrugged. Had she been unwanted, like him? Is that why he felt at home with the Kotari?

"Look," Pel said, pointing into the forest. Clustered on the crook of a tree were seven dark-furred creatures, their faces shiny black, with round brown eyes and soft, stubby noses. One pursed its lips into an O and let out a long, ululating call.

Kiran stared in wide-eyed wonder. "She was right."

"They are so cute," Bria cooed.

The monkeys followed the raft as it glided downriver, swinging from branch to branch, grabbing hold with human-like hands, using their long tails to steady themselves.

Without warning, the sky seemed to open and rain fell in a torrent, coming in sheets so thick they couldn't see across the river. Water poured from Kiran's hat and ran down his back. They dragged the raft to shore.

Kiran grabbed a waterskin and tried to catch it. The water splashed around the small opening. Little went in.

"Hey, look at this," Jandon hollered. He had a giant leaf held over his head, a palm frond he had tugged from its stem.

Kiran grabbed the other waterskins. "Roll the end," he shouted over the pounding of raindrops. "Like a funnel!" Together, they filled the waterskins and everyone gulped their fill of fresh water.

With his knife, Roh cut more of the large fronds. Kiran found some branches and they tied the leaves together, creating a shelter. With a little effort, they were able to fasten it to the raft, one of the leaves turned downward for collecting rainwater, and they were back on the river.

As soon as the rain stopped, Kiran anticipated relief from the heat, but the air turned steamy and the humidity hung thick in his mouth.

They floated down the river hoping for more rain that did not come. The air remained sticky wet, a stagnant, humid heat that oozed from the green depths. Nothing dried here. Everything they had was soggy and smelling of mildew. Their wet clothing clung to them. Occasionally, they'd find a puddle of water, held cupped in a leaf, but it was usually only enough for one or two of them to wet their mouths. There was never enough to refill their waterskins. They became ever watchful for side streams.

As they drifted deeper and deeper into the jungle, plants and vines with leaves in all shapes and sizes grew entwined around enormous trees, merging with their branches into an endless expanse of impenetrable green with no horizon and scant glimpses of the sky. After three days, they could no longer find the sun and lost all sense of direction in the chaos. They were at the mercy of the capricious river, twisting and turning through this foreign landscape.

By day, the forest was silent, showing no sign of inhabitants whatsoever, human or otherwise. They had assumed, in the thick of wilderness, there would be animals to hunt. They even tried their hand at fishing, but were unable to catch even a single fish. They soon realized that any food that may be available in the jungle was out of reach, high atop the trees in the canopy, where they could see the monkeys feasting, but could not reach themselves. At ground level, there was nothing to harvest.

The only creatures in abundance were the buzzing insects that came out in droves at dusk, swarming around their heads, getting in their mouths and nostrils. When the high-pitched Eeeeee-Eeeeeeee of the night bugs started, they knew it was time to make camp. If a sandbar couldn't be found, they'd push through tangles of branches for high ground.

Kiran dreaded the night. He would lie wrapped in his damp bedroll, listening to the cacophony of nocturnal creatures, every sense alert. Over the incessant chitter of countless insects, he'd hear low, guttural growls and thumps that raised the hair on his neck. Then a high-pitched shriek would slice through the night, piercing through the din of the jungle, and all life would halt in a deathlike silence, waiting in breathless anticipation. Then the bugs would ease back into a slow, steady hum. By the time morning finally came, with the nerve-wracking cries of the monkeys, he was thankful to get back on the raft again.

Kiran had no idea what to do about Bria. In the past, she had always been more reserved around the others than when they were alone, but now she was even more distant and withdrawn. She slumped where she sat. He tried not to stare, but couldn't help himself. She would chew her food, stopping to stare off into the distance, a look of regret in her eyes. He wanted so much to tell her how sorry he was. He ached to see her smile, to hear her contagious, uninhibited laughter. He thought he might drown in her sorrow.

His only consolation was Pel's effervescent optimism. The boy's uninhibited nature was infectious. He regaled them with tales of faraway places. He told them of giants covered from head to toe with shaggy white hair who lived in the snow-capped mountains and came down to surrounding villages once a year to steal babies from their cribs. He went on about a tribe of hunters, men with enormous genitalia who tossed their wives and daughters off cliffs, sacrificing them to their gods. He talked of man-size bats that lived in forests like these, creatures that would creep into a hut at night, tiptoeing on their hind legs, and climb onto their sleeping prey, sinking their fangs into their victim's flesh without waking them, sucking their blood dry.

Kiran wasn't sure what to make of his stories. Pel knew more about the world than he did, that was for sure, but was he just telling stories to keep them entertained? He certainly had a knack for drama; everything seemed exaggerated. Still, Pel spoke with conviction, as though he had witnessed these events first hand.

Jandon followed every word, quaking. Bria ignored him altogether and Roh tolerated him with the same amused grin he always wore.

When Pel started on about sea creatures that talk, Deke scowled and with a harrumph said, "Pel, I believe you could very well be the best teller of tales I've ever met."

Pel stopped mid-sentence and looked at Deke. "Hey, before we left, you mentioned a dwelling place at the edge of the world. What did you mean?"

"Well, *we*, Pel, are not on some fairytale adventure. We seek the Voice of the Father who dwells on the far side of the world, near the sea."

"The voice near the sea. Do you mean the Oracle?"

Kiran piped up. "The Oracle?"

"Yes, She who is all-knowing. Everyone seeks Her guidance at some point."

"She lives by the sea?" Kiran asked.

"Oh, yes. She is sought by men the world over for her prophecies. You should see Her palace. Oooooh. It's much more luxurious than the Guardian's. And Her court of priestesses." He raised his eyebrows. "Well, they are fine to look at." He glanced at Jandon and they shared a knowing nod.

"This Oracle is a woman?"

"Is She ever."

Deke made an exaggerated eye roll and turned his back to Pel.

"How do you know this?" Kiran urged.

"I used to live there," he said, matter-of-factly. "Well, not with the Oracle, but in the city. It's really a long story, I—"

"You lived by the sea?" Kiran interrupted. "On the edge of the world? Facing the setting sun?"

"Uh huh. Oh look!" he pointed, jabbing in the air with gleeful enthusiasm. "Pull over! Pull the raft ashore."

Roh and Kiran looked at each other and shrugged. They pushed the poles against the river bottom and the raft glided to the shoreline. Pel leaped from the raft and darted into the leafy jungle. The others waited, uncertain what to think as he disappeared from view, thrashing through the brush.

Kiran leaned over to Roh and whispered in his ear, "Do you think he tells the truth? About the Oracle?"

"I don't know," Roh whispered back. "I was wondering if he ever shuts up."

They waited, staring into the tangle of green.

Bria scratched her face, red and swollen with bug bites.

Finally, Pel burst from the foliage, arms loaded with leafy branches.

"What the blazes are you doing?" grumbled Deke.

"Oh, you'll thank me," Pel said with a mischievous grin. He dropped the branches into a pile on the raft. "Off we go," he said with a flick of his wrist. "Onward."

Roh shook his head in disbelief and shoved the raft back into the current.

Pel plopped down on the raft and started plucking the leaves from the branches. He shoved a few leaves in his mouth and chewed. "Bria, would you kindly find a pouch?"

Bria nodded, reaching for the packs, keeping an eye on him as though she didn't know what he might do next.

"Here, try these," Pel said, handing Kiran a handful of leaves.

"I really want to hear more about the city by the sea," Kiran said, uninterested in the leaves.

"Sure, sure. Whatever. But first, give these a try." His eyes grew bright. "Go on now."

Kiran held the leaves in his open palm, examining them. They were thin, oval-shaped, almost opaque with a green tint. He put one leaf in his mouth and chewed. It had a pleasant, pungent taste.

"Go on now, all of them," Pel said. "Trust me, you'll like it. I call these Kiki leaves. They give you a…" He thought for a moment, looking up out of the corner of his eye. "A cheerful mental lucidity," he said with a grin. "Chewing these leaves can stave off your thirst."

"I don't know why you're so stubborn," Deke said. "There is water all around us."

Kiran took one look at Deke and shoved the rest of the leaves in his mouth. As he chewed, a pleasurable numbness filled his mouth, easing the gnawing thirst. "Tell me more about your home, the city by the sea," he said to Pel.

"You like the kiki leaves?"

Kiran nodded.

"So, what do you want to know?"

"Everything. The city. The Oracle."

"There's not much to tell, really."

"Why did you leave?"

Pel clamped his mouth shut and turned away. For the first time since Kiran had met him, Pel had nothing to say.

At last, they came upon a shallow, muddy rivulet, oozing from the bank. Pulling the raft to the shore, they disembarked and tried to walk along the shoreline back to the spring. The entire forest floor was spongy and rotten, the top layer dark, rich compost. Long, flat liana criss-crossed their path, sharp thorns protruding at every angle, snagging on their clothing and cutting their skin. They dipped and twisted to avoid the spiny vines.

At the spring, Kiran brought cupped hands to his lips. "It's bitter," he said, his face screwed up in a pucker.

"Bitter?" asked Pel. "I know what to do. Wait here." Once again, he disappeared into the thick tangle of vegetation, thrashing through the underbrush. He emerged with an armload of branches. He dropped to his knees and dug in the mud with his bare hands. Cramming the leafy branches into the mud, he made a small dam where the water formed a tiny puddle, the sediment settling to the bottom.

"How do you know all this? How to get the water, about the Kiki leaves?"

Pel shrugged.

"This is good," Roh said. "Let's make camp here. We can drink our fill, then leave in the morning with full waterskins."

They agreed and spread out, trampling down the foliage to make a comfortable camp and a short path back to the raft. Roh and Pel carried packs and dropped them in the center of the clearing. Deke helped but had to stop, coughing and out of breath. He sat down next to the packs, sweat dripping from his forehead and chin, his face ashen.

"Are you all right?" Roh asked.

"Yeah, yeah. It's nothing, just the heat."

Roh started a fire from sodden wood and they stood around as it sputtered to life. Pel offered a sack of nuts.

Jandon rubbed his stomach. "At least with the Kotari we had hot food."

Bria gave Jandon an eye roll. "I'll be right back," she said, turning to head into the jungle.

"It's not a good idea to wander off," Pel warned. "You should stay close."

She stopped, hands on her hips. Then she turned and slipped through the foliage, out of sight.

Jandon watched her go, then stepped next to Kiran. "What's going on between you two?"

"What do you mean?"

"What do I mean? Are you kidding? The tension is enough to strangle a cat."

Kiran swallowed and looked away. Roh was down the path toward the raft, trying to get his attention. Using the Lendhi hunting sign to stay quiet, he motioned toward an unsuspecting animal, grazing in the underbrush downriver about fifty feet. It was nearly as big as a yearling lamb. An animal that size would provide food for them for days.

Roh eased to a crouch, reaching for the knife in his boot. Suddenly a giant snake dropped from a tree branch and sank its teeth into the neck of the wild beast. The animal reared back, squealing. He grunted and bucked as he fought to get loose, but the hold of the snake was too strong. The creatures tumbled over one another in a grisly struggle, the beast flopping on the slippery riverbank as the nearly twenty-foot long snake slowly but methodically wrapped itself around him.

Within moments, the snake had itself completely coiled around the beast and locked in a death hold, slowly strangling him in a mass of blood and mud. Kiran cringed with horror as the beast gasped for his last breath.

"I'm sleeping on the raft!" Pel said, scooping up his pack and running for the raft.

"Agreed!" The boys said in unison, grabbing their belongings.

"Hold on!" shouted Kiran. "Bria, where's Bria?" A shiver of terror shot through him.

"Right here," she said, emerging from the tangle of leaves, brushing at her sleeves. "I've never seen so many bugs. What's all that noise?"

She looked around, searching for the source. Her gaze stopped on the snake. Her eyes grew wide and her mouth dropped open.

"Get on the raft!" Kiran shouted.

Bria's eyes shifted to Kiran and she nodded, grabbed her pack, and launched into a dead run.

They shoved the raft from the shore and piled on, tossing their packs in a heap in the center.

"Have you ever seen anything like that?" Kiran asked Pel, his arms shaking as he shoved off with the pole.

Pel shook his head, his face gone pale.

"From now on, we stay on the raft. Only stop on sandbars."

"Oh no," said Deke.

Kiran turned to look at him. He had his hand to his nose, blood oozing out. "What happened? Did you bump your nose?"

"No," he said. "I don't know."

Bria handed him a cloth from her pack. "Are you feeling all right?"

"No, I…" He looked at the other boys. "I just have a headache. It's nothing."

Bria put her hand to his forehead. "You're burning up."

Deke swatted her hand away. "Leave me be, girl!"

"Heads up," said Roh, digging his pole in the muddy river bottom, bringing the raft to a stop. "Which way do we take?"

There was a fork in the river ahead. To the right, the jungle closed in on itself, forming a tunnel of darkness. Puffs of steamy air swirled on the surface of the water like the warm breath of a giant, living beast.

"To the left looks like the main branch," Roh said.

"But which goes in the direction of the setting sun?" Jandon asked. "I can't tell."

"I think we go to the right," said Bria. "The Script said to take the way less traveled, remember?"

"Uh uh! That's the Forest of the Widhu," said Pel, shaking his head. "No way am I going that way. They are bloodthirsty cannibals. They'll cut off your heads!"

"The Widhu? What are you talking about?" asked Kiran.

"Only danger that way. Trust me. They bite you with their fangs, injecting deadly venom that makes your insides burn up and you slowly suffocate to death. Or they hunt you down and chop off your head. That's how they steal your soul! No way. I'm not going that way." He crossed his arms. The Torans looked to each other. "And that's not all. There are fish with mouths full of razor sharp teeth. If they get the scent of one drop of blood, they attack in a frenzy, and bite by bite, they eat you alive, right down to your bones."

"Why didn't you mention this before?" Kiran asked.

Deke spoke then. "He didn't mention it because it's not true. There is no need to argue or debate. The Great Father has declared His will clearly in the Script of the Legend, as it is told: *Alas, you will be faced with a crossroads; Choose the way less traveled.* We, as faithful Torans, know that the Script is the absolute, authoritative Law. We do not challenge it. It is our duty to follow where the Father leads.

"We cannot let ourselves be paralyzed by fear, though some have wandered from true faith and forgotten that His watchful eye is ever upon us." He glared at Kiran. "At every turn, we have been tested— tested by the savages of the plains, by the raging river, by the tyranny of the Guardian. Now our faith is tested once again—not by the wicked, though we must beware, and not by temptation, though we have learned there are many in this world—but by the face of fear." He glared at Pel. "We must move forth despite it.

"And so," he paused to cough, "our path is clear. It is not for us to determine which direction we take; it is to decide whether or not we follow the Great Father or wallow in faithlessness. This is our path, and to deny it is to deny His authority. So, let us go forth, for our destiny is before us, as was foretold."

Kiran sat back. Deke was right. There was no question which way to go. And who was truly the leader. Deke's faith was strong, unwavering, and he acted with steadfast devotion. *He's the Seventh Elder. He must be,* Kiran thought. "I'm with Deke," he said.

Jandon nodded and Bria did, too. Roh simply shrugged in acquiescence and, using the long pole, shoved the raft back into the current.

"Hold on!" shouted Pel. "Let me off the raft!"

"You want us to leave you here? Alone?" Roh asked.

"Anything is better than going that way." He shuddered, his eyes bulging.

Roh eased the raft to the bank.

Pel's eyes shot back and forth from Roh to the riverbank.

"Well?" Roh said. Everyone else stared, waiting.

Pel jumped off the raft and scrambled up the muddy bank.

Roh stuck the pole in the side to push off. "No, no, no!" hollered Pel. "Don't go!" He plunged into the river to get back on the raft. "Listen to me. Listen to reason! It's too dangerous to go that way."

"Well, that's the way we're going," Deke said and nodded to Roh.

Roh pushed out again. Pel plopped down on the edge of the raft, his arms crossed. "Fine, but mark my words."

As they eased toward the right branch of the river, Bria rearranged their packs so they would be able to sleep while underway. Deke sat straight-backed, facing forward while Jandon lay on the back of the raft, staring up at the clouds, his fingers trailing through the water. Roh deftly maneuvered the raft, eyes in constant motion on the river ahead for danger.

Around them, the forest was deathly silent. The only sound that could be heard was the sucking noises Pel made as he chewed on his lower lip.

24

Deke took the pole from Kiran as they entered the channel. The current slowed, the river widened, and its surface turned smooth. Towering trees jutted straight up out of the water and formed a ceiling of leaves high above the river where a few tiny shafts of sunshine filtered through, lighting the dark chamber with a pale sepia, the mist rising like smoke from the sacred incense. In an instant, Kiran was back in the Temple, Old Horan murmuring: *Someone must go.*

"This is creepy," said Jandon, his eyes in constant motion as he rose to take the pole from Roh. A warm fog enveloped them in the muted murmurings of the jungle and the scent of stagnant mud. Spider webs dripped from dead tree branches, thick with moisture. "Are you sure this is the way, Deke? I've got a bad feeling about this." Stillness surrounded them, a palpable calm, as if some silent predator lurked within the dense foliage at the edge of the river.

Deke coughed, a heavy, raspy hacking from deep in his lungs. "Of course, I'm sure," he said in a hoarse whisper, then coughed again, trying to clear his throat.

He and Jandon eased the raft along on the floor of water, navigating around the sprawling tree trunks, leaving an inky-black path through swirls of green algae.

"Look," Jandon whispered, tugging on Kiran's tunic, "Look there." He pointed into the tangle of foliage that hung at the shoreline.

Kiran saw nothing but green leaves. "What is it?"

"A face. In the woods. Didn't you see him?"

Kiran looked again. "No, I don't see anything."

"But it was just there. I swear it."

"I told you," Pel piped in. "This place is nothing but evil."

Deke said to Jandon, "Your imagination has gotten the better of you. There is nothing there. There's not even a sound in the forest. It's dead calm."

"But…" Jandon kept scanning. "I was sure I saw something."

Deke glared at Pel. "So how did you hear of these headhunters, anyway? Have you ever seen them yourself?"

"Huh?" said Pel, twitching. "Well, no. But everybody knows to stay out of the swamp."

"Uh huh." Deke nodded. "And the fountain you mentioned, the one you were seeking to heal your leg. Did you ever find it?"

"No, I told you."

"And how did you hear about that?" Deke asked, his eyes fixed on Pel.

Pel squirmed under his gaze. "Well, I just heard about it. I don't remember how exactly. Everyone talks, you know."

"Uh huh," said Deke, nodding, a fake smile on his face.

"I don't care what you think. I'm going to find it someday." He looked over his shoulder. "If I get out of here alive,"

Deke launched into another fit of coughing.

As the day wore on, Kiran could not shake an uneasy feeling. He scanned the riverbank as they floated past, trying to spot anything threatening amid the shadows. Jandon was right. They were being watched. He was sure of it.

Deke asked Pel to take the pole, complaining of a headache. He sat on his pack and coughed and coughed. If there was anyone or anything in the forest, there was no question; they knew the Torans were there.

As dusk settled, the fog took on an eerie, yellow glow and the night turned chill. In the stillness, they floated along, listening to the lapping of the water on the edge of the raft.

With a start, Bria sat upright. "Do you hear that?" she whispered, her voice shaky.

From somewhere in the distance came the pounding of drums. Everyone held their breath, alert.

"It's the headhunters. They're on the hunt," Pel whispered.

"Shhh," Roh and Kiran said simultaneously.

Roh turned his head side to side. "I can't make it out," he whispered. "Where's it coming from?"

Then the drumming stopped. They waited, but did not hear the drums again all night.

Every night, they glided along, never seeming to come closer to the drumming. It was as though the drums followed them down the river, working to unravel their nerves.

The rains came every afternoon, and afterward, they'd pass through cool pockets of air, giving them fleeting bouts of respite from the oppressive jungle heat. But there was still no food to be found. As the days dragged on, Kiran could think of little else but food. If he took a few bites of the rationed stash, his stomach felt worse than if he hadn't eaten at all.

A heavy gloom settled on the group. Reciting the daily Verse was forgotten. No one spoke of the quest. The thought of getting to the Voice now seemed like a far off dream, vague and obscure. The reality was the swampy morass they were in—opaque, musty, and airless—and the constant fear of the Widhu, eating away at their resolve. Kiran had fleeting thoughts of giving in, of diving from the raft and floating away into the green oblivion. It seemed easier than the constant fear that gripped his stomach. The possibility that they may not return home alive was as real as the empty food bags.

Every little thing, no matter how small, became something to be concerned about. Kiran developed a rash on his feet. Standing to take his turn at the poles became painful as his feet turned from pink to bright red and cracked. Skin flaked on the sides and back of his heels. Within a few days, the skin was peeling off in chunks around his toenails and the tops of his feet were fiery red. He knew he should keep them dry, but the raft was always wet.

Deke's condition turned worse. When he coughed, it gurgled like vomit in his throat. It made Kiran sick to hear it. Deke's skin turned ashen and his eyes yellowed. In the miserable heat, he lay on the raft, wrapped in his blanket, shuddering uncontrollably from fever, complaining of a tender stomach. At times, he could barely get off the raft and get his pants down before his bowels let loose.

One afternoon, through the mix of jungle smells, Kiran caught the faint odor of wood smoke. Then the river made a sharp turn. On the shore, amid a tiny patch of cleared land stood a structure that was clearly manmade. Wood poles, lashed together and stuck in the ground, supported platforms with palm-thatched roofs built high above the ground—huts on stilts.

The tiny village appeared abandoned, as though the inhabitants had simply vanished into the silent forest. Roh dug his pole in the river bottom to halt the raft.

Pel looked up at him with wide eyes. "What are you doing?"

"Hello!" Kiran called.

Pel swung around and glared at Kiran.

Roh pulled the raft along side wooden posts that had been driven into the river bottom.

"This is a bad idea," Pel said, perched on the edge of the raft. "We shouldn't be here. Don't go in there."

Kiran was already off the raft and poking his head in the doorway of a hut. Bria was right behind him.

In the center of the compound stood a cooking shed with a stove made of baked mud brick. Roh put his hand over it. "They've not been gone long," he said.

Next to the stove was a table, its surface cut with knife marks. Bits and pieces of a cabbage-like plant were scattered on the ground next to a water bucket. Kiran picked up the half shell of a round, woody pod about the size of his open palm from a pile on the ground next to the table. "This looks like their cooking area," he muttered, tossing the empty shell on the ground.

"Look at this!" Jandon was trying to pry open a pen constructed of sticks. Inside was a turtle the size of a dinner platter.

"Don't touch that," Roh warned.

"Are you kidding? Look at the meat on it."

Roh simply stared. Jandon shrugged, letting go of the pen. He shuffled away, heading around the back side of the huts.

Bria stopped short, turning back toward the jungle. She motioned for them to listen. "I hear something. In the forest."

Roh nodded. "They're letting us know that *they know* that we are here."

"Do you think it's a warning?" Kiran suggested. "They have no reason to be afraid of us."

Roh's brow creased with concern. "True, but do they know that?"

"Look at this," Pel called from the water's edge. He had hauled a small, open-weaved basket out of the water and was holding it up for them to see. "Fish!"

Deke tried to sit up to see, but collapsed back down on the packs.

Bria went to check on him.

"There's another one over here," said Jandon, standing downriver, pointing into the water where one was lashed to a pole, bobbing in the current.

Kiran said to Roh. "How do we make them see we mean no harm?"

"Kiran, Roh, look at this!" Bria called. She was hovering over Deke. They hurried to her side.

Bria had Deke's tunic pulled up. Rosy spots covered his chest and belly. "His stomach is rumbling. Look how bloated it is." She looked up at the boys, her face flush with fear. "This can't be good."

"Have you ever seen this before?" Roh asked her.

She shook her head. Kiran squirmed. He took a step back, looking down at his own feet. They were red. Rosy red. Was it the same sickness?

Deke mumbled something and grabbed at his clothes, sweat dripping from his forehead.

"He's burning up," Bria said. "He can't go on like this. He needs to rest. We should stay here." Deke was asleep now, a coarse rattle coming from his chest as he breathed.

Kiran scanned the forest. "Maybe they know how to cure him."

Roh said, "Or maybe they'll chop off our heads."

"If they were going to attack, wouldn't they have done it by now?"

Roh glanced at Deke sprawled on the raft. "Maybe they know what ails him and they don't want to catch it."

"More fish over here!" yelled Jandon.

"We have to try," Kiran said. "He needs something to eat."

Roh looked at Kiran a moment, then nodded. "You're right," he said. He yelled to Jandon. "Take only two. Bring them here. I'll get a fire going."

Kiran sat down beside Bria. A mix of emotions crowded in on him at once.

She turned toward him. He could feel the weight of her stare, but did not turn and face her. He would be forever haunted by the look in her eyes that morning when she had left him lying on the ground, the scent of their lovemaking still on him.

"Do you have anything to say to me?" she finally said.

Every moment of every day since they had left the Kotari, he thought of what he would say. On the long days on the river, he had rehearsed this moment, over and over in his mind, waiting for the time when they would be alone together, planning every word he would say to her, to tell her how sorry he was. But now that the moment was here, all thought left his mind and he feared that if he opened his mouth he'd be a babbling fool. He took a deep breath and turned to face her. "I miss your smile."

The corner of her mouth quivered, but her stare revealed nothing. He felt each second crawl past, waiting for a sigh of regret or a flash of anger in her eyes, anything. Finally, she turned her head deliberately so that she no longer saw him. The silence was agonizing. He had to say something. "I'm sorry."

She swung around. "Do you think I blame you? That you seduced me? Well, go away with good conscience." She swallowed hard, fighting back tears. "My decisions are my own. Don't feel you have some obligation—"

"But Bria, I—"

"I take responsibility for my own actions." A tear ran down her cheek. "I am not some barn whore." She hugged herself, shivering despite the hot, humid air.

"A whore? Bria, no. I..." His insides squeezed. "It was the Guardian, the Kotari. We must have been bewitched somehow. My mind was not my own."

She glared at him. "So you don't take responsibility? You say it was some," she bit her lip, "some force against your will?"

"Well, no. Yes. It was just, the drink, maybe it was a potion. My head was fuzzy."

Her expression turned to hurt. "Are you going to tell me you didn't want to?" Her face crinkled with pain.

"No. I mean yes, I wanted to...I... But I would never—"

"But you did," she said flatly, all feeling gone.

"And now, you have lost... Bria, I..." Their eyes held. No words came. He trembled, his heart crumbling. How could he have hurt her like this? He felt hollow, as if his soul had been ripped from his body. "I wish we'd never stopped on that island and none of this had happened."

"But it did." She sat up straighter, pulling her shoulders back. She thrust her jaw forward.

"We could run away, right now. We could live with the Lendhi. They would take us; I know they would."

"So you would run and hide?" she said, disappointment in her eyes. "You don't make change by running away."

He shook his head. "But we could live as we believe."

"You don't know what you believe."

Her words hit him like a slap.

"I will go home. And I will hold my head high," she said, but he could tell she was holding back tears.

"You're right. We'll go back together. I'll make a claim, one of the abandoned farms on the hillside, and work hard, I promise. I can make it work. I know I can." He sighed. "If I had someone to tend my sheep."

In the time it took for her to respond, Kiran had raised a flock of sheep, had the rows planted, the harvest in.

"Kiran, you're not making sense. You've always wanted to be an Elder."

"I don't need to be an Elder to be happy." He turned to face her. "Bria, if we were home, right now, I'd ask for your hand."

She shoved herself backwards, her eyes on fire. "What makes you think I'd accept?"

His mouth went dry. "I wouldn't…assume. But, Bria…I…" *I love you,* he wanted to say, but the words stuck in his throat.

"I know," she said, as though she had read his mind. "But it's not enough."

She held his gaze. He tried desperately to read her eyes.

Roh came toward them. "The fish are ready."

Kiran nodded, avoiding Roh's gaze.

That night, the sky was clear and the current in the river picked up speed. Kiran and Roh took their turn at the poles. Bria and Jandon flopped across their bags, asleep. Deke twitched in delirium. Pel was still awake when the drumming started. He jerked upright, his bright eyes alert. "They're close," he whispered.

Kiran looked to Roh. "This is our chance."

They pushed the raft to shore. "Let's hope they're friendly," muttered Roh.

"Friendly? Uh uh. No way. There's nothing friendly about them," Pel muttered.

"How can you be sure?" asked Kiran.

"Trust me, I'm sure."

"Well, we don't have a choice. We're starving and we have to do something about Deke. Maybe they can help."

"No way." Pel crossed his arms and stared at his feet.

"I'll go with you, Kiran," Roh said.

"What? I'm not staying here all alone," Pel said.

"But you'd be with—"

"Uh uh, if you're going, I'm going."

"But we shouldn't all go," Kiran whispered.

"If you're going, well," Pel sighed. "I should go."

Roh stood with his hands on his hips. "Pel, what is this all about?"

Pel looked to Roh, then back to Kiran. "I ah, I may be able to speak their language."

"Why didn't you say so before?"

"Because I figured you'd do something crazy," he huffed, "like want to talk to them."

Roh shook his head. "Fine, I'll stay. But be careful."

Kiran crept through the tangle of bushes, blind under the new moon, following the sound of the drums.

Behind him, Pel muttered some unintelligible phrase, over and over again. "Moo-day-shoo, gun-der shah. Moo-day-shoo, gun-der shah."

Kiran whispered, "What are you saying?"

"We come in peace."

"Oh. Good idea."

"And a prayer to the God of War."

Kiran paused. *God of war?* This was not the time to question Pel. Through the leaves he saw the flickering light of a fire. "Hold your tongue. I want to get a look first."

Pel nodded and followed right behind him as he crept to the edge of a clearing, the drums pounding out all other sound. Hidden in the shadows, he got a clear view of the people by the light of the roaring fire. What he saw made him gasp.

They were naked.

The women were huddled together, their breasts hanging exposed for all to see, their only garments a roping of knots and beads strung around their waists. The men circled them, gyrating in a wild frenzy, wearing nothing but a length of twine at their waists. Their faces were painted with dark lines and dots. Some had bones pierced through their nostrils while others had narrow sticks of wood impaled in their earlobes. They glared at the women hungrily. The men, he saw now, had pointy fangs for teeth.

"They have fangs," he whispered in Pel's ear. "Have you ever seen anything like this?"

Pel shook his head, his mouth hanging open.

Kiran wondered if they should reveal themselves. He felt like a gawker, hiding in the bushes, staring at these strange, naked savages. What had Roh said when they were captured by the Lendhi hunters? If he caught someone in the grass, he'd kill him. Perhaps he shouldn't stay hidden. But something kept him rooted where he was.

"Look," Pel whispered. "There." He nodded toward the house. It was built on stilts, off the ground like the huts they'd seen, only this one had a long, narrow roof with no walls.

"What it is?"

"In the rafters."

"What? I can't see."

The drumming stopped and the boys' heads snapped back toward the fire. Three men with live snakes wrapped around their necks came out of the darkness, carrying sticks with what looked like bloody hunks of meat impaled on the ends. When they got closer to the fire, Kiran got a better view. His hand flew to cover his mouth. "Those are human heads!"

His stomach dropped and his knees buckled beneath him, but he couldn't look away. He grabbed hold of Pel to keep his balance. Pel swayed. Kiran glanced at him. His face had gone pale. Kiran turned back, drawn to the gruesome scene.

The head-bearers marched toward the fire, dipped the heads in buckets of blood, and raised them high in the air, letting the runoff flow over their bare chests and the snakes that hung there, then swung around in circles, spattering everyone with blood. Men and women alike pushed and shoved in a melee, grabbing at the heads in a bloodthirsty passion, licking the blood that dripped from them.

Kiran's stomach squeezed and he bent over and vomited in the grass. He stood up, light-headed.

"Are they doing what I think they're doing?" Pel whispered.

Kiran swallowed hard, the taste of bile burning in his throat. "What?" A man had ahold of a bloodied woman and was dragging her into the bushes. Another man grabbed a squealing young woman around her waist and carried her off in another direction. Before Kiran could answer Pel, a headhunter with a woman in his arms was headed right for them.

Kiran took a step back and stumbled. He got to his feet and right before him was the headhunter, clamping his sharp teeth over his tongue in a frenzied ecstasy, a bloody froth on his lips. The headhunter saw Kiran and stopped dead, his wild eyes fixed on him. They stared at one another. Kiran's heart pounded in his ears.

"Misu," the man gasped. He shoved the woman toward Kiran and fled, shouting, "Misu! Misu!"

"Run!" Pel yelled.

Kiran spun around and ran as fast as he could, blindly crashing through the forest. "Roh, Roh!" he yelled. "Push off! We have to go!"

When Kiran burst out of the forest, Roh was ready, pole in hand.

"What happened?" he asked, shoving them out as Kiran jumped on board. Pel was right behind him, knocking branches out of his way.

"Go, go, go!" is all Kiran could get out as he fell to his knees, his heart pounding in his chest.

"They're right behind us," Pel shrieked, plowing through the water to get onboard.

Jandon sat up, awakened by the noise. "What the blazes?"

Deke moaned and tried to sit up.

Kiran felt something fly by his face. For a moment, he thought it was a bird. Then he heard the thwack as a tiny arrow hit and stuck in the raft.

"Holy god of war! They're shooting darts at us!" Pel cried, trying to crawl under their packs.

"Get down!" Roh commanded.

Kiran tried to crouch over Bria to protect her from the arrows, but she jumped to her feet and grabbed the other pole.

"Get down, I'll get it," he said.

"I've got it. I've got it." Her hands gripped the pole.

A shrill whoop, loud and clear, ripped through the forest, then excited voices, guttural clicks and chirps. The headhunters were running along the riverbank. The jungle was hushed into silence, as if every living creature sensed the danger.

Thwack! Thwack! More darts hit the raft.

"Can't you go any faster?" cried Pel.

Roh froze where he stood, staring at Pel, wide-eyed.

"What's the matter with you? Go!" Pel yelled.

Roh's knees crumpled and he slumped onto the raft.

Jandon grabbed the pole as it slipped from Roh's hands. The raft caught in the current and careened around a bend.

Kiran rolled Roh over on his back. A dart was stuck in the side of his neck. Kiran grabbed hold and yanked it out. "He's barely breathing," he cried. "What's wrong?" Kiran turned to Pel who stared, speechless. "What happened?"

"It's poison," Pel finally said.

"Poison?" Kiran fell back on the raft, hardly able to breathe. "What do we do?"

"Uh…" Pel tugged at his hair, grasping for thoughts.

Kiran grabbed him by the shoulders and shook him, shouting, "What do we do? You know. I know you know!"

"Salt. I think salt."

"Are you sure?"

"Yes, yes. Salt."

Kiran ripped the ties from the packs, grabbing for his own. He dumped out the contents, searching for the pouch. "Here it is!" He tore the pouch open. "What do we do with it?"

Pel stared at him, eyes blank.

"What do we do with the salt!"

"Rub it on the wound."

Kiran took a handful of the salt and put it to Roh's neck. Roh lay limp. "He's stopped breathing."

"We have to give him breath."

"What?"

"Breath. The poison, it, it, it steals your breath. You have to help him breathe."

"How do I do that?"

"I'm not sure. That's all I know. He, he needs air."

Kiran took Roh's head in his hands and blew into his mouth. "The air is just coming back out his nose."

"Well, plug his nose," Bria urged.

Kiran pinched Roh's nose closed and blew into his mouth once more, watching as his chest rose and fell. He took another breath and did it again. "How many times?" he asked Pel.

Pel shook his head.

No one spoke a word as Kiran blew air into Roh's mouth, feeding him breath after breath as they floated down the river under the dark cover of night.

Finally, Bria took Kiran by the arm. "Kiran, it's no use."

"I'm not going to let him die!" he cried, then blew another breath into Roh's mouth. And then another. And then another until finally Roh sputtered and gasped and breathed on his own.

"Wha..." Roh wheezed.

"Don't try to talk," Kiran said, sitting back. "Just breathe." He kept his hand on Roh's chest, monitoring every breath.

The hum of chittering bugs had returned, the sign of a calm, peaceful night in the jungle.

"I think we've outrun them," Jandon whispered.

Kiran couldn't let go of Roh. *He's all right,* he told himself, and started to shake.

At the first hint of dawn, Roh broke the silence. "Thank you," he whispered to Kiran.

"I'm glad you're all right," Kiran said. "You gave us quite a scare."

"I could hear you talking. I could see you. I just couldn't move a muscle. It was eerie," he said with a shudder. "Then everything went black. What happened?"

"I don't know," Kiran said. From the end of the raft, he plucked a wooden dart. It was no longer than his hand with red feathers on the end. He turned to Pel. "But I bet Pel does."

Pel shook his head. "I don't know."

"You're lying. You've been lying to us from the beginning." He grabbed Pel by the collar and held the arrow in his face. "You tell me right now. Tell me what you know."

"I've told you everything," Pel cried, his eyes focused on the arrow.

"How did you know about the poison? How do you know their language?"

Deke started to shake violently.

"He's delirious," Jandon said, dropping his pole to take hold of Deke. "I can't hold him down. We need to get him off the raft."

"I'll pull over there," Bria said. She dug the pole into the river bottom, turning the raft toward a sandbar.

Kiran let go of Pel and jumped into the water to help.

By the time they got the raft pulled ashore, Deke was thrashing about, drool oozing from his mouth.

Bria sat next to him, wiping sweat from his forehead and trying to cool him with a wet cloth.

Kiran turned back to Pel. "You can start by telling us what is wrong with him."

"How should I know?"

"I want the truth. Right now. Or we're leaving you here. Alone."

Pel shrank where he stood.

Deke's convulsions started to subside. Bria called to Kiran. "He's asking for you."

Kiran glared at Pel, and as he turned away, said, "I expect answers."

He went to Deke's side. "What, Deke? What is it?"

"Maybe…" Deke gasped for air. He gripped the edge of the raft with his right hand. "Maybe it was…the water," he wheezed. His eyes rose to meet Kiran's and, for one instant, his whole heart was revealed—he had doubts, too. Faster than a thought, the shadows claimed him again. Spasms wracked his body.

"It's all right, Deke. It will be all right." There was nothing left to do. As sure as the sun sets every night, life was leaving him.

When the convulsions subsided, Deke lifted his eyes again, determined to tell Kiran something more. "You…" He swallowed hard, and drew in a deep breath, the rattle echoing in his chest. "You…" His eyelids fluttered and shut.

Kiran drew in a breath and held it, fearing the worst. But Deke was still alive, the low, course rattle of his breath the only sign. "Stay with me now."

Deke's head flopped to the side, his breathing a raspy moan.

Kiran looked over his shoulder to the others who hovered there.

"There must be something," he whispered.

They stared back at him with blank expressions.

He turned back to Deke. Something was terribly wrong. Spit bubbles had formed in cracks at the sides of his mouth. Kiran lowered his head to Deke's chest. There was no heartbeat. But it couldn't be. He flipped his head over to listen with his other ear. Nothing. He pulled away. He grabbed Deke by the shoulders and shook him. He let go and Deke slumped to the ground with a thump.

Deke was dead.

25

"We have to bury him," said Bria.

Jandon glared at her. "But we don't have an Elder to perform the rite."

Kiran turned to Roh, but he was gone. He had found high ground and was on his knees, digging with a stick.

Pel's eyes darted up and down the river. "Whatever you do, you better make it quick. I'll go help Roh," he said and scampered off through the brush.

Jandon paced in circles, tugging at his hair. "But we don't have the funerary pole. Or the blessed seeds."

Kiran sat on the edge of the raft, staring at Deke's lifeless body. He knew he should feel something—sad, upset, angry—something. But he just felt numb. "Jandon, it's all right," he said, searching his mind for something. "Aldwyn told me once that the rite could be performed without the seeds," he lied. "And any pole will do. It's the…" he glanced around the forest, then down at Deke, looking for inspiration, "it's the manner in which his arms are folded that is most important."

"Really?" Jandon seemed to calm.

"Yes, and we must be sure he faces the setting sun."

Jandon nodded, pacified.

Bria took hold of Deke's arms and laid them across his heart. "There is something here," she said. She reached inside the collar of his tunic, tugged at the cord at his neck, and pulled out a Pyletar. She looked up at Kiran with a questioning expression.

"That must be his father's," said Jandon.

Bria slipped it from around Deke's neck and handed it to Jandon. "You hold on to it," she said.

Jandon's mouth dropped open. Toran custom was to leave a body as it lay. Removing anything from a corpse was not done.

"We'll return it to Elder Morgan when we get back home," Kiran said.

"Fine," Jandon said, taking the Pyletar. He shifted from one foot to the other. "Then don't you think…?"

"What?" asked Bria.

"The stones his father gave him."

Bria ran her hands along the seams of Deke's tunic and found where they had been tucked into a seam. Kiran got his knife from his pack and handed it to her. She slit open the fabric and they fell into her hand. "There are scribe marks etched on the surface. What do you make of it?" Bria asked, handing the stones to Kiran. "Doesn't that look like writing?"

Kiran examined them closely. "I see the marks, but I don't know what they mean." He looked at Jandon.

"He said his father told him to find more, as many as he could." Jandon shrugged. "That's all I know."

"Well, you should hold on to them," Bria said to Kiran. "Maybe the words will come to you."

Roh appeared by his side. "The ground is too wet to dig very deep."

Jandon started shaking his head. "How can Deke be dead? He was the Seventh Elder. Wasn't he? How can this be happening? There's no hope. It's all over." He glared at Roh. "We need to turn back and head home."

Bria looked to Jandon and back to Kiran. "Maybe he's right," she said, a quiver in her voice.

Jandon slumped to the ground next to Bria and put his arm around her. She leaned into him and he held her as she cried. A fire exploded in Kiran's head. He raced up the bank to Deke's grave, his stomach churning. He hated himself for what he had done, for losing her the way he had. He dropped to his knees, took the stick in hand, and struck the mud, again and again, gouging the bottom of the hole.

Roh came along side him. "I already told you—" He stopped short, looked back toward Jandon and Bria, then sat down next to the grave. "Listen, Kiran. Everyone is upset right now, but we're not turning back. We need to bury him and move on." He scanned the forest as he spoke. "We are not alone. Remember?"

Kiran let out his breath. Roh was right. He tossed the stick aside and slumped down next to Roh. He stared into the grave they had dug. "But without Deke—"

"Deke wasn't meant to go any farther."

Kiran turned to face Roh. "How can you say that? We don't even know if we are going the right way."

"We're going the right way."

Kiran paused, studying Roh's expression. "How can you be so sure? The Script is so vague. What if we get there and we don't find the Voice? Pel comes from the sea and he doesn't know of the Voice. How can that be? Something's not right." He sighed. "I don't know what to think."

"It doesn't matter what we think. What matters is what we do." He got to his feet and shook the muddy leaves from his trousers. "Your problem is that you think faith is about believing in something." He offered his hand. "We were sent to do something and we are going to do it." Kiran took his hand and Roh pulled him to his feet.

Kiran stared at him. "What is faith then, if not belief?"

Roh smiled. "Perseverance, my friend," he said, patting Kiran on the shoulder. "Perseverance."

Together, they went back to the sandbar and took hold of Deke's body. Roh lifted under his arms and Kiran lifted his legs. Jandon and Bria walked on either side, helping to hold him up as they shuffled up the riverbank and laid his body in the shallow grave.

Pel had gathered a pile of branches and palm fronds. Together, the young Torans placed them over the grave, then stood with their arms crossed, staring at the mound.

"What do we do now?" Jandon said, his voice a whimper.

Pel shifted uneasily on his crooked leg, his eyes swerving through the forest.

"I know the funeral verse," said Bria.

Jandon glared at her. "What? How? You're not an Elder. You don't speak the Tongue of the Father."

Roh put his hand on Jandon's shoulder. "Let her speak," he said.

"No!" Jandon dropped to the ground next to Deke's grave, hugging himself, rocking back and forth. "We have strayed too far! This is wrong, all wrong. Women do not pray!"

"Um," Pel looked over his shoulder. "You're being awfully loud."

Jandon glared at Pel. "We're all going to die!" He jumped up and shouted in Pel's face, "We're going to die! We're going to starve to death because of you!"

Pel shrank back, shaking his head. "But I told you not to come this way. I told you."

Roh stepped between them. "What's done is done." To Jandon, he said, "Right now, we need to get moving."

Pel nodded, relieved.

Roh shook his head, jabbing his finger in Pel's chest. "You'll tell us all you know or we'll pull over and leave you alone in the jungle like Kiran said. Do you understand?"

Pel's face fell. He nodded and headed to the raft.

Back on the river, Kiran took the pole in hand, his focus on the river ahead. Roh stood next to him, working his pole to avoid a rock, while Jandon and Bria clung to the raft, looking back to where Deke lay in an unmarked grave.

Once the raft was moving in the current, Roh turned to Pel. "Now speak."

"I was, uh…" He chewed on his lower lip. "I was taught a few words of their language and other stuff."

"What do you mean? Who taught you their language?"

"I was sent here, to teach the Widhu proper worship of the true gods. But I didn't want to." He fidgeted with the straps on the bags. "I just wanted a way out."

"Out of what?"

Pel slumped in resignation. "My father made me join the Order. But the men there…" His face soured. "I just wanted out. So I volunteered. It was the only way. They gave me what I needed to travel." He sat up straight, his eyes wide. "I was supposed to live with them. Can you imagine?"

"But you never did?"

"No way. You saw. They are savage killers. I'm not crazy."

"So, you've never met them before?"

"No. I just know what I was taught, which wasn't much. There was a man who made contact with them and survived. He was part of the Order. We learned from him, but he wasn't right, in the head, you know."

Kiran nodded. "Last night, the headhunter was scared when he saw me. Why? What did he say?"

"Oh," Pel giggled. "He thought you were an evil spirit."

"An evil spirit? Why in the world would he think that?"

"Dunno, but I'm sure that was the word he said."

There was a long silence.

"That's all I know. I swear it," Pel cried.

Kiran looked at Roh and they nodded in silent agreement. Pel was telling the truth.

"Now what do we do?" Jandon said. "This is hopeless. We're going to die out here in this forsaken jungle."

That's a good question, Kiran thought, staring off into the endless green, his stomach cramping from hunger. On the muddy bank, he spotted a woody pod. "Stop!" he shouted. "Pull over."

Roh pulled ashore on a patch of sand. Kiran leaped from the raft and ran back along the shoreline to find the pod. He picked it up and examined its tough, woody exterior. It was heavier than he expected, as heavy as a rock of the same size. He glanced around, searching for a way to crack it open. He placed the pod against the base of a tree and struck it with his foot. It took four strikes before the hard shell cracked open. He picked it up and pried the two halves apart. Inside were hearty nuts, nestled in the shell like the slices of an orange.

The others had secured the raft and were watching him. He held the pod out for everyone to see. "We are not going to die," he said, smiling. "We can eat these nuts."

"Hold on," said Roh. "How do you know they're safe?"

"Don't you see?" Kiran said as he worked to smash the shells off the individual nuts. "We don't have to meet the Widhu, or talk to them, to learn from them."

Bria and Roh exchanged curious glances.

"At the Widhu camp, there was a pile of these shells in their cooking area. They must be edible. There were also leaves of that cabbage-like plant. We've seen it all along the riverside. And remember the baskets where you found the fish? There was a hole on one end. They must have been some kind of fish trap. We can fish."

Jandon took a handful of the nuts and chucked them in his mouth. "They're good."

"We will survive," Kiran said, smashing open the rest of the nuts for everyone to eat. "And we are going to make it." He craned his neck back and scanned the canopy. "Jandon. I think the pod came from that tree, the tallest one. Do you see?"

Jandon tilted his head back.

"Find more of those trees and you will find more nuts," Kiran said. "Can you do that? Gather as many as you can."

Jandon nodded and headed out, stumbling through the forest, his eyes on the treetops.

Kiran turned to Bria, handing her some nuts to eat. "Do you think you could make a fish trap like the one we saw?"

She nodded. "I can try." She left to collect the grasses she would need.

"Pel," Kiran continued. "Why don't you take the waterskins and look for water. In the trees, a stream, wherever you can find it without roaming out of earshot. We can't always count on the rain."

"Will do," Pel said, his head bobbing as he hobbled to get the waterskins.

Kiran turned to Roh. "We need to keep moving. Would you please check the roping on the raft, make sure it is sound?"

Roh nodded, a smile forming at the corner of his mouth.

Together, they walked back to the raft where Roh declared the roping secure and went to help Pel. Kiran sat down on the edge of the raft, took the Script from his pack, and read it through once more. It spoke of the river, a crossroads, then an upward struggle. He was sure that was what it said. But how could that be? Rivers don't travel upward. Were they to leave the river then? But where?

He dwelled on the line: *Drink of it and be merry, for it is your salvation.*

Jandon staggered toward him, holding up the edges of his tunic which was filled with the nut-pods. He got to the raft and let go. The nuts tumbled into the sand with a clatter of thumps.

"You found some. This is fantastic," Kiran said as he rolled up the scroll and tucked it back in his pack.

A smile returned to Jandon's face. "There are a few more. I'll be right back," he said.

Bria arrived with an armload of twigs and grasses. She plopped down on the edge of the raft and started to weave the pile into a fish trap. "I think this might work," she said.

"I know it will," he told her.

She had him hold several twigs so she could wrap the grasses and get the base started. Roh and Pel emerged from the jungle, waterskins in hand. "We found a trickle of a stream," Pel reported. "All are full and ready to go."

Roh and Pel helped Kiran bag the nut-pods and tie them to the raft. Jandon returned with a few more. He held one up and cheered, "The Great Father provides!"

"And Kiran has the Script to guide us," Bria said with a smile, the first Kiran had seen in days. "The Great Father watches over us."

Kiran stared at them, trying to make sense of their renewed faith. Was this what Roh meant? Faith was simply to persevere? Is that what they were doing?

But Deke's faith had never wavered. He followed the Way, without question. As the Script commanded, he had drunk from the river. But now he lay in his grave. How could that be? Guilt weighed on Kiran like a huge stone. If only he had argued more, made him understand Manu-amatu's warning. But he had known Deke would not bend. His conviction was not shallow; it was ingrained in him, a part of him. Nothing could have saved him from it.

Now they were on the river, and at the fork, had taken the way less traveled, just at the Script directed. But were they meant to? If not for the Script, they'd have no direction at all. Then which way would they have gone?

Kiran picked up one of the nut pods and rolled it in his hands. Had the Great Father provided the food, now, in their time of need, or was it here all along and they hadn't seen it because of their own failings, their sheer ignorance of the jungle?

Jandon slapped Kiran on the back. "To the Voice of the Father!" he cheered. "The headhunters are behind us now. Everything will be all right!"

Kiran offered a faint smile and looked away.

With their bags loaded with food, they shoved the raft back into the flow of the river and climbed on board. Kiran laid his head back, closed his eyes, and listened to the solemn tones of the river flowing around branches that dipped in the current, wishing he could feel as sure.

Near dawn the next morning, the terrain changed abruptly; the river narrowed and the jungle walls crowded in around them. Before they realized, they were rushing through a tunnel of rock with white waves crashing over the raft, pummeling them from all directions.

Pel grabbed hold of the raft with a shriek.

"Here we go again," said Roh.

"Just hold on," Kiran told Pel.

The river turned sharply and the raft rode up the side of a rock wall. Bria slipped and Kiran reached for her. Together they were washed off the raft and into the roiling river. Kiran kept hold of her skirt as they were swept through the roaring rapids. He desperately grabbed at branches and vines at the river's edge. But the force of the water was too strong, and the branches snapped in his hands. The current spun them round and round, then dragged him to the bottom, ripping Bria from his grasp.

Then the river dropped beneath him and he was falling, weightless, the water pushing him downward in a long agonizing drop until he plunged into a churning abyss and all went black.

Kiran tasted sand, gritty on his tongue. He lay face down, the roar of falling water pounding in his ears, his soggy clothes heavy on his back. He tried to lift his head, but the world started to spin. *A few more breaths.* He lifted his head again and tried to focus. What happened? The raft. He and Bria had slipped off the raft. Bria! He sat upright. Pain shot through his temples. He slumped back down, taking a breath. In his left hand was a torn swatch of fabric. Her skirt. He had to find her. He lifted his head again and the pain throbbed in his veins. *A few more breaths.*

He opened one eye. There was movement, someone there. He tried to raise his head again, but gave up, lying back down on the sand. Someone walked around. People. No. Was he dreaming? He rolled over on his side for a better view. Monkeys. Giant monkeys, the size of humans, walking upright. Six or seven of them. Two were hunched at the edge of the river, reaching for something in the water. Kiran lay still, watching, trying to focus. Above the sound of pounding water, he heard a noise behind him and rolled over to look. At the waterfall, a large male grunted and swayed back and forth from foot to foot, his movements a rhythmic dance. He picked up a rock and threw it into the water, then let out a high-pitched hoot and, in three quick steps, was up the side of the waterfall. He grabbed a vine and swung out into the spray. The monkey-man launched from the vine, grabbing at branches as he swung back downward, and continued his dance on the shoreline, passing by Kiran, circling round and round until finally he plopped down on a rock and looked up, staring into the cascading water. Kiran recognized the look in his eyes. He had seen it before: when the followers attended worship in the temple, when the Lendhi gathered around Manu-amatu, when the Kotari gazed upon the Guardian.

A smaller one of the creatures, a child it must have been, crept toward Kiran, its knuckles on the ground, walking on all fours. The child sat in the sand next to Kiran and swirled a twig in the water. She paused, looking at Kiran with curious, brown eyes, her face so like a human's Kiran couldn't believe his own eyes. She poked him with the twig. He stared back at her. She held his gaze and Kiran saw intelligence, like his own. These were no ordinary animals. The creature before him was a thinking, cognizant being. She poked him again. Was she prodding him to get up?

Behind her, the others were moving back and forth from the riverside, their gait awkward and stumpy, their long arms swinging. They were carrying something. The nuts. They were carrying the nuts away. *Our nuts.* Kiran pushed himself up on his knees. At his movement, all heads turned his way. The large male leapt to his feet and charged toward Kiran, running on all fours, shrieking. Kiran froze. The animal was nearly on top of him when he veered off and grabbed hold of a tree trunk and swung around the base, shrieking and grunting. He thrashed through the brush, shaking branches and grabbing sticks, throwing them at Kiran as he stamped at the ground with his feet.

Kiran sat stone still. He didn't know what else to do.

Something behind Kiran caught the male's attention. At once, all the monkey-men turned and scampered off, disappearing into the forest.

Kiran swung around, causing his head to spin again.

"Are you all right?" It was Roh.

He closed his eyes a moment to stop the dizziness. "Yes, yes," he answered. "I think I hit my head. Are you all right?"

He opened his eyes. Bria and Jandon were with Roh. He felt such relief that he closed his eyes again and slumped back down on the sand. Bria rushed to his side. "You're not all right," she said.

He pushed himself up to sitting position. "I'm fine," he said, gazing into her worried eyes.

"Where's Pel?" asked Roh.

Kiran looked around. "I don't know. What happened?" He rubbed his temple.

"We went over the waterfall, that's what happened," Jandon said, his voice a higher pitch than usual.

"There he is," said Roh. At the bottom of the falls, Pel lay sprawled over a piece of wreckage that spun in a torrent of angry water. The raft was smashed to splinters on the rocks around him.

Jandon gasped. "The raft! It's gone. Broken to bits!"

Roh was already fighting the surging water, heading toward Pel. Bria was right behind him. Together, they towed the wreckage from the roiling water, dragging Pel to shore. He was barely conscious. They placed him on the sand next to Kiran. Bria slapped his cheeks, trying to revive him.

His eyes blinked open and he looked up at her. "By the gods, I'm alive!" he shouted, leaping to his feet. "You people are crazy!" He frantically brushed sand from his clothes as though trying to regain some composure.

Bria's eyes grew wide. Roh roared with laughter, his hand at his stomach. Kiran had never heard him laugh with such abandon and he started to laugh, too. Pel stared at them with disbelief, then plopped down on the sand and giggled like a little girl. Then they were all laughing. Jandon howled until tears came to his eyes. For a long, glorious moment, Kiran forgot they were stranded in this forlorn jungle.

"What are we going to do now?" Bria asked.

"I don't know," Roh replied, unable to contain his chuckles.

Kiran gave in to another round of laughter, snorting and crying. "Thanks, by the way, for scaring off the monkey-men," he said, trying to get himself together. "I wasn't sure what to do."

"Monkey-men?" Jandon stared, eyebrows raised. He launched into another bout of chortling laughter.

"You didn't see them?" Kiran looked to Roh.

Roh shook his head, a smirk plastered on his face. "How's

your head?"

"My head is fine." Kiran ran his fingers through his hair. "I saw these creatures. Giant monkeys that walked like men." He got up and moved to the rock where the monkey-man had been sitting. "They were right here," he pointed toward the ground. "It was amazing, actually. I think they worship the waterfall."

"Worship? Animals?" Jandon scoffed. "You must have clobbered your head pretty hard."

"Well, they were intelligent enough to take our nuts."

"What?" Pel jumped to his feet. "Where?"

Kiran gestured toward the woods. "That way."

Roh grabbed Pel by the arm. "Hold on, chatter pants. Not so fast. They could be dangerous. Besides, now that we know what to look for, we can find more." He gestured toward the pile of wreckage. "We need to gather our things and determine what we've lost."

As suddenly as they had begun, they stopped laughing and got to their feet, sober and fully aware of their situation. Roh started to untangle the ropes from the pile of wreckage.

Kiran looked up and saw his pack, hanging by the strap, snagged on a jagged rock near the top of the waterfall. He staggered back a step and sat down on the rock. As soon as he sat down, he saw it; arced across the center of the falls, suspended in the mist, was a shimmering rainbow.

"Come, look at this," he called to the others.

They gathered around him. "It's a sign from the Great Father," said Jandon.

Bria smiled at Kiran. "Everything will be all right," she said. Her eyes held his for a long moment.

"I knew we'd have to go a different way eventually," Kiran said.

"Look," Roh whispered. "Your monkey-man."

On the edge of the forest, the male crouched on all fours, peering at them through the foliage.

"Look at those eyes," Bria said. "He's beautiful."

Suddenly, the creature jerked up on his hind legs, standing fully erect, his head turned downriver. He held there for moment, turning his head, first this way, then that, as though trying to locate a sound. His eyes grew large and he dropped to all fours and was gone.

Kiran drew in a breath. *Something's wrong.* Instantly, he was fully alert, scanning the forest in the direction the monkey-man had looked. Dark-skinned men burst from the woods, a dozen or more, armed with cudgels and hatchets. "Savages!" Kiran swung around. There was nowhere to hide, nowhere to flee. He braced for a fight, fear coursing through his veins.

Bria ran into the river. One savage veered off from the force, chasing her. He grabbed her by the hair and yanked her down.

"No!" Kiran screamed as a savage slammed him to the ground and shoved a bag over his head.

26

"Bria!" he called. A switch cracked across his chest.

Then he heard her. He knew her voice, without question. But the sounds she was making were not natural. Something was wrong, terribly wrong. "No," she screamed, over and over again amid the sounds of grunts and laughter. Kiran thrashed on the ground, fighting with the straps at his wrists, at his ankles, choking on his own hot breath inside the bag. He had to get to her.

Someone kicked him in the stomach. The air left his body. He curled in a ball and lay still, straining to listen above his own gasping. Rage burned in his gut and spread through his body, exploding at his bound hands. He got to his knees and yanked and tugged at the straps, clenching his teeth with fury, every muscle in his body stretched to the point of breaking.

But it was no use.

Her cries dissolved into submission.

Kiran slumped face down in the hot sand, smothering his agony in the canvas bag. He could not save her. "No, no, no," he sobbed. *How could the Great Father let this happen?*

He was hauled to his feet, his wrists tied to something. A pole?

The bag was ripped from his head. He blinked grains of sand from his eyes and looked around for Bria.

Jandon was right in front of him, his back to him. Bria was ahead of Jandon. They were all tied to the same pole, held horizontally between them.

Her face was stained with dirty tears, her cheek purple where a man's fist had landed. Her lips were swollen and bleeding, her tunic torn and hanging on her in tatters. Kiran yanked at the bindings at his wrist. *Crack!* came the whip once more.

Jandon flinched.

This can't be happening! Kiran fought to force down the panic that surged through his body, threatening to overwhelm him.

Roh was next to him, to his left on the other side of the pole, watching everything, counting the men, assessing their strength, strategizing; Kiran was sure of it. He wished he had Roh's calm fortitude. Right now, he was too angry to think.

Through gritted teeth, he sucked in a deep breath and examined the solid leather straps that bound his hands and attached them to the pole. They were secured so tightly that his wrists were white from the pressure. They weren't going to come loose.

There were fourteen savages, all of them armed, their skin black as pitch. These were not the headhunters they had seen upriver. These barbarians were taller and built of solid muscle. Each wore a woven harness strapped to his torso that held his weapons at the ready and all his supplies on his back. The apparatus, Kiran could see, allowed the savages to move through the jungle with speed and stealth.

They reminded Kiran of the Javinians, yet the weapons these savages carried seemed specifically designed to hunt men.

One prodded Kiran, sputtering in a strange language—guttural, brief, as though he didn't really want to speak. Kiran didn't understand the words, but the message was clear—move.

"Ah-oo, notaraby, Ah-oo notaraby!" Pel repeated in his high-pitched, piping voice. He was strapped to the pole opposite Bria. He turned to look back at Roh and Kiran over his shoulder. "Either they don't speak the language of the Widhu or they don't care," he said, shaking his head with surrender. A savage whacked him on the back of the head with his cudgel and he dropped to the ground, hanging by his wrists. The man grabbed him by his elbow and hauled him back to his feet.

The barbarians pushed and shoved the Torans, forcing them to march into the dense tangle of the jungle, leaves and branches scraping at their skin. They fought to stay on their feet as they slogged through the mud, jerking and tugging at the pole as the five tried to move as one.

Kiran struggled to make sense of it all. Where were they being taken? And for what reason? What did these men want of them? They had done nothing to these people, whoever they were. He tried to stay calm. After all, when he and Bria had been captured by the Lendhi, everything worked out. But when he looked at Bria, he knew, this time was different. He wondered how much she could endure. But she kept up, and kept her head down. It was Pel who tripped and fell from exhaustion and was forced to his feet again and again.

Maybe he could find a way to communicate with them, to make

them understand he meant no harm, that this was all a mistake. But when he tried to speak, the whip came down hard, cracking across his back, causing such excruciating pain he had to gulp for air.

He clamped his mouth shut and trudged on, wondering how much more they would have to endure as the savages pushed them deeper and deeper into the jungle. With no food in his stomach and no water to drink, the stifling heat drained what little strength he had left until, at last, when he didn't think he could take one more step, they came upon a trickling stream and the savages stopped to rest. The Torans were forced to the ground. Kiran's legs were wobbly from fatigue and he slumped to his knees. The flesh on his wrists had rubbed raw and his arms felt numb.

He kept his eyes on their captors, wondering what would happen next. One of the savages, who appeared to be the leader, grunted orders and two of the other barbarians went to work, starting a fire. Another dipped a wooden container in the stream and walked by the Torans dumping the water over their heads. Kiran opened his mouth and gulped it down, nearly choking on his thickened tongue.

Another of the savages walked the edge of the stream, searching for something. At last, he pulled a machete from a sheath he had slung over his back and chopped at the forest floor. Bunches of the cabbage-like plant were tossed at their feet. Kiran sighed with relief, thankful for something to fill his stomach and ease his gnawing hunger.

A third savage came round. Kiran thought he was going to cut them from their bindings so they could eat. But instead, he checked each one, making sure they were still tight and secure.

Kiran and the others had to lean over and eat right from the ground. They're feeding us like sheep, he thought, his anger inflamed. Why not just kill us? Why keep us alive? He eyed the men and their weapons and their purpose became clear. These savages weren't protecting their territory.

They were capturing slaves.

As soon as night fell, their bindings were checked again, and all but two of the men took their weapons in hand and disappeared into the dark jungle. Kiran risked a quick glance at Roh whose eyes mirrored his own. They had to escape.

Kiran looked to Bria, trying to make eye contact with her, but she stared off into the darkness, her eyes barren of all expression. She had retreated far into herself, resigned to their fate it seemed, a mere shadow of the spirited Bria that he loved. Kiran's insides tightened. He wanted to kill each one of these savages with his bare hands for what they had done to her. He tugged at his bindings once more.

The two savages who were left to guard looked up from the fire and laughed. One had a scar that ran the length of his cheek, giving his face a permanent scowl. He got to his feet and grabbed Bria by the chin. She tried to pull away, but he yanked her chin around to face him, fierce lust in his eyes. The savage ran his tongue up her neck, his eyes on Kiran, taunting him. Kiran shook with rage. His vision turned blurry. His throat constricted. He wanted to scream at this evil savage.

"Don't show your anger," said Roh, his voice loud and clear. "It will only encourage him."

The savage leaped to his feet and kicked Roh in the side of the head. Roh slumped to the ground. Bria let out a gasp. With a huff, as though he'd become bored, the savage turned and went back to the fire.

Roh slowly lifted his head and spat a glob of bloody saliva on the ground. For a long time afterward, no one dared to move. Kiran hung his head, seething in an empty, impotent rage.

Soon, exhaustion overtook him. He dreamed of a dark shadow, smothering him in blackness. He tried to run, tried to hide, but no matter where he ran, it followed, hanging over him, surrounding him. Finally it pinned him to the ground, the pressure in his chest too much to bear.

He came awake with a start, soaked in sweat.

The barbarian guard closest to him, the one with the scar, was sound asleep. Kiran stretched to get a look at the second guard. He was asleep too. He worked at his bindings, tugging and tugging, back and forth, until they became bloodied and slippery and he thought he could slip one hand out. He gripped the pole with his left hand and worked his right. If he could just get one hand free. But it was bound too tightly.

Frustrated, he slumped in defeat, warm blood trickling down his arms. How could this happen, he wondered. Was this what the Great Father intended? For Bria to be… How could He!

Something moved in the forest. Kiran sat upright. The two guards came awake. One whistled and a whistle came back. It was the other savages, back with a new captive, a headhunter. He was shoved to the ground and lashed to the pole between Pel and Roh, opposite Jandon. Awake now, Jandon shifted, leaning as far away from the man as he could. The savage turned to Jandon and drew back his lips and bared his sharp fangs. Jandon shrank back.

Kiran squirmed, eyeing the bloodthirsty headhunter in the firelight, so close now, visions of bloody heads filling his mind. When the man turned and saw Kiran, his eyes grew large and his mouth dropped open. "Misu," he whispered and started to tremble. Kiran felt a pang of compassion for him. Bound and tied to the pole, he looked less savage than small and tired and just as terrified as the rest of them.

The headhunter hung his head and sang a low, sorrowful song.

"What is he saying?" Kiran whispered to Pel.

"I think he is praying to his gods for mercy," said Pel. One of their captors smacked Pel in the mouth with the back of his hand.

Kiran looked to the headhunter and back to their captor, angry. Why hadn't they hit the headhunter? He wanted to scream: *Unfair!* But he could already feel the crack of the whip. He laid his head on his hands and listened to the mournful song until the sun came up again, and the world filled with steam. The savages prodded with sticks, forcing the Torans to their feet and on the march again.

He had to find a way to escape. If only he could talk to Roh.

They were taken due south, as best Kiran could make out. He fought feelings of hopelessness and a choking fear that he would die here in the jungle at the hands of these barbarians. At times, he struggled against the impulse to give in to it, to let fear overtake him and resign himself to his fate. He would start to think of nothing but the nightly halt, longing for the daily drink of water, then his anger would well up again and his mind would race, trying to find a way to escape. Before he knew it, ten days had passed.

He gave up trying to free his wrists from the bonds as they marched. Even if he could, he'd never get past the men. There were just too many of them. Besides, he wouldn't leave Bria. There had to be another way.

Having Roh next to him gave him strength. Roh would never give up. Every moment of every day, Roh would be thinking, plotting, planning. Together, they would find a way. They had to.

The headhunter sang and sang, but his spirits did not save him. It must have brought him solace, though. The barbarians allowed it. Perhaps singing kept their captives calm and complacent. *Maybe I should sing to the Great Father,* Kiran thought. He knew the Tongue of the Father, after all. But would He listen? Would He save them? Kiran could sing the one song that was sung every week at worship, the Song of the Father, but he only knew that one in the common tongue. No one would be listening.

Kiran stopped dead, jerking the pole. *That's it!* One of the savages turned and smacked him on the back of the head. He dropped his eyes and started walking again. Did these savages understand his language? If he sang, would they assume that he was singing to the Father for mercy? Could he sing, like the headhunter, without getting whipped?

He braced for the whip and sang out, "Glory to the Great Father, la la la la." No whip came down on him. "I'm singing. We can sing!" He looked to Roh whose eyes grew bright. He understood immediately what Kiran had realized.

One of the savages glared at Kiran, a skeptical look in his eyes. Kiran sang out the Song of the Father, knowing it had a distinct rhythm and melody. Then he slipped in a line: "Bria, are you all right?" She did not respond. She didn't even lift her head.

Roh joined in, adding his own line. "Kiran, you are a genius, la la la la."

"Yes, yes!" Kiran sang. He was so relieved; he wanted to cry.

Roh sang. "Pel, sing to the headhunter, la la la la, and find out what he knows."

Pel turned and nodded. A flicker of hope returned to his eyes.

After a long, melodic exchange with the Widhu man, Pel switched back to the language of the Torans, singing, "He says we are being taken to the land of hot sand. We are now slaves of the man-god who builds mountains of death."

"What does that mean?" Jandon warbled.

"Don't know. But he says no one ever comes back."

In the silence that followed, the headhunter, as if to accentuate the point, yowled a long, sorrowful lament.

The jungle gave way to chaparral and then, in the late afternoon, the savages climbed atop a knoll, dragging the Torans with them, and sat in the shade of a scraggly tree overlooking a vast, grassy flatland.

Kiran shifted and squirmed, trying to stretch his sore muscles. Roh sat stone still, only his eyes moving. Jandon moaned and fidgeted, tugging on the pole and Bria slumped to the ground, her eyes closed. And poor Pel—Kiran didn't know how he'd make it much farther.

At least we are out of the wretched jungle, he thought, gazing across the flatland. Wind whispered across the fields, soft on his face. For a moment, Kiran closed his eyes and imagined he was back home, breathing in the cool breezes that blew up from the sea.

Their captors made camp. Kiran wondered why they chose this particular spot. There was no water. No shelter. They were out in the open, exposed. It didn't make sense. None of this made any sense. The headhunter must be wrong, Kiran told himself. No one could build a mountain. That was nonsense. If no one ever came back, as he had said, how could he know if there was truth to any of it?

As their captors worked, Kiran noticed them constantly scanning the horizon.

They were waiting for something.

Then, across the savannah, something without form or definition appeared on the horizon, a dark patch against the light sky. Kiran watched it take shape as it inched toward them through the shimmering heat. In the sky above, vultures swung back and forth, gliding on the air over the dead sun.

As the thing came closer, it was clear that it was not one thing, but a long caravan. Out front, animals lumbered toward them, some with tall spindly legs, laden with packs, others, heavy and muscled, like the beasts of the Great Meadow, harnessed and forced to tow giant wagons. Kiran stared in awe. These barbarians had subjugated animals!

His awe turned to shock when he saw, at the head of the procession, a creature so amazing he couldn't believe his eyes. "Look at that! It's half-man, half-animal," he said aloud, without thinking. A savage slapped him, but he couldn't take his eyes from the creature with the head and torso of a man atop the body of a beast. He had heard tales of these kinds of liminal beings, spawn out of the depths of Eternal Darkness—an evil twisting of two souls. But he never dreamed he'd actually see one.

As the procession came closer, it turned, forming a half circle, and he could see now the two massive wagons were cages on wheels. Inside, gripping the bars, were hordes of monkey-men, their eyes pleading like enslaved captives.

Behind the second wagon, a long procession of men shuffled along, two by two, each man's wrists bound and tied to a long rope. Kiran's heart started to race. He counted nearly seventy slaves.

The caravan halted in the distance. The half-man, half-animal being continued forward, climbing the incline toward them, a small entourage following. When the savages were turned away, watching, Roh leaned close and whispered in Kiran's ear. "We don't have much time."

A guard swung around and glared at the weary group tied to the pole.

The creature came to a halt and, with a jerky movement, the man separated from the beast and jumped to the ground. Kiran gasped. It wasn't one being. The man had been riding the animal!

The man was clad in a long, brown robe of animal hide, which Kiran realized now, had covered his legs. He approached the Torans, eyeing them closely. With an air of detachment, he turned on his heel and shouted at their captors, pointing in the direction of the jungle. Kiran was sure he was scolding the savages; the leader's face was flush with hostility. The barbarians grunted to each other, debating some decision. Finally, all but the two guards headed back toward the jungle.

Roh started singing the chorus of the Song of the Father. Then he eased into a plan. "Once the guards fall asleep, Kiran, you slide my knife from my boot and cut everyone free. When he does, keep your wrists at the pole, though, so if the guards wake, they'll think you're still tethered. I'll get them to chase me. Then you quietly slip away. Make sure they are both chasing me before you go."

Kiran started to interrupt.

Roh shook his head. "It's the only way. There are too many of them to fight. Do you understand?" He waited for everyone to nod. "I'll lead them in the opposite direction, leaving a trail, so when the other barbarians return, they'll track me."

The guards were engaged in a brusque exchange with the robed man.

Roh whispered to Kiran. "You take Bria and run. Don't look back. Just run as fast as you can. Get her far away from these vile men. If one of them comes after you, you'll have the knife. Slit his throat."

Kiran nodded. They'd run, as fast as they could. If he had to kill to protect Bria, he wouldn't hesitate. He looked to each of the others, pondering the plan. "I'm not sure Pel can make it."

"Then leave him," Roh said with such cold regard Kiran was taken aback.

"And how will you—"

"Take care of her. Do you understand? Get away."

The look on his face was unmistakable. Roh knew exactly what he was doing. He might not survive, and if he did, he'd still be enslaved. Kiran shook his head. "There has to be another way. We can't leave you."

"You can and you will. My destiny is here, in this act. When you return to the village, tell them what I have done, so that honor may be restored to my family."

Kiran stared at Roh, unable to find words.

"Tell me you will do this," Roh said with an urgency he'd never shown before. "You get to the Voice and return."

The Voice? Kiran searched Roh's eyes, confused now. Did Roh believe in the Voice? After so many conversations, so many shared thoughts, he still wondered. Roh had argued with Deke, more than anyone. Kiran had always assumed he had doubts, too. But now, sitting next to him, it was clear; Roh believed, without question. He was willing to sacrifice himself because of that belief. "But what if—"

"You will," Roh assured him, as though it was a certainty of which he had privileged knowledge. "It is you. I know it is you."

"Me? But how—"

"Of all, you will persevere."

Kiran paused, held by Roh's intense gaze.

The night grew quiet. The robed man climbed back up on his animal and rode back toward the caravan.

Kiran looked Roh straight in the eyes and nodded.

Roh smiled then, that long, drawn smile that never quite curved upward.

Night closed in and the young Torans were enshrouded in darkness. An unusual stillness settled on the camp and it seemed an eternity before both guards were snoring. Roh gave Kiran a nod and lifted his foot to Kiran's hands. He strained against the wrist straps, stretching his fingers until he was able to push against the hilt of the knife and work it out of Roh's boot. His tongue felt like leather in his mouth. He turned the knife over and moved the blade up and down, cutting into his wrist bindings, his heart pumping hard inside his chest. Once the blade broke through, he went right to work, cutting Roh free.

One of the guards woke and was getting to his feet. In an instant, Roh jumped up and lunged toward the sleeping guard. He grabbed the cudgel from his hands and struck a blow on the side of his head. For a moment, Roh eyed the other guard coming toward him as though trying to decide if he could win a fight with him. When the guard got close enough, Roh dove to the ground, swinging the cudgel, and cracked him in the ankle. The guard shrieked as he doubled over in pain. Roh got to his feet, lumbered down the hill, and plunged into the bushes. The guard glanced at Kiran and the others. Kiran sat still, holding his wrists at the pole, his heart thumping in his chest. The guard took a step closer in indecision, then turned and limped after Roh, shouting in the night.

Kiran dropped his wrists and reached for Bria. "Now," he whispered and tugged at her bindings, sawing at the leather with the knife.

Jandon whispered, "But Roh said to wait."

"He's out cold. We've got to go. Now!"

Her straps broke free. He went straight to work on Jandon's straps. Within moments, they were free. Then he went to Pel.

The other guard sat up, shaking his head, trying to focus now.

Pel's straps broke free and he tried to get to his feet, but slumped back down. The guard grunted. Bria and Jandon grabbed Pel under his arms and helped him to his feet. "Go!" Kiran shouted to them. "Leave him!" His gut wrenched with guilt.

Bria looked at him, disbelief in her eyes.

He turned away and his eyes met those of the headhunter. He hesitated. They had to go. Now. But the man did not deserve to be enslaved. Pel did not deserve to be enslaved. No one did.

The guard was up on his knees, grumbling.

Jandon and Bria were still standing there, staring at him. "Go!" he shouted as he put the knife to the headhunter's bindings. The guard crawled toward him as he sawed and sawed at the leather.

The guard grabbed him around his ankle. He glanced up. Bria and Jandon were running toward the jungle. The strap broke free as the guard yanked his foot out from under him and he dropped to the ground. His chin slammed into the dirt. The guard was on his feet, dragging him toward the fire. The headhunter was gone. Kiran dug his hands into the ground and flipped over on his back, kicking at the guard with his other foot. The guard rammed his shoe against Kiran's throat. He gasped with pain.

From nowhere, the headhunter was there with a vine wrapped around the guard's neck, strangling the life out of him. When the guard slumped to the ground, they nodded to each other in shared relief.

The headhunter picked up Pel, slung him over his shoulder like a knapsack, and sprinted for the jungle, motioning for Kiran to follow. Kiran got to his feet. His legs burned, but he ran.

27

The headhunter moved like a shadow through the night. Kiran struggled to keep up, breathing so hard his chest nearly burst. All he could hear was the sound of his own feet, crashing through brush, and his heart hammering in his ears.

He kept his eyes to the ground, scanning for low branches and vines. He couldn't fall. Not now. Behind him, he heard the shouts of the guard, alerting the other savages. They were out there. Somewhere. He had no idea how far they had gotten. His lungs were screaming. He was weak from lack of food and water. He stumbled and fell, hitting the hard ground, ramming his shoulder into a root. Pain shot down his arm and he let out a yelp. He cursed himself; the other savages could be anywhere nearby.

He got to his feet again, Roh's knife in his hand. The headhunter was there, urging him onward. He stumbled forward, moving again. He had to find Bria. But how would he ever find her now? The jungle was immense. Would she try to head back to the waterfall? They had traveled for days, how would she find the way in this thick maze of green?

The headhunter slowed. Kiran came alongside him but the man took Kiran by the arm, holding him back. Something moved in the forest. The headhunter set Pel down and dropped to a crouch. Kiran dropped down behind him. The headhunter pointed.

Bria and Jandon were cowering behind a shrub. Kiran felt such relief he nearly knocked them to the ground in his rush to hug them both. But his heart sank when Bria pulled away from him.

Without a word spoken, they followed blindly, trusting the headhunter, as he led them deeper into the jungle. Pel stumbled along on his own. Every screech of an owl, every croak of a night thing, made Kiran's heart skip a beat.

Every once in a while, the headhunter would stop and listen intently, then motion for them to move on, reminding Kiran of Bhau and how careful he had been; but compared to this man, Bhau was clumsy and awkward. This man knew his world, was a part of it, like the creatures that inhabited the treetops. He was sure of his path, though it always seemed in the opposite direction Kiran thought to go, making Kiran painfully aware of how out of touch he was with his surroundings. He didn't belong here. He belonged back home, in the village, tending his farm, not running like a hunted animal through this steamy jungle.

Where had everything gone wrong? How could he have let this happen? Without Roh, nothing seemed real, like it had all been a twisted dream. Without Roh. He couldn't bring himself to accept that Roh was gone now. He couldn't get the image of his face out of his mind, the look in his eyes, the determination. He had been sure that Kiran was the one. It was absurd. How could he have let Roh persuade him?

He thought of turning around, of heading back to free him. But he knew Roh would not forgive him if he got caught. So, he tried not to think and focused on running, on getting away. When he ran, he didn't think; and if he didn't think, he didn't have to think about Roh. So Kiran ran on, following the shadow into the darkness.

Near dawn, they came upon a stream. Pel and the Torans dropped to their knees and brought cupped hands to their mouths. The headhunter took a drink, his eyes scanning the forest. Kiran wanted to rest here. He felt weak and dizzy with fatigue. But the headhunter seemed adamant they move on.

Once they were a safe distance from the stream, the headhunter halted the group and motioned for them to sit down. Kiran reached for Bria's hand, but she flinched and he let go. He turned away, trying to hide his rage. *Damn them to Eternal Darkness!*

The headhunter rooted around in the humus at the base of a decaying tree trunk. When he found what he sought, he stood up and held out his hand. Five giant maggots, as fat as his fingers, wriggled in his palm. He pinched one between his thumb and index finger and tossed it into his mouth. It squished and popped as he chewed. Kiran's stomach flipped. The headhunter lifted his hand again, emphasizing his offering with an encouraging grin. "Mootoo," he whispered.

"What is he saying?" Jandon asked Pel.

Pel was leaning on Jandon's shoulder, too exhausted to answer.

"Mootoo," he said again, shoving his hand at Kiran.

Before he could change his mind, Kiran plucked a grub from the man's hand and shoved it into his mouth. It was chewy, like a piece of fat. The juices oozed onto his tongue and he gagged, but managed to swallow, his eyes watering. He cleared his throat and said, "It's not bad."

The headhunter nodded with satisfaction and offered the grubs to the others. Without hesitation, Bria snatched one from his hand and popped it into her mouth. Jandon squirmed.

"This may be the only food there is," Kiran said. "You must eat."

"Why should we trust him?" he sneered. "Maybe he's trying to poison us."

"He ate one first."

"So! Maybe…" Jandon faltered. He took some time to find the courage to place the fat maggot in his mouth, then made such strained faces as he chewed that the headhunter laughed out loud.

With a grin of satisfaction, the headhunter went to search for more grubs. He came back with another handful and surprisingly it was enough to fill their stomachs. He gestured for them to sleep now.

Bria curled into a ball and closed her eyes. Kiran wanted to hold her, protect her. She was so quiet, touching her was the only way to assure himself she was there. But he knew he could not. The best he could do for her now was get her out of this forsaken jungle.

He nudged Pel. "Ask him if he will take us to the waterfall."

Pel spoke in a sleepy mumble.

The headhunter screwed up his face.

Pel spoke again and the headhunter's eyes grew wide.

"What is it?" asked Kiran.

"I'm not sure. He seems to know the waterfall, but surprised we came from there."

"Will he take us?"

Pel spoke with the headhunter again. "He says since we set him free, he owes us a debt. He will take us."

The headhunter gestured for them to go to sleep.

"One more thing," Kiran said to Pel. "What is his name?"

"Butu," the headhunter said, pointing to himself. "Boo too."

"Butu," Kiran repeated. "Thank you."

The man nodded before Pel could interpret the words, as though he understood.

When Kiran awoke, he felt refreshed, better than he had felt in several moons. They had napped through the heat of the day. Pel had regained some strength, too, and they set out again, moving along at a good pace.

Even during daylight, in the dense jungle, Kiran lost all sense of orientation. At any change in direction, he assumed the waterfall was the opposite way. But he followed, trusting Butu's word.

Periodically, the headhunter would stop to collect nuts, insects, or mushrooms, showing the Torans which could be eaten. Kiran was astounded at the food that was available in the jungle, knowing now that it had been present all along while they floated on the river, starving. If only they had known where to look.

Near dusk on the fifth day of their escape, they emerged from the thick jungle at the river's edge, the sound of pounding water just upstream. Kiran and Jandon rushed to the base of the waterfall and found what was left of their packs, right where they had left them. Kiran dropped to his knees in relief.

"What's she doing?" asked Jandon.

Kiran spun around. Bria was on her knees in the river, scrubbing her body with sand and rocks.

Kiran ran to her. Fresh blood flowed down her arms and legs where scabs had broken open. "Bria, what are you doing?" He took her by the arm. She glared at him, biting down hard on her lip. In her eyes he saw all the pain she had been hiding, how she had suffered. She yanked her arm from his grasp and plunged deeper into the river. "Stop. You're hurting yourself. Stop it," he begged. He reached for her again and she pulled away, swinging her fists. He tried to deflect her blows, but she was too fast. He wrapped his arms around her and held her tight. She kicked and screamed and they fell into the shallow water. "You're all right, Bria," he soothed. "You're safe now." She collapsed, sobbing in his arms. He rocked her, stroking her hair. "You're all right. I'm going to get you far away from here. I promise."

He held her until her sobs subsided. Jandon left them alone and Kiran fought to keep his own tears from flowing. Inside, he was screaming, *why, Father, why!* But he kept whispering to her that everything would be all right.

When she finally fell asleep in his arms, he motioned for Jandon. "We leave at daybreak," he whispered. Jandon nodded.

Jandon sifted through what remained of their belongings. He salvaged what rope they could. He and Kiran wove it into harnesses for themselves, then tied what supplies they had left to their backs. There were two waterskins and they fastened them so they could be tipped up without detaching them from the harness.

Meanwhile, the Widhu man sawed at a stick with a bit of dead vine. The friction caused a small pile of kindling he had gathered to smoke. He was starting a fire.

"Pel, tell him I don't think we should do that," Kiran said.

Pel interpreted Butu's response. "He says not to worry. He will know if they are nearby."

"But he was caught once before."

Kiran watched his expressions as Pel listened. "He says he was… uh…" He leaned forward and whispered, "Busy with a woman. Now he's not distracted."

"Where's the woman? Why didn't they capture her too, then?" Kiran asked, then waited for the response.

With wide eyes, Pel said, "He killed her."

Kiran leaned forward, unsure whether he heard correctly.

"A Widhu woman would rather die at the hands of her lover than be taken against her will."

Kiran winced. He glanced at Bria and the yellowed bruise on her face. His gut tightened. Was that how she felt? Would she have rather been dead?

"He says he builds the fire to honor her, that the smoke will carry his prayers to the spirits of the sky."

Kiran watched the smoke rise from the tiny pile of kindling and sent his own silent prayer.

As darkness surrounded them, Butu gathered some green vines and smashed them to a pulp with a rock. He gestured for Jandon and Kiran to wade into the water downriver. After all Pel's stories of the creatures that dwelled there, they were reluctant, but the headhunter was insistent. He tossed the mash into the river and immediately fish started floating to the surface, belly up.

"Look at that!" Pel shouted in amazement.

There were more fish than they could carry. They tossed the stunned fish onto shore and Jandon went to work, chopping the heads while Kiran used Roh's knife to gut them. The headhunter gathered some thin reeds he used to skewer the fish and grill them on the open flame. On the hot rocks he had put in the fire, they placed the remaining fillets and covered them with large green leaves to partially smoke and dry them.

Soon the air was heavy with the savory scent of grilled fish. Kiran could hardly wait until the skewer was taken from the fire and passed around. Once the food was in his belly, he sat back and for the first time started to relax.

There was a noise in the forest. He looked to the headhunter and held his breath, waiting. The headhunter made no reaction and Kiran eased out his breath. The sound came again and this time he recognized it. A woodpecker, tocking on hollow wood.

In the firelight, he looked at Butu, really examining him for the first time. The man did not sit, rather he squatted on the ground. The lines and shapes on his face were not painted on, as Kiran had first thought, but permanently scarred. Rows of raised dots adorned his cheeks, as if small stones were implanted beneath his skin. The bones in his ears had been there a long time, the skin grown around them. His sharp teeth were the most curious.

Butu noticed he was staring. Kiran pointed to his own teeth, then to Butu's.

Butu spoke and Pel interpreted. "He thinks his teeth are beautiful, I think. Says he is a man."

"A man? Are you sure that's what he said?"

Pel shrugged. "No."

Butu continued to explain.

Pel shook his head. "I'm not sure I'm understanding. He says they filed his teeth down that way when he became a man."

"He let them do it?"

"Why are you here?" Butu asked through Pel.

Kiran sat back. The question was unexpected yet so relevant. Why am I here? he thought and looked up at the roaring waterfall where his pack was still hanging, the Script inside. "We seek the Voice of the Father," Kiran finally answered, his own voice sounding stiff and wooden to him. "We are headed toward the setting sun."

When Butu responded, his voice sounded hollow, as though

haunted. Kiran stared at him for a long moment in silence. "He wonders why you go to the Land of the Dead," Pel whispered.

Jandon's eyes grew wide. "Land of the Dead?"

Kiran was too tired to be concerned. He'd been through too much. He only knew that he was to keep going, regardless of this man's warnings or Jandon's fears. "We must leave in the morning and continue on," he said to Pel. "As soon as I climb up there and get my pack."

Bria sat up and looked directly at Kiran. "No!" she shouted, her eyes wide with fright. "It's too dangerous."

"All right, Bria," he said in a soothing voice, suppressing his elation that she had final broken free of her grief-stricken silence.

"The worst moment of my life was when you left me and climbed the canyon walls. When the blood gushed down from above, I thought you were dead," she cried.

Kiran stared at her. He knew, in that moment, that she loved him, and he could feel it as powerfully as the sun that warmed his face.

Pel sat up straight. "You saw a waterfall of blood? A real waterfall of blood?" he asked, his head bobbing, anxious for her confirmation. "Where? Tell me how to get there."

Kiran tried to calm Bria, but Pel yanked on his sleeve. "I waited all that time at the Kingdom for the fountain to run with blood. I must find it. Tell me. Tell me where it is."

"Uh, upriver, from the Kotari, in the canyon. I don't remember exactly. Two days travel maybe," Kiran said, not taking his eyes from Bria. He paused, realizing what Pel had just asked. He turned to him. "You're not thinking of going back there, are you? You'll never find it. The blood only ran when it rained."

Pel's face fell.

"Besides, I assumed you'd guide us to the city by the sea."

"To the city?" Pel said, pushing away. "Oh no, I'm not going back there."

All at once, Kiran realized how selfish he had been. Pel was on his own quest, with his own fears and misguided views of the world. Only he was seeking the waterfall of blood. "Up river from the Kingdom of the Kotari, the rock walls are steep, but beyond, you pass through a narrow gap. From there, the walls open to a more gradual slope. It is there that I climbed and Bria saw the waterfall of blood. There was a rock formation that looked like the tower of our Temple. Perhaps you can find it. How you will travel, I don't know. We rode the river downstream."

"I'll find a way," Pel said, his eyes bright with the joy of renewed hope. He turned and, with his usual enthusiasm, spoke with Butu, chattering away for a long time while Kiran and the others waited.

Finally he turned back. "Butu says he will show you a path that will lead you out of the jungle into a savannah of low brush, then into a forest of giant trees. From there, you'll have to cross the dunes to get to the sea."

Kiran paid close attention, putting the directions to memory. "What dangers should we watch for?"

"When you are on the savannah, watch for pit monsters. They lie in wait in underground lairs. You can't see them until you're upon them. You must be very careful where you step."

Kiran sat back, surprised.

"Pit monsters?" Jandon gasped. "Bhau was killed by a Mawghul, hiding in a pit."

"So you know."

Jandon dropped his head in his hands. Kiran stared at Pel. He didn't know what to say, what to think now about Pel, about the other stories he had told them. Were any of them true? Was there really a city by the sea? Pel could speak with the headhunter. That part was true. But what else was and what wasn't?

Now restless to move on, when Kiran lay down, he couldn't sleep. He rose and took a coal from the fire, wrapped it in a green leaf, and cast it afloat in the river, sending a silent wish for Pel to find what he was looking for. The leaf twirled in the current, then tipped, and sank to the bottom. Kiran frowned.

He had hoped to send one for Bria, too.

When Kiran awoke, the headhunter was dancing in the morning mist, singing to the waterfall in placating tones.

"He says this is where the creation mother made humans and taught them to dance for Her," Pel whispered. "Before you enter the sacred mists to get your pack, he needs to invoke Her indulgence."

Out of respect, Kiran and Jandon sat with Pel on the rock next to the river, waiting.

When Bria finally rose from her sleep, she went right to the river and threw up her dinner.

Kiran rushed to her side. "Are you all right?"

"I'm fine," she said, spitting into the water.

When Kiran put his hand on her back, trying to soothe her, she pulled away, her face fear-stricken. "Please, don't. Don't touch me." She swallowed hard.

An iridescent blue butterfly bobbed along the river's surface and landed at his feet. He reached for it and caught it in his cupped hands. Its wings fluttered against his skin. He reached out to show it to Bria, thinking it would make her smile, but it made such a violent attempt to escape, he had to set it free. It danced on the wind in happy flight.

Bria started to cry.

"What's wrong?"

"Roh," she whispered, watching the butterfly flit away.

His chest constricted. He stared into the swirling water, looking for answers. He had followed the Script and come so far seeking the Voice. Bhau was gone, and Kail, and Deke, and now Roh. What would happen to Roh? He could hardly think his name without breaking down. He thought of all that Roh had given up. And for what? He went over their conversation again in his mind. My destiny is here, Roh had said. But why was he so sure? He had insisted. No, he had forced Kiran to go on. Kiran shook his head. What had he been thinking? And what had he meant when he asked Kiran to restore honor to his family?

He went straight to Jandon. "What happened to Roh's family?"

"What are you talking about?"

Bria came along beside them.

"I know you know. Before we left, Deke said something about him being a bad seed. What did he mean?"

"Oh that. Well, about a year or so before we left, Roh's betrothed claimed she was raped and—"

Bria flinched.

"Raped?" Kiran said.

"At first, folks figured she was lying, you know, trying to hide her sin of fornication."

Kiran felt a lump growing in his throat. He didn't dare look at Bria.

274 • Kimberli A. Bindschatel

"But then Roh's father disappeared. They say he did it and he was banished from the village." He shrugged. "At least that's what they say."

Bria's eyes narrowed and she glared at Jandon. "Of course that's what *they* say." She huffed. "Elder Wregan does as he pleases. *They* say and do whatever *they* want, take what is not theirs to take, regardless of whose lives are ruined." She rose to her feet, turned her back on him, and walked away.

"What got into her?"

Kiran stared at Jandon, incredulous. "Don't you see?"

"What? Elder Wregan? You don't believe that do you?" Jandon leaned toward Kiran. "I mean, you know how girls lie about those things."

Kiran drew back and punched him in the stomach. Jandon doubled over. Kiran stomped away, rage pumping through his veins. He went to Bria, tears in his eyes. "I'm sorry. I'm so sorry."

She sat down on the rock, saying nothing. He sat down beside her and looked up at the waterfall and the towering ledge where his pack hung snagged on a protruding rock. The thought of climbing up to get it made his stomach turn watery. But he had to get the Script, then get her away from here. He remembered the giant monkey, swinging across, from vine to vine, with no effort, no fear.

Bria whispered, "You can't climb up there. There has to be another way."

"I'll go," said Jandon. Kiran swung around to face him. Jandon dropped his eyes. "Then maybe you can forgive me."

Jandon scrambled up the rock wall next to the falls. At that moment, Kiran didn't care if Jandon fell and he hated himself for it. Beside him, Pel was calling, "You're almost there. Almost there!" Jandon was stretched across a cascade, hanging on with one hand, reaching for the pack, water pounding over his head.

"Just a little farther," Pel shouted.

Jandon swung out, reaching, and when his hand grasped the pack, his other hand slipped and he tumbled downward into the churning pool below. The others raced along the water's edge as Jandon was carried downriver in the current. He popped up in the center of the river, spitting water, holding up the pack. He swam to shore, shook the water from his hair, handed Kiran the pack, and with a nod, said, "To the Voice."

They moved briskly, anxious to leave the jungle behind. Kiran never took his eyes from the faint path Butu had shown them for fear if he looked away for one moment it would be swallowed by the jungle and they'd be lost.

They hardly spoke, knowing that silence was their best defense against being captured again. When they stopped for the night, they took turns sleeping, each keeping watch. Kiran grew tired of the quiet. He was tired of being scared, tired of running, tired of starving, tired of never getting any closer to the dwelling place—and tired of not knowing why he had been sent or the truth about the Seventh Elder. Aldwyn had told him so many things that night before he left, but the memories were all jumbled in his head. He had said clarity would come with time. But hadn't it been long enough? Wisdom from humility, he had said. But hadn't they suffered enough? How many more sacrifices would have to be made?

Jandon and Bria were the only ones left. Jandon was no leader. He didn't even want to be here. Bria? Could it truly be her? No woman had ever been an Elder. Yet Roh had clearly said, take Bria and run. He hadn't mentioned Jandon. Was he just worried about her or was it more than that?

Kiran noticed Jandon's ankle was swollen and discolored, the old wound inflamed.

Jandon shrugged. "I must have knocked it on a rock when I fell from the waterfall. Don't worry about it."

"Don't worry? You're limping. You can't just ignore it."

Jandon's expression turned hard. "What choice do I have?"

Kiran paused. Jandon was right. They had to go on. Like Roh, they would do what they had to do. Without question. Without hesitation.

Kiran would have given anything to believe like Roh. But could he ever? Was that the reason he had been sent? To find faith? He'd never be an Elder if he couldn't find a way to truly believe. It was simple, he thought. If he could get to the Voice, to see for himself. Then he would know for sure. But something haunted his thoughts. Something Aldwyn had said. Or was it Manu-amatu?

Maybe Roh was right. Maybe it didn't really matter what he thought. Maybe the only thing that mattered was to persevere. To get to the dwelling place. No matter what.

After two days of travel, the jungle turned to savannah and they were finally, once again, under broad, blue skies. Kiran felt like he could breathe again. No more wondering what might be stalking them behind every leaf or branch.

But as they traveled on, the moon waning, the silence between them grew. Bria's behavior became more and more odd. She'd swing between sudden bursts of rage and long periods of moody silence. And she was tired all the time. Kiran had to shake her awake in the mornings and urge her to get moving again after bouts of nausea. He smiled with his eyes, trying desperately to reach her. She'd stare back at him, emptiness in her eyes, as if she were a completely different person. He had no idea how to help her.

One afternoon, they came upon a grove of trees, their bright orange leaves swirling on the wind. Is it harvest time already? Kiran wondered. Had he truly lost track of that much time? As they got closer, he saw they weren't autumn leaves but hundreds of thousands of butterflies that skittered and bobbed, each seeking a foothold among green leaves. Tree upon tree was covered with the black and orange triangles, multiple layers deep, and the sky was alive with soft wispy fluttering of gentle wings.

Bria went ahead, gazing up in delight at the spectacle.

Kiran whispered to Jandon, "What if she has what Deke had?"

Jandon stared at Kiran for a long moment in silence.

"She didn't drink the water," Kiran went on. "I know she didn't. She'll be all right. She's just tired, that's all. She'll be all right."

Jandon nodded.

Their journey in the savannah lasted about seven days, then the terrain turned upward and they were climbing into the mountains. The trees grew taller and taller. They walked on, Bria with her head down, Jandon limping along, and Kiran wondering what would happen next, when they entered a forest of trees taller than he ever imagined trees could grow. Soon his neck was stiff from looking up to marvel at them. In silent wonder, they walked on beneath the massive canopy, over and around logs, across trickling streams, listening to the twittering symphony of chirping birds. The air was sweet and clean with the scent of new growth. Kiran lost track of the sun once more, only catching glimpses of rays filtering through the treetops.

Jandon thought he found a trail amid the web of ferns and grasses and they decided to follow it. By late afternoon, fireflies glinted and pulsed around them, their twinkling lights a reminder of home.

As they crested a rise, Kiran stopped a moment to listen. Something didn't feel right.

From above came a gentle voice. "If you come in peace, you are welcome."

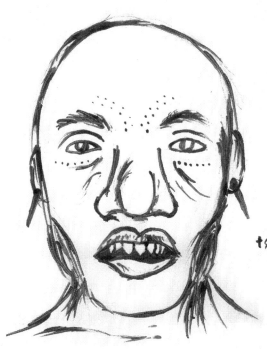

Butu
teeth filed sharp
bones in ears

huts of the Widhu
headhunters

from the tallest trees
harvest from the ground

edible nuts

fish trap

tie down in deep
water, facing
downriver

monkey-brown fur,
black face
haunting howl

food

kiki leaves

stave off hunger and thirst

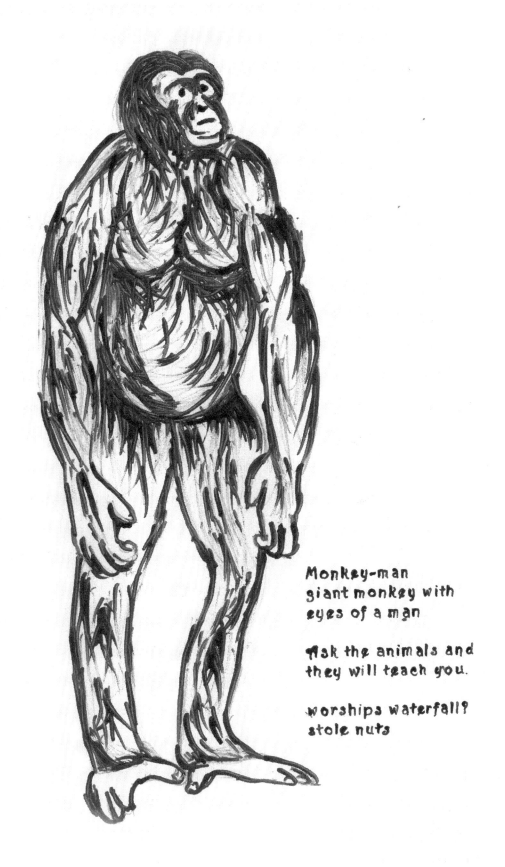

Monkey-man
giant monkey with
eyes of a man

Ask the animals and
they will teach you.

worships waterfall?
stole nuts

28

High above their heads, in the crook of a tree branch, stood a woman wearing a fluttery white tunic and brown, woven pants that cut off just below her knees. Her hair cascaded around her face in soft, brown curls. Kiran blinked to be certain she wasn't an apparition.

She called down to them again. "If you carry no weapons, you may join me. I was just about to sit down for a meal."

"We mean no harm," Kiran said, "and we would be most grateful for something to eat." He turned to Jandon and whispered, "Stay alert."

Jandon shrugged. "Alert for what?"

"Take the stair," she said, waving them toward the base of the tree. Kiran hadn't noticed until she pointed toward it, but sure enough, a thick vine spiraled around the trunk, bending and flattening every few inches forming stairs. A second, smaller vine clung to the tree trunk above, serving as a handrail.

Bria did not hesitate. She took hold of the vine and started up. Kiran took a deep breath, then another. After Jandon hobbled awkwardly upward, Kiran gripped the vine, keeping his eyes fixed on the stairs as he followed.

When he finally reached the landing where the woman greeted them, he had to lean against the tree trunk to steady himself and catch his breath.

"Welcome. I am Aurora," the woman said. She had rosy cheeks and creamy white skin. There was a warmth in her soft, brown eyes that made Kiran feel as though he'd come home.

The woman gestured toward another staircase. "This way." Jandon gave Kiran a questioning glance. Kiran shrugged, glancing upward. From this vantage point, he could see tiny treehouses nestled in the great trees throughout the canopy.

The higher he climbed, the more houses came into view, all connected by a web of branches, braided together, forming bridges from tree to tree.

The stairs led to an open, porch-like room with a low plank table surrounded by soft pillows and set with wooden bowls filled with berries and nuts.

Aurora motioned for them to sit.

Bria plopped down on the nearest pillow.

Jandon and Kiran moved past her. Kiran chose a spot where he could sit with his back against the solid trunk.

Aurora joined them. "Please help yourselves," she said, gesturing toward the food. "What brings you to the Weikaito Forest?"

Instantly, Kiran's mind went back to the day they had arrived in the Kingdom of the Kotari. He was certain now that Angei-Ami had betrayed them, taking their story to the Guardian so he could use it to twist and distort his message, drawing them into his web, before separating them to slowly enslave their minds. Kiran wouldn't let that happen again.

He stared at Aurora without expression. "We're just passing through."

"Well, while you are here, our home is your home." She handed Bria a bowl. "You look famished."

Bria thanked her with a smile and took a handful of berries.

"We serve those in need. Rest here and regain your strength. Stay as long as you'd like." She paused as if waiting for them to say more. When they didn't, she went on. "You have traveled a long way."

"Yes, a long way," Kiran said, forcing a smile.

"If you are lost—"

"We're not lost," Kiran interrupted, then realized he'd been rude. "But thank you."

"Do you know the way to the dunes?" Jandon asked.

Kiran shot him a warning glance.

"The dunes?" She sat back, her eyebrows raised in surprise. "Are you headed to the city by the sea?"

Kiran shifted in his seat. "We are just travelers who will thank you and move on."

"I see," she said with a kind smile. "Forgive me, but you don't seem to be prepared to travel the dunes. If indeed that is your plan, I must warn you, the sun is harsh and the wind unbearable. The sands shift constantly. It is a very dangerous place. Many have lost their way." She looked from face to face, waiting for a response.

The Torans remained silent.

"No matter," she said. "You are safe here among the trees." From below, as if an affirmation, came the soft fluttering of leaves on the forest floor.

Until that moment, Kiran had almost forgotten how high they were. "So this isn't just a hiding place, you live up here?"

"This is our home." She said the word with special reverence as she glanced around her room. "We care for the trees and they take care of us. The forest is Mother to all." Kiran followed her gaze and noticed with awe: the room was part of the living tree, its branches woven into a roof. The floor was made of woven branches as well. Somehow, the branches had grown into shape, forming the shelter.

Beyond, among the treetops, Kiran caught glimpses of faces popping out to spy on their unexpected visitors. They reminded Kiran of the squirrel on the mountain and the monkey-man by the falls— cautiously aware.

Aurora noticed Jandon had emptied his bowl. "Have more," she said. "We have plenty."

Jandon hesitated, looking over the food on the table. "Do you have any meat?"

She replied with a gentle smile. "We nourish our bodies with the fruits of the forest, not the flesh of another living being."

"Huh?" Jandon curled up his lip, confused by her answer.

"If we harm one, we harm all. So, you see," she turned to look into Kiran's eyes, "if you mean no harm, you are safe here. You have nothing to fear."

Kiran held her gaze. He liked this woman and this peaceful abode. She seemed kind and genuine. In some inexplicable way, she belonged here in the trees, somehow a part of this place, as though she embodied the essence of the forest itself. He felt he could trust her. But how could he know for sure?

"You are tired, I can see." She was looking at Bria who was fighting to keep her eyes open. "Let me offer a place to rest. We can talk in the morning."

"No. Thank you," said Kiran. "Really. If we could just refill our waterskins and be on our way, we'd be most grateful." He wanted to get his feet planted firmly back on the ground and move on.

Bria looked to Kiran and nodded. She tried to get to her feet, but slumped back down again. Aurora glanced at Kiran, but said nothing.

When Jandon rose, his pant leg was bunched around his thigh, revealing his injured ankle.

"My, that is a serious wound," Aurora said.

Jandon whipped his eyes toward her and bent to shove down his pant leg.

"Let me take you to our healer. I'm sure she can help."

Kiran's stomach tightened. "No—" he caught himself, "I mean, we'd prefer to stay together. We'll all go." He took Bria by the hand and helped her to her feet.

"As you wish," Aurora said. "Your journey has been a difficult one. No doubt you have met many who were… unkind." She placed her hand on his arm and looked into his eyes. "We are not them."

Kiran turned to Bria. Dark circles had formed under her eyes, her hair was a tangled mess, and she slouched where she stood. "Thank you," he said, managing a smile. "I don't mean to offend. You are most gracious, though we are strangers."

"Who is a stranger but a friend we have yet to meet," she said, her warm smile melting his resolve. "Perhaps it would be better to summon the healer here, in the morning, after you've had a good night's rest."

Kiran nodded.

She took Jandon by the arm and helped him across a suspended walkway.

Kiran hesitated. They must have been fifty feet above the ground. He took a deep breath and stepped out onto the bridge. He was surprised at how solid it felt. Quickly, he made his way across to the other side to another tiny treehouse.

Hammocks lined with soft, inviting pillows were strung from overhanging branches. "Sleep well, my friends," she said and slipped away.

Bria and Jandon crawled into hammocks and were fast asleep. He gazed at Bria, lying peacefully. He ached to embrace her, to take her in his arms and smother her with soft kisses. But he knew she would refuse him; it was as though she'd crossed over to another place, on the other side of a great chasm that Kiran would never be able to reach.

Of all the things Kiran had done on the journey, he never dreamed he'd sleep cradled in the boughs of a giant tree high above the forest floor. He eased into a hammock and it swayed back and forth, rocking him to sleep.

In the morning, Kiran lay in the hammock in a drowsy half sleep, listening to a beautiful symphony. The birds of the forest sang together, their melodies woven into a tapestry of sound.

From across the way, Aurora called out, "Good morning! I hope you have slept well." She was making her way across the bridge. "I have breakfast for you."

"Ah, thank you," Kiran said. "We very much appreciate your hospitality, and don't want to be rude, but after the meal, we must really be on our way."

"Certainly," she said as she set a tray on the table. As promised, there were berries and a whole host of nuts and breads and honey.

Kiran turned to wake Bria. She was gone. His heart leaped into his throat. He spun around. "Where is she?"

"She asked for a bath. Early this morning."

"Where? Take me to her."

"But the baths are—"

"Now! Take me to her now."

"Certainly. This way."

Just then, Bria came to the top of the stair. He rushed to her. "Are you all right?"

"I'm better." She smiled with her eyes. "I'm better." She walked past him to the table and sat to eat, her clean scent lingering in the air. He sighed with relief, able to breathe once more.

Jandon rolled from his hammock and limped across the floor to the table.

An old woman with a doughy face and soft eyes was ambling across the bridge toward them. "Oh, here is our healer now," said Aurora. Right behind her, carrying a canvas bag, was one of the giant monkeys Kiran had seen in the jungle. His eyes grew wide.

Aurora caught his gaze. "There is no need to be alarmed. She won't hurt you." She paused. "You have seen others like her before."

"We have seen them." Kiran's heart started to race. "Is she, is she your slave?"

"Oh my, no." Her laughter sounded like the soft twitter of a bird.

"These creatures are our cousins. We offer them refuge. The men of the south see only their physical strength." The creature approached and wrapped her arms around Aurora. "But we know the beauty of their souls. We have found many wandering alone and near starvation, separated from their loved ones by the slavers. We invite them to live here with us. This is Fifi." Aurora hugged the healer woman, too. "She has taken to our healer and follows her, helping where she can." The healer nodded her agreement. "We care for them and they for us." Aurora sighed and gazed out over the railing. "If only it could be that way with all our forest neighbors."

Kiran couldn't take his eyes off the creature. She was just like the ones he had seen at the waterfall, walking with the same awkward gait. When the animal set down the bag, she moved her hands in the air, making a series of odd gestures. Aurora nodded and gestured back.

"Are you communicating with her?" asked Bria, her eyes bright with curiosity.

"Yes," Aurora answered. "They cannot speak like we do. So we use a language of hand signs to communicate. I've asked her how her little one is feeling today." She pointed to a tiny ball of fur held in the creature's arms. Bria's face brightened. The animal sat down next to Bria. The baby opened its huge brown eyes and crawled from her mother's arms into Bria's lap. Bria giggled with delight. She cradled the babe in her arms and it nuzzled her face, making a little sucking noise. Bria glanced at Kiran, her eyes wide with joy, and he had an overwhelming urge to wrap his arms around her.

"You must stay off it or you may never walk normally again," the healer told Jandon. "You should rest at least two moons."

Kiran spun around with a gasp. "Two moons!" He and Jandon exchanged a look of surprise.

"Are you sure?" Jandon asked.

"I suppose we could spare a few days. But two moons," Kiran mumbled.

The healer gave Jandon a salve to rub on his ankle and suggested he rest in the hammock.

Aurora nodded toward the empty waterskins. "I know you are anxious to make preparations. Shall I show you to our well?"

Kiran looked back to Bria. She was cooing and tickling the baby. He drew in a long breath. The air smelled of fresh spring buds, cool and sweet. He looked back to Aurora. He knew he should be cautious, but something about her reminded him of Kalindria and he felt a pang of regret. He should have trusted her. Not everyone is harmful, he told himself. *Listen to your heart.* He nodded and picked up the waterskins.

Once they had descended the vine staircase and were back on the forest floor, Aurora walked beside him. "If you tell them they must go, they will follow you."

He shook his head. "I'm not the leader."

She nodded. "Nonetheless, they follow you."

"They are just tired right now. You were right. They need some rest."

"Indeed," she said. They walked on in silence over green moss. Kiran reached down to touch it, to feel the soft, velvety texture.

"It is a great burden, being a leader," Aurora said, her voice faraway.

He plopped down on the moss and looked up at her, surprised. "You're the leader of the Weikaito? But you're—"

"I'm what?" She smoothed the front of her tunic. "Not dressed for the role?" She laughed. "I am no different from anyone else. Yet, they look to me for answers. They have great faith in me, though I never feel worthy." As she eased to the ground to sit on the moss beside him, Kiran noticed a glistening pendant dangling from her neck. He had only seen a stone like that once before, the morning before he had left the village.

"But you must have the answers," he said. "You carry a magic stone."

"Magic?" She took it in her hand and ran her fingers over the smooth surface. "This? No. It's just a beautiful rock." She twirled it in the sunlight and it sparkled, flashing different colors. "I carry it as a reminder that, though we think something is clear, if we look from another angle, we might see it differently."

Kiran thought he understood. "Everything looks different from the other side, or on a different day, or in a different season."

"You speak like a true leader."

He didn't respond. They were Aldwyn's words, not his own.

"Most people need to know someone has the answers. In your group, that someone is you."

"I'm not even a true Toran," he mumbled.

She waited, silent.

"The Elders didn't designate a leader. You see," he paused. "There were seven of us, sent on a pilgrimage. We have been traveling now for eight moons. We, well, we aren't even sure if we're on the right path. We had to leave our village in haste. We weren't prepared. Bria and Jandon are the only ones left."

"And you."

"But I was only sent to record the journey."

"And how do you know this? You were one of the seven sent, were you not?"

He shrugged.

She waited for him to go on.

He looked down at his feet. "I'm the only one who can scribe. Aldwyn taught me in secret. So you see, that must be why I'm here."

"Kiran, you have great strength, yet you are humble. You are cautious, yet not afraid to make a decision." She waited for him to look her in the eyes. "You have the character of a great leader."

He felt his cheeks warm.

"Do not be mistaken: regardless of the intent of your Elders, leaders cannot be designated. Leaders are those whom people *choose* to follow." She gestured toward the treetops, toward Bria and Jandon. "They choose to follow you."

Kiran gazed back up at the tree for a moment, then rose to his feet. "I was following you to fetch water," he said. He didn't know what else to say.

Down a short path, they came to the well. Rocks had been gathered and stacked to form a shallow pool where water bubbled up from the ground. Encircling the pool were intricate wooden carvings of flower blossoms with multiple layers of petals. "These are beautiful," he said as he knelt down to fill his waterskin.

"The water lily is the manifestation of the divine essence. She is born mired in muddy waters, far from the sun. In time, she reaches the light and transforms into a pure white beauty." Aurora ran her fingers along a petal of one of the carvings and closed her eyes. "She inspires us to seek the light, for that is the greatest aspiration." She stared into the water, a faint frown lingering at the corners of her mouth and he wondered what she was thinking about that created such a look of sadness in her eyes.

"Aurora, do you really think...is it possible...what I mean is...I am just an orphan boy, the bastard son of a heathen."

"Were." She gestured for him to rise to his feet. "Look," she said, her gaze dropping to the water's surface. "There is wisdom in water."

He rose to see his own reflection. He didn't recognize himself. Before him was not a boy, but a man, weary and drawn.

Back up into the trees Aurora went and Kiran followed. When he entered the treehouse, the healer was talking with Bria. She had brought crutches for Jandon and he was hobbling across the bridge, trying to get used to them. Kiran paused in the archway.

Aurora whispered to him, "She will be all right. She is strong." Kiran turned to face her, feeling transparent, as if she understood his every thought and emotion. "So is your love for her." He nodded, his eyes returning to Bria. "She will be safe here. Cared for."

"It won't be long and we'll be on our way."

She bowed her head. "Yes, of course."

Bria noticed Kiran had returned and ended her conversation with the healer. The woman rose and with a bow turned and followed Aurora down the walkway.

"Do we have to leave soon?" Bria asked him.

Kiran hesitated. Aurora was right, he thought. How did this happen? Not so long ago, Bria would have stated her opinion, argued for it. Something had changed in her. Or was it him? Maybe he had become the leader. But did that make him worthy of the robes of an Elder? I'm still a heathen bastard, he thought. Suddenly he felt utterly alone, deep inside, where no one could reach. Bria was right here with him, but he couldn't talk to her.

"Did she show you the well?" she asked.

He nodded. *And so much more.*

Late that afternoon, the forest came alive with the soft murmur of rain and the rich scent of green leaves. Two women came across the walkway with two young boys and a baby girl toddling behind. The first woman set down a basket and heaved a sigh. "My, I am getting old. Well, let's have a look at you." She twirled her finger, gesturing for them to turn around. Bria, Jandon, and Kiran did as she directed. "This should do." She handed Jandon a fresh tunic and sifted through her basket for another one for Kiran.

The other woman held a pair of short cropped pants up to Bria. "Hmmm," she muttered, dropping the pants back in her basket and riffling through it. "Take these," she said, holding out another brown pair.

"This is so kind, but I couldn't—"

"Oh, don't you worry now. We share and share alike." She gave Bria a gentle nudge. "Go on, now. Try them on."

Bria went behind a dividing wall to change and emerged with a bright smile. "I've never worn pants before."

"Ah, well," said the woman. "I'm glad you are delighted."

"Come along now," the first woman said. "Everyone is gathering for the banquet."

"Banquet?" Kiran shook his head. "Thank you, but we don't want to impose."

"Impose?" said the woman with a chuckle. "You misunderstand. The celebration is in your honor." She paused. "To welcome you to the Weikaito forest."

"Oh," he said. Kiran, Bria, and Jandon shared a surprised look and turned back to the women, smiling and nodding.

The kitchens and dining hall were built on the ground with smooth stone floors, a stone fireplace, and half walls to protect the forest from fires. The entire Weikaito community had gathered, nearly one hundred and twenty of them, the air abuzz with greetings and gossip, each one anxious to meet the Torans. They lined up to shake their hands and pat their backs. Two young boys with identical blond curls were hopping in line, piping, "My turn! My turn!"

Jandon whispered to Kiran, "They must not get visitors often."

There were too many faces to remember and the women's and the men's clothing was practically identical—white tunic, brown knickers. Among them, Kiran counted eighteen monkey-men, and just as Aurora had said, they were part of the family.

A robust soup of roasted mushrooms and leeks was served with warm bread. It felt good to be among people again, laughing and talking. On a raised platform, a boy played a wooden flute and a girl strummed an instrument similar to the lyre of Kiran's village. The Weikaito ate and drank and sang along with festive cheer, clearly happy to have a reason to host a party. Kiran imagined, had they had a farewell banquet in the village, it would have been like this one.

A song ended and the flute-playing boy announced to the crowd, "And now, for our guests, *The Ancestor's Footprints*." He launched into a vibrant, catchy jig. The people cheered and clapped to the beat. The lyrics spoke of the beauty of the landscape—the plants, rocks, sand, water holes. Kiran hummed along, enjoying himself.

For the rest of the evening, he danced and sang, relaxing in the company of the kind-hearted folk.

When the festivities finally came to a close, and the Torans returned to their room and readied for bed, Bria sat down next to Kiran. "I like it here," she said.

"Me too," he said, the *Footprints* song still playing in his head. "Me too."

Two days later, after the morning breakfast, Aurora called for Kiran.

"I have a gift for you," she said, smiling.

"A gift? But you've already done so much."

"It has been my pleasure. Come. I want you to meet someone as well." Kiran, curious now, followed after her, across the branch bridges from one treehouse to the next, through the intertwined canopy they called home. They came to a large house he hadn't yet visited, high above the others with a stunning view of the valley. "Salista," she called as they entered. "I've brought Kiran."

Kiran's eye roamed, taking in his surroundings. This was not a home but some kind of working area. There were individual tables with candles set on each one.

Salista shuffled out from behind a shelf. "Ah, yes. Welcome, Kiran." She was short and plump with a wide smile and small eyes set too close together. "Take a seat," she said, patting the top of a stool at one of the worktables. Kiran glanced at Aurora. Salista shuffled back behind a wall of shelves and emerged with a wooden box in her arms. She set it on the table in front of Kiran, then heaved herself up onto the stool next to him and crossed her arms, resting them on her belly. "Go on now. Open it."

Gently, he raised the lid. "It's a codex," said Aurora. Aldwyn had told him of books, tomes that contained the stories of many scrolls, but he had never seen a real one. He hesitated, looking to Aurora. She nodded to continue.

He reached in and took the codex from its box. It was square-shaped with a woven cover. Individual folded pages were sewn together with thin twine and could be turned one at a time. He ran his fingers along the edge of the first page, feeling the texture. "This isn't vellum," he said.

"Paper," Salista told him. "Made from trees."

He flipped through the pages. Each was blank. He looked back to Aurora, confused now.

She went to the shelf and returned with a cup of writing sticks. "This codex is yours, to record your story."

He swung around to meet her eyes. "Mine?"

"You are a scribe, are you not?"

He looked down at the book in his hands. "Well, yes, but…"

"You may work here. Anytime you'd like. Salista tells me there is room."

"Thank you," Kiran said. "Thank you!" He couldn't contain his delight. An entire book! He would transpose the Script first, then, while Jandon healed and Bria rested, he would record every important detail of the journey so far.

This was what he was meant to do.

29

Kiran stared at the mildewed scroll spread open before him as though, if he waited long enough, its secrets would be magically revealed. There had to be more, something he was missing. The elaborate calligraphy, the intricate designs painstakingly scrawled in the borders—any seemingly insignificant part of it could hold meaning. He imagined the Elders gathered at the Temple, whispering by candlelight, pouring over the Script in their deliberations. Were they just as puzzled, trying to make sense of it? Or, if they were here now, would they have known if they were on the right path?

Aldwyn had said he would find the way and learn the truth on his own. But how? There were so many things he didn't know, didn't understand. The only thing he knew for certain was that he was the scribe.

When he had first arrived in the Weikaito Forest, he was exhausted from simply trying to survive. But now, he worked diligently in the workshop, writing and drawing in his new codex, recording all he had learned so far—the story of creation from the Lendhi, warnings of the Guardian and their escape. Salista even taught him a way to record the Weikaito song he enjoyed so much, *The Ancestor's Footprints*.

But he struggled with the sensation that time was slipping through his fingers. Every day he told himself that it wouldn't be long and Jandon and Bria would be ready to travel again.

One morning, after they'd been in the Weikaito forest for nearly two weeks, Bria came to tell him of an upcoming celebration that would occur at the full moon. She wanted to witness the miracle the Weikaito called the Blooming of the Lilies. "For three days each spring, everyone joins in the festivities," she said. "When the lilies bloom, it marks a new beginning. During the celebration, any couples who desire to be wed simply take part in the ceremony. They don't have to ask permission of anyone. No Elders, no parents. Not even the Great Father. Can you imagine, Kiran?"

"That's nice, but we've stayed too long already," he said and could see right away that she was disappointed. "But perhaps it will be a good omen," he said. "Then we'll head out."

She paused before nodding agreement.

When the day of the festival finally arrived, there was an excitement in the air. People bustled back and forth along the walkways and up and down the tree trunk stairs, carrying baskets and blankets.

Jandon, Bria, and Kiran set out through the forest with the crowd, walking along the bank of a stream toward the Lily Pond. They came to the top of a rise and saw in the valley below where the stream met another and the two intertwined as though in a lustful embrace, merging into one, then spread wide to form a placid pond. Large glossy green lily pads floated on the surface, each as wide as a man is tall, the edges curled up, forming a rosy lip around the circumference. Maroon buds floated amid the gigantic round leaves, rocking with the gentle lapping of tiny ripples.

At the edge of the pond, Kiran sat next to Bria on a bed of soft green moss to wait for dusk. The grasses along the pond's shore were a tender new green and alive with the tocking of frogs and the throaty warble of tiny birds, flitting through the bushes. Yellow butterflies with paper-thin wings skimmed the glassy surface of the pond. The air had an earthy, indefinable scent that reminded Kiran of warm spring days back home that made him ache for their innocence. He'd give anything to see Bria smile once more, the way she would when her eyes sparkled. If only they could go back in time and start again.

The wind calmed and the lengthening shadows turned soft as the last rays of sunlight reached across the valley, turning everything golden.

As the moon rose, and night finally settled on the pond, the buds began to open right before their eyes. The brilliant white petals stood erect and released an intense fragrance, like sweet apple cider, that permeated the night air, then slowly unfurled, spreading their petals to receive the full light of the moon. Soon came the monotone hum of thousands of beetles flying to and fro about the pond in their frenzied quest to enter the innermost sanctum of the blossoms. "The beetles must arrive by a certain time," Bria whispered to Kiran, "or they'll miss their one chance."

The night grew darker, the full moon brightened, and all watched with reverence as one candle was lit, then another, then another, the flame shared round the pond, as the bard told a tale of the sacred water lily and her hero, the beetle.

When the bard finished her story, the sweet strumming of the lute joined the buzzing of the beetles and the Weikaito came alive, dancing and singing in celebratory merriment. Food and drink were shared, though Kiran was careful to drink only from his own waterskin. The party reminded him of the Harvest Festival back home, everyone having a good time and enjoying each other's company, chores set aside for the duration.

The celebration lasted until dawn, when the first rays of sun peeked over the horizon. All gathered around the pond once again to watch the blossoms close, trapping the beetles inside. Then, a few at a time, they wandered away to settle down to nap on soft mosses in the sun. "Now, I'm told, we wait for the farewell to old and the celebration of a new beginning," Bria said and turned to find a place to lie down. He followed her, wanting to be with her every moment he could. She chose a spot and he lay down next to her, their shoulders touching. When she didn't pull away, he took her hand in his and held it as they dozed off to sleep.

Kiran awoke as the sun was dropping behind the trees. Beside him, Bria whispered, "It won't be long now. At nightfall, the beetles will be off to fulfill their destiny. But first, the wedding." She was smiling and he nodded, happy that she was happy. She pointed to a towering cedar at the edge of the pond. "That tree is Adoette, the sacred tree. Those who choose to be wed will circle it, symbolizing their commitment to one another." A young bride and groom, both dressed in flowing green gowns, circled the tree, three times around, both carrying something in their hands. "Each has made a doll," Bria explained, "a likeness of themselves, from their own clothing." The young lovers presented the dolls to Aurora. As she recited a prayer, she tied them together with a white ribbon. "Now they are bound. The couple will go together to hide the dolls in the woods. They will bury them in a secret place that only they know about, so that no one can separate their love," Bria whispered, a tear in her eye. Kiran took her hand in his and squeezed.

Aurora offered the bound dolls to the couple, and, when the bride and groom took hold of the little bundle, the people cheered. "They are now wed," Bria said. She looked up at Kiran, her eyes watery. "Isn't it romantic?"

He wanted to take her away to their own secret place. But she had made her feelings about marriage clear. He stood stone still, unsure what to say, unsure what she wanted him to say. So he said nothing.

They went back to sit in their spot by the pond. She drew her knees up to her chest like a child, shivering in the cool night. Kiran opened the blanket and wrapped it around them both, holding her close to him, feeling optimistic. Bria seemed happy, almost like herself again. He pressed his cheek against hers and felt her breath, hot on his neck. He'd forgotten how having her so near affected him. His breath came in tiny pants. His hand went to the back of her head and he gently pulled her head against his chest and twirled his fingers in her hair.

She turned and looked up at him, her eyes heavy with weariness. "Tell me again what our life would be like if we were back home and I had accepted your hand."

His eyes warmed with tears. "We would have our own little farm. And we would have beautiful babies with rosy cheeks and your green eyes. And I would love you until the end of days."

"Ah, that is a pleasant dream." She smiled, a faraway look in her eyes.

"Bria, I…" Their eyes met and held. "Bria, I love you. I don't care about anything else. Nothing else matters. I love you."

"I know," she said. "I love you, too."

She closed her eyes and kissed him. He trembled, wishing life could stop right here and now so he could live in this bliss forever.

All at once, the blossoms opened and released the beetles to the wind.

Bria watched them fly away. "Do you see, Kiran, how the blossoms have changed from white to pink overnight?"

He nodded.

"I'll never forget this night," she whispered as she laid her head on his chest.

After a time, her breathing slowed and he knew she was asleep. He jerked upright. "Bria, the full moon."

Gently, she took his hands and wrapped his arms back around her. "It doesn't matter," she whispered. "Not anymore."

He awoke in the treehouse to the soft serenade of the woodland birds. In the night, everyone had returned to their rooms. Almost everyone, he thought, as he glanced at Jandon's empty hammock. Bria was awake, sitting in the chair next to his bed, her eyes filled with tears.

He sat up and took her hand in his. "Bria, what's wrong?"

She shook her head and let the tears flow down her cheek. She dropped his hand, rose from the chair, went to the edge of the platform, and leaned on the railing, gazing out into the mist. Kiran went to the railing next to her. Beams of sunlight streamed down through the mist, giving the forest a soft yellow glow.

Her eyes drifted around the treetops. "This…is what I've always…"

His heart sank. "You want to stay."

His statement hung in the air between them.

Kiran looked down at his hands. "I thought you just needed some time to rest."

She turned to face him. "You and I both know, even if I make it, they won't accept me. Not a woman."

"Of course they will. How could they not?" He took her hand in his. "Bria, you are just as worthy of the robes. They'll see. We'll make them see."

She forced a smile. "That's just it, Kiran. I no longer care what they see." She gazed out into the mist. "Things…happen. People change."

He glanced around the forest. It was peaceful here. Women were respected, equally. There were no Elders telling her what she could or couldn't achieve. He thought of his last conversation with Kail, how she had been so sure she had found exactly what she had been seeking, how the words of the Guardian had fulfilled all of her expectations, how being his bride had fulfilled her aspirations.

Maybe we seek what we believe, he thought.

His eyes found hers again. Her face looked drawn, her eyes heavy with regret. For a long moment she was silent, holding his gaze. She had more to say, he could sense, and he tried to brace himself for whatever it might be. She looked away, her eyes swaying back and forth as if she were trying to find the words. She turned and paced to the chair, then back to the railing.

"Bria," he said, taking her by the hand. "You're just feeling—"

Her eyes met his. "You need to go."

He let the air escape from his lungs and his shoulders slumped in resignation. She was staying. And he had to go on. Without her.

There was a part of him who wanted to argue with her, to tell her he could stay with her and be content here with a life together, that he could let the quest go. But he knew he'd be lying. To her. To himself. What she said was true; she had simply put it into words before he could admit it to himself, the same way she always seemed to know what he was feeling about her.

Suddenly the forest seemed to draw in on him. He grabbed hold of the railing. He wanted to beg her to go with him, to tell her how terrified he was.

She waited, her eyes on him. He started to say something, then saw her expression. She brought her finger to his lips. "It's your destiny," she said.

"But you and I—"

"The villagers are counting on you."

He let out a breath. "Bria," he whispered. "I'm no hero."

"Listen to me. We all would have died without you. You found food, you came up with a way to collect water. You saved Roh's life. You were the one who realized we could sing. If it weren't for your bravery, we might never have escaped." She tapped him on the chest. "Kiran, you did all that. You." She kissed him on the cheek. "You're already a hero."

He had to turn away, to hide his tears from her. He wasn't worthy. Not of her praise. Inside, he'd been just as scared as the others. He had only done what he had to do. He had only been trying to… to persevere. He took a deep breath. Isn't that what Roh had been trying to tell him? To go on, despite his fear? Roh must have been terrified, running from the slavers, not knowing whether he would live or die. But he had done it anyway, and saved them.

Kiran raised his chin and brought his shoulders back, his resolve hardened. He would make Roh proud. He would make all of them proud. He turned back to face her. "I will come back for you."

For a moment, she showed no reaction. Then she simply nodded.

He realized then what she must have already known, that he might never see her again. Might never hold her again. Might never… Suddenly he couldn't breathe.

She hugged him tight, then drew back and smiled a broad, happy smile. "Let's get your things together."

She handed him his rucksack and started gathering his few belongings. He stuffed them in the pack, then pulled them out, and repacked them again. He dropped the pack on the floor and looked at her. Everything was happening too fast. "Bria, I..."

Jandon came hobbling across the walkway on his crutches, carrying something under his arm. "Going somewhere?"

Kiran looked to Bria, then back to Jandon. "We've waited too long. We need to get going," he said.

Jandon looked down at his foot. "I know."

"It will be all right. We'll take it slow, but we'll get there."

Jandon looked at Bria, then back to Kiran, his expression solemn. "We both know I'm not meant to go," he said. "If I had to face the Voice, I'd probably turn to stone."

"But—"

"Bria asked me to get this for you." He shifted his weight to one foot, took both crutches in one hand, and handed the codex to Kiran.

Kiran looked to Bria, then back to Jandon. "But I hadn't decided yet."

Jandon shrugged.

Kiran was speechless for a long moment, staring at his old friend. He put his arms around him and whispered in his ear, "Take care of her."

"I will. I promise."

Kiran held his gaze, searching for more to say. He glanced at Bria, then back to Jandon and a jealous fear crept into his mind.

"I know what you're thinking," Jandon said, slapping him on the shoulder. "Don't worry. Bria's too smart to ever fall for someone like me." He gave Kiran a half grin.

Kiran smiled back and laughed. They had been through so much and he never stopped to think about how scared Jandon must have been all along, especially when Deke died. Jandon hadn't even wanted to come in the first place. It was unfair to blame him for any of it. Jandon hadn't changed a bit. He was still the simple farmboy who liked Kiran when no one else did. "I will miss you, my friend."

"And I, you. You will make us proud." They embraced once more and Kiran fought back tears. When he pulled away, Jandon said, "Oh, I almost forgot." He pulled at the cord around his neck and slid the Pyletar over his head. "Take this."

Kiran took it in his hands. "But you—"

"Just take it." Jandon shrugged. "Maybe he meant for it to be blessed or something."

Kiran nodded and put it around his neck.

"While I was out, I saw Aurora. She said to meet her by the well."

"Did she say what she wanted?"

Jandon shook his head.

Kiran turned back to Bria. "Whatever it is, I suppose I need to tell her of my plans. I'll be right back." He set the codex on top of his pack and headed for the stairs.

Several of the Weikaito family were gathered at the well. Aurora stood next to an animal with a flat back and shaggy, white fur, similar to a sheep, but taller and lankier, with long, curved ears. Strapped to its back were two water containers made of tree bark and sealed with pine pitch. "It is a very long way," Aurora said. "The sun will come round forty times before you reach the sea. You cannot carry all that you will need alone. This is Medira," she said. "She's a great companion and can carry enough food and water for the two of you."

"This is very kind," Kiran said, looking to all the encouraging faces. "I don't know what to say. Jandon must have told you I'm going, but I am not yet prepared to travel the dunes. I don't know—"

"Ah, but you do." Aurora took a step forward, reaching out to someone standing behind Kiran. He spun around. Jandon and Bria had followed him down from the treehouse. Bria was holding his codex out to him. Aurora took it from her and opened it to the page where he had inscribed *The Ancestor's Footprints*. "Sing the song and you will find your way."

The others started to hum the tune as though sending him in merry farewell.

Aurora hugged him and whispered in his ear, "All you have to do is take the first step." She pulled away and gave him a broad smile.

His head was swimming.

He turned to Bria. Her eyes were filled with tears. He reached out to her, touched her cheek, and ran his finger along her jaw, trying to etch her image into his memory to hold forever. His gaze lingered on her soft lips, then her green eyes. He had forgotten how bright her eyes could be. How they seemed to sparkle when she smiled. "When I see you smile, I know I can do anything," he whispered.

She rewarded him with a larger one. "I have something for you," she said, taking from her pocket two tiny dolls. She handed him one that was made from her skirt. "It's…" She wiped back a tear. "It's me." She hugged the other little doll to her chest. He could see that it was made from his old tunic. "And I will hold you… close to my heart… until…"

He pulled her to him and kissed her with abandon, his heart filled with longing. He wanted to hold her for eternity, but knew that no matter how far he traveled, he would be forever bound to her.

When she pulled away, he looked down at her beautiful face "Bria, I don't need—"

She put her fingers to his lips. "Some things we have to find out for ourselves." She handed him his pack and nodded toward the setting sun.

Day after day, as he walked the shimmering dunes, he lost all sense of time and space. Nothing in life seemed solid anymore, just waves of unending, undulating sand, sculpted by the whims of the wind. The only sign of life was an occasional snake, its head protruding from the sand, its body hidden below, or little piles of sun-dried grasses, whisked around by the tiny whirlwinds that spiraled across the dunes.

At night, alone in the vast expanse of darkness, with nowhere to hide, nowhere to flee, he felt naked, as vulnerable as a baby, and slept curled in a ball next to Medira, his dreams invaded by visions of snakes, their bloody heads on sticks. Worst of all was the recurring dream of himself, wandering the dunes for eternity, alone, staggering through the sand, shouting for the others, knowing he'd never see them again, sent to die alone in the sand, his bones left for the birds to pick clean. He would wake in the morning, shivering in the chill, with only Medira to comfort him, her ears perked upward.

He'd look for his tracks from the day before. There were never distinct footprints, only a faint hint of his passing. He'd take off his boots and shake the sand from them, brush the fine dust from between his toes, then put his boots back on, get to his feet again and walk on.

He plodded west, day after day, fighting the wind under the silent sun, with nothing to see but sand and sky, nothing to do but think, acutely aware of the void. The nothingness pulsated with profound emotion and his mind began to drift with the sand, up and away, for lengths of time without measure, from the ceaseless striving toward the Voice, back to the forest and Bria, to live out their lives together in the harmonious world of the Weikaito.

The urge to quit, to turn back, came on him in waves. Then he would imagine his village, dry and brittle, swept away like dust on the wind, and he'd be left weak and shaken by the visions, gripped by fear that if he ever did made it to the Voice, it would be too late. His mind retreated into a dark state of detachment, as though his soul had fled into a deep recess of his being. His life back home in the village became a surreal, dream-like image of the distant past, fading now into a mirage.

At times, he thought how easy it would be to lie down, stop walking, to give in, to escape to the bliss of sleep. He was sick to death of thinking, of words, of not knowing the meaning of the Script. He wanted it over. But he was haunted by the image of Roh and his indomitable will, and the promise Roh had compelled him to make. He would not quit, not while he could still draw breath.

One morning when he awoke, he thought he smelled the salt of the sea carried on the wind. He counted the scratch marks he had been making on his walking stick, once again, to be certain of the days that had passed. He had spent forty days and forty nights, as Aurora said the journey would be, but in every direction he saw nothing but rolling hills of sand. Then he noticed, toward the setting sun, a mound speckled with reeds of grass. He picked up his pace and trudged to the top.

In the distance stood a city of buildings like none he'd ever seen before. Beyond, lay the sea.

the Lily and the Beetle

Long ago, at the end of days,
before the beginning of days,
Lily rose from the abyss
of the primordial waters,
seeking light.

The full moon shone down on her.
Beetle, attracted to her beauty,
came to greet her.

She opened herself to him
and the two became one.
Then he took her divine essence
and spread it through the forest.

Now the sun sets, and rises again,
fine and slow,
Lily transforms.

There is no death.
She passes to another world.
As winter thaws
and spring comes anew.

Why, Great Father, do you forsake me to this agony? I cry out to You, but You do not answer. I will see You with my own eyes. Why must I continue on? I know that you can do all things. Oh, Great Father. Speak to me now. Why must I suffer? What will happen if I die here under the sun? Oh, that I might collapse and end my days now. Do I have the strength of stone? What I feared has come upon me. The days pass and so do the desires of my heart. As a mountain erodes and crumbles, as water wears away the soil, so is a man's hope destroyed.

Oh, how I long to understand the mysteries of the Great Father. Am I to carry every question like stones in my pocket? What a burden the Great Father has laid on men—to endure, without certainty.

You say, wisdom is for those who seek the sun. Have I not roamed the land at your service? I have kept to the Way without turning aside, my feet closely following the path. If I am truly not worthy, why did I not perish at birth? Why is life given to a man whose way is hidden?

Oh, Great Father, hear me! Let all men hear me! The spirit within me compels me to tell what I know. Let me speak, then let come to me what may.

I have seen many ways to worship under the sun. How can only one be right and the rest meaningless? I know the destiny of the man who blindly follows. What he trusts in is fragile; what he relies on is a spider's web. He leans on his web, but it gives way; he clings to it, but it does not hold.

The sun rises and sets, then hurries back again. The wind blows round and round. I am but one, tiny grain on a vast sea of sand. But this I have learned. It is not only the old who are wise, not only the aged who understand what is right. It is the spirit in a man that matters.

My eyes have seen all this, my ears have heard and understood. Is this not what I was sent to see and hear and know?

The Ancestor's Footprints

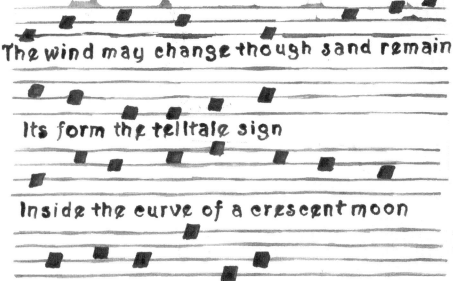

The wind may change though sand remain

Its form the telltale sign

Inside the curve of a crescent moon

The sun and sea align

Book Five

Losing an illusion makes you wiser
than finding a truth.
~Ludwig Börne

30

The air shimmered around the city and for a moment, Kiran thought it was a mirage. A sprawling mass of white buildings with roofs of all shapes and sizes and colors rose up against the blue skyline, covering the hillside as far as the eye could see. It dwarfed any settlement he'd ever seen or could have imagined.

Amid all those buildings, all those people, how would he find the Voice? He had assumed that once he got to the edge of the world, everything would be clear, that all would be obvious, that the dwelling place of the Voice would be right in plain sight.

"Now what do we do?" he said to Medira. She flicked an ear and took a step. He followed and they made their way steadily forward.

As they got closer, he could see the harbor. Dozens of boats bobbed on the waves. A breeze blew up from the sea and he was sure he could hear the low rumble of waves crashing on the beach. To the south, a roadway meandered along the shoreline and into the heart of the city. A steady stream of wagons and animals traveled in both directions, to where and to what, he could not guess.

At the city's edge, they passed beneath an arch and into a maze of earthen streets lined with buildings made from stone blocks with tiled roofs. The clatter of wheels and the clickety-clack of hooves mixed with hurried voices. From under broad, colorful canopies, shopkeepers shouted into the crowd, tempting women to browse their markets filled with baskets of fresh fruits and vegetables, barrels of drink, and all sizes of wooden boxes. Children ran and played in the streets. Everything seemed crammed too close together and saturated with the sweat of men and the odor of their animals.

Kiran blended in among the throng of bodies. There were so many people; no one noticed or welcomed him. He didn't know which way to turn, where to go, but somehow Midira seemed to have a direction in mind, so he followed her, wandering through the streets. They entered a district with fewer shops and more residences, the buildings old and dilapidated, made of weathered boards and wood-shingled roofs. Chickens and other small animals scurried about under foot. At one house, a woman veiled in long robes was sweeping her porch. She watched Kiran walk past, suspicion in her eyes. A rut, running with sewage, cut across the street. He pulled his tunic up over his nose.

Medira picked up the pace. They rounded a corner and came to a ramshackle stable with crooked slatboard walls. Medira went straight to the trough to lap up a drink of water.

Kiran sat down on a wooden box in the shade to rest, wondering where to go. A door slammed opened in the back of the stable and a man with shaggy red hair and a belly that hung over his pants waist stumbled across the threshold. "Damn," he muttered as he fumbled with his pants and urinated into the straw.

Kiran eased from the box, thinking he could quietly slip away.

The man's head swung around. "What do you want, boy?" he grumbled, eyeing Kiran up and down as he flicked a tiny sliver of wood back and forth in his lips. He took his time adjusting his pants and turned to face Kiran, hand on his hip.

Kiran faced him head on, unsure what the man would do. "Hello, sir," he said. "I, ah…"

The man yanked the splinter of wood from his mouth. "Out with it," he growled.

"I came with Medira," Kiran said, gesturing toward the animal. She turned, her ears perking up at the mention of her name.

The man noticed the animal then and his lips spread into a broad smile. He stroked her neck. "Welcome home, old girl." He scratched his face through his thick beard. "You brought her all the way across the dunes, eh?"

Kiran hesitated, then nodded. "Yes. How did you know?"

"Just a guess," he said with a grin. He slapped Kiran on the back. "You look thirsty. Go on in." He gestured toward the door. "The least I can do is offer you a pint. Tell Marion that Artus sent you."

"Uh, sure." Kiran wasn't sure what a pint was, but the man seemed friendly enough.

"Well, go on. I'll unburden Medira here and be right along."

Rusty hinges groaned as Kiran pushed open the heavy wooden door. He stepped into a dark room and waited for his eyes to adjust. Hanging on wooden pegs driven into the wall were three woolen coats. Bunches of dried herbs hung from the rafters. Sitting atop a couple of bins were tall, brown earthenware jars with narrow necks. Rows of barrels were stacked along the far wall.

Through another door, he could hear the low rumble of men's voices. He pushed it open and stood in the doorway, looking into a crowded room alive with chatter and laughter and the savory smell of a bubbling stew. Men sat around tables, drinking from mugs.

A robust woman with rosy cheeks stood at the bar, wiping the top with a rag. Her hearty laugh filled the room. She noticed Kiran and waved him in. "What'll you have?"

Kiran stared a moment, unsure what she was asking him.

"Looks like you could use a pint," she said, enunciating each word.

Kiran nodded.

"Shy one, are you?" She slung the rag over her shoulder and gestured toward a stool at the counter. "Well, take a seat. Relax."

Kiran dropped his pack to the floor and climbed up on the stool. Two men, leaning on the bar next to him, mugs in hand, eyed him up and down. One wore a beard that was too scraggly to hide a face pocked with old acne. They both smelled of fish. Kiran nodded in greeting and they turned back to their conversation.

The woman grabbed a mug from behind the counter, lifted it to a spigot in a barrel that lay on its side, and filled it full to the top with a rich, frothy brew. As she slid the mug across the counter, she seemed to reconsider. With her hand still holding the handle, she said, "I'll be needin' your money up front."

Kiran looked at her. "Money?" He shook his head, confused.

She pulled the mug back. "Yeah, I kinda figured. Where you from, lad? You one of them outlanders?"

"Outlanders?"

"You look like one." She leaned back, one hand on her hip. "You smell like one."

Kiran's eyes flitted around the room as he leaned toward his armpit and took a whiff.

The woman roared with laughter, her hand going to her stomach. "Well, young man, what have you got worth tradin'?"

He shook his head. "I…" Then he remembered the pouches of salt Aldwyn had given him. He dug around in his pack, pulled a pouch from its container, and presented one to her.

"What have we here? Salt? Ha," she said with a chuckle. "So, you're a time traveler." She dropped the pouch on the counter in front of him and cocked her head as though waiting for the punch line. When Kiran didn't respond, she shrugged.

"Artus sent me," he said.

"Oh he did, did he?" She examined him anew through narrowed eyes. "You're welcome to wait for him." She lifted the mug and drank it down. "I've got work to do," she said and sauntered away.

Kiran spun around on the stool and watched her as she went from table to table, pouring mugs of ale for the men. Occasionally, she'd serve a bowl of stew from a pot that hung over a crackling fire in the hearth on the far wall.

Over the ruckus, he listened to the men sitting next to him. "I'm telling you, he swears the creatures could talk. Swam right along side the boat."

"The oaf fell in love with a mermaid," the other chuckled.

A mermaid? Kiran thought. A swimming creature that could talk? Where had he heard that before? *The Irichoi*. Takhura, Jandon's Lendhi maiden, had told him about them. He turned to ask the men about it when the door to the stable opened and Artus ambled in.

"Marion, did you give the boy an ale?" he asked.

"He's got no money," she grumbled.

The man heaved himself onto the stool next to Kiran. "Two pints, my dear," he told her with a wink.

Hands on her hips, she squinted one eye, then heaved a sigh. She grabbed two mugs, filled them to the brim, and slid them across the counter.

Kiran brought the mug to his lips. The ale smelled bitter. He took a sip and raised his eyebrows. The old man took the toothpick from his mouth with one hand, lifted his mug with the other, and poured the ale down his throat like a man dousing a fire. As he slammed the empty mug on the bar, he thumped himself on the chest with the side of his fist and blew out his breath in a rumbling belch as if to purposefully insult anyone within earshot. He wiped his dripping beard with the back of his hand and shoved the toothpick back in his mouth.

"So, got a name?" he asked.

"Kiran," he said and sniffed the ale again, debating whether he wanted to take another sip.

"Well, young Kiran, what brings you to my door?"

Kiran thought he sensed some sarcasm. He tipped back the mug and took a long draught of the ale, stalling before he answered, wondering if he could trust this man.

He had made it this far, to the edge of the world. But he had no idea where to go next. He needed help from someone.

He decided he had no choice but to trust him. He gulped down another couple swallows of the drink. "I've come on a pilgrimage," he said, setting down the mug.

"Ah, of course you have." Artus slapped his hand on the counter. "You hear that, Marion? The boy's here on a pilgrimage."

"I knew it," the barmaid said. She leaned toward Kiran. "You have that faraway look of a dreamer."

Kiran looked to Artus. "A dreamer?"

"Don't pay her no mind," he said. "Everyone's searching for somethin'. How can I help?"

"Can you tell me where to find the Voice of the Father?"

Artus eased back on the stool and looked at Kiran as though seeing him for the first time. "The Voice of the Father, eh?" He fiddled with the toothpick in his mouth.

All of a sudden, Kiran was overcome by a wave of dizziness. He tipped back the mug and gazed at the swig of ale left in the bottom, then looked up at Artus. He shoved back the stool. "I've had enough of your kind of magic."

"Magic?" Artus threw his head back and roared with laughter. The men standing at the bar turned and snickered. "There's nothing magic about getting drunk." He slapped Kiran on the back so hard he nearly knocked him off his feet. "Sit down." His eyes turned serious. "No one's trying to do anything but make a new friend." He took hold of Kiran's mug, tipped it up, and chugged it dry. "No magic. Just tasty malt." He burped. "Though some call it the nectar of the gods. I tell you, it will cure what ails you. And make you forget your troubles."

Kiran hesitated, unsure what to make of this man, then eased back onto the stool.

Artus leaned on his elbow, facing Kiran, serious again. "So, you were saying, you're on a pilgrimage…"

Kiran nodded.

"And this Voice. Is that all you're seeking?"

Kiran thought for a moment. He reached into his pocket, took out Deke's two stones, and placed them on the counter. "I'm also looking for more of these."

Artus looked at Marion and something unspoken passed between them.

"What is it?" Kiran asked. The two men beside him had stopped talking and were staring at the stones.

Artus scooped them up, grabbed Kiran by the wrist, and placed them in his hand. He leaned forward and said to the men at the bar, "Mind your business." He whispered in Kiran's ear, "You'd do well to keep those coins in your pocket." He scanned the room as though looking for something. "That's a lot of money."

"Money?" Kiran shook his head.

Artus shifted on his seat. "Let's go check on Medira, shall we?" He placed his hands on the bar and lifted himself from the stool. "C'mon."

Kiran grabbed his pack and followed him back out to the stable.

"Sit down," Artus said, gesturing toward the wooden box. He found another one in the corner of the stable, set it next to Kiran, and sat down. "I can see you've got a good heart. I was young and ambitious like you once." He lifted an eyebrow. "I bet you've got some sweet girl waiting for you back home." He sighed as though his own memories made him weary. "Now listen to me. If you want to make it back to her, you have to use your head. Do you understand?"

Kiran stared. He had no idea what he'd done wrong.

"All right now, tell me the whole story." He shifted his weight on the box. "Tell me the truth and I'll do what I can to help you."

Kiran took the codex from his pack and opened it to the first page. "I have followed the Script. But I fear…"

"What? You fear what?"

"That I've translated it incorrectly."

"I see," Artus said, examining the page.

He listened patiently as Kiran told him of the quest, how he and the others had been sent to save the village, and how Aldwyn had given him the scroll.

"And what does it say?" Artus asked.

Kiran read it to him.

Artus took the toothpick from his mouth and pointed to the codex with it. "You came all this way on that?"

Kiran nodded. "We found the river. But the valley and the peak…

I don't know... I've followed the setting sun."

Artus leaned against the wall, shoved the toothpick back in his mouth, and chewed on it for time before he said, "I'm sorry to tell you. I don't know of this Voice. I wish I could help."

"Do you know of the Oracle?"

"The Oracle? You've traveled ten moons to see the Oracle?" The old man shook his head and muttered, "Well, that explains a lot."

"You can take me to her?" Kiran asked, feeling hopeful.

"Yes, but I don't think—" He drew in a long breath. "She's a fortune teller."

"Maybe she knows how to find the dwelling place of the Voice."

Artus paused, his eyebrows knit as though he were searching for words. "Kiran, it doesn't work that way." He waited for Kiran to respond, but Kiran said nothing. "She babbles and people interpret it to mean whatever fits their needs. I'm not sure that's what you're lookin' for."

"Pel said she knows about prophecies. Maybe she knows about the Seventh Elder."

Artus gripped the edge of the box and pushed himself up to stand. "Well, who am I to say? If you want to see the Oracle, then by all means, go see her."

Kiran looked down the street at the maze of twists and turns. "Which way do I go?"

"I'll draw you a map of the city," Artus offered.

"A what?"

Artus chuckled, shaking his head. "A map. Let me show you." He took Kiran's writing stick and his codex. "May I?"

Kiran nodded.

"Think of it as though you were looking down at the city from the sky."

Kiran watched, fascinated with the concept, as Artus sketched out lines for streets and shapes representing buildings, explaining each as he drew them. He handed the codex back to Kiran. "Now, remember what I told you. Keep those coins in your pocket. And be careful. The city attracts all kinds of people seeking all kinds of trouble."

Kiran yawned as he nodded.

"On second thought, you'd better wait till mornin'. You can sleep here in the stable."

Kiran thanked him.

"Good luck, boy," Artus said and sauntered back through the door.

Kiran found the corner in which Medira had lain and snuggled up next to her. He took the tiny doll that Bria had given him from his pocket, held it close to his heart, and fell fast asleep.

When he opened his eyes again, he didn't know where he was or what had brought him here. He felt groggy, as though awakening from a long dream.

"Sleep well?" came a voice.

Kiran jerked upright. Artus was sitting on the box. Kiran let out his breath, tucked the doll away in his pocket, and rose to his feet.

"Still intent on seeing the Oracle?" Artus asked.

"Yes, sir," Kiran said, taking hold of his pack.

"I was thinking I'd come along. If that's all right with you? I don't have anything better to do this morning anyway."

Kiran nodded.

"Listen, I'm going to be honest with you. I don't believe in this Oracle and her cryptic messages. But I can see you're stubborn." He rose from the box. "Some things we have to find out for ourselves."

Kiran gazed at Artus, Bria's voice echoing in his mind.

"Let's get going then," Artus said, and led the way.

As they walked, Artus showed Kiran many things he hadn't seen the day before: buildings with elaborate porticoes supported by towering columns graced with fine sculptures of women in flowing robes; an amphitheater built in the side of the hill, all of stone, where the cityfolk acted out stories and held meetings; a water bridge that, Artus explained, was connected to underground tunnels, built to carry water throughout the city from the hills above.

Kiran marveled at the massive construction. "I can't believe men would toil to build such a thing. Is there no river? No streams?"

"Yes, of course," Artus said. "But water is a necessity and the rains are fickle. Streams can run dry. In the hills, there are cisterns to collect the water and keep the flow constant, so that we are not made to rely on the whims of nature."

"I see," Kiran said, curious now about the detailed workings of the system. Artus told him that was all he knew about it.

At last, on the outskirts of town, atop a steep hill, they arrived at the Palace of the Oracle. Hundreds of people milled about the lawns. "C'mon," Artus said, pushing through the crowd. "Let's find the end of the line."

An old woman grabbed Kiran by the arm. "I can read your fortune," she said with a grin, revealing a mouth full of rotten teeth. "You seek love. I can see it in your eyes."

Artus stepped between them. "Mind your business," he said, shooing her away.

"But the boy seeks answers." She shook a small leather pouch and dumped the contents on the ground. Five seashells lay scattered at her feet. "Ah, I see what you are seeking," she said, looking up at him, her eyes wide.

"I said, mind your business," Artus told her, more strongly now. He took Kiran by the arm and steered him through the crowd.

"Wait," Kiran said. "Why were you so rude?"

"Rude? She was just trying to get your money."

"My money?"

"Yeah. Some people will tell you what you want to hear, just to get something from you." He frowned at Kiran. "Boy, you really are naïve. Good thing I came along."

Kiran looked back for the woman. She was already tossing the shells for someone else.

Artus tugged him toward a long, covered colonnade that led to the entrance of the palace, where the line had formed. As they passed under an arch, something caught Kiran's eye. Engraved in the stone were the words: *He who has eyes, let him see. He who has ears, let him hear. Blessed are those who understand with their hearts.*

"What do you think that means?" he asked Artus.

"It's your journey, son. What do you think it means?"

Kiran read the words once again. *Listen to your heart,* he thought. *To listen to your heart.*

A few more paces along the colonnade, a crowd had gathered before a tiny, makeshift theater. On the stage were seven dolls with realistic features, each adorned in intricately embroidered costumes. They hung from strings on which someone hidden above tugged, making them come alive, their arms and legs moving as though they were real miniature people in a miniature world. The dolls were lined up before a golden throne. From behind the stage, a voice thundered, "Who deems thyself fit to reign? Come forth and present thy worth."

"What is this?" Kiran asked Artus.

"It's just the old parable of the seven virtues."

"Seven?" Kiran said, turning back to the stage.

"C'mon, you need to get in line if you are to see the Oracle today."

"Wait. I want to see this."

A flute played a soft melody as a puppet with pink cheeks and flowing hair, stepped forward from the group, her tiny skirt swaying as she walked. "'Tis I shall reign," she said. "For I am chaste."

"No, 'tis me," said another, pushing her out of the way. A drum beat played, bum, bum, bum. "For I am the strongest and most courageous among thee." He dropped to one knee and raised his muscled arm.

Then from the side, with the strumming of a lute, another doll came skipping round the stage and bowed before the throne. "Humble obedience is most revered. 'Tis I who is the worthy one, though I do not ask for it."

A fourth doll marched across the stage, his tiny boots clicking. "Step aside," he said. A bell rang four times. "For I am the hand of justice."

Kiran blinked, his eyes fixed on the arrogant little puppet. A gnawing feeling crept into the pit of his stomach.

The instruments played in a cacophony of sound, the rhythm out of sync, as the four dolls danced and twirled, vying for the throne. The tempo increased until a fifth doll joined the dance. Her sing-song voice rang out over the music accompanied by a tinkling harp. "Love and kindness, I provide." Kiran's hand went to the little doll in his pocket.

The sixth puppet joined the fray with the bah-boom of a large drum. "Dance, dance, dance. But hope shall reign tonight."

They twirled and twirled, faster and faster. Bah bah bum, bah bah bum. Kiran felt dizzy, trying to make sense of it. The whole world was suddenly out of focus, the colors blurring together.

The seventh doll descended from above with the whoosh of a rattle. "'Tis faith that is needed most."

The doll spun wildly among the others, round and round, as the instruments beat out a frenzied clash of sound. The music stopped and they all fell down before the throne. Each struggled to get up on his own, but could not. Then, one doll reached out to the one next to him for help, and that one reached for the next doll, then the next one to another, until all seven puppets were holding hands and, together, they rose to their feet as the music played in glorious harmony. The crowd cheered and applauded.

Kiran stared at the miniature stage long after the show was over.

"Are you all right?" Artus asked.

"There were seven," Kiran said, his eyes fixed on the tiny throne. "Seven."

"It's a parable, Kiran. It's a common story. It's been around for ages. Don't tell me you've never heard it? The moral of the seven virtues?"

Kiran turned and looked into his eyes. "Virtues?"

"It's not enough to have one. We are to strive to have all seven. Each of us. To be good, I suppose. To be worthy."

Kiran took his codex from his pack and opened it to the last page he had written. He turned back to the stage. He tried to swallow, but his throat felt coated with sand. "To be a leader."

"Yes, I would say that, yes."

Kiran slumped to the ground. He leaned forward and held his head in his hands.

After a time, when the crowd had dispersed and the tiny stage had been packed and hauled away, Artus said, "If you want to see the Oracle today, we should get back in line."

Kiran lifted his head from his hands. "I don't need to see the Oracle." He rose to his feet and hefted the pack unto his back.

"Where are you going now?"

"I have no idea."

Kiran wandered the city, lost in thought, until finally he made his way back to the only place he knew. Marion was at work, putting chairs up on the tables so she could sweep the floor. Artus was at the hearth ladling a bowl of stew.

Kiran slumped down on a stool and dropped his head on the counter.

Marion heaved herself unto the stool next to him. "Find what you were lookin' for?"

He couldn't make sense of his thoughts, his fears. Everything was jumbled in his head. "There were seven." He shook his head. "I just don't know anymore." He raised his head enough to meet her eyes. "The prophecy, what if it's—"

"Prophecy?" Marion shook her head. "Sounds to me like you've been chasing the shadow of a ghost,"

"What if?" He sat up. "What if they were all wrong?" He was shouting now. "What if it isn't true?" He stared into her eyes, fighting back tears. "What if everything is all just..." He slumped back down, holding his head in his hands. "Oh, what am I saying? I'm all mixed up. I don't even know if there is a Script of the Prophecy. I mean, Deke said so. But..."

"Listen, boy," said Marion. "I know what you seek."

Kiran's eyes snapped to meet hers.

"But that which you seek can never be found. For the moment it is sought, it ceases to exist."

The door flung open, startling them. It was the two men who had been standing next to Kiran at the bar the night before. "Good morning," the one said.

The other man saw Kiran and said, "Ah, just the man we've come to see."

Kiran glanced at Marion and saw an edge of concern in her eyes.

"Pub's closed. You boys'll have to come back later," she said.

"Oh, we just want to talk," said the bearded one to Kiran.

Marion kept her eyes fixed on the two men as she eased from the stool and moved behind the bar. Artus joined her, setting his bowl of stew on the counter.

The men drew up the stools on either side of Kiran, sat down, and leaned toward him. "Couldn't help but overhear last night. Seems you're looking for something." Kiran glanced at Artus who made a subtle shake of his head. "I got to thinking about that symbol," the man pointed at the Pyletar hanging from Kiran's neck. "I've seen it before."

"Where?" Kiran asked, curious now.

"On an island across the sea. We was thinkin' we could get you passage there." The other man nodded his agreement.

Kiran looked to Artus questioningly. Artus shrugged. He turned back to the men. "But I see no island in the sea."

"Well, you can't see it from here. But it's on the map. That's why you'd have to take a ship, of course."

"A ship?" Kiran narrowed his eyes. "You must think I'm a fool."

"No, not at all. We can show you the map."

"Don't listen to these scoundrels," Artus said. He rose to his feet, his shoulders back. "Let me guess. You'll help him get on this ship in trade for two gold coins. Am I right?"

The two men glanced at each other and didn't answer.

Artus stepped from behind the bar. "Out with you. Be on your way. He doesn't have the coins any longer anyway. The fool spent them for a dose of nonsense from the Oracle." The men looked at Kiran, then back to Artus. "Now be off with you," Artus gave them a nudge out and shut the door behind them.

Kiran stared after them. "I don't understand. Why would they tell me that?"

"What did I say, now? People with tell you what you want to hear, just to get your money."

"They would send me on a ship to plunge over the edge of the world?"

Artus cocked his head to the side and scratched his chin. "Kiran, that's not—"

Marion slapped her hands on the counter and said to Artus, "I think it's time you take him to meet the Scholar."

31

The home of the Scholar was built of stone, perched atop a cliff with a view of the sea. At the door, they were greeted by a young man who spoke in hushed tones. He led them into a room to await the Scholar, then disappeared through a door that, Kiran assumed, led to a second room. It was a strange home. There were two chairs and nothing else. No cooking hearth, no bed that he could see. The air had a stuffy smell, heavy with the musty odor of old dust.

"Why are we here?" Kiran whispered to Artus.

"I told you. The Scholar possesses great knowledge."

"You think he knows where to find the dwelling place of the Voice?"

Artus pursed his lips. "Just wait and see."

Kiran sat back in his chair and crossed his arms, then shifted forward and crossed his legs. A fly circled the ceiling, trying to escape with a determined bizz-buzz, bizz-buzz.

At last, the door creaked open and a short, wrinkled old man appeared, leaning heavily on a cane. "Kiran is it?"

Kiran quickly assessed the man. His eyes were soft and honest, his face like soft putty, his frail stature unintimidating. Kiran nodded.

"So, what brings you to me?"

Kiran looked to Artus. Artus replied, "Well, the boy here needs some guidance."

"That so?" the Scholar said.

"I'm on a pilgrimage to the Voice of the Father," Kiran told him.

The Scholar frowned at Artus. "A pilgrimage? Why bring him to me?" The Scholar looked at Kiran as though examining every inch of him.

Kiran squirmed. He looked at Artus, then back to the Scholar. "I, ah, thought he would be here. But now, well, I don't know where to go. And those men, they told me of an island, out there, in the sea, but how could that be?"

The Scholar placed his cane to turn and head back through the doorway. "Perhaps you should go and see for yourself. Artus can help you get passage on a ship."

"But the ships, they fall off the edge!"

"Ah, I see now," the Scholar said, turning back. "Your pilgrimage has brought you here, to the edge of the world? Is that right?"

Kiran nodded.

"And now, someone has told you this is not the edge of the world, and you want to know the truth."

Kiran stared. He wasn't sure. Was that what he wanted to know?

"Yes, yes. Well, no need to be concerned. Common misconception. Indeed, the world goes on. It is not flat, but a big round ball. So, take to the sea if you are still seeking. Time on the open ocean is good for putting things into perspective."

Kiran stared. What was this man saying? A big round ball?

As though reading Kiran's mind, the Scholar added, "There is no edge."

"No edge?" Kiran sat back. This couldn't be true.

"It is so large, that you cannot see in the distance. It only appears to fall away. But as you travel on, you always continue to see out in the distance. Do you understand?"

"I suppose," Kiran answered, trying to imagine how it could possibly be so. He remembered walking on the flatlands, thinking he could see the edge in the distance, but as they kept walking and walking, the hills had appeared on the horizon. Kiran's eyes grew wide and his mouth fell open. He was right!

"So, you see? There is no edge."

"That means the dwelling place could be farther in the direction of the setting sun. On an island, as those men said, then." He stared at the old man's face and his mouth slowly dropped open. *Wrinkled with time and crippled with wisdom.*

"Could be." He leaned on his cane and made for the door. "Best wishes in your travels."

Artus said, "Uh, that's not all."

"No?" The Scholar sighed and leaned against the doorframe.

"The sailors claimed they had seen his symbol on a map." He nudged Kiran. "Show him your pendant." Kiran presented the Pyletar to the Scholar. With a furrowed brow, the old man examined the symbol. Artus went on, "They said it's on an island in the far reaches of the sea. You see?"

Without looking up, the Scholar asked, "Where did you say you've come from?"

"The Toran village. On the far side of the world, toward the rising sun."

"Toran?" The Scholar looked up so quickly he nearly lost his balance. "Toward the rising sun?"

Kiran nodded. "Yes, on the edge, sir—" he caught himself. "I mean, yes, on the sea."

The Scholar seemed perplexed. "But you... how did you get here?"

"I walked," Kiran said, matter of fact. "Well, mostly I floated on a raft. I have traveled now ten moons and—"

"Would you excuse me a moment?" He turned away without waiting for an answer and hobbled through the doorway, taking the Pyletar with him.

Kiran leaped from his chair, his head swimming. "Do you think he is the wise man? Do you think he is the Voice? He knows things... about the world. Maybe it's him. What do you think? I mean, his house here, we are on the top of a hill. A peak. Yes, it could be him. Artus, what do you think?"

"I think you need to simmer down." Artus folded his hands in his lap.

Kiran paced the floor, holding the doll in his hands. The fly circled the ceiling. Bizz-buzz, bizz-buzz. Kiran thought the old man would never return. Finally, he heard the clip-clop of the Scholar's cane. "Would you care to join me for tea?"

Kiran's eyes lit up and his head bobbed up and down. He shoved the doll in his pocket.

Artus rose to his feet and gave Kiran a wink. They followed the Scholar through the doorway. An entire wall was lined with shelves stacked with books, hundreds of leather-bound tomes, full of knowledge. A thick codex lay open on the Scholar's desk.

The old man pointed to a couple chairs. Artus moved a pile of books from one and plopped down in it.

"Please," the Scholar said, gesturing for Kiran to take a seat. "Let's start at the beginning, shall we? Tell me about this pilgrimage. What is it you are seeking?"

"The Voice of the Father. He dwells somewhere here, on this edge. I mean..." Kiran thought a moment. "Perhaps I've, uh, misinterpreted it."

"Misinterpreted what?"

Kiran paused. "I have a scroll, part of the Script of the Legend. It has been my guide."

The man's eyes lit up. "You have this scroll with you? Here?"

Kiran took the scroll from his pack and presented it to him.

A sparkle of delight came to his eyes, like one who has found a long sought-after treasure. "May I?" he asked, gesturing to remove the mantle. Kiran nodded, then waited as the man unrolled the scroll and read every line. Finally, he looked up, his eyes assessing Kiran. "So, you made your way here by following the description in this scroll?"

Kiran felt uneasy, though he wasn't sure why. "Yes. I was sent by the Elders."

"Hm…" The Scholar reached for a piece of paper on his desk and scribbled something on it. "So you were chosen?"

"Yes, seven of us. But, well, there is only me now." He thought of the seven puppets, twirling round the golden throne. "I think maybe—"

"Seven you say?" he pondered this a moment, as if it had great significance. "Tell me about these Elders and the temple. How is it run? The structure of leadership?"

"There are six elders. Aldwyn is the Eldest."

"Six you say?"

Kiran nodded.

The Scholar leaned forward on his desk and thumbed through the pages of the book. "Not seven?"

"Well, there is the Seventh Elder. Of the prophecy."

The Scholar looked up. "The prophecy?"

"We await the Coming of the Seventh Elder."

"Interesting." The Scholar flipped through more pages, then landed on one, his finger trailing across the page as he read.

"What is it?" Kiran asked.

"Huh?" The Scholar looked up at Kiran, his eyes slowly trying to focus. "Oh, yes, yes. We'll come back to that."

Kiran glanced at the page of the book the Scholar held open and recognized the words. Then he remembered—the Scholar had read the Script when he handed it to him. "You can read the Tongue of the Father."

"The Tongue of the Father?"

"The Script. It is written in the Tongue of the Father. It is the *divine* language. For Elders only. How is it that you read it?"

"Your Script was written in Skarta, the ancient language of the Mriti."

"Skarta? The Mriti?" Kiran said, confused.

"Yes, the Mriti were an island culture, the birthplace of the Toran religion." He paused, raising an eyebrow. "So, the Script is interpreted and the Way governed by the Elders. Is that it?"

Kiran stared at the Scholar for a long moment.

"Let's move on. So the Elders must have given you directions then?"

"Well, actually, they didn't." Kiran tried to focus, but he couldn't shake an uneasy feeling. "See, before they could explain, Javinians attacked. We escaped, but—"

"Javinians?"

"Wicked heathens who live in the forest." As the words left his lips, they didn't feel right. He thought of Kalindria and how she had tried to help, of Manu-amatu and how Deke had called him a heathen.

"Hm. We have no record of natives in that area. You call them Javinians?" He scribbled on his paper again.

"Natives?"

"You said they live in the forest." His eyes were fixed on Kiran as though he meant to extract every drop of information. "Do you interact with them? Trade things?"

"Do you mean since the Time of Dissension?"

The Scholar raised his eyebrows. "The Time of Dissension?"

Kiran sat back. "Yes, when the Javinians rebelled."

"Ah. What happened exactly?"

"Well, it was generations ago."

"But you know the story?"

Kiran nodded. "Elder Javin spoke out against the Way. He..." Kiran paused.

"He what?" the Scholar urged.

"He made the most blasphemous claim."

The Scholar leaned forward, his eyes wide. "And what was that?"

"He denounced the Seventh Elder, saying He would never come." Kiran thought a moment. "But he had the Script of the Prophecy, the stolen scroll. Wait, that doesn't make sense."

The Scholar shrugged. "Go on."

"He encouraged the people to withhold tithes. He said the Elders could work their own farms, like everyone else."

The Scholar sat back and crossed his fingers under his chin. "I imagine the Elders didn't like that very much. What happened next?"

"A fury of flying demons blocked out the sky."

"And you witnessed this?"

"Well, no. I wasn't born yet. I told you. It was many generations ago"

"Yes, yes. But you describe it as though it is fact."

Kiran paused.

"Is that what you believe?"

"Well, the Javinians brought about the wrath—"

"I understand that is what the Torans believe. But what do *you* believe?"

"Well...I..."

"Have you ever seen such a thing? With your own eyes?"

He stared at the Scholar for a long moment. He had seen a flock of birds so large it blocked out the sky.

"Go on. What happened next?"

"Javin and his followers were banished from the Temple."

"They were banished because the demons appeared? Or because the Elders didn't like to be questioned?"

Kiran shifted in his seat, feeling like a butterfly pinned to a board. Why was he asking these questions? He looked to Artus. "Artus said you could help me."

"Yes, yes." He sat back in his chair. "I think I can. But first, I want to be sure I understand a few things. I don't want to give you bad advice, you see. So, tell me about the journey to get here."

Kiran let out his breath. "As I said, there were seven of us. Bhau was killed a few days after we left, in the meadow beyond the forest, by a Mawgh—" He paused. "I mean, he fell in a hunter's pit. That's when we met the Lendhi clan."

"The nomads of the flatlands? Tell me about them. I'm told they are without religion."

"I thought so too, at first. But they understood things about the land, as though, I don't know, they lived as though the land itself was sacred."

"They worshipped the land?"

"No. I think they loved the Great Father, just as we do, only called Him by a different name. It was as though they felt His spirit lived among them, as trees, as the animals, as the wind. I'd never thought of it that way. It was quite…profound."

"It sounds as if you respected them."

Kiran looked the Scholar in the eyes. "If you met them, I'm sure you'd see—"

"I'm impressed. Most people hold on tightly to their beliefs, seeing any other views as an affront to their own."

"Aldwyn says wisdom comes with humility."

"This Aldwyn is very wise."

Kiran nodded and had to look away. He missed Aldwyn so much he had to fight back tears.

"But you continued on?"

Kiran told him of their time with the Kotari.

"I've heard of this *Guardian*. He preys on people and their need to believe."

Kiran paused. "Did you say *need* to believe?"

"All men suffer from it. Religions come and go. The deep-seated need to believe is what remains. Some men are excellent at exploiting it, masters of telling people what they want to hear, guiding them to see what they want to see."

Is that what the Guardian had done? Kiran wondered. Told them what they wanted to hear? Shown them what they wanted to see? "No. We were under some kind of magic spell."

"Magic spell?"

Kiran cringed, flushed with memories of the night with Bria. He drew in a breath. "It was the drink!"

"Drink?"

"Oh no! I helped Kalindria make it."

The Scholar sat up in his chair, his eyes wide.

"But I didn't realize—"

"You know how the drink is made?"

"Yes." Kiran took his codex from his pack and thumbed through the pages. "I wrote it down." He found the page. "Here it is," he said, pointing at the recipe.

The Scholar reached for the codex. "May I?"

"I suppose it would be all right," Kiran said, handing the book to him.

The Scholar immediately called for someone from the next room. A man came in—the same man who had greeted him earlier—and set down a tray with cups of tea. The Scholar whispered to him and he took the codex in hand and went to sit at the table across the room. "He's going to copy the recipe, if that's all right with you?" the Scholar said.

"I suppose," Kiran muttered.

"Please continue."

Kiran told him of their escape, their time on the river, and how they came to a crossroads. "Pel warned us that it was dangerous. But we had to follow the Script." Kiran paused, that feeling back again. "That's where we were chased by headhunters."

"Headhunters? Were you in the territory of the Widhu?"

"Yes, that's what Pel called them. How'd you know?"

"The Brotherhood has tried to build a relationship with the Widhu, but it's been tenuous. The natives of that region have the best medicines in the world. Their knowledge of the local plants is extraordinary. They have many concoctions to cure life-threatening illnesses and we want to learn them."

Kiran felt a stabbing sensation in his stomach. "They could have cured Deke?"

"It's possible. If they didn't kill you first."

Kiran exhaled a long breath. "We tried to make contact with them. We came to a settlement. But it had been abandoned."

"It wasn't abandoned. They hide when they fear outsiders. They were probably in the bushes nearby, watching you. Had you been hearing drums?"

"Yes, drums, yes."

"They use drums to communicate over long distances. It's quite fascinating, actually." He looked back to Kiran. "But you said you were chased?"

"Yes, we tried again to meet them. But this time, we accidentally surprised them during some sort of bloody ritual. They had heads on stakes. People's heads!"

The old man scratched his chin, gazing off into space. "Perhaps they thought they had already killed the intruders."

"We fled. Then went over a waterfall and were captured by slavers. But we got away." He thought of Roh, running into the jungle. Suddenly he didn't want to talk anymore. "Can't you just tell me what you know about the Voice of the Father?"

The Scholar leaned back in his chair and stared at Kiran for a long time before answering. "Yes, about that." He drummed his fingers on the book. "When you first mentioned this *voice*, I thought it was some kind of message or the name for the messenger. I didn't recognize your symbol either. But when you told me that you're a Toran, well, then I remembered."

Kiran sat upright in the chair.

"There was a Toran temple here, in the city. The seat of the patriarch. Other temples were built in the outer regions, at trade outposts and—"

"Well, then," Kiran pushed himself up and out of his chair. "That must be the dwelling place. That's it! That's where I need to go."

"I said it *was* here. The building still stands. But it is no longer a Toran Temple. It is now owned by the Brotherhood."

Kiran stared. "What are you saying? The dwelling place is no longer here?"

"Let me explain and I believe it will become clear." He gestured for Kiran to sit back down. "You see, each of the rural temples had six Elders. The seventh was likely a representative sent from the main temple. He probably carried messages from the patriarch, hence the voice. That's commonly how it is done."

"So, you're saying…?"

"Your village was an outpost for some form of trade, I presume."

Kiran sank back in the chair. "Salt. Aldwyn said we traded salt."

"Ah yes. Salt deposits were found in the ground just south of here many, many years ago and the trade ceased. The elder probably no longer had a way to get passage. Perhaps all those years ago, your forefathers were told to expect him. All this time, they've awaited the seventh elder."

"So, the Coming of the Seventh Elder…the prophecy?"

"The stuff of legends," the old man said, then cleared his throat.

"But how?"

"Time," he said, as though it were obvious.

Kiran shook his head.

"These things don't happen all at once. It's a culmination of little changes with each retelling. The truth gets washed away."

"Like a river over rock," Kiran whispered. "How do you know all this?" he asked, his breath ragged. "Is it in that book?"

"Go ahead. Have a look," the man said. Kiran rose from his chair, went to the man's desk, and looked down at the open page. It read: *A*

History of the Toran Religion. He drew in a breath and looked up at the Scholar who was easing back into his chair. "We thought you were all long gone. Your village is the last of the Torans." The old man's voice sounded musty, as if it rose from the pages of the book.

"But here in the city, all these people…"

"There are many different ways to experience the world, different views of reality, different religions. Everyone is just trying to make sense of the mysteries of the world, to understand the unknown. The world in which you were born is just one way of being, one way of understanding what *is*." He leaned forward, engaging Kiran with his eyes. "But you already knew that."

Kiran held his gaze, his hand shaking. Hadn't these ideas crossed his mind? Hadn't he thought these same thoughts, somewhere deep in the shadows of his mind?

"Go on," the man nodded.

Kiran turned to the first page, then the next, then the next. The Verses were there, the Songs, the stories Aldwyn had taught him. He flipped through the pages to the end. "Is that it?" he asked. "All I see here that I haven't read before is this page outlining the hierarchy of the Temple. But there is nothing about the prophecy, the seven chosen I mean. There was a reason the seven of us were chosen. I thought maybe…"

"What? You thought what?"

Kiran looked up at the Scholar. "I thought it would be here, in your book. When Javin rebelled, he stole a scroll from the Temple. Since he had claimed the Seventh Elder would never come, I assumed there was some evidence in that scroll. But then today, I saw a puppet show. Do you think the scroll he took was the moral of the seven virtues? And the prophecy is just—"

"Could be. Time has a way of twisting the truth."

Kiran flipped to the page with the Script of the Legend. "But the Voice. The Script is here, word for word as in the scroll. I understand how your explanation of the Seventh Elder could be… true. But the Voice. The Script clearly states—"

"Yes, yes. This Script you've been following." He cocked his head to the side. "Well, I don't know how to tell you this. You see, it's like the parable of the seven virtues. It's not meant to be taken literally. It's an allegory."

"A what?" Kiran took a deep breath, trying to get his thoughts in order.

"It's not uncommon in religious texts." He paused as though giving Kiran time to consider what he was telling him. "Allegory communicates an idea by means of symbolism. It's about the imagery, the message, not the literal words that are used." The Scholar pointed to Kiran's pocket. "Like the doll you carry. I assume it represents someone you love. You don't love the doll. It is a symbol of her. Does that make sense?"

"I suppose," he breathed. His shaking hand went to his neck where the Pyletar had hung.

The Scholar handed it back to him. "This is a symbol as well. A pyramid and a sphere. Something you can see, you can touch, representing an idea."

"Yes," Kiran said, his voice a whisper. "The Sanctuary on the Mount with the moon above at the Time of the Coming of..."

The Scholar was nodding his head, his fingers tapping on the edge of his desk.

Thoughts cascaded through Kiran's mind like sand sliding down a hillside. "So the Script...the path and the river...the sun...?" His mind went wobbly. "But the Voice?" The heat of the room seemed to rise. His stomach twisted into a knotted tangle of his worst fears.

Anger welled inside him. "But Aldwyn, the Elders, they must have known." His eyes snapped up to meet the Scholar's. "Why? Why would they send us? Bhau and Deke, dead. And Roh! All for nothing. Nothing!" He stared at the last page of the book, his heart beating fast. Shadows started to grow at the edge of his vision, crowding inward. "There must be more. An explanation. There must be!" He flipped back through the pages, the sound of the curled paper like the crinkle of dead leaves. "There must be some mistake."

"Kiran, I'm sorry."

The bizz-buzz of the fly screamed in his ears. The tap of the man's fingers pounded in his head and it was as though a crack was opening in the floor beneath him, then the ground was heaving and dropping away below, and he was falling, spiraling away from all that he had known, all that he had ever believed. He couldn't breathe. The musty odor of the book was so overwhelming, he suddenly felt like he was going to throw up.

He grabbed his pack and the codex and plunged through the door. Outside, he fell to his knees, gasping for air.

He scrambled to his feet and ran, as fast as his legs would take him, with no direction, no path to follow. He ran until he could run no more.

Kiran found himself back at the alehouse. All he wanted was for the drink to take him away from this world and make him forget, to fill the hollow ache in his heart, and escape the feeling, to end the agony of it all. He brought the mug to his mouth, tipped it back, and gulped down the brown liquid, spit forming in his mouth to wash away the bitterness.

He stumbled across the room to the hearth and stared into the flames. His whole life—the only thing he'd ever dreamed of—had evaporated before his eyes, everything lost. All for nothing, he thought, and threw the codex into the fire.

In the third year of the drought, seven Toran pilgrims set forth into the Land Unknown, seeking the dwelling place of the Voice of the Father.

Jandon, son of Hagen, a humble man and friend to all. Injured, living in the Weikato forest.

Deke, son of Elder Morgan, a man dedicated to the Way. Died on the river.

Kail, daughter of Alicion, the Flower Bearer, a woman of virtue. Remained in the Kingdom of the Kotari.

Bhau, son of Sanders, a man of great strength and courage. Died on the flatlands.

Bria, daughter of Laird, a woman of strength and love. Injured, remained in the Weikato forest.

Roh, son of Taniek, a man of honor, with hope in his heart. Captured by slavers.

Kiran set out across the dunes.

He who has eyes, let him see.
He who has ears, let him hear.
Blessed are those who
understand with their hearts.

Parable of the Seven Virtues

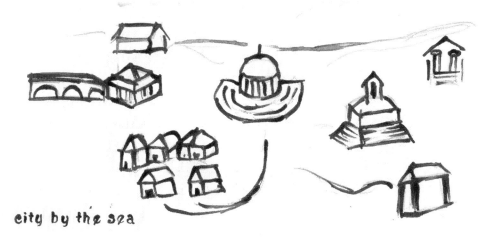

city by the sea

from a pool in the hills, down a conduit,
fresh water flows into the city

And there was written
therein: The History
of the Toran Religion

32

For a long moment, Kiran didn't know where he was. All he knew was the pungent odor of animals and a pounding in his head. He raised his heavy eyelids and saw Artus sitting on a crate, looking at him.

"Kinda liberating, ain't it?"

"What?" he grumbled. His mouth felt like he'd eaten sand.

"That moment, when you realize you don't have to see the world the way you've been told to."

Kiran shook himself awake and pushed up to a seated position, thoughts and feelings coming back in waves of clarity. It was as though he had been living in a dark cave, trying to make sense of the shadows, and now he was blinded, having been turned to face the light of day. Something had left him. A feeling. A question he had carried with him for as long as he could remember. It had been a part of him. Now there remained an emptiness, an overwhelming void, looming in the absence.

He was truly an orphan, with no home, and nowhere to turn. He clenched the doll in his hands.

Artus handed him a mug of water. "So, what will you do now?"

Kiran chugged down the drink. He'd been heading in one direction for so long; he'd never considered another. He thought back to the beginning, back to that moment on the hill, before he had left home. It had been only ten moons ago but felt like a lifetime. He had been a child—naïve and full of hope. Everything seemed possible. There had been one path before him, if only he would have the strength to take it, to see it through to the end.

If only he could persevere.

He winced. Roh had given everything. And for what? Nothing was as they thought. If only they had known.

He sat up straight. "I have a duty," he said. "To my village. I have to go back. I have to tell them what I've learned." He rose to his feet and slung his pack over his shoulder, his mind racing through a plan. He turned to look for Medira, wondering if he could take her back across the dunes.

"And what do you plan to tell them exactly?"

"They need to know the truth."

"The truth. Ha! Whose truth?"

Kiran stared at Artus, confused now. "The prophecy was a misunderstanding, a misinterpretation. There is no Seventh Elder. And the Script—"

"So you'll just stroll back into the village and tell them, eh? Like Javin did?"

"But I'll tell them what I've found, what I've learned. I'll tell them what I've *seen*. Then they'll see, as I have."

Artus was shaking his head. "Eh, people see what they want to see." He yanked the toothpick from his mouth and pointed it at Kiran. "That's what believin' is."

Believing, Kiran thought. He'd seen it in Kail's face. Nothing would have changed her mind. And Deke. He had been so sure about the river, about the Script. It was the Toran Way. Faith without question.

Kiran slumped back down. Deep inside, he had always known this moment would come. He was exhausted. He needed Roh. He needed Bria. He needed help. "What do I do?"

Artus paused a long moment before responding. He reached behind the crate, pulled out the charred codex, brushed it off, and handed it to Kiran. "I think you should do whatever your heart tells you to do."

Kiran sighed as he took the codex from Artus and stared at its cover. He was the scribe. Wasn't that why he had been sent? Aldwyn had told him this was to be a quest for knowledge and understanding. He was to seek answers. Even if they weren't the ones he had been expecting.

His hand went to the Pyletar that hung from his neck. This same symbol, he thought, on a distant island. Was it some other trade post? Maybe there were other Torans there, and they had the answers. "Do you think those men really saw the Pyletar on a map?"

"Maybe." Artus bit down on his toothpick. "I know someone, an old sailor friend I trust. He travels the sea for trade. He might know for sure."

"This friend. You've seen him sail away, out of sight, yet come back again?"

Artus nodded.

"So it could be true, how the sea goes on and on." He ran his fingers across the cover of the codex. "What if I go out on the sea, still to find nothing? What if none of this matters and it's too late to save the village anyway? What if everything I've ever been told is wrong? Not just the Seventh Elder, but—" he swallowed hard, "everything?"

"There's only one thing I know for sure."

Kiran raised his head.

"Never let anyone else tell you what to believe."

Kiran looked down at the codex he held in his hand, then at the doll, still clenched in his other. Her voice came softly in his head, *Some things we have to find out for ourselves.*

Kiran walked into the street where he could hear the muffled roar of the surf in the distance. It sounded like a voice, beckoning him to come.

The waterfront docks bustled with fishermen hauling in nets and crates. The smell of fish hung over everything. Flies buzzed everywhere. Artus seemed to know right where he was going. Kiran followed without a word as he left the wooden planks and made his way south to a sailing vessel that was hauled out on the beach.

An old man greeted them. His leathery brown skin looked as though it had been dried in the sun over years and years, but his eyes were vibrant and welcoming. Artus introduced him as his old friend, Lu-paia.

Kiran showed him the Pyletar. "Have you seen this before?"

The man stepped back.

"So you have seen it," Artus said.

Lu-paia closed his eyes in acknowledgement. "I know of this place."

"The boy seeks passage there."

The man shook his head. "Dark spirits haunt those cliffs."

Kiran exchanged a knowing glance with Artus. "I'll take my chances."

Lu-paia's eyes narrowed. "You are either very brave or very crazy."

Kiran offered him one of the gold coins. "Either way, will you take me?"

The man looked at Artus, then back to Kiran. "We set sail as soon as there is a favoring breeze."

Kiran said his goodbyes to Artus, promising to go straight to the alehouse upon his return and waited.

As he stared out over the sea, trying to imagine how an island could be hidden over the horizon of blue, the waves rushed up the beach, curled into foam around his bare feet, then broke into patches of froth. As the sea inhaled, drawing the water back to gather strength once more, he decided he could do nothing now but wait and see.

In late morning, when a warm, gentle wind came blowing across the bay, the old man declared, "To the sea we go once more."

The boat was double-hulled, made of a light, buoyant wood, with an open deck, all lashed together by rope. It had two tall masts and a long steering oar astern and a canoe strapped to the side. As Kiran boarded the vessel, he was told to stay clear of the ropes and sails, so he found a nook to sit in, tucked out of the way.

There were three others on board, two men and a teenage girl. They all looked like Lu-paia with bronze skin and pearly white teeth. Kiran sensed an edge of curiosity in their eyes, but they did not question Lu-paia.

As the boat eased out of the bay, the triangular sails filling with wind, Kiran fought the urge to jump overboard and swim back to land. Riding on a raft was one thing, but was he truly going to take to the sea? His heart thumped in his chest. *You wanted an adventure,* he told himself, and laughed out loud.

Once they hit the open sea, fear clenched his throat as the boat rolled and rocked, side to side and up and down. He had to grab hold to keep from falling to the floor. A wall of water would rise up before them, then roll under the bow, lifting the boat aloft, and they'd ride the top of the wave, skimming along the foamy ridge, then plunge down again on the other side, only to tilt and climb the next crest, the salt water spraying his face. He looked to the others on board. They were calm and peaceful, as if this were perfectly normal.

The swells grew heavier and heavier. Suddenly, Kiran felt his stomach squeeze in his throat and he vomited over the side. The world started to spin and he retched once more. The girl was by his side. "It'll pass," she was saying. "You'll be all right. Just keep your eyes on the horizon."

"You mean the edge?" He grabbed hold of her arm.

She gave him something to chew. It was spicy and tart, but he chewed. When they were a distance from shore, the sea at last calmed to an easy roll.

By late afternoon, the city began to sink below the horizon. Kiran gripped the edge of the boat as the last of it disappeared, leaving nothing but blue upon blue in every direction. *It's all right. The island is there, it will be there,* he told himself.

When the sun set, the sea turned oily black and the stars shone above in a moonless sky. Kiran lay in his bedroll, listening to each creak and groan of the ropes as the boat heaved in the sea. If he relaxed and let his mind go with the rhythmic flow, pulsing up and down, he imagined they rode on the breath of a giant.

A half moon rose on the horizon, lighting the sky, its reflection rippling across the water. The same moon that hung over his village, the same moon that Bria now slept under, he thought. He reached into his pocket and held the little doll. *I'm going to make it,* he told her. *And then I'm coming back for you.*

"That's an interesting token for a grown man." The girl nodded toward the doll.

Kiran tucked it back into his pocket and shrugged. "Thanks for helping me earlier."

"I am Leikela," she said with a smile. "I prepare the meals."

He nodded.

She stared at him. He turned away. "Sleep well," she said and crawled into her own bedroll at the stern.

The days passed in what felt like an eternal drift as they trekked across the open sea. Lu-paia did not seem to sleep, but remained trance-like, all his concentration needed to navigate. Sitting in his special seat at the stern, he used the sun by day and the stars by night. He knew the secrets of the winds and how to read the waves as they moved across the hull; to him, the swells were the pulse of the sea. Leikela whispered to Kiran, saying Lu-paia could conjure islands out of the mist, simply by imagining them.

During the day, they sailed through schools of fish in the thousands—large and small, dark and silvery. Most amazing were the fish that could fly. Kiran couldn't believe his eyes. Amid the blue-green waves, masses of glittering fish would shoot from the water and fly in a straight line, gliding through the air, their large fins spread like wings, until they hit a wave and vanished beneath the surface. Often, one would come hurling through the air and land on deck, flopping about helplessly. A sailor would use it as bait for the bigger fish, which were the main source of food on board.

Kiran was reluctant to eat from the sea. It was taboo in his village.

"Don't be silly. You must eat," Leikela insisted, dishing him a portion.

"But the lesions. I can't."

"Lesions? Ha! An old wive's tale."

He hesitated, then shook his head.

"Then you will starve." On the third day he relented, having no other choice.

One day, they encountered a school of fish the size of men that jumped and frolicked in the playful manner of children, twisting in the air and flopping on their sides. "They aren't fish," he was told. "They breathe like us." They'd surf at the bow of the boat, as though trying to race, then twirl and spin away, emitting pops and squeaks, a chattering that sounded like voices.

"Do they talk like us, too?" he asked, thinking again of Takhura's story of the Irichoi.

The men just laughed.

One night, under the new moon, with only the stars lighting the night sky, glowing specks flashed in the water, tiny shining lights that spread across the surface like a million fireflies. Several times, Kiran caught sight of two round shining green eyes, emerged from the water right next to the boat, glaring with an unblinking stare—phantoms of the deep. Some nights, balls of light the width of his spread arms would be visible below the surface, flashing at irregular intervals like lanterns. It was a fantastical world, beyond his imagination. He had never dreamed such things existed. Lu-paia and the crew seemed not to notice, so common were the sights to them.

Kiran liked to lie on the foredeck, looking up at the stars sprinkled across the firmament, though it made him feel lonely, like he too was just another tiny light, lost in the vast darkness of the night sky. Every night he'd doubt his decision to come. Then every morning, he'd wake with the same determination to continue. In between, he dreamed of being home, with Aldwyn. With Roh and Bria. With all this over and done.

If the sea was calm, he wrote in his codex, his legs dangling over the prow, his bare feet in the green seawater. Gradually, he began to understand what the Scholar meant when he said the ocean was a good place to put things into perspective. The boat did not fight the waves, rather flowed with the natural harmony of the sea, a freedom he'd never felt before. Instead of being a feared abyss, the endlessly retreating horizon, where the blue sky met the blue sea, drew the boat steadily forward, carrying him on his quest.

One late afternoon, after they had been at sea for nearly sixty days, the crew became excited when a large black bird with a forked tail glided overhead, then circled round and down, skimming over the wave crests where it snapped up a flying fish. It was a sign, Kiran was told. They were nearing land.

The next day, larger flocks of sea birds circled the boat until dusk, when, after a long day of fishing, they all flew toward the setting sun, screaming as they went. At dawn, a solitary cloud hung in the sky directly in the path of the vessel, and by late morning, a patch of green cropped up out of the blue sea. Kiran was overwhelmed with relief and wonder. It was true! Land! As the boat steadily approached, the sun rising astern, he could see individual treetops and rows of tree trunks shining in the sun.

People milled about on the beach. Some were launching canoes and paddling out to sea, waving and shouting in welcome. Lu-paia anchored the vessel on a reef surrounded by crystal clear water where the sea bottom was covered with what looked like underwater mosses and oddly shaped plants, red and orange and green, with tiny fish darting about, in every color of the rainbow, bright and shiny. The sailors unlatched a canoe and paddled Lu-paia to shore then one came back for Kiran and Leikela. When Kiran reached the snow-white sandy beach, he dropped to his knees and thrust his bare hands down into the sand. Land! He had lived to see it. He moved to the shade and flung himself flat on his back and looked up at the blue sky. He had made it. White birds circled above on the warm drafts. He breathed in the aroma of the forest as the winds ruffled the leaves of the trees and the waves lapped on the beach.

He sat up straight. There was no mountain here. This island was a patch of sand in the middle of the ocean. He got to his feet and ran straight into Leikela. "There's no mountain. This isn't the place."

She giggled. "Here we trade. Soon," she patted his arm, "Lu-paia will pull your place out of the sea."

In two days time they arrived at another small island, then a day later, another. By week's end, in the late afternoon, signs of land appeared in the distance—a barely imperceptible texture spanning the length of the horizon. As night fell, Leikela whispered to him to get some sleep. But he shifted in his seat as they sailed onward. Under the bright moonlight the dark cliffs rose out of the sea.

At dawn, for as far as they could see in either direction, sheared cliffs towered into the sky. Lu-paia pointed to the tree-lined ridge. "It is there. The place you seek."

A raven swooped down from the cliff and passed overhead, squawking in welcome. Kiran's heart started to race. He couldn't believe it. Finally. *When you reach the peak and stand on the edge of darkness...* He had found the peak.

Lu-paia's eyes moved over the water. "But it is as I had feared."

"What do you mean?" Kiran asked, anxious now by Lu-paia's tone.

"It is not the will of the gods," he said. "We cannot sail in. Too many rocks."

Kiran looked to the cliff once more. "What about the canoe?"

"I cannot ask this of them. The men fear the dark spirits."

But there are no dark spirits! Kiran plopped down on the deck, his head in his hands. He laughed out loud at the irony.

He rose to his feet and looked over the edge of the boat. He could swim in white water. He'd done it before.

"I will take you."

Kiran spun around.

It was Leikela. Kiran didn't know what to say, how to thank her. He simply returned her nod and it was done.

The canoe was built for two paddlers with an outrigger attached to one side, which was made to skim the surface of the sea for stability. Kiran looked out over the choppy sea, then to the canoe.

The girl smiled and gave him a nod of confidence. They dropped the tiny craft into the water, climbed aboard, and paddled hard, keeping their bow turned toward the crest of the waves.

"Why did you agree to take me?"

She gave him a hint of a smile. "If I return alive, my bravery will bring honor."

"If you return alive?"

She nodded. "It is a full moon. The dark spirits will be few." She broke her rhythm for a moment and he turned to face her. "I could see you meant to swim."

He turned around and dug his paddle into the water.

As they approached, the massive rock wall grew before his eyes, swarming with seabirds darting in and out of crevices on the jagged face. He had hoped to find an incline that was terraced, like the canyon where he and Roh had hiked. But the face was a sheer vertical for as far as they could see.

"You're sure this is the place?"

"It is as Lu-paia said."

He craned his neck and looked up at the cliff towering above, his heart in his throat.

He'd have to climb.

Upon the face of the water, driven by
force of wind, into the blue horizon,
we did go among flying fish.

33

As the tiny canoe rolled in the sea, and the waves crashed against the rock wall throwing a white spray high into the air, he stared up at the jagged cliffs, overcome with terror. He felt like telling Leikela of his fears, but he knew if he did, he would panic. In a strange way, it felt comforting to be faced with a simple choice. Climb or go back. Persevere or give up. It made him see his goal with greater clarity and honesty than he had ever experienced before. He had to get to the top of that cliff.

"We'll ride in on a wave and you'll have to jump as I bring the canoe about," she shouted. "I won't be able to hold it steady."

He took a deep breath and nodded. If she misjudged the wave, the canoe would be smashed into the rocks. If she couldn't get him close enough, he'd drown in the churning surf.

On the next incoming wave, she dug in hard with her paddle and kept the canoe pointed forward as they rode the crest toward the wall. He slipped his pack onto his back, grabbed hold of the sides of the canoe, and rose to his feet, trying to keep his weight low until the right moment. The wall rose up before him, closer and closer, until she yelled, "Now," and without a thought, he launched into the air and smacked against the wet rock face, his heart hammering in his chest. The white froth soaked him as he slid down the slimy, algae-covered surface, groping for a handhold. His feet were underwater before his left hand clamped onto a crevice. He grabbed hold of a nubbin with his other hand and pulled himself up until he got his foot on something solid. The ocean surged and a mound of churning water pushed from below, engulfing him, then drew back, its force threatening to pull him from his hold. He had to get higher. And fast.

He looked straight up the wall to the cliff above. His throat constricted and he gasped for air. He thought back to the climb in the canyon and Roh, sitting on the ledge above. Take it steady, he had said. Kiran clamped his teeth together. Steady. Persevere. One step at a time. He wedged his toe into a crack and pulled his body up with his right hand, his left searching for a new hold. When he found one, he hesitated a moment, stretched against the wall, gripping the rock above him at full reach. The waves pounded below his feet. He took a breath and pulled himself up farther. Sweat ran from his forehead and down his neck. He found another spur for his right toe, then raised himself another length. He was one step closer.

Gripping the rock, he looked over his shoulder, blinking the salt spray from his eyes. "But how will I...?" His heart sank. They had made no plan, no arrangements. Leikela was paddling out to sea. "When will you come back for me?" he hollered, but his words were drowned out by the pounding of the waves. She simply waved with her paddle and continued on. He turned back to face the rock. He couldn't think about that now.

He tested each foothold with light kicks and tugged on each handhold—cracks, spurs, tiny ledges—to be sure they were solid. He couldn't afford to make a mistake. One slip would send him to the bottom of the wall. He ascended, one slow movement at a time, never looking down, cutting back and forth across the rock face, all the while repeating, like a mantra: persevere, persevere.

The climb became a blur of endless rock, its textured surface etched with figures and faces—Bria, Roh, Aldwyn—speaking to him from the shadows. At every rise, every step, they were there, urging him onward.

At last, he reached a wide ledge and sat perched, high above the sea as waves crashed far below. He slid the waterskin over his shoulder and gulped down half the contents, then took off his pack and rubbed his sore shoulders.

A giddy sensation came over him and he leaned out over the drop and stole a glance to see how high he had climbed. The sea was over fifty feet below. His stomach clenched and his head spun. He shoved his back against the wall. *What were you thinking? Don't do that again!*

At that moment, from far up the cliff, came a deafening crack. A mist of scattering pebbles showered down around him and a rock the size of his boot went whizzing past his ear, accelerated toward the sea with a low whistle, and smashed into the rock below as he looked on, transfixed. Then a hail of tumbling rock came crashing down around him, louder than thunder. He rammed himself against the sheer rock face, his arms covering his head, as heavy blows pummeled his hands, thudding into his neck and shoulders and whacking against his back. He was sure the whole side of the cliff was collapsing and he was going down with it.

Then all was silent. For a moment, he was too stunned to think. He clung to the ledge, paralyzed with fear. He took several deep breaths, trying to slow the pounding in his chest.

He knew he had to move. He resisted the urge to look back down. He looked up. He simply had to find a way. The answers were there. He knew it. *When you reach the peak…*

The top of the jutting ledge was twenty-five feet above him, the last segment rearing up so steeply he had no idea how he could possibly make it. Sweat ran down his neck. He took a few deep breaths. *Get on with it,* he told himself and slipped his pack back on.

When he looked up again, he saw a path of handholds as clear as if it had been drawn. The summit was within reach. Before he could talk himself out of it, he grabbed a hold and crept up the sheer rock face, moving like an overgrown spider, until he was just below the final, jutting ledge. He reached up as high as he could, but couldn't grip the edge to pull himself up any farther. He tried to shove his hand into a crack in the rock, but it was too narrow. His strength pushed to the limit, his fingers gone numb, he needed something solid he could hold onto. *If only Roh were here to help me.* Then he remembered. Roh's knife. He slid the blade from his boot and shoved it into the crack.

Barely breathing, he pulled himself upward as his legs dangled uselessly in space below him. His foot found a nubbin to push farther up. One more reach and he swung up and over the ledge.

He lay with his head in the gravel, numb with relief. There was no place higher to go. He had made it. He had climbed to the top. Relief washed through him, leaving him light-headed and weak, as if he had used up the last reserve of energy within him.

When he was finally ready to move on, he reached for the knife, but was barely able to touch it with his fingertips. He tried to wiggle it from the crack, but it slipped from his grasp. "No!" he screamed as it hit the rock wall and bounced outward, spinning round and round until it dropped into the frothy sea below. Instantly, he hated this malevolent and lonely place. What had he been thinking? How foolish to think he had accomplished anything. Roh was supposed to be here, by his side, and Bria holding his hand. Now he was here, alone, angry for all that the quest had taken from him. Would it ever end?

He looked out over the sea. Lu-paia's boat was out of sight. He was at the top of a rocky cliff, by the edge of a sea, farther from home than he could ever have imagined, with no idea what to do, where to go, where to turn. He didn't even know if he had arrived anywhere worth going.

He knew only one thing. He wasn't about to sit here, waiting for the sun to lead him on. Whatever was here, he would have to face it. He stood up and headed into a copse of trees.

Not far in, the trees gave way to an open meadow of lush green grasses, resplendent with wildflowers, purple and orange and yellow. Above, a raven soared, calling on the wind, *cur-ruk cur-ruk.* On the far side stood a stone archway covered in ivy. His spirits soared. There was something here. He had found something. An entrance. He hurried across the meadow and through the arch into what appeared to be a courtyard. To his left was a small cavern, to the right, against a rock wall, was a fountain, gurgling with life. He halted, his heart pounding in his chest. *A great pool of glorious reflection...* Could it be? Beside the pool was an altar, on top of which was a Pyletar. His breath caught in his throat. At its pinnacle was a sparkling stone cradled in a thin iron basket, just like the one in the Sanctuary on the Mount. Kiran trembled, overcome with joy. Had he found the dwelling place? At long last? He had imagined this moment a thousand times.

He went to the altar and bowed in reverence. A tiny pile of autumn leaves swirled in a spiraling dance at its base, then died as suddenly as they had begun, settling on the surface of a shallow puddle, distorting the surface. Then he saw it. At the base of the Pyletar, carved in the wood. An X. His heart stopped. How...how could that be? He shook his head. *But it can't be...* He dropped to his knees and ran his fingers along the mark. In the back of his mind, a voice echoed: *the world goes on... a big round ball.* Had he come all the way *around* the world? Was he truly in the Sanctuary on the Mount, the same place he had visited that fateful day, so long ago?

A voice, low and raspy, smothered the silence. "What are you doing here?"

Kiran's throat tightened. He spun around, rising to his full height. He met the gaze of a pair of eyes so dark, so intense, that he stumbled back a step. A barely perceptible gasp escaped his lips. "You're..."

Standing before him was Elder Morgan.

Kiran blinked, but there was no mistaking it. He glanced around the Sanctuary, trying to get his bearings. Of course this was it—the sparkling pool of water, the ivy-covered archway—now, green with life.

"Answer me, boy! What are you doing here? How'd you get past the bridge guards?"

"I…" Kiran glanced toward the archway and the bridge he knew was beyond.

"You wicked Javinians have desecrated the sacred Sanctuary for the last time!"

"Elder Morgan, it's me."

The man took a step closer. His eyes grew wide. "Young Kiran?" His hand went to his chest as his mouth dropped open. "The rains have come. But you…it can't be." He stepped back, lowering his eyes. "So you've faced the Voice."

"I sought the Voice. But I…" Kiran heaved a sigh. "I didn't find what I expected."

"The Great Father is ever surprising in His infinite Grace. And now you have returned, with His blessing." He looked around the sanctuary. "Where is Deke?"

"Returned? No. I came by sea."

"What?" He glanced in the direction of the sea. "What are you saying?"

"I'm saying…" Kiran took a deep breath. "I thought this was, well, I got to the edge, but it wasn't. You see, the Script of the Legend is just a story, an allegory. There is no Voice."

Elder Morgan reeled backward. "What is the meaning of this?" He looked around the sanctuary. "What's going on here?"

"I'm sorry. I didn't mean to—"

"Where is my son?"

Kiran looked down at his feet. "Gone. Everyone's gone but me."

"Everyone?"

Kiran's eyes met his. "Deke lies in his grave, sir."

Elder Morgan blinked twice, then swallowed. "What happened? Who put him there?"

"No one. I mean, we buried him, but his death was, well…" Kiran took the Pyletar from around his neck and handed it to Morgan.

The man rolled the pendant between his fingers. "All for nothing," he whispered.

"No, no, it wasn't all for nothing." Kiran shook his head, trying to get his thoughts in order. "Aldwyn told me to seek knowledge. Elder Morgan, I have. I've learned so much, so many things we had wrong."

Morgan's eyes snapped back to Kiran. "*Wrong?*" He shook his head. "Enough." A tiny blood vessel pulsed in his temple. "This is nonsense. All of it." Morgan took a long breath, then stepped forward and laid his hand on Kiran's shoulder, his face a mask of virtuousness. "You are a very confused young man," he whispered, pity in his dark eyes. "Come with me now and never speak of this again. Serve the Father, with humility, and everything will be all right. So long as you never speak this blasphemy again, we won't forsake you. As with Old Horan."

Old Horan. He had been chastised, teased, an outcast among the villagers. Was that to be Kiran's fate? *But I know the truth!*

As though he'd read Kiran's mind, Morgan said, "This is heresy."

Kiran looked past Morgan to the archway. "But Aldwyn told me—"

"Ah, yes. Aldwyn. This all makes sense now." He rocked back on his heels and looked Kiran up and down. A wry grin came to his face. "I didn't want to believe it. But here you are, proof in flesh and blood. Aldwyn's bastard."

Kiran stumbled backward. His mouth went dry. "Aldwyn is… *Aldwyn* is my father?" He reached for the rock wall to steady himself. The pulsing gurgle of the stream echoed in his head and his legs started to shake. His eyes dropped to the ground, searching for any insight, any memory, anything that made sense.

"Where have you been hiding all this time? With that Javinian whore mother of yours?"

A chill ran through Kiran. He tried to respond, but his voice crackled in his throat. It was true. He knew it. Aldwyn. Kalindria.

"He thought his plan was so clever, sending you." Elder Morgan shook his head. "And he thought once the rains came you could stroll into the Temple and announce you've returned, is that it?" He leaned forward and hissed through clenched teeth, "I know what you seek."

Kiran swallowed hard. "I seek the Truth."

"You don't know what Truth is. I had in my heart to accept you. But you lack the conviction of real faith. You were offered the test and failed."

"You knew about that?"

"You're nothing more than a heathen."

Kiran took a deep breath, trying to find calm, and in that suspended moment, between exhaling and inhaling, when the breath left his body, realization dawned. He pulled his shoulders back, thrust his chin forward, and looked Morgan in the eye. "I know what you fear."

"You know nothing." Elder Morgan pulled back. He straightened his cloak. "No matter. Aldwyn has already reaped the punishment of his sins. And you will too."

"What's happened to Aldwyn?"

"The Great Father sees all. You will suffer His wrath."

"Tell me what's happened to Aldwyn!"

"The prophecy will be fulfilled. You will see. When my son returns."

"I told you, Deke is dead."

"Lies. All lies." Beads of perspiration clung to Morgan's forehead.

"Your son is dead."

"Not another word," Morgan growled.

Kiran stepped forward, his face inches from Morgan's. "Your son died because of his stubborn faith." He was too angry to stop. "He was clinging to it like a child at his mother's leg."

"Lies!" he spat. "My son lives! He has to."

"You have the missing scroll," Kiran realized as the words left his mouth. The hierarchy of the Temple. The one page in the Scholar's book that Kiran had not recognized. *In the absence of the seventh elder, a son shall take his place. An Elder's son.* "You're the one who had a plan all along."

"You want all the glory for yourself!" Morgan's eyes flared with rage and Kiran saw in those eyes what he should truly fear. Not the Mawghuls, or wind demons, or witches, or headhunters. The demon who stood before him was more menacing than any he'd ever faced. "I cannot let you tell these lies." Morgan turned toward the archway and shouted, "Guards! Guards!"

Kiran's thoughts flashed back to the Kingdom of the Kotari and the Guardian, his guards locking him away in the cellar. He glanced toward the sea. He couldn't go back that way. He glanced toward the pines where he and Jandon had been. He turned on his heel and ran.

Needles scraped at his face as he pushed through branches. Morgan was right behind him. He squeezed through the crevice in the rock wall, then scrambled up the incline, around the corner, and up onto the ledge, side-stepping to the farthest point.

Morgan got one foot on the ledge and faltered. He clung to the rock wall, his face gone pale.

Kiran took a breath. "What's wrong? Afraid of heights?"

Morgan clenched his teeth together. "Your plan will never work. You've got nowhere to run. You're a heathen bastard and always will be."

Kiran looked across the chasm. The lone pine was gone; the rock it had clung to had crumbled away. "I am the son of an Elder." He turned back to face Morgan. "The time of fear and ignorance is over. My parents had to suffer your oppression, your bigotry, your shallow-minded hatred because of some old, misinterpreted words." He spit over the edge. "You say I don't know what Truth is," he thundered on. "But I know this. It's not what's written on some ancient scroll that matters. It's what's in your heart."

"You dare to challenge the Way? You'll never be a true Toran!"

"So be it. I've got nothing to prove to *you*," he said.

And he jumped.

34

As he plummeted downward, he could see the raging river below, frothy white. For a fleeting moment, he thought of the hands that were supposed to catch him. Then with a bone-wracking jolt, he plunged into the churning water. He tumbled in the maelstrom, powerless against the force of the current. He didn't try to get to shore. He rode the torrent, gasping for air, fighting to keep his head above water as the river carried him toward town. He had to get to the Temple before Morgan. He had to talk to Aldwyn.

He let the water take him. He became one with the flow, giving himself up to the power of the river. Then hands were groping for him and he was hauled to shore. He lay on the bank, heaving with exhaustion. When finally he caught his breath, he looked up to see a man he recognized, but could not recall his name. His four sons stood behind him.

The man gasped. "You are Kiran," he said and dropped to his knees and bowed his head. "We have awaited your return, Blessed One."

Kiran managed to sit up.

The four sons followed their father to their knees. "Bless you," the man spoke with head bowed. "When the rains came, we knew the Great Father had not forsaken us. Bless you. Bless you! You have saved the village."

"No, no," Kiran shook his head.

"And now, at the harvest moon, you have returned." He nudged one of his sons. "Norbert, run ahead to the village and tell the Elders the Seventh has come." The boy stared at Kiran, mouth agape. "Do it now," the man ordered. The boy jumped to his feet and took off running.

No, this is all a mistake, Kiran wanted to say, but something stopped him. The boys were staring at him with bright young eyes. He shook his head. He had to get to Aldwyn; he'd know what to do. Kiran tried to stand, but pain shot up his leg.

"Give him a hand," the farmer told his sons. Two of them lifted Kiran to his feet.

"I must get to the Temple."

The third son nodded and ran to the barn. He returned with a hay cart. "We'll take you."

Kiran thanked him and sat down on the back of the cart. His feet dragged on the ground as it bumped along the road to town. Tall grasses swayed in the breeze, sparkling with dew. Birds swooped in the air, bees buzzed on the wind. The valley looked reborn, fresh and alive, as if there had never been a drought at all. Nothing was as he remembered; yet it was exactly the same.

On the far hillside, sheep grazed, as lazily as any other day. Among them was a shepherd girl. Kiran took the tiny doll from his pocket, wrung the water from it, and ran his fingers along the face. *What am I going to do?* he thought. What could he say, how could he possibly explain? Artus was right; they'd never believe him. It would only cause him grief and worse, banishment. Maybe that was what he deserved all along. Maybe it was right that he should be punished, to atone for it all.

He squeezed the doll in his hands and fought back tears. *I should have stayed with you.* He had the impulse to jump off the cart and sprint into the woods, to find a way back to her. But running wasn't the answer.

From his pack he took the container of salt, dumped its contents on the ground, then tucked the doll safely inside. His destiny was here. He owed it to Roh. He owed it to himself. No matter what, he had to tell the truth. But how?

The cart turned a corner and the valley spread before him. The Temple dominated the landscape, the tiny village lost in its shadow. How different from the city, he thought, with its diversity of buildings and people.

On the road ahead, a crowd of villagers was approaching, shouting with glee. "Praise the Father! He's come!"

Kiran rose from the cart and limped forward to greet them, trying to figure out what to do, what to say. Followers knelt at his feet and wept with joy. Wide-eyed children gathered round, reaching out to touch him. "Kiran! Kiran!" they chanted. Then more voices joined in, surrounding him with praise. People came out of their doors to see, chanting his name. Before long, there were so many people, he couldn't get through. He glanced back toward the Sanctuary on the

Mount, then toward the village.

"I must get to the Temple," he said.

Before he realized what was happening, he was swept up in their arms and raised to their shoulders. "Praise Kiran, the Chosen One!" they shouted as they carried him along. The crowd swelled and he felt like he was back on the sea, riding the crest of a wave. Amid the sound of his own name, he was carried right to the front steps of the Temple. The door swung open and three Elders stumbled toward him with expressions of disbelief. "It's true," Elder Beryl stammered and dropped to his knees.

Elder Cenewyg grasped at the Pyletar at his neck. "The Seventh Elder," he whispered. His mouth went slack. Elder Markin's eyes grew wide and he turned and disappeared through the doorway.

"Praise the Father! The One has returned! Praise the Father! The One has returned!" the people cheered. Kiran pushed through the mob, trying to escape the chanting.

Someone grabbed him by the shoulders, spun him around, and whispered in his ear, "If you are wise, you'll mind your tongue. Choose your words carefully." Kiran drew back to look into the clear, cogent eye of Old Horan. Kiran nodded and as he started to turn away, he caught sight of Morgan coming down the road, staring right at him.

The bells rang out above—ding-dong-ong-ong-ong, ding-dong-ong-ong. Morgan glanced up at the bell tower, then back to Kiran, his eyes lit with a burning hatred.

Kiran spun around. To Elder Beryl he said, "Aldwyn, where's Aldwyn?"

Elder Beryl's face fell. "I'm afraid—"

"Where is he?"

"He's in the garden."

Kiran ran through the Temple chamber and out the back door. He found Aldwyn slumped on a bench. "Aldwyn!" he cried as he ran toward him. Aldwyn barely raised his head. "What's happened? Are you all right?" Aldwyn made no response. The left side of his face was slack. His left eye drooped and drool seeped from his lip. Kiran's knees went weak and he slumped onto the bench beside him.

Then he saw her. Kalindria was coming down the path, a cup in her hand. Kiran drew in a breath. He looked to Aldwyn, then to Kalindria, then back to Aldwyn again.

358 • Kimberli A. Bindschatel

She stopped a few paces away, her mouth dropped open, and the cup slipped from her fingers. "Kiran," she gasped, covering her mouth with her hands.

He rose to face her. "I knew it was you."

She nodded, tears in her eyes. "How? How did you know?"

"My heart told me." He took her in his arms and held her tight.

The back door of the Temple swung open and the chanting spilled into the garden. She pulled away and brushed a curl from his eyes. "They are calling for you?"

He nodded. "How did you get back here?"

"A friend came for me. We've been back a few days. But that is a story for another day. Is Bria with you?"

His stomach clenched. "No," he shook his head. "I...she...I have a lot to tell you as well." He turned back to Aldwyn. "What's happened to him?"

"I don't know. It was before I returned. One morning, when he did not arrive at the Temple, someone was sent to his home. He was found like this."

Kiran knelt on the ground in front of Aldwyn. "Does he know what's happening? Does he know it's me?" He fought back tears.

"I'm not sure. I think so."

"Aldwyn, it's me. It's Kiran." Aldwyn jerked back as though trying to wake from a bad dream and Kiran thought he saw a hint of awareness in his ancient eyes.

Ding-dong-ong-ong-ong. Ding-dong-ong-ong, the bells rang, then echoed across the valley, bidding all come. The chanting of the villagers grew louder. "Praise the Father! The One has returned!"

Kiran took hold of Aldwyn's hand and searched his eyes. He seemed to be laughing and crying at the same time. "Aldwyn, I need you. I don't know what to do." He leaned closer. "I don't know how to tell you this. Aldwyn, it's not as you thought. I got there. I made it to the edge of the world. There is no—"

Aldwyn squeezed his hand, a flash of warning in his eyes.

Startled, Kiran turned around and saw Elder Beryl coming down the garden path. He was beckoning Kiran with a wave.

Kiran turned back to Aldwyn and whispered, "I need your help."

"All is ready. Your followers await," said Elder Beryl, lowering his eyes as he approached.

Kiran glanced at Aldwyn, then back to Elder Beryl. "All is ready for what?"

"For the ceremony, of course."

Kiran looked to Kalindria. She had no response.

Elder Beryl took Aldwyn by the arm and helped him to his feet. "Let's hurry now," he said.

Kiran took hold of Aldwyn's other arm and together they walked him to the Temple. Kiran struggled to gather his thoughts, grasping for what to do. When they stepped through the door, the chanting grew louder, "Praise the Father! The One has returned!" Kiran's knees started to shake. He glanced around, looking for an escape.

He shuffled Aldwyn into the scroll room and sat him on a stool. "I'd like a moment with Aldwyn," he said to Elder Beryl. "Alone."

The Elder hesitated. "But your congregation awaits."

"I understand," Kiran said as he closed the door.

He paced across the tiny room and back, wringing his hands, then stopped and faced Aldwyn. "What am I going to do?"

Aldwyn made no response.

Kiran dragged a stool to the wall, jumped up on top of it, and gazed through the crack. The Temple was filled with villagers chanting his name. He ran his hands through his hair, grabbed a handful, and tugged in frustration. He jumped down from the stool. "All right. I can figure this out." His gaze fell on the tiny pile of scrolls. "There has to be something here," he said and reached for one.

A hoarse grating noise came from deep in Aldwyn's throat. It sounded like someone calling from the hollow depths of an old well, dry from drought.

"What? What is it? Tell me," Kiran begged.

With an excruciatingly slow effort, Aldwyn raised his right hand and motioned in the air.

"What is it?" Kiran sat on the stool next to him. "What are you trying to tell me?" He searched Aldwyn's eyes. "Please, I need your help. Don't you see? It's all been a mistake. There is no Seventh Elder. There is no Voice of the Father. I was still seeking. I thought I was on the other side of the world. Then I ended up in the Sanctuary. How do I tell them? How can I tell them the truth? I'll be banished like Javin. I'll be shunned. Aldwyn, Elder Morgan threatened me!"

Aldwyn's eyes flared and he trembled.

Kiran took hold of his arm, afraid the old man would fall from the stool.

Aldwyn brought his right hand, shaking as he lifted it, to rest on Kiran's heart.

"My heart? Listen to my heart? I'm trying Aldwyn. But, I can't go out there and face them. What will I say? Listen to that." He gestured toward the door. The chanting was growing louder. "They think I've succeeded!"

Aldwyn's eyes flickered. His hand dropped to the table and he dragged his finger across the surface.

"What? Are you writing? Are you trying to write something?" Kiran took the candle from the wall and brought it to the table. In the dust, was the letter V.

"V? V-what?"

Aldwyn moved his hand in a circular motion, forming an O.

"V-O... The Voice?"

Aldwyn slumped, the hint of a smile in the curve of his lip.

"But I told you." Kiran clenched his teeth in frustration. "Aldwyn, there is no Voice."

Aldwyn lifted his hand once more to Kiran's chest and tapped, determination in his eyes.

"But you don't understand." Kiran shook his head. It was no use. Aldwyn was a mere shadow of his former self.

Kiran was on his own.

There was a knock at the door.

Kiran opened the door to Elder Beryl standing before him dressed in his finest robe. "The time has come," he whispered. He gestured to two young men behind him who entered the room and helped Aldwyn to his feet.

Kiran took a deep breath, nodded, and followed him to the Temple chamber.

The chanting reverberated through the Temple. "Praise the Father! The One has returned!"

The Elders were lined up, waiting in the wing. Elder Morgan had donned the special robes and stood with his arms crossed, the skin on his red face pulled so taut it looked as though it were about to burst.

Elder Beryl nudged Kiran from behind.

"I don't see Elder Wregan. We can't start without him," he

whispered, trying to stall.

"Elder Wregan was killed two days ago."

"Killed?"

"Javinians must have gotten to him." His hand went to his neck. "His throat was slit."

"His throat slit? Is that common with the Javinians?"

He shrugged. "Who else would want him dead?"

Kiran's mouth fell open. *A friend came for me,* she had said.

"Don't you worry about that now. Your followers await," the Elder urged, gesturing for Kiran to move forward.

Elder Cenewyg took Kiran's pack from his back and set it down in the corner. Elder Markin placed a white tunic over Kiran's head and pulled it down to fit. Then Elder Beryl took him by the arm and led him to the edge of the platform to face the congregation.

At once, the room fell silent and all eyes were on him. His heart beat heavy in his chest. His throat went dry. A lone voice rang out, "Praise Kiran!" The sound of his own name reverberated through his body like a haunting echo. *I'm not worthy!* he wanted to shout back.

Elder Cenewyg appeared before him, holding a vest made of the highest quality sheepskin, fashioned together with twisted linen. The Elder fastened it to Kiran, tightening it around his chest until he could barely breathe. Next, he placed the Pyletar pendant around his neck. Kiran stared at it, feeling nothing. So many times when he was a child, he had imagined standing here, accepting the vestments. He was to be ecstatic, filled with joy. Instead, his knees wouldn't stop shaking.

Elder Beryl approached, the robe in his arms. It was made of pure white wool, hemmed at the collar and the edge of the hood with a floral motif embroidered with purple and scarlet yarn. He and Elder Markin lifted the cloak and placed it on Kiran's shoulders. It felt heavy on his shoulders. The scent of wool filled his nostrils and he shuddered; he couldn't breath.

The congregation watched, waiting. He wiped the sweat from his brow and an icy chill came over him. Aldwyn had been trying to tell him something. *Something...* That something haunted him, the answer just beyond his grasp, as elusive as a firefly on a warm autumn night.

He knelt at the altar and stared into the candle's flame, hoping for inspiration as the smoke carried his whispered pleas skyward. High above, at the cusp of darkness, a spider crawled along the rafter. Kiran watched, his mind numb with anguish, as it inched downward on a silken strand, glistening in the candlelight. Did she ever question the Truth? he wondered.

Truth, he thought now. The word itself had lost all meaning.

Kiran swallowed hard. The villagers waited, as though collectively holding their breath. He stared out into the sea of faces, saw their eyes lit with reverent bliss, and he knew, sure as he breathed, that in those eyes was the answer. In every set of eyes he had encountered—the Lendhi, the Kotari, the Widhu, even in the monkey-men next to the waterfall—he had seen the same hope, the same faith. He had seen it in Kail's eyes when she refused to leave the Guardian; he had seen it in Roh's eyes when he had told Kiran to go on, to persevere. He knew it was a part of them like the sun was integral to the day.

All he'd ever wanted was to belong, to be accepted. He breathed in deeply, trying to slow his racing heart. What was he going to say? What would he tell them?

Artus was right. They'll never believe ME.

A wisp of wind crept across the altar. The candle's flame wavered a moment. Then it sparked back to life in a burst of light and Kiran knew what he must do. Somehow, deep in the recesses of his mind, he had always known. As if someone else had made the decision long ago, as if it wasn't his own. As if it were already destined.

Kiran closed his eyes, took a deep breath, and made one last glance skyward. In the shadows above, the spider carried on, weaving her own destiny.

He rose to his feet, went to his rucksack, and pulled out the box that held the codex. Morgan's eyes narrowed. Kiran turned back toward the congregation, set the box on the altar, and removed the book.

The Temple pulsed with hushed anticipation. He lifted his eyes. A drop of sweat trickled down his temple.

He held the book out before him and read aloud.

And the people heard the Voice of the Father.

Go forth on your path, as it exists
only through your walking.
~ Saint Augustine

Author's Note

Every extraordinary geographic and environmental phenomenon described in this book actually occurs on Earth. Argillite sediment, when freed by heavy rains, can turn river water blood red. In the Amazon jungle, howler monkeys incite terror with howls that can be heard for miles.

The whitewater rafting came from my own experience, but a friend was in the Grand Canyon during the rare occurrence of a thunderstorm and the ensuing flood. His video and testimony inspired my description.

The descriptions of the various cultures Kiran encountered are compilations of behaviors and beliefs from different real world cultures, modern and historical. The Toran village was inspired by the story of the Greenland Norse as presented by Jared Diamond in his book, *Collapse: How Societies Choose to Fail or Succeed.* At an isolated trading post, the people failed to adapt to the habitat, were in constant conflict with the natives, held on to their cultural traditions regardless of their practicality, and held a taboo of eating from the sea. The fictional Toran village is also an example of how some historical societies collapsed due to poor farming practices, which caused erosion and localized drought.

The behavior of the Kotari people and the coercive persuasion techniques used by The Guardian were inspired by the research of Dr. Margaret Thaler Singer as described in her book, *Cults in our Midst.* I've always been fascinated with the nature of belief and therefore cults, in particular, for their seemingly extreme ideas of the divine.

The darts of the headhunters were coated with curare, a substance made from an Amazon plant, which causes paralysis in the respiratory muscles of the victim. Curare is used in modern medicine as an anesthetic. A full recovery is possible if artificial respiration is administered. First explorers to the Amazon region believed salt to be an antidote, but that was a myth.

The idea for the song, "The Ancestor's Footprints," came from the Dreaming-tracks of the aborigines of Australia. Sometimes called Songlines, these were invisible pathways that stretched across the Outback. Aboriginal myths tell of Creation Beings who sang the world into existence. If you sang the songs, the lyrics described the landscape and you could find your way.

In some ways, *The Path to the Sun* is about survival. Anyone can be taught survival skills, but in any given circumstance, as Lawrence Gonzales says in his book, *Deep Survival*, "...it's not what's in your pack that separates the quick from the dead. It's not even what's in your mind. ... it's what's in your heart." Gonzales goes on to describe the attributes of a survivor. Interestingly, as I set out to give my protagonist those attributes, I found Kiran, as I had conceived of him, already had them.

Most of all, in this story, I share my love of nature and respect for animals. I've always wondered: if we are the so-called "moral animal," why do we treat other animals with such disrespect? We rarely recognize their intelligence and the vast amount of knowledge we could gain, if only we would pay attention to them. When I was a child, I first learned that Dr. Jane Goodall had discovered that chimpanzees make and use tools, an activity long thought to be exclusive to humans. Then, she witnessed something much more profound: chimpanzee behavior she recognized as awe, the beginning of religion.

As for the monkey-men of my story, (as Kiran describes them with his limited experience), may we someday share our lives with those other than human, in peace and harmony, and treat them, not just with the compassion they deserve, but with mutual respect. I will leave it to you, my reader, to decide if that is possible. I encourage you, as Aldwyn did Kiran, to listen to your heart.

Are you a **TEACHER**? Download the free classroom guide at:
http://www.thePathtotheSun.com

A **BOOK CLUB** discussion guide is available for download at:
http://www.thePathtotheSun.com

Thank you

To my mom and dad, for nurturing my creative spirit and my love of nature. To Rachel and Bruce for their dedication to my story and always challenging me to strive for excellence. To my teen authors group for cheering me on. To Linda Smith, for many things, but most of all for being my friend. To Laurie Scheer for all the encouragement and expert advice. To Christopher Mohar for his editorial magic. To Barbara Schue for her kind words and copy edits.

To all my first readers, whose insight and feedback was invaluable: Aubrie, Nicole, John, Kathleen, Matt, Scott, Steve, Anthony, Onlee, Mella, Linda, Mary, Ellen, Harriet, Laura, Meghan, Devin, Heather, Molly, Suzette, Crystal, and Gary.

A special thank you to Marie for always knowing when I need a hug or kick in the butt, and for always, always being on my side.

Finally, to Ken, for believing in my dream. There is no greater gift.

Thank YOU for reading *The Path to the Sun*

Share **YOUR** thoughts—on the story, on philosophy, the universe, the meaning of life—whatever inspires you or makes you wonder. Let's ponder together at: **http://www.thePathtotheSun.com**

If you join the discussion, you'll also get great perks, like special promotions, early releases, discounts, and more.

If you enjoyed this book, **please** post a positive review on this book's page at Amazon.com or Goodreads.com.

About the Author

Born and raised in Michigan, I spent summers at the lake, swimming and chasing fireflies, winters building things out of cardboard and construction paper, writing stories, and dreaming of faraway places. Since I didn't make honors English in High School, I thought I couldn't write. So I started hanging out in the art room. The day I borrowed a camera, my love affair with photography began. Long before the birth of the pixel, I was exposing real silver halides to light and marveling at the magic of an image appearing on paper under a red light.

After college, I freelanced in commercial photography studios. During the long days of rigging strobes, one story haunted me. As happens in life though, before I could put it to words, I was possessed by another dream—to be a wildlife photographer. I trekked through the woods to find loons, grizzly bears, whales, and moose. Then, for six years, I put my heart and soul into publishing a nature magazine, *Whisper in the Woods*. But it was not meant to be my magnum opus. This time, my attention was drawn skyward. I'd always been fascinated by the aurora borealis, shimmering in the night sky, but now my focus went beyond, to the cosmos, to wonder about our place in the universe.

In the spring of 2010, I sat down at the computer, started typing words, and breathed life into a curious boy named Kiran. Together, in our quest for truth, Kiran and I have explored the mind and spirit. Our journey has taken us to places of new perspective. Alas, the answers always seem just beyond our grasp, as elusive as a firefly on a warm autumn night.

Made in the USA
Lexington, KY
05 July 2014